Assassins

Assassins

The Fourth Age: Shadow Wars, Book I

David N. Pauly

Dedication

To my loving wife, Minh Ha, who made this possible, and my brother James, the first to believe.

Contents

Last Day of the Third Age

Bran's diminutive figure lay under a magic cloak given to all the Walkers by Aradia, Elf Queen of Phoenicia. Months of planning, hardship, and pain would be rewarded, or he along with his friends would die here in *Plaga Erebus,* the dark kingdom of Magnar. Ash spewed up from the *Brunna Hatan*, the fountain of hate, where Dark Lightning crackled and hummed, at the top of its metallic peak, just a mile from their position. The ash spread outwards from the terrible fountain creating a gloomy pall that covered the sky, blending day into night.

Dark lightning crackled behind them, flickering all along the borders of Magnar's realm of nightmares, forming an impenetrable barrier obviating the need for border guards. Nearly all of the Dark Elves and Men comprising Magnar's army of conquest lay dead upon hate filled battlegrounds across the great lands known as *Nostraterra.* Most of the remnants gathered at the *Sanguine Templar*, the enormous temple complex only miles from the fountain, sacrificing captives from all the races, fueling the Dark Lightning. Others roamed the confines of the land patrolling between the temple and the fountain, guarding against any interference while Magnar brooded and festered in malice, plotting his resurgence.

Aradia, Elf queen of Phoenicia, driven from her realm into exile in the human realm of Eldora used her magic to find a small rent in Magnar's lethal defenses, allowing the Watchers to penetrate step by step avoiding all contact with the guardians of this dark kingdom. Horses could not fit through the small stone archway that was the only ingress to this land and the Elven cavalry waited upon the hills just outside the shimmering fence of death, waiting for their chance to rescue the Walkers upon their success.

Now, with a slight increase in light, the day was beginning, they must strike soon, or risk detection this close to the fountain. One of Bran's fellow Walkers, the Dwarven King Gneiss approached leaned down to whisper,

'It's time Bran; stay behind me while I see if I can breach this infernal pipe.'

Gneiss and Bran moved to the edge of a freshly dug hole only three feet down, where the top of a subterranean pipe lay, flowing with the raw magic supplying the Fountain. Bran's three closest friends from their homeland of Platonia were gathered close to Bran, chosen from amongst their fellow Gracies to bear the water of life from their Spring of Hope to this terrible place. The four men from Eldora lurked nearby, their bows at the ready as they covered the rest of the party. The three Dwarven engineers, accompanying Gneiss had located this section of pipe, which was close enough to the surface to be breached, digging the hole. Now, the magic of the Dwarves must sever the hard metal of the pipe for Bran to complete his mission.

Gneiss took an ornate ancient war-hammer from his pack, its' head made of solid Platina a priceless metal mined by Dwarves, and Gneiss muttered an ancient Dwarven spell. Withdrawing a gleaming crystal cylinder, capped in Platina which shone with hundreds of changing colors and tiny shapes, Gneiss inserted it into a socket in the top of the hammer.

Muttering for everyone to stay back but his fellow Dwarves, Gneiss struck down through the hole in the ground hitting the pipe with a tremendous metallic crash. Small bits of black metal spewed up into the air from the hole, and Gneiss lurched backward, pulled by the Dwarves.

'Now Bran!' said Gneiss.

Bran and his three fellow Gracies approached the hole and peering down Bran saw a large rent made in the dark pipe, where a thick dark red liquid swirled its' way to the Fountain, the smell of rotting flesh emanating from the fissure was nearly overwhelming. '*Death, in liquid form.*' thought Bran, '*so Aradia was right.*' Gracie lore held only Life can defeat Death, and now Bran uncapped the jar of blue liquid—the waters of life carried from Platonia. His fellow three Gracies held him around the waist as he poured in the waters, and for a moment nothing happened; Bran feared that he had failed.

Suddenly the liquid in the pipe turned from red to a purple-white, welling up from the pipe into the hole, as the ground beneath their feet shuddered. The Fountain's muttering flicker visible above their heads stuttered and went out, an unearthly quiet descended upon the land. Then, the Tower exploded in flickering sheets of shimmering energy, blue-white bolts discharging up from the ground and into the sky in actinic courses, running along the ashes of the surrounding desert. The deafening roar was pierced again and again by the sharp cracks of fresh bolts emanating all around. Bran dragged up from the hole was pushed to safety by his Gracie friends, when a great rush of gas and liquid vomited forth from the hole, claiming two of his friends. Their escort of men grabbed Bran and his friend Arwel, propelling the Gracies to run as fast as they could, following the Dwarves towards the borders of the land, hoping for rescue by the Elven cavalry.

Seconds turned to minutes as Bran ran as fast as his short legs could manage, the bolts of Dark Lightning flashing across the ground and the sky. Bran paused at the top of a small rise, gasping for breath turning to watch the Fountain discharge its energy upon the *Sanguine Templar*. The entire temple structure was covered in streams of the dark lightning when suddenly it exploded upwards and outwards; dark red blocks of stone hurtled hundreds of feet skyward before crashing down again. The magic of the *Sanguine Templar* faded, its dark red glow failing at last. Now, the Fountain spewed its magic outwards, the bolts lashing further and further from its peak.

'Run, Bran, run.' Cried Gneiss and turning to look ahead, Bran saw that the Dwarves were in front, with the men bringing up the rear. The smell of ashes, of ancient dust and decay, filled Bran's nose, as a bitter alkali taste choked his tongue, acrid vapors filling the air, making it difficult to breathe. Wheezing, he ran down the slope of the rise, seeing the dark hills where the cavalry surged down from the hills, the deadly fence vanquished. A leap of hope unlooked for soared in his chest,

'*We did it, we destroyed Magnar and Platonia is safe and soon I will return home.*' He thought but one last bolt of dark lightning caught him, its dark blue threads burning across his face and body. His left ear erupted in a cacophony of great sound and he writhed upon the ground in agony. Arwel had caught most of the blast and was ablaze, the men behind him vanishing forever. As Bran lay upon the sands of *Plaga Erebus* he saw dark ash filling the sky, his feeling of triumph over the destruction of the fountain replaced by hopelessness and despair as he realized the price of victory. Bran thought he would die until the strong arms of Gneiss grabbed him and dragged him towards the distant hills, where he saw with his last sight a small column of horsemen racing towards them across the bitter desert.

* * *

When Bran woke, he felt the terrible pain shoot through his body, he screamed aloud, arching his back off the ground. He lay on his back, naked inside a silken tent, with a young Elf sitting on a nearby stool.

'My lady, he is awake!' cried the Elf.

'Here, my young Gracie, drink this potion it will help with the pain.' said the Elven healer Drindar.

Supported by Drindar, Bran gratefully gulped down the thick cloying liquid. The pain began to subside almost immediately, but the potion only took the edge away, and it was all that Bran could do to keep from screaming again.

A tall blonde Elf woman entered the tent, her high cheekbones and sapphire blue eyes, gave her face an unearthly beauty. Aradia was clad in light grey robes that clung to her slender figure, but she carried a small bundle with her under one arm. Now, she approached Bran and said,

'Bran, you are mortally wounded, without Elven magical aid you will die by tomorrow. You have said that your people forbid the use of magic, but if you wish it, I can slow the poison within you.' said Aradia.

Bran thought for just a moment, unable to speak through his teeth that he clenched against the pain, and then nodded.

'Drindar, leave us, I will call for you when I am finished.'

The Elven healer left the tent and Aradia opened her bundle, removing a slender crystal rod that appeared to generate a small pink light. Kneeling at Bran's side, Aradia placed the flute to her lips and she began blowing air through it like a normal flute, but now the pink light strengthened, tendrils moving from the flute towards Bran's body, in tune with a warm rich melodic tone emanating from the flute. The pink lights expanded and entwined him within a magical net, where the light touched his flesh. He felt the pain subside, and he could finally relax his jaw to try and speak when Aradia shook her head slightly without losing contact with the magic flute.

Several minutes later, Aradia stopped, her serene features now set in lines of fatigue, as she placed the flute back in her bundle. She looked down at Bran and saw that the purple lines of dark lightning that had flickered and gleamed when she entered the tent were now barely visible. The open gaping wound across the Gracie's chest was beginning to close, but Aradia knew that this was only a temporary respite.

'Bran, can you hear me now clearly?'

'Yes my lady,' said Bran exhausted by his wounds.

'The healing powers in this Breath Crystal are unique, and while they have stayed your death by reducing the poisons from the Dark Lighting, the crystal is not strong enough to save your life. There is an alternative; you can take ship with me to El-valon, the immortal homeland of the Greater Elves. There you will be healed by the master healers, but the magic will fade if you try and leave Elvalon to return here to Nostraterra. Your death would come swiftly. However, by living in Elvalon, surrounded by our magic, your life will have no natural end.'

'But I want to go home, to see that my people are safe; not go into exile even if I live forever!'

'It will take four weeks at the fastest ride on horseback to get you to Platonia, and that is as long as I can keep you alive. You would have a day, maybe two to see your land before you die an excruciating death. You must choose now which journey you wish to make.

Bitterly, Bran said 'So my choice is either to die in my home or go oversea forever. Can you guarantee me that I will survive the voyage to Elvalon?'

'No, all I can do is take you there by the fastest ship remaining in Elven hands and hope that I can get you to the Master Healers before you die on board the ship.'

'Hope, there is that dreaded word again, all I "hoped" to do was save Platonia from destruction.'

'You accomplished this Bran; Magnar is no more and while you lay unconscious, word has reached me that Platonia was not attacked and remains inviolate as it always has. Truly your task is done.'

'I will go with you my lady to your homeland; I can only hope that I find peace there.'

'Rest then Bran, for we leave for my ruined city of Phoenicia within the hour. I will have Drindar come in to clothe you and prepare you for the journey. We must hurry.

As Aradia left the tent, Bran wept bitterly for his friends and his impending exile, before sliding into a fitful sleep.

Chapter One

Arrival

Aradia awoke to the smell of rain blending with the hiss of fragrant seas coming through a small open window in her cabin. The fact that the window was open for the first time in four days told her as much as the absence of both the howling shriek of wind and the chaotic lurching motion of the ship *Silver Foam*: the great tempest was over. She was safe from a shipwreck.

The rhythmic rocking of her bed should have soothed her back to sleep, but instead, she fretted over her dying friend Bran lying in a neighboring cabin. Bran was a Gracie, people who had once been Men, but they had been changed long ago by a mysterious plague. Persecuted for their diminutive stature—they were shorter than Men, though taller than Dwarves—they had found refuge in Platonia, an island surrounded by a fierce river whose powerful spirits had bestowed their protection upon the refugees. There they had lived in peace and harmony for time out of mind … until the shadow of Magnar had fallen upon them. Though Gracies were slender as reeds, their appearance belied a physical and mental fortitude not present in other races, as Magnar had learned to his sorrow. But even so, Bran had been taxed beyond these limits and Aradia had pushed the ship and its crew into the heart of the storm, racing against time to save Bran.

Now, dressing quickly, she drank a small cup of water when there was a knock on her door.

'Enter,' she said.

Jerus, the Elven healer, opened the door and stood before his queen; his portly build and short stature at odds with the tall slender build of other Greater Elves. The usual warm smile and caring eyes beneath light brown brows that usually filled Jerus' face was missing replaced with an ashen color, and faint sweat on his forehead.

'My lady, may I speak with you?' asked Jerus with a slight bow. Aradia nodded her six-foot frame towered over Jerus, long blond tresses flowing down to her waist her sapphire blue eyes fixed him with a penetrating stare. 'Bran is dying, isn't he, Jerus?'

'Yes, my lady. His wounds are beyond my ability to heal. I fear that he will not survive until we reach Elvalon.'

The queen's exquisite features, sculpted cheekbones above a perfectly symmetrical mouth, tensed into a grim mask as she turned to Jerus, 'Let us go find Raghnall.'

Climbing up a light ladder, Aradia rapidly walked to the stern of the ship, while around were the sounds of Elves repairing the ship from the rigors of the storm. A cool cloudy day, filled with mist and the faint crying of a seagull, was a welcome change from the days of the unrequited tempest, but Aradia knew that if the wind was too calm for too long, Bran would die. Aradia now saw Raghnall, the only Air Spirit known to have assumed corporeal form. He had ventured to Nostraterra in defiance of his own kind, who, for reasons of their own, had prohibited all direct contact between Air Spirits and mortals. Raghnall bore the form of a Greater Elf. He stood nearly seven feet tall, with bright silver hair. Only the faint shimmer that occasionally blurred his outline marked him as other than what he appeared to be.

'Raghnall, you told me the Air Spirits would allow me to take Bran to Elvalon, where he could be healed if I consented to their demands.'

'My lady, the Air Spirits consented to Bran's arrival in Elvalon, but they never guaranteed that he would arrive alive.'

Her pale cheeks flushed red with anger. 'I will go to him now and see how he is. Jerus in half an hour have Bran's bandages changed, along with his clothes and bed linen, remain here until then.'

Aradia strode across the deck, furious that the Air Spirits had taken advantage of her situation and her motherly love for Bran. She had been forced to surrender her freedom and nearly all of her magical powers in an effort to save Bran. She'd initially believed that the Air Spirits would honor both the intent and the letter of their agreement; that Bran would live until their arrival in Elvalon and then be treated by the most senior Elven healers. But now Aradia realized that the preeminent powers of the Greater Elves had their own plans and that she had made a bargain with entities far beyond her control or understanding, subject only to their own whims. '*Well, if they want to argue the terms of our agreement, then so can I,*' she thought with great determination.

She climbed down the ladder and knocked on Bran's door. Hearing no answer, she entered and saw Bran more unconscious than asleep. The Gracie tossed and turned, moaning faintly. The stench of his wounds permeated the air; green pus oozed from the top layer of his bandages, while stronger threads of purple light crawled over his face. Aradia reached within her robes and brought out her healing pipe again, knowing that each time she used the flute, its powers were less effective. The poison from the Dark Lightning contained magic that seemed to adapt to Aradia's magic, countering the effects of the healing notes, bringing death closer and sooner to Bran than Aradia had once thought.

The Breath Flutes were conceived by Aradia and produced by her husband Justinus soon after their arrival in Nostraterra. Their collaboration had borne fruit once before when they had designed new Air Crystals, unknown to Aradia's grandfather Phaidan, patriarch of the Greater Elves. Phaidan, jealous of her skill and innovations demanded she and Justinus reveal the techniques that they had invented so that he might have mastery of all Greater Elven magic. Refusing to submit, Aradia and Justinus instead lead a rebellion of other young Elves, determined to create a new kingdom in Nostraterra, free from interference.

Placing the flute against her lips, Aradia smiled darkly as she thought of Phaidan's face going purple with rage if he ever discovered that she and Justinus had transcended the very nature of the Air Crystals. Air Crystals were meant to move through the air, allowing the magic of the Air Spirits to flow through them, creating the magic of the Greater Elves. Instead, the Breath Flutes received their air from Aradia, allowing her to imbue her exhaled air with her own magical powers, creating magic uniquely hers. If Phaidan ever learned of this new form of magic, he would place her in prison until she surrendered all of the secrets of its use and making. Phaidan would brook no rivals to his magical supremacy or his role as king of the Greater Elves.

Aradia placed her lips against one end of the flute, and a melodious sound filled the cabin, and the strands of pink light did their work again, but this time, the effect was not as great as before. The poisoned threads lost much of their vibrancy and many of them faded away, but they would return stronger than before, winning the war over Bran's body. The terrible odor retreated, however, and Bran lay easier in his bed, enjoying a restorative sleep.

Aradia placed the flute back into her robes and thought of the other, similar flutes that lay hidden aboard ship. If they were discovered when she arrived in Elvalon, there would be little mercy for her. While all on the boat were loyal, she suspected that her baggage would be carefully searched upon her return, but with the aid of the *Silver Foam*'s captain, one of her most loyal followers, she hoped to be able to hide the flutes until she dared to use them again. Spent and hungry, she left Bran's cabin as Jerus and another Elf entered Bran's cabin to clean his body and change his bandages. Aradia returned to her own cabin and bathing and dressing, she climbed on deck in time for lunch with the ship's captain Sarton, joined by Raghnall and Jerus. As she ate, she asked Sarton 'How is the ship, when can we get underway again?'

'My lady we have hove too for the past 6 hours, and we should be underway safely in three days, I dare not risk the safety of the ship.' replied Sarton.

'How long until we reach Elvalon?'

'My experience tells me that we should have a steady north wind for the next week, so with a little luck we shall arrive in six days.'

Turning to speak with Jerus, she asked, 'Does Bran have six days?'

'No my lady, I am amazed he has lived this long, at most he will die within four days.'

'Sarton, when is the earliest that we can get moving again?'

'The main mast is sprung, and our bowsprit broke off; six hours would see us able to make way again, but even without another storm, strong waves or wind could spring another leak. Without finishing the repairs, the ship stands little chance of making Elvalon.'

'As soon as you are able to make sail again, do so.'

Sarton opened his mouth to object, when Aradia cut him off 'We and every other person in Nostraterra owe their lives to Bran, the least we can do is risk ours to save his.'

Nodding his acceptance and acknowledging the debt to Bran, Sarton turned and bellowed orders to the Elven crew 'Finish the repairs to the mast, reinforce the plug in the starboard leak, jury rig a bowsprit, I want to make sail by sunset.'

Aradia retired below for a brief nap, knowing that she would have to risk using her forbidden magic again to circumvent the machinations of the Air Spirits to try and preserve Bran's life until they reached Elvalon. But now time was her enemy and once again she would wrestle with fortune, but this time not to help herself but her friend.

* * *

Three days later, Bran was carried aloft to the port rail, close to death yet again, his wounds fomenting disease and oozing, barely able to see through the haze of pain, when he felt his chest contract, the breath leaving his frail body. Black spots swarmed before his eyes, a chill grayness covered his eyes, as if he were enveloped in rain clouds on a hillside.

Suddenly Bran felt a cool, invigorating draught placed within his lips, he swallowed reflexively, and the fog fled. Life, along with cool air, flowed back into his battered frame. Never had he known such joy in the simple act of breathing. Bran tasted sunshine and the fruits of the garden, smelled the sweet clover moving beneath the buzzing sound of bees laden with pollen. As suddenly as the flavors had appeared within his mouth, they were gone, replaced with a newfound strength that coursed through his limbs. Today he had tasted death for the second time, and this time it had seemed so empty, so empty. He hoped he would be spared its cold embrace in Elvalon, but even more, he longed to be free of the pain of his body.

Coming fully back to himself, Bran realized that someone had called his name. He blinked away the last of the mist obscuring his vision and turned his head to the left, where he saw his friend Raghnall.

'Are you all right Bran?' As Raghnall spoke, Bran saw a flash of gold in his hand. It came from a small crystal phial that shone as if a newly risen sun was trapped within it. Raghnall spilled the phial into a pocket in his robes, as Bran responded.

'Is that…' he began.

'The Cordial of Phoenicia, so powerful that only today, could you take another drop without the liquor burning your body away. The effects will last only until sunset; pray that we get you to Elvalon in time. Look now while you still have the strength to see.'

Bran turned away from Raghnall and looked over the port rail of the ship. Cerulean waves hissed as they caressed the hull, welcoming it onward into strange seas the timbers had never known. Dawn was breaking, and to the east, a golden glow filled the sky. Shafts of rose and pink, saffron and salmon streaked across the sea, blending with darkened waters. Silver-white foam climbed upward from the crests of waves, blown westward to fall like heavy raindrops upon the sea.

Bran's heart gave a great leap as he saw a range of white-tipped towers impossibly high against the still midnight-blue sky of the south. In their lee lay green isles, their living presence felt like a mother's kiss on a child's scraped knee. Peace and hope radiated from them. Bran saw small ships put out from their shores, tacking into the northerly breeze, eager to greet their brethren from the distant shores of Nostraterra. The crew responded redoubling their efforts to keep the ship afloat long enough to reach land. Above all were the towers of Myrddin, the city of the Immortal Lands. The towers rose from white castles and battlements, their tops covered in crystals that sang with the morning breezes.

'You are the first mortal to hear the music of immortality,' said Raghnall.

Bran was astounded at their song, music that came to him in the flutes of birds, the pipes of musicians, and the voices of otherworldly spirits mixed in with the noises of wind and weather. The sounds culminated into a great symphony of life and hope portending tremendous magic and power flowing through this land.

As the day wore on, the ship drew nearer to the isle, and the Elves in the first welcoming boat swarmed up the sides of the ship like squirrels up an oak tree. Many presents they brought, and their clear voices bid all welcome to the undying lands, but Aradia cut short their welcome bidding them return to Elvalon and summon the master healer to meet them at the dock as soon as possible. Several Elven mariners remained on board the *Silver Foam* aiding in the repairs as their small sleek craft turned back to Elvalon its silver lateen sail billowing out from the mast, racing before the wind to summon help for Bran.

Raghnall and Aradia remained on deck as they helped Bran into a hammock. Jerus examined Bran briefly, turning to Aradia, and said in the Elven tongue,

'Three hours after sunset my lady, that is all the time he has left. Would that he could have gone in the small boat, but the rougher voyage would have finished the work of Magnar's poison.'

'Then let us sail as fast as we can.'

Sarton stood nearby and gave the order to get every trace of speed out of the beleaguered ship, heavy objects and extra supplies were thrown overboard, their fresh drinking water pumped over the side. Fresh groans and snaps were heard by Aradia coming from the wounded main mast. Glancing at Sarton with an unspoken question, Sarton replied.

'My lady this ship must reach harbor by nightfall, or we will founder.' Mentally urging the ship on, Aradia watched the island steadily grow larger. Hearing Bran's breath coming in shorter rasps, Aradia wondered if any of them would be alive tomorrow.

* * *

An hour before sunset, the ship reached the quays of Solana, the great harbor on the north shore of Elvalon. There a great throng of Elves had gathered to greet them, as Sarton drove the sinking ship alongside the pier knowing he had to beach the ship on the soft sand close to shore as they would never remain afloat at the dock. Aradia heard the ship shudder and groan, the mainmast slowly toppling forward until it crashed upon the deck, the Elven sailors jumping free from the tangled rigging. The ship scraped to a halt and listed towards the pier on its right side by ten degrees. Elves had run alongside them, and ropes were tossed to the ship and a boarding ramp was hastily brought up and lowered to the deck of the *Silver Foam.* Bran was bundled ashore and taken into a tent bearing the flag of the Master Healer that had been hastily set up on the pier and was lost to Aradia's sight.

Aradia now saw her grandfather, Phaidan, High King of the Greater Elves emerge from the crowd. He towered a foot over Aradia, his raven black hair starkly set against his extraordinarily pale face. His deep, rich, melodious voice spoke with disdain and contempt.

'So granddaughter, you have returned to the land of your birth after leading a rebellion against my authority, do you have anything to say for yourself?'

Gritting her teeth and suppressing the rage that she felt towards the man who had always held her back from her true potential, she said 'Grandfather, accept my apology for my transgressions, I ask nothing for myself only that Bran be treated for his wounds and allowed to live here in Elvalon.'

'I can see the fire in your eyes, and I don't believe that you have repented in the slightest from your arrogant folly. Still, the first reports reached me yesterday about the tiny mortal in your charge. He accomplished what you could not, destroying Magnar and the evil magic in his realm. He will be treated by our healers and if he survives he will live in Elvalon for eternity. You will pay the agreed price for his care. Go now to my kitchens, you are the lowest scullery maid there, with no rights of the royal family. After one hundred years, your behavior will be reassessed and if you have not re-offended, you will be freed from the kitchens and placed on probation for another century as a lady in waiting. Make any presumption to resume your rebellious nonsense and you will spend eternity scrubbing dishes, and your mortal friend will age and die in a matter of days. Now go from my sight.'

Aradia could do nothing but bow her head in acceptance, hoping that someone would tell her tomorrow whether Bran had survived his healing treatments. She found herself wondering if she had made the right choice in coming here, wondering if the sacrifice of her rank and magical powers would be worth the cost. Still, morally she had no choice but to be Phaidan's loyal servant, as Bran's future held her hostage to the King's will.

Chapter Two

In Paradisium

Fourth Age: Year 100–Spring
One hundred years after returning to Elvalon, Aradia stood on the pier in the bay of Solana, conflicting emotions clouding her thoughts. Dawn was breaking over the eastern edge of the harbor, illuminating the homes and businesses clustered on the small hills that ringed the harbor in a half moon. The sounds of the harbor coming to life were all around her. The slap of oars from a small boat ferrying crew and cargo to an outbound fishing boat came over the water along with the strong smell of fish from nets drying along the shore.

Here, she thought. *Right here on this pier is where it all began. I stood on this very spot and vowed never to return … and yet here I am.*

Early in her youth, Aradia had led a rebellion of talented young Greater Elves who chafed against the conservative restrictions of the Elven Council denying them permission to experiment with Elven magic. Phaidan was the first and only Greater Elf given the secrets of both making the Crystals and how to use them by the Air Spirits. As his family grew, Phaidan made certain that the crystal-making skills were confined to Greater Elves, not of his line, who possessed no magical abilities to use the crystals. Phaidan did not want anyone to threaten his complete monopoly over the use or creation of Elven magic. Aradia from an early age showed tremendous magical talent, but Phaidan, brooking no rivals, would not teach her all that he knew, so to expand her skills and learn, she began experimenting with different movements of existing crystals, usually with disastrous results. Specific crystals were designed for individual tasks, and Aradia was terribly frustrated until she met Justinus, best and brightest of the apprentice crystal makers. Justinus possessed a similar curiosity, but he too had been forbidden by the Master Crystal maker to deviate from traditions handed down over millennia.

Aradia and Justinus then made a fateful choice: Justinus would make new crystal designs, and Aradia would experiment with them in secret. Swiftly, their efforts bore unexpected fruit as they fell in love with one another, but Phaidan discovered their activities and demanded the surrender of the crystals: worse, he forbade Aradia from seeing Justinus again, as Justinus was not a member of Elven royalty. Refusing to bow to her grandfather's demands, Aradia gathered other young Elves who yearned for independence and set sail for Nostraterra, where they would be free to be themselves.

Departing from this pier in open defiance of the Council, Aradia, and the other rebels had been convinced of the superiority of Greater Elven knowledge and culture. Aradia had wanted to civilize what she considered to be the primitive, barbaric, races of Nostraterra; to build a kingdom of her own far from the oversight of the paternalistic males, led by her grandfather, who formed the Council. She, along with her followers, would lead all the races of Nostraterra into a new enlightened age from a city she would found and rule as its queen. Aradia, Justinus, and the other Greater Elven rebels created the city of Phoenicia on the southern coast of Nostraterra, the most beautiful advanced city in the mortal lands, startling the other races of Nostraterra with their tremendous magic. Aradia and the other Greater Elves were forbidden to interfere in the affairs of the other races by the terms of the Spiritual Peace commanded by the Elementals who created the world.

According to Phaidan, when Nostraterra was newly formed from the void, the Elemental spirits had warred with one another, each vying for supremacy, creating individual portions of the world, yet seeing them destroyed by other Elementals. The futility of their actions eventually persuaded them to cease the pointless war, and each agreed to influence part of Nostraterra, with lesser Elemental spirits building specific areas under individual Elemental control. Earth chose to forego putting her power into many lesser elemental spirits, creating only a few lesser elementals, while instead creating a race of mortal creatures, Men that would breed quickly and use the secrets of the elements of the earth to eventually dominate Nostraterra. Fire chose to have many lesser elementals, but he kept the peace with the other Elementals by having only distant, mysterious contact between his Lesser Elementals and his mortal creatures. These mortals of the fire Elemental, known as Dwarves, would initially be few in number, live much longer than the creatures of earth, and slowly build their realms, hoping to outlast the brief lives of Earth's creatures. Water, gentlest of the Elementals, wanted no domination of Nostraterra, only the right to create life wherever and whenever she chose to do so. She spread her power far and wide, with only one lesser Elemental to abide in Nostraterra, creating immortal beings, the Lesser Elves, who would care for the forests and beasts. Air, strongest of the Elementals, had a large group of lesser Elementals at his command, but his very strength was his undoing, as the other Elementals allied against him most frequently. He chose to create the strongest beings to people Nostraterra, immortals superior in magic and skill above the other beings. To retain the uneasy peace amongst the Elementals, he was forced to agree that his creatures would never intervene directly in the affairs of other beings and that his lesser Elementals would communicate rarely with his creatures, the Greater Elves.

The Elementals created their creatures and set their individual plans for eventual supremacy in motion, content to wait for eons if need be for their beings to defeat the others. Only if the peace was broken, directly or indirectly, could they act personally or send their subordinate spirits to act in their stead. Constant maneuvering and jostling for power kept the Elementals on edge, suspicious of one another's actions. This mistrust manifested itself within their creatures, and each race of beings looked to the others with suspicion. But the world was young, and Nostraterra was vast: the great conflicts between the races were yet far in the future when the first mortal creatures awoke and began to fulfill the plans of their creators.

Now, returned to Elvalon, Aradia reflected on how arrogance and pride had been her downfall. Too late she'd discovered that even immense talent and undying personal strength could not lead a world if its inhabitants did not wish to be led. Prohibited from direct intervention in the affairs of mortals by the Elven Council and the Air Spirits, Aradia was forced to work indirectly, confounded and stymied by the ignorance and fear, greed and selfishness inherent in the peoples of Nostraterra. Only when the Great War enveloped Nostraterra did the other kingdoms call for her help, and then it was too late.

Justinus, searching for new materials to make stronger crystals at the edge of the Plaga Erebus, was ambushed in the first skirmish between Magnar's forces and the Greater Elves. Justinus and his entire mining party vanished, presumed dead.

Fifty years to the day that Aradia received this terrible news, Magnar launched his attack. The outer portion of the kingdom of Phoenicia was sacked and looted, leaving only the eponymous capital city on the southern shores of Nostraterra intact. Aradia wept for her husband but took solace that her city, and her people, most of all her son, Marcellus, remained safe. Aradia bitterly remembered the choice forced upon her by the Elven Council: flee with the few ships she had, abandoning most of the Elves of Phoenicia, or intervene in the war and lose her powers. Unable to betray her subjects or even the ungrateful peoples of Nostraterra, she had stayed to fight for her people and her kingdom. She felt so certain that her choice to stay and fight had been the correct one. But her certainty and inner peace were breached as quickly as the city's defenses as the hordes of Magnar sacked and looted the city while Aradia found her magic inexplicably useless against Magnar's sorcery. Fleeing with the tattered remnants of her people, Marcellus leading the van and Emedius, weapons master of the Greater Elves, guarding the rear, she found temporary refuge in the Great Forest of the Lesser Elves.

There she was met by an Air Spirit sent by her grandfather. Stripping her of all her traditional magic, the spirit offered her a final choice: return to Elvalon, beg forgiveness from the Council, and spend a year in humble compliance to her Grandfather's will, or remain a powerless Elf woman, queen of a ruined city and a ravaged people. Raging in defiance, she refused to return to Elvalon, determined to regain her powers through methods known only to her. And such had been her intent ... until Bran was brought to her, dying from terrible wounds. After all the pain and loss Aradia had suffered, this was a tragedy she could not endure. Secretly she used a flute created by Justinus for healing and played the small crystal instrument, staving off Bran's death. The Breath Crystals, as Aradia and Justinus called them, were few in number, but Aradia had not been given the powers to use them by the Air Spirits, instead of learning them on her own.

Remorse for leading her people from the safety of Elvalon to disaster, and grief at the loss of her husband and her kingdom, overcame her desire to remain free. Guilt coursed through her mind as Aradia realized the tremendous suffering she had inadvertently caused by her arrogant presumption that she could change Nostraterra for the better. Distraught and hopeless, magically destitute of her traditional powers, Aradia had been determined to save at least one innocent life, and thus she had asked Raghnall to petition the Air Spirits to aid Bran. The Air Spirits had agreed, but their conditions, backed by the Elven Council, had been dire. Aradia was forced to accept even more humiliating terms than she had been offered before. Now Aradia would become a submissive lady in waiting, losing her royal privileges and titles for one hundred years, but Bran would be allowed access to Elvalon, to heal and become whole again.

Now, today, her sentence had been removed at last, and she had been restored the use of her traditional powers … though forbidden to experiment with new forms of Elven magic. She had come here, to where her long downfall and suffering had begun, to watch the sunrise on what she believed would be a new life, one in which she had learned from the errors of the past. One in which she could be happy again. Complete.

No one troubled her solitude, and she basked there in the morning light, feeling as if the dawn were breaking inside her as well as without. But she did not linger overlong, for had agreed to meet Bran at his house close to the harbor. It was late morning when she arrived at Bran's simple home, located in a quiet courtyard adjacent to a small market where the hum of Elves going about their business was faintly heard. She knocked and was told to enter.

Ducking her head, Aradia avoided the low ceiling of a dwelling fit for a Gracie. Clean white-plastered walls in a rustic style with wooden beams greeted her eye. A simple couch stood against one wall. This sitting room was also Bran's dining area, and Aradia smelled the simple fish stew that Bran made for his lunch, the aroma drifting from a pot that hung above the glowing coals of the fireplace along the wall near his kitchen. Daylight streamed in through open windows.

Bran offered her refreshment, which she declined. Crossing a small rug woven of clean rags sold cheaply in the markets, she sat on the low, cloth-covered couch, her knees nearly level with her chin, and looked at Bran in the sunlight. How young he looked! Far from the prematurely aged and wounded Gracie who had disembarked the ship one hundred years ago. The Air Spirits had actually kept their word. 'Well, how are you, then Bran?' she asked.

'Fine, my lady, I am as healed as my wounds will allow. But my dreams remain dark and foreboding.'

Knowing that Bran would likely never recover completely from the terrors of his adventures, the pain of his physical wounds, and the loss of his dearest friends, Aradia counseled him as she always did to focus on the present and the future. 'The past, dear Bran, is eternally written. No magic can change it.'

'I know this objectively, my lady, but it still haunts me. However, that is not what I wanted to discuss with you today. For the past two weeks or so, I have had a recurring dream of Gracies in thralldom and Platonia overrun by outcasts and vagabonds. I am afraid now that my sacrifice was in vain and that my home is in great danger.'

'Why do you believe your dreams are anything more than that?' asked Aradia.

'I have never had a dream that repeats itself night after night. I believe in my heart that what I see is true. We Gracies have always relied on our rivers to protect us from the outside world. Even before I departed, there was some concern amongst us that an attack by the Alchemists of Men could overpower the River Spirits who guard us against outsiders. If Men successfully overcome our River Spirits, then we will be forced to rely on the goodness of Men to honor their treaty giving us Platonia in perpetuity for our part in destroying Magnar. Who will look after the Gracies if Men fail in their promise and allow others to take Platonia for themselves?'

Aradia replied, 'When we left, one hundred years ago, nearly all of the Alchemists had been slain in their efforts to defeat Magnar. Many of their secrets were lost, according to the Men of Eldora. Even the two Earth Spirits who, according to legend, taught the Alchemists of Men their knowledge had fled Eldora to parts unknown long before Magnar attacked the world. Only the Earth Spirit who values life and the growth of animals and plants remains among Men, and even he has gone missing. What makes you think that Men could now attack your River Spirits and force your land into submission?'

'My dream is persistent, my lady. I do not know what else to say other than that.'

'Why would Men covet your small lands? Nostraterra is vast, and even now I am certain that Men have not filled all the corners. Besides, the Men of Eldora and Kozak are for the most part honorable and true. They will protect your land against intruders in thanks for the great part that you played in freeing all of Nostraterra from the terror of Magnar.'

'If there is one thing I learned during my journey to the dark land, it is that most people, when given half a chance, will take from others simply to have something that someone else does not—Magnar being the greatest example of such selfish desire. Please, my lady, will you take me to the place of your visions so that I may see for myself that Platonia is safe?'

Aradia frowned. 'Though I mentioned this place to you, Bran, I also told you that I am under complete restriction to use any magic by the Council, including using the Acies,' she said, referencing the massive crystal set in the Tower of Sight to which Bran had referred.

'I may be much older than I look,' Bran said, 'but I have not yet lost my wits. Rumors of your pardon swirled through the market when I went shopping this morning. It is common knowledge that your sentence is over. The restriction has been lifted, your powers and authority reinstated. You can help me if you wish it.'

Sighing, Aradia said, 'Yes, my restrictions are lifted, it's true. But if I wish to keep my new status, I must abide by the law. No one but a member of the royal family is allowed to use the Acies, and it is strictly forbidden for all but Greater Elves to communicate through them.'

'I do not want to talk to anyone, my lady, just look through it a single time. You can direct it to allow me to see Platonia. I lack the knowledge, desire, and skill to communicate with anyone. I just want to see. My access would be only with and through you, so what harm could it possibly cause? I have not asked for any favors from you Elves in the two hundred years I have been here. Surely, after so long, I might be permitted a brief glimpse of home.'

Confounded by this clear logic, Aradia was uncertain what to do. Part of her thought of sending for permission from the Elven Council, but as this was a minor matter; it might take weeks or months to receive a response. After all, her appeal for clemency had been pending before the Council for three years before she had finally received the news this morning. The Elven Council derived its power from the Air Spirits who communicated through Seven Sacred Crystals of Air. The Spirits' voices were notes of music, various tones that were open for interpretation by the Seers of the Elven Council. Aradia knew that the only method of communication was to make similar sounding tones through a sending crystal played by the only Crystal Master, one of the oldest Elves in Elvalon, with air supplied from bellows by his two apprentices. At least two millennia of training were necessary before an apprentice had sufficient skill and knowledge to become a Master, forming random notes and tones into messages complex enough to pique the Air Spirits' interest. The Air Spirits were notorious for ignoring most requests from the Elves, and when they responded, a simple answer was highly unusual, and only when their preeminent law of non-interference was at risk. Thus the three Seers of the Council interpreted the messages from the Air Spirits and frequently disagreed with each other. The only fact that had remained constant for the past millennia was a strict policy of isolation, in which the Air Spirits refused to aid any Elves that left Elvalon for Nostraterra.

Besides, Bran was correct: she would not be violating Elven law in any significant way that she could see. So what if he looked upon the forbidden crystals? And who, if not Bran, deserved a bit of mercy, a glimpse of home? Still, if she did this thing for her old friend, she must be careful and consult with some authority in Elvalon to make certain that she was not punished again.

Saying nothing, Bran looked haunted by his dreams, and she was moved again by great pity for him.

'Very well. Tomorrow, I will meet you here just before dawn. But we will meet with Raghnall on our way to the tower and abide by his opinion in this matter. If he says that you may not see through the Acies, then we must petition the Elven Council and await their reply, no matter how long it will take.'

Bran nodded his assent, as this was the best outcome that he could reasonably expect.

The next morning, in darkness, Aradia and Bran passed swiftly across the city of Myrddin to the hill on which stood the Vistus Castellum, the Tower of Sight. Waiting for them at the foot of the hill was Raghnall, his lined face grave but not foreboding.

Raghnall was the only Air Spirit who had taken corporeal form in the history of Elvalon. He had done so in an effort to aid Aradia and her rebel group millennia ago. In punishment for defying the ban on Air Spirits aiding material beings directly, Raghnall was forced to remain in this form indefinitely, allowed access to some of his former powers, seemingly at random, but not allowed to transform back into spiritual form. Raghnall had told Aradia long ago that he believed the Greater Elves would someday play a decisive role in defeating evil in Nostraterra and that he was willing to make this great sacrifice in aiding her and the Greater Elves in the creation of their city of Phoenicia.

Now Aradia spoke with him and asked his thoughts on taking Bran to the Acies. Raghnall was long in thought, and his eyes lost focus as he appeared to commune with a higher power. Aradia saw Bran shuffle uncomfortably as the seconds became minutes and the minutes nearly an hour before Rahall's gaze returned to Aradia and Bran.

'I consulted the Air Spirits, and while theirs was not a unanimous decision, the consensus is that you are correct, Aradia. Bran's aid in defeating Magnar is renowned even in the spirit world, and allowing him to see his homeland is part recompense for his great sacrifice. Such is the view of the majority of the Air Spirits. However'— and Raghnall's features took on a stern aspect—'if Bran communicates with anyone or anything in Nostraterra in any fashion, you and he will be severely punished. Is this clear, Bran? There will be no mercy if you break this command.'

'Perfectly clear, Raghnall,' replied Bran, whose ruddy, cheerful face now drained of color.

'Then you both may proceed with me. I will inform the guards at the base of the tower that you are both allowed to enter the room of the Acies.'

A great beacon had been placed atop the tower to hold the light of the sun and moon at all times. It lit the sea for dozens of leagues at night so that any ships tarrying in the darkness need not fear to lose their way. Bran marveled at the immense crystal tower two hundred feet tall, built of white, hard stone whose pipes and flutes powered the beacon. The crystal tubes, imbued with the magic of the Elves, took energy from the very air and changed it through sound into a great heat and light.

The beacon waxed and waned as the wind coursed through the beautiful tubes. A deep, powerful song was sung by these tubes, often plunging in tone to beneath hearing, resonating in the body with powerful waves. Indeed, even the Elves could not long withstand the power of the song of this mightiest of crystal towers. Guards were exchanged several times per day, yet still, the tower took its toll, and the Thunder Elves, as the guards and beacon tenders were known, came to look old in a land of perpetual youth.

With Bran and Raghnall beside her—the Gracie appeared lost in marveling—Aradia climbed the steps to the tower entrance. There Raghnall stopped and addressed the guards, informing them that Aradia and Bran had the permission of the Air Spirits to enter into the Chamber of the Acies.

The guard captain was relatively young, perhaps millennia in age, and he was rather short, with weak, watery features under his dark hair. His thin voice matched his stature. 'My lord Raghnall, while I take your word that the Air Spirits have given permission, I must have permission from the Elven Council for this mortal to proceed with lady Aradia."

Raghnall shot him a glance of cold condescension. 'Young one, the Elven Council draws its authority directly from us Air Spirits. Lady Aradia and her guest have neither the time nor the inclination to wait on a slip of parchment from the Elven Council. We Air Spirits have allowed this visit. Now stand aside.'

Looking uncomfortable but acknowledging the authority of Raghnall, the guard captain bowed and stood aside, 'My lady, you and your companion may proceed. Here is a pass to present to the guards on duty outside the Acies Chamber.'

'I shall wait here,' said Raghnall.

Aradia nodded. 'We will not be long.'

In silence, Aradia and Bran climbed the circular stairs that led up the tower. Six Elven guards greeted them at the entrance to the chamber and, after briefly examining Aradia's pass, bowed and opened the doors.

Aradia knew the history of Elven magic better than any Elf but her grandfather and her brother. Great was the skill of the Greater Elves in the Ancient Days when magic was fresh and ran freely in the world. It was then that they had built the great city of Myrddin in Elvalon. Her grandfather had drawn forth the magic from the air necessary to create the Acies, and the finest Elven crystal wrights had built the magic devices when they were still young in their craft, before their final masterworks, the Crystal Towers of Air, were born of their hands and hearts, forming the heart of the defenses of Elvalon.

Beyond the door lay the master crystal pipes of the Acies. There were other lesser and Greater Acies within Elvalon, one Greater Acies in Phoenicia, and four lesser Acies scattered throughout Nostraterra, originally given by Aradia to the men of Eldora.

Lesser Acies, while transmitting images to the user, only allowed communication when another person was using an Acies. More powerful Acies would allow the user to send messages to others, though the recipient of the message could not respond directly to the sender. Only the master Acies here in the tower allowed the user to directly communicate with another if they were not using an Acies in return. Moreover, all of the Acies would present images of past and present and future, though only a highly skilled user could distinguish between certain of these images. The Elves who were allowed to possess them used the Acies as messenger devices. The Greater Acies could be directed by the user to an extent, depending upon the mental strength of the viewer, and could communicate with both other Greater Acies to a limited degree and with nearby lesser Acies with only minor difficulty.

Aradia was going to use the Master Acies herself to see if she could, what was occurring in Nostraterra, and then focus its powers on Platonia. As she and Bran entered the room, she knew in her heart there would come a time again when the purposes of the Council and her own purposes were in direct conflict. She hoped only to have enough time to be beyond the reach of the Council before she returned to Nostraterra to resume her desire to bring order to that chaos.

Enormous open windows filled the outer walls of the room, giving Aradia a view of the endless ocean to the north, and the lands of Elvalon to the east and west. The breeze was much stronger up here, blowing almost constantly from one direction or another. The sweet smells of the flowers of Elvalon wafted into the room with the ever-present salt tang of the ocean. This high above the surface, on an isolated hilltop, the only sound was that of the wind; sometimes cheerful, occasionally mournful, the sound came with each gust as it danced and swirled around the room.

The room itself was simply furnished. Chairs were set along one wall, and there were a small step ladder and one gold circle inlaid in the floor about two feet in diameter where one stood to use the Acies. The large crystal pipes of the Acies hung down from the ceiling in an ornate, chaotic mass, glinting in many different colors as the sunlight that streamed in from the eastern window was refracted and reflected in an endless light that constantly changed.

Bran stood a few feet back from the center of the room as Aradia moved around the collection of pipes, which was over ten feet in circumference, hanging down from the simple ceiling above it. Many valves were within her reach, but others required the use of the ladder, and Bran was soon moving the light wooden ladder on wheels as Aradia commanded. Bran looked on in confused wonder at the Acies: some of the crystal cylinders resembled flutes, with a myriad of small holes where air would flow and resonate, while others were larger, nearly ten inches across and ten feet long, responsible for the deepest sounds of the set. Still, others were tiny, smaller than even Bran's fingers, and made no noise that Bran could hear.

'My lady, how does it work?'

'By opening and closing the valves and stoppers, I can generate an infinite variety of tones, but most of these are useless except to create a sense of mood or create an enticing fragrance in a home. There are small crystal sets, sold by my family, that require no magic; just place them in an open window, and they will generate one effect, perhaps the smell of new-made bread. Please move the ladder two feet to the left, Bran, thank you. But the great, complex sets, such as this Acies or the Beacon crystals, can do much more. As you saw as we arrived, the massive towers strung along the coast project enchantments of the Elves across the water so that none but the Greater Elves can come here. Now please let me concentrate: the exact combination of tones is quite complex; I will need all of my thoughts focused on the task to allow you to see Platonia. Just move the ladder when and where I tell you.'

'Yes, my lady.'

Aradia focused on the final subtle combination of tones needed to produce distant visions in the Acies—a combination known to only a few Elves of the royal house of Phaida. Though it had been more than two centuries since Aradia had stood here, in the Chamber of the Acies, she had not forgotten the knowledge that was her birthright.

With only final small adjustments necessary within her reach on the ground, Aradia had Bran sit in one of the chairs in the room as she twisted knobs to create the silvery-sounding tones that indicated the crystals could and would produce their visions. Suddenly a sphere of light burst forth from the Crystals, forming a globe many feet in diameter, and Aradia heard Bran gasp in wonder. Most of the pertinent information was only visible within the golden circle, and Aradia knew that Bran could only see the odd vision from his vantage point a few feet from her side. The magic had a will of its own, and while it could be directed to a degree by someone as powerful as Aradia, the images it chose to reveal were not always of the present, but instead could be of the past or the future.

'My lady, may I look now?' asked Bran, screwing up his courage.

'Please do not interrupt, Bran,' Aradia replied without glancing up. 'I must now engage my will with the crystal set. Otherwise, it will generate random images from all over Elvalon, Nostraterra, and even the ocean. Once I have adjusted the Acies, I will first have a look around Nostraterra to satisfy my own curiosity. Then, when I am finished, I will focus the Acies on Platonia and sit in the chair next to you. Then you can step into the circle and see your homeland. But for now, please be still.'

Aradia stood in the golden circle looking into the light sphere immediately beneath the crystal set. At first, she saw little, only the sea and views from the other Acies located in Elvalon. Slowly, she became able to direct her gaze, and ever northward did she press, until she cast her glance toward Phoenicia, where her cousin Celefin, Lord of Phoenicia, dwelt with Emedius, weapons master of the Greater Elves. Seeing him, she was able to use her many gifts to read some of his thoughts and learned much concerning the Greater Elves who yet remained in Nostraterra.

Then the sphere took her farther afield from Phoenicia. She saw swirling smoke, trees that were in motion, Gracies on short horses, some with weapons, and bedraggled Men standing in weak sunlight. These images were confusing and disturbing, as the Acies was unclear as to the sequence of the events and their specific location. Still, the images seemed to validate some of Bran's concerns.

Bored of sitting, Bran rose from his chair and slowly walked around the sphere, watching idly as occasional images flashed into focus and then disappeared. The only image that made sense to him was one where Gracies appeared engaged in combat. The rest showed places unknown to him and the faces of people that he did not know. Impatiently, he waited for Aradia to finish with her search, reminding himself that he would soon partake of magic that was not even rumored amongst Gracies, much less accessible to them.

Aradia concentrated harder on bending the magic of the Acies to her will, and the sphere took her northeastward to the Ice Mountains, where she could see into many of the Dwarven mines, but not into the minds of the Dwarves. She saw enough clear visions of Nerea, the great Dwarf Mine, to concern her gravely. Looking north to the Dwarves of the Bastion and those of the Sandy Hills, she caught her breath in fear as an ancient dark magic took new form, fluttering wingtips crackling with lightning as it embarked on a new reign of terror and destruction, the ancient enemy of the Dwarves stalking them again with terrible new weapons.

'No, it cannot happen again, not after all these years!' she muttered to herself.

Looking away from the sphere, she paused and, seeing Bran's hopeful gaze, shook her head, then returned her gaze to its depths. This time she was able to focus her thoughts more clearly and looked into Eldora, the realm of the Westmen. Many images of Men flickered and died, each more foul than the last. Corruption vied with debauchery and treachery as Men took what they wanted from themselves and from others.

'So, this is the legacy of the Westmen,' she thought with disgust. 'This is what we all fought and died and sacrificed for: the rule of Men at the last.' Though sickened by what she saw, she was surprised by it. The scenes only reinforced her fears that Men would lead Nostraterra into decay and destruction, even those of the north. 'Why?' she asked herself silently. 'Why are they acting like this now?' her mind drawn to a hidden source of great power far to the east in Nostraterra.

Suddenly, she heard Raghnall's voice in her mind even though he remained outside the tower, '*Cease looking eastward Aradia, turn now to answering Bran's questions*.'

Ignoring his command, she bid the crystals to help answer her question and they into the Eastern Waste of far Azhar. Here she saw hundreds of people, Elven in origin, but dressed in skins and rude clothes, the Dark Elves, chaotic allies of Magnar banished after the end of the war. Gathered together, they praised a giant humanoid figure garbed in blue robes. Its features were hidden by a large hooded cowl. She could guess nothing of its race and origins. Shimmers of light and darkness came from its outstretched hands, glowing and fading, serpentine bands of radiance and emptiness vying with one another in their quest for supremacy. The blue hands, with claw-like fingers covered in scales, were like nothing she had ever seen or heard of before. They manipulated the intertwining bands, holding them together somehow, despite their apparent opposition in kind, even as they twisted and turned their way outward from the figure.

'Perhaps there is a similarity in function,' Aradia thought. 'The mirrored reflection of the same will or purpose that takes different hues and forms, facets of an unknown power of thought and focus.'

Many of the Dark Elves were touched by these emanations, and some writhed in pain as they died. Still, others began to change into forms that had no clear shape or purpose. One thing was certain: none of those who came into contact with the billowing strands of nightmare were able to survive without catastrophic change to their corporeal forms.

Feeling the evil presence of this figure, but seeing nothing clearly of it besides its clawed blue hands; she pulled her gaze away, directing it to a second nearby figure. This one was also garbed in coarse robes of a dark, nearly midnight blue. Its hands were also blue, though of a darker hue, and its face and form were likewise concealed beneath robe and cowl. But Aradia felt on some unknown level that this being was mightier than the first blue shape she had seen.

This second figure unlike the first stood utterly still, without any overt display of magical energy. Yet it exuded a sense of power that made Aradia shiver. Little could she see of its interactions with its subjects or slaves, but the bodies of the Dark Elves, moving in a rhythmic, sequential dance, testified to its influence over them. Aradia felt sure that those bowing before this second figure were wholly its creatures, devoid of individual will or thought.

Swaying as though in an ecstatic trance; the worshippers turned their faces to the sun and silently screamed. Raw rage was written there. It seemed to Aradia that their hatred was so great that it must extinguish the sun itself. For it was plain that they needed only one sun: the blue-garbed figure around which they orbited.

Pulling terrified animals, birds, and wild dogs toward a crude altar, the Dark Elves slew them all, slashing their throats and anointing themselves with the warm blood of their victims, offering the hearts to the darker figure before them. The creature gestured slightly, and those closest to it fell screaming, their bodies melting and blazing in the darkening sky.

Now more Dark Elves dragged a young female, a child of Man, to the altar. She seemed drugged, or at any rate did not struggle or cry out as her heart was torn from her body by the fingers of the supplicants and held up, still beating, to the blue-garbed figure. This time the creature did not slay its worshipers but instead imbued the closest with an unearthly black-purple hue. As dark light flickered across their limbs and upturned faces, they grew in stature, their faces gleaming with an almost sexual rapture even as their eyes became blackened slits and their fingers elongated and twisted, turning into claws. All the while, they sang silently to the maker of their madness.

All at once the cloaked head rose; its face still concealed, yet Aradia felt the hidden gaze reach out to her across the vast distance that separated them. The creature removed what appeared to be a large black gem, nearly the size of Aradia's hand, from its cloak and held it in front of its shadowed face as it stared in Aradia's direction. A chilling stab of malice thrust at her mind as the figure tried not merely to contact her through the Acies but to overwhelm her defenses. It knew she was watching, of that she had no doubt. And it meant her no good. The strength of its dark mind, unknown and unheralded, was astonishing. She felt a shadow, an echo, of the madness and hatred that dwelt there, and a dark hunger that yearned to feed on her soul. The creature would possess her if it could.

But Aradia was not so easily defeated, though it had been long indeed since she had battled mind to mind in this way. Fortifying her thoughts from all of the long, hard years of struggle in Nostraterra, she used her renewed powers to snap the outstretched tendrils of hateful cunning that searched for her without eyes. As soon as the pressure lifted, and before the attack could be renewed, she pulled back, retreating from the most powerful evil mind she had felt since the days of Magnar.

Wrenching herself from the sphere of light, Aradia withdrew her gaze and collapsed, exhausted, onto a chair.

Bran rushed over. 'My lady, are you all right? Should I summon the guards?'

Powerless for several moments, she could say nothing but waived her hand toward Bran and the sphere, which Bran took as a signal that she was merely tired, that he should enter the circle. He took this opportunity to gaze into the sphere itself, believing that Aradia had left it focused on Platonia for his use.

Dragging the small ladder into the golden circle, he climbed to its top rung. There, balanced precariously, he gazed into the sphere. But instead of the pastoral fields of Platonia, he beheld a terrible blue-cloaked figure holding a black gemstone in front of its hidden face. Dark blue rays of energy shot from the gem and through the sphere, striking Bran in the face and running up and down his body. Never had he known such pain. He screamed as the crackling sounds of lightning filled his ears and a horrible smell of burning meat rose to his nostrils. Only briefly did Bran realize that his body was the source of these sounds and smells.

The guards outside the room heard Bran's terrible screams and rushed into the room. One went to Bran's aid as the other, seeing the terrible purple rays of energy slash into the Gracie again, moved to close the valves on the crystal set. As he pulled the last valve shut, a final blast of energy emerged, slaying him where he stood. Still, his falling body completed its action, shutting down the Acies. The other guard, meanwhile, ordered his fellows to carry Bran from the chamber. The Gracie's unconscious body twitched as streamers of dark energy faded, sinking into his flesh.

Aradia rose from her chair and took a step toward Bran then, intending to aid her friend, but her reserves of strength were gone. Black spots swam before her eyes, merging, spreading over everything, and she knew nothing more.

* * *

Later that day, Aradia lay upon a couch in her chambers. The curtains were drawn to protect her eyes, which were unusually sensitive to light in the aftermath of the attack. She still could scarcely believe what had happened. The blue-clad creature had sent its magic through the Acies. That should not have been possible for anyone. What was the creature, and why had it attacked her? The strength of it, the sheer violent hatred she had sensed, caused her to shake, assailed by fear such as she had never known, not even when she had faced Magnar.

Just then, a knock came at the door. She heard it openthen sensed more than saw Raghnall and her brother, Dorphin, enter.

'How do you fare, my sister?' asked Dorphin in a voice at once gentle and sorrowful.

'Bran,' she croaked, with no thought for herself. 'How is he?'

'In great pain,' responded Raghnall coldly. 'The dark magic that attacked him lives in his flesh still. He will last only a matter of hours maybe a day or so. He is paying for your incredible arrogance in ignoring my command, with his very life. I hope that you are satisfied with yourself.'

Weeping bitter tears, Aradia begged Raghnall to aid Bran, asking him to use the power of the Air Spirits.

'Do you not think I haven't tried?' Raghnall replied angrily. 'Unfortunately for Bran, the magic that invests his body will not respond to any magic available to the Elves, and the Air Spirits have denied my request for aid and temporarily have taken away my powers for my role in allowing this catastrophe to happen. I cannot save him. No one can. Bran will die, as the world intended before we ever brought him here.'

'I must see him,' she said. 'I must try to—'

'You have done enough,' Raghnall broke in. 'Bran is beyond your help now. You should be more concerned about the Council.'

Aradia felt a thrill of fear at that. 'What do you mean?'

'They have decreed that you are to be placed under close watch for a year and a day. During this time, you will not have access to the Acies. Nor shall you be permitted to use any of your Elven magical skills.'

'I broke no Elven law!' croaked Aradia angrily. 'How dare they punish me? Shall I be relegated to cleaning kitchens again, or do I have some dignity and respect left from my family and the Council?'

'Silence!' thundered Raghnall, and Aradia heard in his voice that she had gone too far. 'Even now, you repent nothing. You have learned nothing. I told you that while you were allowed to use the Acies yourself and allow Bran to see his homeland, you were not to allow Bran to communicate with anyone in Nostraterra. Once we Air Spirits felt the tremendous dark powers close to where you were looking, I commanded you to stop, but you refused and look what happened? You broke the law of the Air Spirits, and my plea on your behalf condemns me as well. Any hope that I might receive more if not all of my powers back has been summarily rejected. Selfish, sentimental woman, you have allowed an unknown creature with terrible powers access to Elvalon. Who knows what this creature might be capable of now? All Elves are forbidden the Acies until we Air Spirits can create safeguards against this most terrible magic.'

At that, Dorphin spoke up. 'You will always have my love, sister, but your action was incredibly foolish and, yes, selfish. Now there is fear in the Council that, as Raghnall says, thanks to you, whatever you saw has learned a way to breach the magical barriers that protect Elvalon. Now, this creature may attack other Elves who live here, as it did you and Bran, or, worse, may suborn them into doing its bidding. That is why your punishment is so harsh. Don't you see? They are afraid you might be under the influence of Dark Magic.'

'The only influence I am under at the moment is anger,' she said. 'And that mostly at me for allowing Bran access to the Acies. It is my fault that he is dying. Take me to him in the morning if you will, Dorphin. I should be strong enough to see him then.'

* * *

By the next morning, Aradia's eyes were able to tolerate dim light. Wearing a hood, she was escorted by Raghnall to Bran's chamber, where the Gracie lay in his bed. As soon as she entered, she saw the horrible pulsing of purple energy below his skin, like a crawling bruise. The sheets of his bed were filled with putrescent ooze whose foul odor assailed her with almost physical force.

Ignoring it, she pulled free of Raghnall's supporting arm and knelt at the bedside, taking Bran's hand in her own. 'I am so sorry, Bran, that you were attacked,' she said softly. 'If I had thought you would be in any danger, I would have kept you from the chamber and looked at Platonia for you.'

'It is not your fault, my lady,' hissed Bran through clenched teeth. 'I begged you for this chance, and I took it. But unlike the other times, I escaped death, this time I fear there is no other path.'

'Think of it as a gift,' said Raghnall. 'You will soon be beyond the point of pain and heartbreak. You will be at peace.'

'A gift,' Bran repeated and laughed weakly. 'A gift would have been to remain here in Elvalon forever, my pain slowly fading through time, or until I was weary of life. Instead, I have had but a taste of immortality, a taste that is now unjustly taken from me for no greater crime than concern for my people.'

Raghnall seemed intrigued by these words. 'All of your people eventually die, Bran. They can accept it. Why can't you?'

With a weak yet vehement voice, Bran said, 'You may be wise, Raghnall, wise beyond the vision of Men and Elves alike, but you are blind when it comes to the hearts of mortal beings. Can you not guess what I have always wanted?

Raghnall thought a moment, then said, 'No, I cannot.'

'Family,' cried Bran. 'A sense of belonging somewhere; belonging to someone, of believing in something that mattered; a sense of purpose. I was orphaned at an early age. My parents died of an evil plague that came from a Gracie who traded in the far east of Nostraterra. I was raised by distant wealthy cousins. I lacked for nothing, but I did not have any family. I was always alone. I had a few friends, and they provided great comfort at the time, and I didn't understand until much later all that I was missing. I became an acolyte of the Gardens to give myself some purpose and then undertook my dark journey in the hope of preserving Platonia from harm.

'Magnar represented a danger to Platonia, and as long as he lived, my people were in danger. While they were not my immediate family, they were the only family that I knew. I took the Waters of Life to the Plaga Erebus and poured them into the breach hewn into the conduits of Dark Lightning, destroying the power of Magnar: hoping that with his destruction I could return to a home unscathed by war and anguish, that the tramp of boots from evil creatures would not be heard in the quiet fields or family taverns of Platonia. Yet it was not to be. I came here to preserve my life, in hope of peace and healing. Yet that hope, too, has been dashed. I am dying. I am so afraid that my sacrifice and those of the other Gracies will be in vain! Platonia is still in danger—worse danger than ever. I know it! And there is nothing I can do to help.'

'Your sacrifice was not in vain,' replied Raghnall. 'All that you desired to preserve was preserved. Your cousins and Platonia were saved along with the rest of Nostraterra. Take solace in that.'

'Thoughts of what is past cannot assuage my fears of what the future may hold,' Bran said. 'That is what torments me now. What happens after we die, Raghnall? Where will I go? What will I become?'

Raghnall answered softly. 'Your questions have been asked by many mortals. And many are the answers they have given themselves. All the Spirits that oversee Nostraterra demand faith, but they will not give certainty in exchange; unfair perhaps, but then you mortals are myriad mayflies in a perpetual morning that they—'

'I do not mean to be rude,' said Bran, interrupting, 'but my questions have only one answer. I do not belong anywhere. I have been bereft of kin since I was born. Alas, that is my doom. I only wish that somehow it could have been different. The least of all Gracies have a home to call his own: a family and a place in Platonia. He is secure in the knowledge that, at least within his family, he will go on. Here I am only a name in a song, a heroic figure in a larger tale, a small thread in the greater tapestry. Please forgive me for my outburst,' he went on, seeing the effect of his words on Raghnall and Aradia. 'None of this is your fault. You have heard the maunderings of a dying Gracie who only wanted a simple life that was denied him. I fear now more than ever after my encounter yesterday that Platonia is still in danger. Keep my people and my land safe once I am gone, I beg you both.'

Aradia spoke, still kneeling beside him, clasping his hand in hers, tears streaming down her proud face. 'Bran, I do not have the answers to your questions. The Acies showed me only confused images of Platonia. Your people might be in danger now or perhaps in the future. Nothing is certain. But there is a new ship arrived this morning from Nostraterra. We can ask the crew if they have heard any tales. Hold on while we send a messenger.'

'My lady, I am trying to,' said Bran, 'but I feel my life departing quickly now.' With those words, a deep shudder wracked his body. 'I am so cold, my lady. I am so frightened. I can't see anymore.'

His breathing grew thin and rapid, his chest heaving under the blankets, gasping for air. One final word, 'Platonia,' sighing his last breath in Elvalon.

Aradia wept openly for Bran.

After several minutes, Raghnall said, 'Go in peace, my friends, for the spirit of our beloved friend is now departed. Let us honor him with our memories. There shall be a feast in his honor within Boreas, the holy grove of air, in seven days' time, his body interred in fragrant earth as is the custom of his people, but his coffin will be interred in marble at the foot of the sacred mountains.'

* * *

Later that day, Aradia found Raghnall standing on one of the small hills contained within the city, looking out over the waters of the harbor. Raghnall turned toward her as she approached, nodding in acknowledgment of her presence.

'Did you ask the Elves who came from overseas if there was anything to substantiate Bran's fear?' asked Aradia.

'Not yet,' he replied. 'I was waiting for them to sleep and wash away the burdens of the mortal lands.' After pausing for a moment, Raghnall asked, 'Why was Bran so afraid his sacrifices had been in vain? Despite the attack of the dark creature, it is located far away from the civilized regions of Nostraterra and no threat to Platonia. Besides, Magnar is no more. The Hraban, his terrible Black Cavalry, perished before the walls of Titania. The great Southern army that was once united in purpose and destruction fled in disarray, pursued by the armies of Men. All of the Elemental Spirits and wizards that aided Magnar have been defeated, their avatars and bodies destroyed. The Dark Elves, who survived the war, were sent fleeing into the utter east. Even if they are allies of this blue creature, there is no indication that they will attack Platonia. None of the great evils that once sought to dominate Nostraterra survived the fall of Magnar. Bran succeeded beyond his knowledge. Not only did he help destroy the Fountain, but he saved his own land from destruction. He asked us to protect Platonia after his passing, and I intend to do so, but until this attack, I did not fear that any Dark Magic was left in Nostraterra. Men are the most powerful race there now. They, too, lost much in the war. I believe that they will do well by the rest of Nostraterra.'

'How can you believe that the powers of Men are preeminent and all other ancient powers removed after the attack upon Bran and me?' Aradia asked in turn. 'Clearly, even an Air Spirit can be mistaken, or perhaps deluded. As the attack showed, there are still beings greater in power than Elves alive and well in Nostraterra. While the beings may now be in the far-east, how long will they remain there? Even if those terrible blue creatures stay put, there are mortals in Nostraterra who covet what the Gracies have and will stop at nothing to possess it.'

'Most Men are honorable and trustworthy,' Raghnall said. 'Are you saying that the rule of Men, even those such as the Westmen, is flawed? That they are incapable of governing themselves?'

'No,' answered Aradia. 'I am saying that while Men are capable of governing themselves—although that, too, is open for debate—there is no guarantee that Men will govern the other creatures of Nostraterra with wisdom. Not only the other mortals but all the Elves in Nostraterra will fall under their sway. What of them? Even Celefin, Elf Lord of Phoenicia, and my son, Marcellus, must bow to the weight of Men. Men alone of all the races of Nostraterra survived the Great War essentially intact, their cities still standing, their people alive and well. All other races will have to determine how they will live under the dominion of Men. Men, given half a chance, have always fallen into darkness. How can I expect them to succeed this time? Will they become benevolent leaders or despicable tyrants? Regardless, they will have power above all others in Nostraterra, and where will that power lead them? These are the questions I will be asking the Elves who have returned,' said Aradia. 'Will you join me in asking them?'

'I will do so within the boundaries of my authority,' said Raghnall. 'You would be wise to exercise great caution in this matter. While I will not betray your confidence to my Air Spirit brethren, you walk a fine line between independence and exile. You have seen that you're impulsive, though well-meaning instincts led you astray. You would be wise not to defy the will of the Council in this regard.'

Aradia laughed. 'I cannot tell you the extent and nature of my defiance of the powers throughout the ages. They neither frighten nor disturb me. I will deal with them when the time comes.'

* * *

The next day, she met Raghnall at the end of the pier in the harbor of Solana. Aradia rose from a white stone bench where she had been gazing out to sea in hopes that her visions and Bran's fears would not be verified by tales from the most recent arrivals from Nostraterra. Raghnall nodded to her and gestured for her to resume her seat, then sat beside her.

'I have spoken with the crew of the ship,' he said. 'It seems you and Bran had reason to worry. Nostraterra is in danger again. When the great evil of Magnar was vanquished, you and I, along with others of the Greater Elves, thought that evil was gone forever from that long-suffering land. One thing we overlooked, however, according to your visions through the Acies and my interviews, is the unifying effect of Evil.'

'What do you mean?' asked Aradia.

'When Magnar was a power in Nostraterra,' said Raghnall, 'Men, Dwarves, and Elves put aside most of their differences and allied in a common goal to defeat him and his army. Now, without such a pervading evil, all sentient beings have been free to revive old differences and create new strife from them. Each race has its divisions, and now, without an external enemy, they may descend into chaos and war. Strong-willed leaders, wishing to enhance their own glory, will emerge here and there, carving out petty realms and tearing asunder the stable fabric of Nostraterra. In the end, our mysterious enemies, whom you glimpsed from afar, may succeed with new dark armies, creating a realm worse than that of Magnar.'

Sinking onto her knees from the bench, Aradia looked up at Raghnall. 'What can we do? I am not yet fully healed, and my magic is forbidden me again for a year, presuming that it will be reinstated even after that time.' Aradia conveniently did not mention her new magic that depended upon the Breath Flutes, but she would have to be even more careful now in practicing than she had been before.

'There is time, Aradia, for us to think of a course of action that will free Nostraterra from the darkness without and within,' Raghnall said. 'We must remember that the Acies, while powerful, will show things that have not yet come to pass and may not ever come to pass.'

'Yes, but the Blue Shape attacked through the Acies. That was no glimpse of a possible future. That was here and now. That was real.'

'True enough. The danger is real. But the future is not set in stone. Still, we cannot tarry. We must speak with your brother, Dorphin, who is sympathetic to you, and take his counsel in great secrecy, lest all our past efforts and sacrifices are rendered useless.'

Interlude

Fourth Age: Year 147—Mid-summer

Creon, King of Eldora and of all the Westmen, gazed implacably down at the man responsible for the breach of peace in Occupied Shardan. Gronthin, a rebellious upstart from the far Shardan province of Parnin, lay as he had for hours now, spread-eagled over an enormous ant hill in the Shardan wastes, his naked brown body coated with honey and sugar. The man writhed uselessly against the ropes that held him in place as the fierce stinging ants of the desert introduced him to agonies that Creon wished only to prolong. The Eldoran king did not bother to disguise his smirk of triumph at the spectacle of this treacherous, callow man browned from both the infernal sun in this land of devils and destitution and from his inferior place in the world.

A thin, dry wind was blowing on the high plateau. Scrub pines and sand dunes sprawled haphazardly under a brilliant, cloudless sky of dark blue. The only sounds were the shrieks and groans and maddened mutterings of the condemned man, and the busy scratching of the pens of the royal scribes as they recorded every detail for subsequent review. The sour and stale odor of sweat from men and horses hung heavy in the air, unmoved by the wind. Only the faint hint of resinous oils from the pines alleviated the stench of overheated bodies, honey, and death.

Gronthin was not the first to taste justice here. The bones of other Shardan rebels and criminals gleamed dully amid the heaped sand of other insect mounds. Skulls scoured free of flesh gazed up at the sky with empty eye sockets.

Creon spat. No matter how much water he drank, he couldn't clear the grit from his mouth. Though he wore the lightest of silks, still he was sweating like a peasant. This was a foul land. No wonder it bred traitors and assassins.

Discontent and evil always sprang from the South, whether it was the terrifying might of Plaga Erebus or the incessant rebellion that lurked within the heart of every man not historically allied to Eldora. Time and again, Creon had crushed the uprisings in Shardan and Hagar, only to see them sprout again, vile weeds in his otherwise tidy garden. The original wars of pacification had gone well, but with a heavy cost. Shardan had fought stubbornly and tenaciously. Only after fifty-nine years of struggle had the great Treaty of Jelani been signed; by the North men from Kozak, the Westmen from Eldora, and the lords of Shardan. The Great Peace of the South, as it was colloquially known, had lasted for decades, until this one rebel leader had threatened to bring it all crashing down by assassinating the King of Shardan and the Eldoran ambassador. Gronthin had been captured immediately after the murders, but the damage had already been done, the example set. He'd claimed to have no memory of the attack, and he had stuck to that absurd story throughout his interrogation, revealing nothing of value. It was that intransigence, as much as his crimes, that was to blame for the grisly manner of his execution.

Now, as the day began to wear to a close, the stream of words from the prostrate, writhing figure became more disjointed and unintelligible. Gronthin suddenly paused and drew in a rattling breath. Creon leaned closer to hear his dying words. Wrinkling his nose at the stench and ignoring the fierce heat beating up from the sands despite the shades held over his back by sweating servants, Creon waited with grim elation for the foul creature's final croak. The creak of leather saddles and the sounds of boots moving as the guards tried to shift their cramping muscles without leaving their assigned positions seemed impossibly loud to Creon, and he began calling out irritably for silence. But then Gronthin began speaking again. His voice was cracked but strong, and his words were in the native Shardan tongue, unknown to Creon.

'What is he saying now?' demanded Creon of his interpreter.

'He is not making any sense, my King,' the man said, looking up at Creon, who, at well over six feet, towered over every man present. 'He is saying, "The dark one is coming, the dark blue one whose powers can move heaven and earth. Atanar save me from the pain, save me from the white men." He continues to repeat this over and over again.'

'Atanar? Who is that—another rebel?'

'I have never heard the name before,' the interpreter replied.

'Bah. He is raving.' Creon looked at Gronthin's brown skin, blistered and red from the ferocious sun despite Gronthin's origin in the deep desert. Gronthin had spent the first hours pleading for mercy and water, then begged for a quick death, before finally lapsing into raspy, intermittently coherent mutterings. Creon noticed that his shadow had fallen over Gronthin's body, and it occurred to him that he might inadvertently be comforting the condemned man. The notion filled him with fresh rage, and he stepped forward, drawing back his boot to deliver a vicious kick to the cowardly assassin who had, however briefly, fanned the flames of rebellion again.

But before he could deliver this final insult, Creon suddenly felt a wave of tremendous fear rise up in him. As the veteran of a hundred battles, he was no stranger to fear, but always he had been its master. Not now. The icy cold terror that raced along his spine was like nothing he had ever felt before.

Without thinking, he turned and ran away from the staked-out man, leaving his aides, guards, scribes, and interpreter behind as he stumbled across the sand and broken stone, breath rasping from sun-dried lips. Only after a few hundred yards was he able to master himself sufficiently to stop. Looking back, he saw nothing that had not been there before the blind terror had overwhelmed him. Angry at himself and feeling conscious of having humiliated himself before his inferiors, he began striding back.

He had not taken more than a dozen steps when he felt the hairs on the back of his arms and his head stand straight up. An incredibly loud, high-pitched sound, such as tens of thousands of mosquitoes might make, pressed upon his skull from all directions. He halted as though he'd run into a wall. But in the next instant, the sound was gone, vanished as suddenly as it had arisen. Creon shook his head. The fear threatened to return, but he fought it off. Some of his guards, he saw, had started toward him. He motioned them back irritably even as he advanced again in their direction.

Then, out of nowhere, a bolt of lightning split the dry desert air just beyond the figure of Gronthin. It hit the sand with a deafening crack, throwing up a cloud of sand and smoke that completely obscured the rebel. The dark cloud did not disperse. It hung in mid-air, a foggy void from which, like some demonic exhalation, a rush of unnaturally frigid air. Despite his distance, Creon shivered at the icy blast. His men, closer, reacted with panic, as did the horses, straining against their tethers and whinnying loudly. One animal broke free and came straight at Creon, fleeing blindly in its terror, just as he had done a moment earlier. Creon had to throw himself aside to avoid being trampled.

He hit the sand, rolled, and regained his feet to a chorus of screams. He turned toward them … and staggered. Not from fear but from sheer disbelief. A vast blue figure, man-shaped yet over ten feet tall; emerged from the fog. A great cloak draped its body; its face was hidden by a large cowl. It hovered above the sands of the desert, and tendrils of lightning emanated from its form, slaying all who were near.

Even as Creon watched, muttering a prayer to the Earth Spirits, a bolt flashed toward him. It fell just short, though the tremendous thunderclap nearly bowled him over. He felt the heat of lightning on his face and braced himself against a tremendous icy wind that began once again to blow from the void. A great black cloud billowed from the shape, concealing all but the figure itself as several men, trying to flee, were slowly and inexorably dragged into the maelstrom. Arrows snapped and hissed toward the Blue Apparition but were reflected back toward the men who had sent them on their way. They screamed as their own arrows cut them down. Creon watched the bodies of the slain float above the sands, seeming to respond to subtle arm gestures of the shape, moving in a macabre dance as it drew them into its blue cloud. Gronthin's tortured form was ripped from the sands, his hoarse voice lost in the tumult as he disappeared within the black cloud.

Then Creon felt the strength of the shape's mind pushing and pulsating against his spirit, hungering for his very soul even as it devoured the souls of the men who were closer at hand. Few men were left alive when Creon, awakening as if from a dream, and angrier than he had ever been in his life so that what fear he might have felt was utterly annihilated in the fires of his rage, strode forward. His guards pulled at his robes, begging him to remain where he was. But Creon ignored them, his gaze fixed upon the midnight blue form. He could hear it calling to him voicelessly, wordlessly, mocking him and offering to contest the mastery of Nostraterra with him, if only he had enough courage.

In answer, Creon drew his ancient sword, Caelestus, forged by the Dwarves of Nerea and given to one of his ancestors long ago. Another bolt of lightning flashed toward him, but Creon parried it with the sword, feeling only a vague tingle as the eldritch energies were dissipated by the timeless edge of his blade. Again ignoring the pleas of his guards, he strode toward the maelstrom, determined to settle the mastery of Nostraterra once and for all. Greater and greater bolts of lightning flickered around the King, and his guards were horrified to see his form disappear into the blue-black cloud of cold and mist.

Chapter Three

Family

Fourth Age: Year 199-Spring

King Creon looked around his Council table, noting that his twin sons, Alfrahil and Daerahil, were sitting upon opposite sides, directly across from each other. The meeting room was nearly fifty feet long and thirty feet wide, located in the citadel of Titania—capital city of Eldora. A dark wooden table ran down its center, its corners rounded in an attempt to soften its clear functionality. White marble veneers covered the dark granite under stones of the walls, and bright, ancient tapestries were hung from a ceiling over thirty feet high. Hundreds of oil lamps hung in clusters from silk ropes suspended from the ceiling, giving the impression of a single bright light. Deep-set windows on either side of the hall let in the mid-morning light.

The only sounds in the room beside the voices of the men gathered were the faint scratching of quill pens on parchment from the small group of scribes seated at a discrete distance behind the table. Servants were quietly setting down glasses of coffee and fruit juice on coasters to protect the surface of the table. The strong odor of coffee, with undercurrents of breakfast pastries and fruit, wafted through the room, competing with the sharp smoky smell of charcoal braziers glowing against the chill of a cold spring morning.

Creon knew that he cast an imposing figure upon the members of his Council, with the possible exception of his son, Daerahil, and for this, there was a good reason. Tall Creon was, tall as the ancient Kings from the earliest days of the realm, and as yet unbent from age. His hair was black and full, though streaked with silver these past fifteen years. His pale face still had that fair Elven countenance he had inherited from his mother, and the glow from his finely formed features was unworldly in its beauty. He had his father's eyes, however, and like polished chips of frozen sapphire, they had the warmth of a shadow penetrating and piercing from beneath a craggy brow. His eyebrows had become a bit wild with age, and it was a look that served him well in these times. The strength of purpose was in his every fiber, and he carried his authority well.

Creon, nearing his two hundredth birthday, ruled from his throne in Titania, one of only two surviving Eldoran cities, the other being the northern city of Amadeus. The other main Eldoran cities had been destroyed in the Great War. Estrellius yet lay in ruins, its remnants bridging and spanning the river Aphon, an empty shell occupied only by its re-constructors. The fate of Hiberius had been even worse. Occupied during the Great War by Dark Elves and other creatures of Magnar, Hiberius had been transformed from a paradise of lush waterways and waterfalls into a dank, polluted ruin. The waters pouring from the city walls and surrounding valley was no longer crystal clear but ran foul and dark, toxic to most life, a breeding ground of deadly plagues that would occasionally spread into the rest of Nostraterra. Creon's only hope for reclaiming Hiberius in his lifetime lay with the Lesser Elves. Possessing magic still secret to the other races of Nostraterra, the Lesser Elves were slowly able to transform the most polluted of waters into clear streams and wells, and since the end of the Great War, two hundred some years before, they had made slow, steady progress in healing the accursed city.

Direct and revealing was Creon's stare, and few could abide his gaze if he fixed his mind upon them. There were none within the land who could lie to the King, and few who would even dare to try. Creon had been born with mental powers, unknown to Nostraterra, honed over a lifetime. Focusing his mind, he could compel all other Men, and even some Lesser Elves and Dwarves, to tell the truth. More importantly, he could read much of their thoughts, making intrigue in his court a very dangerous endeavor. Early in his reign, he had used these powers ruthlessly to expose the politics and plots of the royal court. Disloyal men had been quickly dispatched, their secrets revealed as they literally dug their own graves.

Nowadays, however, Creon rarely used his powers unless there was great need, having learned that some secrets were necessary for any government to function effectively. Yet, even so, there were few in the kingdom who would dare oppose him either openly or in secret.

One of those few was present today. Daerahil, the younger of his sons, was certain to voice his opinions again on the Shardan campaign. His older brother, Alfrahil, would never contradict the King in public, and rarely did so even in private. Daerahil, unlike his brother, had inherited his father's unusual powers, and, like his father, rarely used them, preferring to rely on his intellect and problem-solving abilities.

His two sons were very different in appearance. Alfrahil was tall like his father, yet slender like his mother had been. His soft blond hair fell straight just past his shoulders; the soft blue-gray eyes of his Lesser Elven grandmother were clear and bright in his face, which was lined with the tiniest of wrinkles around his eyes, allowing the appearance of thoughtfulness to dominate his handsome, boyish face. Though he had recently celebrated his seventy-fifth birthday, he looked like a man less than half his age and could reasonably expect another century of life at least. Creon could see hints of his Creon's mother in his son, but the Elven heritage was thinner in him. Creon was glad of it as he rarely missed his mother Persephone, who, denying him her love after his father's untimely death in a hunting accident, returned to her own people, the Lesser Elves, refusing to speak with her son afterward. Seventy-one years later, when he ascended the throne, and even now, after one hundred twenty-eight years, he still felt the pain of that abandonment.

Daerahil was shorter and stockier than Alfrahil. His hair was dark and his eyes brown. His face was tanned darkly and deeply from his time in the Shardan wastes.

'*Yet another reason that he irks me,*' thought Creon now, regarding his younger son in brooding silence. '*He looks too much like those foul rebels and upstarts that he was supposed to suppress. Everyone believes him to be so brilliant, and he himself believes it, yet if he were even half as clever as people say, Shardan would be pacified by now.*'

* * *

After Creon called the Council to order, Lord Zarthir, foreign trade minister of Eldora, went on at length about a recent treaty that allowed some goods from a Frostfields village to pass through the interwoven territories and be subjected to a slightly lower import duty due to the distance that they traveled. Barely stifling a yawn, Daerahil glanced around the table and saw the usual crowd of ministers and their sycophants standing behind them, eagerly refilling wine glasses and placing succulent tidbits on their master's plates.

'*Old, dull, and fat,*' thought Daerahil. '*Only concerned with their profits and their immediate pleasures.*' Daerahil did not include his best friend, Zarthir, in this mix, but even friends could drone on and on.

'*Few of them care for the realm,*' Daerahil continued to muse, '*except for my brother and my father. Yet my father has been seduced by limitless power and now seeks only to subject all of*

Shardan—no, all of Nostraterra—to his will. If he could only see the people of Shardan objectively rather than colored by his hate and loathing, he would understand that nearly all those in Shardan will not accept a foreign overlord. There are those who fight Eldora tooth and nail, fighting with anything and everything to oppose an occupying army. The country of Shardan, however, can be made peaceful and profitable, with little loss of life. Trade and respect for their local customs would bring much of the populace around in renouncing violence. Even where violence continues, rich local merchants would gladly trade in the names of the rebels and collect a reward. Yet Father refuses to listen to my counsel.'

Daerahil had proved that this tactic worked in the Shardan provinces directly under his command, reducing the violence against coalition soldiers by nearly ninety percent. This, however, was regarded as placating the rebels, and his father demanded all violence stop before trade began. *'How incredibly foolish,'* thought Daerahil. *'It is difficult to be peaceful and happy when you are starving and faced with the physical oppression of foreign soldiers day after day. Still, if it were not for my father's counselor, Mergin, I might have enjoyed better success here in the Council.'*

Shorter than most men, barely reaching five and a half feet, but lean and wiry, Mergin sat silently regarding everyone at the table with a calm but predatory gaze. His dark eyes glittered from beneath gray shaggy curls that were receding rapidly now in his middle age. A large hooked nose dominated a face that generally frowned and bore latent marks of terrible cruelty. A sallow complexion belied a Shardan grandmother, a fact that Mergin had buried early in his career, as nothing would be allowed to stand in his way as the King's First Minister. Anyone foolish enough to ask about his antecedents was swiftly and completely discouraged. His cunning mind constantly churned plots and ideas—thoughts he revealed only to a carefully chosen few. Despite his low-born status and lack of formal education, he had proved his worth in a low-level administrative post, and promotion had followed promotion until now he had the King's ear at all times. His ideas and recommendations were taken very seriously by the King and his other Ministers, leading them to be carried out swiftly.

Early on, Mergin and Daerahil had taken an immediate dislike to each other, which had rapidly escalated into a quiet hatred that soon spilled out publicly. Unfortunately for Daerahil, Mergin had first taken over the position of junior minister to the King by extorting and then exposing the larcenous activities of the unfortunate junior minister above him. Within two years, another series of revelations into the personal and public lives of one of the least popular full ministers had allowed Mergin to replace that man, and there had been no stopping him after that. First, he had assumed the tedious yet important task of the assistant minister to the messenger corps, allowing him access to the private messengers that flowed through the realm. Then, after exposing a plot among Shardan sympathizers, he had been rewarded with the position of Creon's First Minister. It was only a matter of time before he had the Messenger Corps report directly to him, so now he was privy to all of the secrets of the land that flowed in from the various intelligence-gathering services. Soon afterward, he was appointed the commander of the Shadows, the legendary messenger assassins. This gave him yet another tool with which to gather information and a small but extremely deadly cadre of men who could and would enforce his will without question.

It was clear that he had become the second most powerful man in the kingdom behind the King himself. His undying loyalty to the King had only furthered his power, and he was able to defeat Daerahil's attempts to sabotage him. Even worse, he was able to contrive several incidents where Daerahil had been less than discreet in his actions and deeds, making them brutally public at the most inopportune moment for Daerahil.

The source of Mergin's antipathy was known to all. Early in his military career, Daerahil had commanded a company of Men, one of whom, Mergin's only son, Jasper, had died in Shardan under disputed circumstances. Mergin blamed Daerahil for the death of his son, focusing his rage against Daerahil whenever he could.

Daerahil knew that his brother, Prince Alfrahil, was the only man beside the King who could contest the will of Mergin with impunity, as the King loved his eldest son above all others and trusted him equally. Alfrahil was quieter and more thoughtful than his brother, fluent in both Elvish and Dwarvish. Having spent nearly five years with the Dwarves and two years with the Lesser Elves of the Great Forest, Alfrahil was invaluable when it came to diplomacy. His absence from Shardan except for a few months of supervised command and his compulsory military training in his early thirties had left him dangerously inexperienced when words failed and hard deeds were required. A skilled diplomat, a hopeless military commander, Alfrahil would depend utterly on Daerahil and the military commanders someday when Alfrahil ascended to the throne.

While not as intellectually talented as Daerahil, Alfrahil used his gifts to see both sides of an issue and find common ground, allowing him to see a path to compromise where others saw only conflict. Alfrahil, decisive in his mild way in most matters, could not stand family quarrels, however, or any form of political infighting, and had tried to smooth ruffled feelings and produce a consensus between his father and brother. Yet when Alfrahil was actually forced to choose a side, his customary decisiveness would evaporate, and he would vacillate between two conflicting viewpoints, making the situation worse.

But though the two brothers had clear differences on how the kingdom should be run, Daerahil bore his brother no ill will. He knew that his father's attitudes were not the fault of his brother, and Daerahil had resolved to continue to support his brother, who would one day be King.

Mentally sighing, Daerahil wished, not for the first time, that the order of their birth had been reversed, with himself as the heir to the throne and his kind and thoughtful brother becoming the senior ambassador and foreign minister of Eldora. Pausing in thought, he glanced at his brother across the table and gave him a tired smile.

* * *

Alfrahil acknowledged his brother's smile with one of his own but saw that there was fresh trouble brewing. Mergin was looking increasingly smug when Daerahil had the impudence to put his head down on the table once Lord Mebron, Outlier Minister of the foreign provinces of Men, began talking. Finally, when Mebron stopped speaking, there was a brief adjournment for the Council members to take care of their personal needs and bid their servants fetch new delicacies and fresh pastries. Alfrahil, knowing what his father and Mergin planned, knew that Daerahil's legendary self-assurance was going to be tested in Council rather than on the battlefield.

While his brother, on an extended leave from his command, expected to return to Shardan shortly and placed in command of the entire army there, Alfrahil, along with Creon and Mergin, knew that this was not about to happen. In fact, Daerahil would not see active combat again for quite a while. Instead, Daerahil was to be transferred and promoted to the General staff of the Eldoran army, where he would learn how to coordinate logistics and supplies rather than plan active military campaigns. Alfrahil would be given nominal command of the Army in Shardan to gain actual experience in the command of men at a strategic rather than tactical level. Alfrahil's one brief command over a company of men early in his youth in Shardan had ended disastrously, with most of his men killed. He had barely escaped with his own life. Regarded as too valuable to risk again, Alfrahil had been withdrawn back to the capital, leaving Daerahil to become a professional soldier.

Yet he knew that the King thought Daerahil had gone native, enjoying all of the delights of the high plateau of Shardan and embracing many of its customs and traditions: most markedly the food and the women. Alfrahil shuddered when he thought of his brother's relationship with a Shardan woman, formerly a prostitute and now his mistress. Alfrahil knew that Mergin was aware of this relationship, but he suspected that the First Minister was waiting for the right moment to reveal it to the King. King Creon was renowned for adhering to strict rank and protocol where social relationships were concerned, and he would refuse to allow either of his sons to marry outside the royal families of Eldora, much less a Shardan woman of ill repute.

More than once, Alfrahil had been tempted to reveal all that he knew to his brother, to warn him while there was still time. But he had held back, for his loyalty to king and kingdom was greater than his brotherly feelings for Daerahil. Now he could only watch with sorrow as Mergin and the King sprang their trap—a trap that Daerahil had not merely stumbled into but had virtually conspired in constructing.

* * *

When the meeting resumed, more and more details, both foreign and domestic, were reported by the various ministers. The most disturbing report came from the Outlier Minister for the Foreign Provinces, Lord Mebron.

'Sire,' said Mebron, 'I regret to inform you that the good citizens of Nexus and other villages north of the mountain spur known as the Thumb, within the Cataract River Valley, have rejected your latest claim that they, as Eldoran in origin, acknowledge your over-lordship. They also decline to pay any further taxes.'

'This is outrageous,' interjected Mergin. 'We should dispatch the Army to quell these upstarts and remind them that they owe their allegiance to Eldora.'

'Perhaps, my good Minister, you can tell me where we can spare the troops to bring these sheep back into the fold?' inquired Daerahil. 'Clearly, the rebellion in Shardan and the skirmishes along the Azhar frontier are keeping all of our men, plus those of our Kozaki allies, fully engaged. Except, of course, in the two provinces of Shardan that I have recently pacified,' he added smugly.

'Prince Daerahil, it is precisely your softness in Shardan that has led these upstarts to rebel against their lawful King, is this not so?' asked Mergin slyly.

This question was directed at Mebron, who prevaricated for a moment before replying. 'Yes, Lord Mergin, they specifically cite the guarantees that Prince Daerahil made to the rebellious Shardan provinces of Kraylor and Voth, which acknowledge the sovereignty of their lords, who pledge fealty unto Eldora. The Council of Traders from Nexus has announced that it has formed a Confederation and thereby ask that any and all foreign troops remove themselves from their towns and farms in any official capacity, though all are welcome to come and trade with them.'

'You are responsible for this, my son?' asked the King ominously. Creon's voice became cold and thin. 'You gave sovereignty to two separate provinces in Shardan? I cannot believe that you would thwart my will in this matter. Your prior actions of placating rebels and criminals already made my next order necessary, but today's news only underscores how quickly I must put a stop to this seditious nonsense.'

Creon hated the peoples of Shardan, despising them as a whole. Their bizarre form of ancestor worship, the stench of their foul food, with its foreign odors and alien spices, sickened him. And if that was not enough, their libidinous, licentious social behavior, multiple wives, and any number of mistresses—or concubines, as the Shardans called them—provoked a never-ending internecine warfare where brother slew half-brother, stepsister poisoned niece, resulting in a social structure even lower than that of the jackals of the deep desert. They were not truly men, Creon thought, but half-men, resembling rutting beasts in the forest rather than civilized people.

In fact, as far as Creon was concerned, only the Men of Eldora were truly civilized. His closest allies, the nomadic Kozaki, were crude and savage, spending all of their lives upon their horses. They, too, had multiple wives, which made Creon shudder. Still, at least their white skin was the right color, and they had always honored their treaties with Eldora, so though they were not generally fit to be seen in Eldora, they did have great value. '*Perhaps*,' mused Creon, '*as time goes by and they adopt more of our customs, the best of them may seem less barbaric and approach our level of sophistication and worth.*'

Other men of the northlands were essentially farmers and herders of flock animals, simple traders, and craftsmen, benevolent, distant neighbors, but not anyone that you would seat at your table. The Dwarves were excellent metal smiths and stone wrights, but like moles and other animals which lived underground, rarely seeing the light of day, they were best left in the dark. The Lesser Elves triggered only dark memories for Creon of the loss of his only true love and the abandonment by his mother. They would be allowed to live their lives in peace, provided that they remained in their forest abode—all of them, that is, save one, whose name was Creon's most treasured secret: he would die a terrible, shameful death.

Someday, Creon hoped during his lifetime, the men of Eldora could bring permanent peace to Shardan and turn their attention to projecting Eldoran power throughout all of Nostraterra, causing all other races and peoples to bend the knee to Eldora. Creon did not think of the Greater Elves in his world view. They were a race apart from Nostraterra, their homeland forever remote, across a distant ocean horizon. The ones who lived in Phoenicia were relics of the past; Eldora was the present and future of Nostraterra.

Now the King nodded to Mergin, and the First Minister cleared his throat and spoke. 'It has been decided, my lords and ministers, that the Shardan campaign has reached a point of stagnation and that a bolder approach must be taken to solve this problem once and for all. Prince Daerahil, you are hereby relieved of command of the First Host of the Shardan army and promoted to command of the Great Host of the army of Eldora. There you will first conduct a rigorous inspection tour, identifying waste and mismanagement, learning the logistics of supply and support for the Army as a whole. You will begin by inspecting the companies guarding the outlands between the city walls and the out-walls, and only after a thorough review of these fortifications will you extend your tour throughout the realm of Eldora. Your inspection schedules will be sent to you after we have reviewed your reports from your first assignment. Do you have any questions?'

Daerahil was speechless. He had expected to be given command of both the first and second Hosts of Shardan, a promotion giving him command of the entire Shardan army. Instead, he found himself 'promoted' to a sentinel position as commander of the Eldoran Army. While any other soldier would look upon it as an actual advancement, Daerahil knew that this position reported directly to the King and his ministers. This meant that he would have substantially less freedom in his movements and reforms then he had when only a Host commander. Plus, he would be mired in Eldora, reporting in and out of the Council chambers at the whim of that vile serpent Mergin; harassing him at every opportunity.

Thinking quickly, Daerahil spoke. 'My Lord King, clearly this idea has originated with you, though doubtless there are many who would disagree with your decision. My brother until recently has held the post of Commander of the Eldoran Army. May I ask where he is to be dispatched?'

'You will address your comments to me, my Lord Prince,' said Mergin silkily.

Ignoring Mergin, Daerahil looked at his father directly and again posed his question. Mergin restated his point with much less silk and more venom in his voice.

That was too much for Daerahil. 'Silence, you vile little worm!' he erupted. 'If you were not my father's treasured errand boy, you would have faced my wrath long ago. I am speaking to my father, the only man that I answer to in this kingdom.'

Anger flashed across Creon's face; this was not proceeding the way that he had intended. Instead of attacking the King's decision and openly defying him, Daerahil had shifted the focus to the authority of Mergin relative to that of the Princes of the realm. Creon knew that he had been outmaneuvered, as the law forbade anyone, no matter their rank, from ordering a Prince of the Realm to do anything at all. Only the King had that authority.

'My son, you will show more courtesy to our faithful Minister Lord Mergin,' Creon said. 'But to answer your question, your brother is today appointed to the General Staff of the Army of Shardan, where it is to be hoped that our royal policies will be carried out both in form and spirit.'

'My lord King, who then will take over my position and see to the reforms of the Shardan campaign?' asked Daerahil.

'Prince Daerahil, your reforms have not achieved the effects that you claim, and they shall be terminated forthwith,' replied the King. 'In fact, in light of today's news, more disorder than I could possibly have imagined has come as a result of your intransigence in this matter. Your royal cousin, Prince Frederic of Amadeus, shall be given command of the first and second hosts of the Shardan army in hopes that my will and that of our Council will be more clearly followed.'

'Frederic?' exclaimed an incredulous Daerahil. 'With all due respect to our royal cousin, he can barely manage the peaceful realm of Amadeus, much less command men in the Shardan campaign. The stories of his errors would fill many an hour if they were read together.'

Creon's face darkened. 'Do not presume to lecture me on the disposition of the commanders at my disposal. Be thankful that I do not hold you more accountable for the dismal lack of progress in Shardan and this new rebellion that I must quell amongst our own trading colonies.'

'Lack of progress, my Lord?' echoed Daerahil. 'Please, majesty, you might not have had access to all of the information from Shardan, particularly if Mergin is deliberately withholding it from you. Let me show you the latest figures of casualties, pacified cities, and towns, and trade revenues from my last six months as commander of the First Host.' Daerahil gestured behind him, and Lord Zarthir prepared to speak on Daerahil's behalf, unrolling the scrolls he had prepared for this meeting. But before he could begin to read from them, Mergin played his last card.

'My Lord,' said the First Minister, 'while I am certain that Prince Daerahil had some minor successes in his endeavors, in addition to giving partial autonomy to two of the provinces that I have mentioned, he failed to instill complete obedience from those foul rebels and even sided with four of their tribal leaders against his own troops on three separate occasions. Worse, he ordered the Royal Governor of Voth to reduce his taxes and recall his own guards to his own barracks so that the Prince's troops could exercise the authority actually given to the governor.'

Daerahil was speechless, for while this information was true, he had thought it had been carefully hidden and that the overwhelmingly powerful results of his actions would deflect any questioning of his methods or orders.

'Is this true, my son?' demanded Creon. 'Have you actually sided with the rebels against the loyal forces of Eldora? Do you govern one of our provinces, usurping our distant cousin, the Royal Governor of Voth?'

'I would not phrase it that way, my Lord. The disputes that are mentioned by Lord Mergin were gross disobedience by three separate Eldoran officials, and the Governor's guards were ransacking and looting the provincial city, fomenting great hatred amongst the populace. I was able to pacify this city and the surrounding province by curtailing the inept, greedy actions of the Governor.'

'So, you willfully admit that you have disobeyed my orders and exceeded your authority,' said the King. 'Is this so or not so?'

'Yes, my Lord,' said a flustered and angry Daerahil. 'But –'

'I have no desire to listen to the justification of your actions. You openly defy my orders, side with known rebels, and now argue about assuming your new command. Even today I hear that your seditious ideas have spread beyond Shardan, creating more chaos and disorder for me to deal with. Be silent for the rest of this Council; we shall speak privately about your actions later. Say nothing until the meeting of the Security Council.'

'What is to be said in private that cannot be said here?' demanded Daerahil. 'My policies and plans are successful. Your blind insistence on total subservience from a conquered people has led us to our current predicament. It is clear that I am the only one who can quell this rebellion. Give me leave, my Lord, to take command of the entire Shardan army, and I will pacify this country and bring our troops back home within a year. Furthermore, the good citizens of Nexus and the trading Confederation exist outside the borders of Eldora and are beyond both our jurisdiction and our control.'

'You dare imply that I am the cause of the failure of the Shardan campaign? You defy me yet again in open Council! Do you claim that these upstarts from Eldora that have founded this vile Confederation have the right to govern themselves? Your contagion will spread like a plague before a dark wind if it is not stamped out! Be gone from my sight, and be prepared to take command of your new post on the morrow. Now get out!' roared the King.

Daerahil stood and was about to reply when he saw the fear in his brother's face and realized that he had been about to go too far. Only a fool would bait a bear in its own den without a viable weapon. Still, such was his fury that he did not trust himself to speak. Without bothering to salute or ask permission to leave, he turned on his heel, intending to leave the room. It was then that he heard Lord Mergin's mocking laughter. He froze and then walked back to this place at the Council table. There he picked up his goblet of wine, moving as if to drink from it, but instead threw its contents into Mergin's face.

'I call you out again, coward, and if you have any honor or backbone at all, you will meet me on the morrow with your sword in your hand upon the field of honor.' he said.

Roaring, Mergin leaped from his chair, but the King ordered silence again. 'Prince Daerahil, you are fined fifty gold pieces for your disruption of the Council chamber and your insult to Lord Mergin. Apologize at once.'

Daerahil reached into his purse and counted out one hundred gold pieces, placing them on the table. The King looked at him quizzically, and said sarcastically, 'It was fifty, my son, not one hundred. Has your time in the desert left you unable to do simple sums?'

'No, Lord, I am merely paying in advance for my next disruption.' With that remark, Daerahil reached over to a jar of pickled fish and hurled its contents at Lord Mergin, splattering one of the other ministers in the process.

'Now I will take my leave, my Lord, and assume my new command tomorrow.'

Ignoring his father's command to return and apologize, Daer-ahil strode from the hall and, without pausing, from the Citadel itself.

* * *

The meeting recessed briefly so that Mergin could cleanse him-self in a nearby washroom personally allocated to him. Enter-ing the room, Mergin saw his ancient manservant, Carlith, who was deaf as a post and thoroughly discreet, standing before him, holding out a steaming washbasin. A new suit of robes lay on a rack nearby. Smiling that his needs had been anticipated, Mer-gin undressed, cleaning himself before putting on clean clothes. Glancing at even this most loyal servant, Mergin did not trust him as far as he could proverbially throw him; Mergin knew everyone and anyone would betray him if given half a chance, as betrayal and treachery were Mergin's closest companions. Mergin trusted no one but himself, for if he ever failed in his tasks significantly, he could be dismissed back to the poverty-stricken village of his birth.

Thinking of the meeting, he began to smile. His plan to pro-voke Daerahil had worked perfectly. Once again, the prince's complete lack of tact and his inability to restrain his temper had proved useful. The First Minister knew that Daerahil was a far stronger prince than his brother, Alfrahil. Yet because Mergin blamed Daerahil for the death of his only son, he loathed the man and opposed any chance that Daerahil might have of be-coming King. But it wasn't merely his personal distaste for the prince that fueled Mergin's hatred. Daerahil's strategy for paci-fying the rebels was folly, a policy of appeasement that could only end in disaster.

Yet he also knew that the weak, indecisive Alfrahil would make an even worse king than Daerahil. While Alfrahil was too weak to make a good king, he was not weak enough for Mergin to influence and control properly. Mergin was of the opinion that the kingship and the role of Eldora in the wider world were much more important than the man who wore the crown, and, not for the first time, he vowed to himself that either a strong man would sit on the throne after Creon was gone, or a very weak man that Mergin could control. Who either man should be, Mergin had not yet decided.

These thoughts Mergin buried deep within his mind, lest the king, with his mental powers, detect them. With his body cleaned and clothes changed, Mergin returned to the Council room for the Security Council meeting.

* * *

Daerahil paused to collect himself on the steps of the Citadel. He knew that he had lost his temper and would be subjected to further recriminations from his father and from Mergin, but he could not sit there and stomach any more of their machinations and outright foolishness. Still, he felt better for putting out into the open what many had whispered, and perhaps there were others on the Council besides Zarthir, including his brother, who would speak on his behalf. Daerahil had few illusions that he would be sent back to Shardan anytime soon, but hoped that at least some of his policies would be kept in place once his deputy had an opportunity to read them to the Council.

From his present vantage, Daerahil could look over much of the city and even beyond. Titania comprised several small hills in a wide natural valley in the Encircling Mountains. These mountains formed a rough circle over a hundred miles wide, with a fertile central area rich in farms and people. The city of Titania filled the wider southern valley between two arms of the mountains that curved east and west away to the north, coming together where the Eldoran city of Amadeus lay in a much sharper valley. A great wall stretched for miles from the last shoulders of the mountains, separating Titania from the fallow grasslands that led down to the river Aphon. There was one aperture in the southern wall, the Great Gate, the sole entrance and exit point for commerce, leading as it did outward from Eldora into the wider world. The City had a smaller, less fortified northern gate that led into the interior realm of Eldora and the six minor royal fiefs that lay there. Inside the walls was the flat land of the natural valley, the plain of Sisera, a vast expanse nearly fifteen leagues wide and ten deep that was surrounded on all sides by mountains. Most of Sisera was given over to farmland, with small hamlets nestled here in there in the enormous sixteenth district, which included all of the valley floor, fields and orchards, vineyards and pastures adorned with the rich tithe of soils washed down for millennia from the neighboring mountains. Fifteen other districts were set about the city, centered around each of the seven hills, with the poorer areas closer to the south wall and the villas of the wealthy on the hills closest to the north wall.

Small rivers ran down from the wild mountainsides to the east and west of the City, providing fresh drinking water as well as an efficient sewer system. The rivers channeled together into a single great canal that had been reinforced with huge, rough blocks of stone, exited the City through a metal grate impassable by any creature larger than a rat. The southern wall was made of indomitable stone, smoothed and without joint or seam, rising fifty feet above the plain.

The valley was essentially flat, crossed with small streams, except for the Great Escarpment, an ancient massif of white granite, thirty feet high, a mile deep, and ten miles wide that nearly bisected the city into two parts. Roads went around this jutting granite ridge on the east and west ends, but the great road from the south gate to the north gate pierced the Escarpment in its center. Before the Great War, incursions of raiding parties from Shardan had shown the need for greater defenses than those provided by the small walls around each hill. A great quarry had been hewn from the escarpment from north to south, extending the width of the formation and plunging fifty feet deep. This stone was moved and formed into the great blocks that comprised the southern and northern walls. A wooden bridge was built, more than a quarter mile long, over the quarry pit, allowing travel in a direct line throughout Sisera.

Within the city were the seven hills of Titania, small, lightly fortified areas of the city which in ancient days had been city-states. The Citadel was within the First District, atop the tallest hill within the city, one-third of the way from the northern wall, just off the centerline of the valley. The smaller walls of the early city-states remained, but besides the Citadel only a light guard was mounted on these smaller barriers. Most of the well to do lived upon one of these seven hills while the common folk such as farmers, orchard and vineyard tenders, and ordinary laborers lived on the flat plain.

It all seemed so peaceful, so orderly. But Daerahil had just experienced for himself how little appearances had to do with reality. Cursing under his breath at the memory of Mergin's effrontery and his father's acquiescence in the humiliation of his own son, Daerahil descended on foot from the Citadel in the First district and made his way through the Second and Third districts.

Tramping along on his own two feet instead of taking his horse gave him a chance to clear his head and let his anger begin to fade away. Citizens of the City ignored him except for those rare few who could identify him without his usual guard detachment and personal banner. Wearing only a tunic and a dagger, he looked like a rich young merchant rather than their prince.

Daerahil paused to catch his breath after walking a mile or so. Seeing that he was close to a Messenger stable, he entered and asked that a horse be saddled for his use. This was swiftly accomplished, and Daerahil swung with relief into the saddle of a sturdy, undistinguished mount and rode the mile to the Hill of Merchants, located east of the Citadel and its battlements and towers. Riding up to the gate that divided the sixteenth district, the plain of Sisera, from the Fourth District, a wealthy merchant district, Daerahil gave his horse to another of the messenger stables that stood near the entrance to this minor wall and gate complex. He then climbed the first of several flights of stairs until he reached the top of this district and walked into a small tavern, the Dusty Cloak, which he actually owned through one of his more private investments. Not even the proprietor, Carus, knew to whom the tavern belonged, only that he must keep an excellent selection of wines on hand at all times, no matter if they sold or not, and that his Frostfields ale must be kept crisp and cold as well.

As Daerahil entered, Carus came to attention and gave his prince a slightly lax salute, as they had come to know each other casually over the past several years. Glancing at the dark stone cabinet that housed his favorite wines, Daerahil gave a meaningful nod to Carus, before ascending to his customary table on the second floor of the tavern, gently nodding and smiling at several of the notable merchants who came here to enjoy wine that they could drink nowhere else in the City.

* * *

While Daerahil was walking to his favorite tavern, the Security Council convened, with Creon, Alfrahil, and Mergin present, along with Zarthir in his role as Foreign Trade Minister, Lord Mebron, and Ferly, the Chief Engineer. Wysteria, the sole woman in attendance, was representing the Alchemist Guild on behalf of her husband, Bufus, the head of the Guild, who was seriously ill and could not attend. Approaching her thirty-seventh year, she was still stunning. Jet black hair streamed back from a high forehead, and her brilliant blue eyes were incredibly seductive, as were her womanly curves and small waist. But it was her mind that was truly formidable. Though her background was common, she had married Bufus, head of the Alchemist Guild, and one of the richest men in the kingdom. The fact that she was here was mildly shocking to Creon, as protocol stated that only the head of a merchant group or minister of a government department could serve as a representative to the king. Mergin, however, had insisted on allowing Wysteria to attend due to her husband's illness, stating that it was she, and not Bufus, who truly ran the Guild, and they might as well cut out the middle-man. Creon acquiesced this once but instructed Mergin to see to it that Bufus was available in the future. The Guild represented the largest concentration of wealth outside the royal treasury, and the Alchemists were the only remaining men who had any understanding of Earth Magic, key too many secret plans of Mergin and Creon.

'Minister Zarthir, your confidential report, please.' said Creon, beginning the meeting.

Zarthir had short dark hair and a beard much thicker than was common in Eldora. Despite his rugged appearance, his personality, small gestures, and speaking mannerisms hinted at feminine characteristics associated with the "delicate men." In addition to his odd personal habits, Zarthir presented Creon with a nearly unsolvable problem: he was incredibly skilled at foreign trade agreements, forging economic alliances with other Men and the other races. He was well known, however, as a complete moral reprobate, throwing lavish parties where he was known to enjoy the company of common joy girls and rumored to enjoy the pleasures of young men as well, facts which deeply offended Creon's sense of moral purity. Still, Creon had to acknowledge that Eldora's coffers had swelled considerably with Zarthir's help, and trade was better than in over a hundred years.

Zarthir's background was another point in his favor. He was from a rich and ancient Eldoran family of the purest pedigree. His father, Parlan, was the heir to an extensive trading business that had grown the family fortune steadily for decades. But just after reaching adulthood and taking control of the company, Parlan had made a critical mistake, taking an enormous risk on a business venture in Shardan that had failed utterly when the caravan carrying the money to finance the venture was ambushed on the royal road to Karban and all the money lost. Facing financial ruin, Parlan had begged Creon to protect him from the creditors besieging him, pointing out that the realm bore at least some responsibility for the loss of his treasure.

Creon, initially inclined to aid him, was stung by the implied criticism of his security and threw Parlan to the mercies of the civil courts. Quickly bankrupt, Zarthir's father ended his life in shame, dangling from a rope in his own house. Many years later, Creon initially feared that Zarthir would bear him anger and resentment over his father's death and probed his mind when Zarthir was recommended for promotion to ministerial rank. Finding nothing at all, Creon was content and allowed Zarthir to ascend to his status. Mergin informed Creon that Zarthir's primary goal was the award of a landed hereditary title, which would protect him according to Eldoran law from any lawsuits save those brought by a Royal Warrant. Creon hinted at giving this to Zarthir, knowing full well that he would never grant such a title to a person so unsavory in his private life. Creon intended to use Zarthir for as long as Zarthir was useful to both Creon and the realm.

Zarthir cleared his throat and began to speak in his odd, lisping voice. 'The two provinces overseen by Prince Daerahil generated more foreign revenue than the other eight Shardan provinces combined. Even if we add in the revenues from our trading missions and customs from abroad, the two provinces of Voth and Kraylor are still the best producers of foreign revenue. Of course, our Customs revenues on imported goods into Eldora from the Dwarves, Elves, and Men not subject to Eldoran law may be far greater, but I do not have those details available. Also, the casualties of Eldoran and Kozaki soldiers, troop transport costs, and training costs for new soldiers and tax collectors is less than a tenth of what it was before Prince Daerahil took over. When you add these figures together, it is impossible to ignore the success of Prince Daerahil's reforms.'

'We will return to this in a minute,' said Creon irritably, 'but despite his successes, my son's transfer will stand. Now,' addressing Minister Ferly, chief of the Engineering Corps, 'about the upcoming mission to Plaga Erebus. Has there been any progress made?'

Ferly was a slight, stoop-shouldered man in late middle age, with dark brown eyes set deeply into a clever looking face. His mind was reputed to be incredibly sharp, as good with engineering and stonework as Daerahil's was at commanding men in battle. His voice, roughened from years in mines and stone quarries, breathing in vast quantities stone and coal dust, rasped.

'We have not yet found a way to break the stone that comprised the Sanguine Templar, the so-called Temple of Blood, but thanks to our friends among the Alchemists, we have made a key discovery, my Lord.' Pausing, Ferly gestured to Wysteria.

Wysteria nodded and stood, as was required of those not awarded an official title. 'Forgive me, Lord, but my husband was suddenly taken ill last night, and I have come in his stead, as instructed. May I proceed, Majesty?'

Even Creon was not beyond her womanly influence and, recalling Mergin's thoughts, nodded his head graciously.

'We have been able to create a way to detect the Dark Lightning safely, Majesty,' she said in a confident tone, her attempt at an upper-class accent nearly flawless except for a slight long extension on some vowels, which betrayed her common origins. 'As you are aware, this energy is pernicious, somehow stored within stones from the Blood Temple, lurking and striking the unwary instantly, causing their death. We have created wooden poles armed with metal devices of our making that reveal where there is a source of Dark Lightning, without causing it to discharge from the rock. Detecting it safely without discharge makes the Dark Lightning approachable, but regrettably, we have not been able to devise a method of breaking the stone matrix, so we cannot yet retrieve a piece of the stone filled with the Dark Lightning for analysis.'

'Thank you, Wysteria,' said Creon. 'This is at least progress on one front. You know of my desire to recreate the Dark Lightning and have it run across our gates and fences here in Eldora. But what about the Blasting Fire? Has the Guild made any progress there?'

Quailing for a moment, Wysteria successfully held her fear in check. Knowing much that even her husband did not know, she replied with the standard answer already known to the Council. 'No, my Lord. The small sample that you gave us from your ancient vaults ten years ago remains under examination, and while little progress has been made on determining its components thus far, we hope that someday we will relearn its secrets. On that note, may I ask a question?'

Startled for a moment, for Wysteria had not been brought here to ask questions but to answer them, Creon said in a curt tone, 'Yes, please do.'

'What of your mission to locate the last of the Earth Spirits? Have you met with any success?'

The Earth Spirits had created the Blasting Fire and given this to men long ago, along with the sciences of alchemy, agriculture and animal husbandry. Content to teach men, these spirits had refused to be controlled by Men and departed Eldora before the Great War. They had not been heard from since. Most Alchemists of Eldora were slain during the Great War, and many secrets were lost forever, including how to create Blasting Fire. Without finding the Earth Spirits again and persuading them to aid Men, Creon knew that science in Eldora would proceed quite slowly.

Now, at Wysteria's question, the king's face took on a look of surprise and anger, while Mergin exploded heatedly, 'How do you know of our mission to find the Earth Spirits? That is a secret heretofore known only to the King and myself!'

'Clearly, my Lord Mergin you are mistaken, as I know of this mission as well,' replied Wysteria with a hint of a smile. 'Suffice it to say that there are those who are beholden to the Guild who hear many things. Perhaps you, Lord Mergin, or you, my liege, spoke once too often about this mission?'

Muttering under his breath that perhaps Wysteria knew too much, Mergin was about to reply when Creon said, 'To answer your question, this secret mission, which is apparently less secret than I hoped, has not found the Earth Spirits, much less spoken with them. You and I will both attempt to find out the secrets of the Blasting Fire. Is there anything else?'

'Just this, my lord—a new contribution from the Alchemist Guild to support your foreign endeavors.' At this, she removed a small pouch from the purse lying at her feet and gently poured the contents into a nearby crystal goblet: Stones as red as blood filled the cup. 'Here, my liege, accept these blood rubies as a gift above and beyond our annual tithe.'

Creon frowned, his face darkening. Though he could not risk offending the Guild by refusing their generous gift, he knew them too well to believe there were no strings attached … even if he could not, as yet, discern them.

'Thank you, Wysteria,' he said with an attempt at a smile. "Is there anything else you have to add?' His tone indicated that she should say no and gracefully resume her seat.

'Only that the Gemsmith Guild has recently agreed to merge with the Alchemist Guild. I trust that this confederation will meet with your approval?'

Backed into a corner, Creon did not know what to say at first. If he rejected the stones, he would lose an enormous amount of unlooked-for revenue. However, if he accepted them, he must also accept the merger of the two Guilds. This would place even more money and power, demonstrated by Wysteria's knowledge of the mission to find the vanished Earth Spirits, into the hands of the Alchemist Guild.

'Yes, Wysteria,' he said at last. 'This match between the Goldsmiths and the Alchemists is well made. You have my approval. Formal documents shall come to you in the next few days.'

Inclining her head with a smile that was at once gracious and triumphant, Wysteria took her seat.

Mergin cleared his throat as if about to object, but Creon interrupted him.

'Not now, Mergin. I will listen to you later. Is there aught else that is relevant to this meeting?'

'Nothing, in particular, Majesty,' said Mergin.

'Very well. This meeting is adjourned until the next, which shall be scheduled by Lord Mergin. I thank you for your attendance. Farewell.'

After the others had bowed and left, Mergin said, 'Majesty I request—'

'Yes, I know what you are about to say,' interrupted the king again, this time with a sigh, 'but I cannot distrust her publicly or the Guild that she actually leads, as her husband is a useless fop, without good cause. Dispatch your Shadows to see if you can bring me evidence of any malfeasance, and I shall bring her back and put her to the question. For now, she and her Guild are far too valuable as an ally to offend, though their continuing acquisition of wealth, power, and information will have to be dealt with at some point, for I see that they begin to think themselves above even the crown. But it is not yet time for that, Mergin.'

'Yes, Lord,' said Mergin. 'I shall send Shadows to watch over her and the Guild.'

Privately, however, Mergin knew that he would do no such thing. He had a secret agreement with Wysteria that was quite beneficial to both of them, and he was not about to jeopardize it.

His performance of indignation and contempt had been perfect: Creon did not suspect a thing.

* * *

Alfrahil, seeing that he was alone with Mergin and his father, felt more confident in speaking his mind and asked what he thought would be a relevant question. 'Father, what has been said today makes much sense, but what about Daerahil's comment that Frederic is not strong enough to assume military command in his place? It is true that Amadeus is full of graft, corruption, and decay. Why the very roads are falling apart! How can you expect Frederic to execute a brilliant campaign of occupation if he cannot even control a single principality in our kingdom?'

Creon said, 'I don't know if truth be told; however, I am willing to let Frederic learn his tasks while he is in place rather than permit your brother's southern empire to grow bigger than it already has. You will be there to help keep an eye on him, so I can only hope that Frederic will not make a mess of things. Besides, the same senior military commanders who will teach you their craft will also closely monitor Frederic.'

'Southern empire? Then you believe those ridiculous rumors that my brother wishes to usurp the kingdom from you now or from me when you are dead and gone? Ambitious, brilliant, and arrogant he may be, but I sense no treachery in him. Do you?'

'Treachery? No. But there is something brewing in Shardan that is not yet obvious to me, something that fills me with disquiet, and I feel that your brother might be responsible … or at any rate, involved, as I have already mentioned.'

'Then put him to the question,' Alfrahil suggested. 'Use your mental powers to determine if he is lying. If he is innocent, let him return to Shardan, where, as we have just heard, he has performed admirably, saving the kingdom both men and money. If he is guilty of treason, you can deal with him accordingly.'

'I only have unsupported suspicion, Alfrahil, not proof that your brother is involved in any Shardan plots. If I move against him and I am wrong, then the army which loves him more than me for his deeds and actions may take his side and refuse to obey my orders, opening the way for your brother to take my throne. Only if he commits an action where I can bring him to trial for treason or sedition can I hope to sway the army that Daerahil is in the wrong, and safely restrain your brother's ambition.'

'Father, my brother is ambitious but loves us both. I do not believe that he would want to take your throne, much less deprive me of my birthright.'

'You have much to learn about the desires of Men and the dark plots they conceive in their hearts, my son,' said Creon.

'If only Blordar were still among us,' said Alfrahil. 'He could investigate my brother thoroughly without Daerahil's awareness.'

'Blordar is dead,' stated Mergin flatly. 'Our beloved loyal master of assassins and former head of the Shadows is dead, his body decaying somewhere under the desert sun.'

'Is that so?' retorted Alfrahil.

'I have told you so,' said Mergin.

'Then why was his body never recovered?'

'Enough, my son,' interjected Creon. 'I believe that Blordar is indeed dead. True, if he were alive, he could help us greatly, but there is no use wishing for the impossible. It saddens me still to hear his name, for he was a friend as well as a loyal servant. Mention him no more.'

Blordar, who had built the Shadows into the feared and effective force that Mergin had inherited and bent to his will, had died nearly ten years ago on a scouting mission into Shardan. A single Shadow had returned from the mission, all but dead, saying that the Shadows had stumbled into a Shardan ambush, which he alone had survived.

Though Creon had immediately dispatched search parties, no sign had ever been discovered of the Shadows or the Shardan raiders who had supposedly killed them.

The unavenged death of Blordar still filled Creon with rage, and now that rage fastened onto the memory of Daerahil's behavior in the Council meeting.

Pausing for several moments, Creon took the unusual step of hand-writing a small piece of parchment, before rolling it into a scroll. Handing it to Alfrahil, Creon said 'Now go and tell your brother of his new restrictions after his deplorable behavior here today.'

* * *

Daerahil sat sipping an exquisite glass of wine and admiring the décor from his private booth on the second floor of the Dusty Cloak. The windows were deep set crystal clear glass, free from bubbles, found in only the most expensive windows. Gentle bars of light shone into the interior of the tavern, covered with sawdust and ground nut shells on the lower level. A set of spiral stairs, with a sturdy porter armed with a large club, was set back against the far wall, leading to a loft accessible only by those who possessed an expensive membership.

The lower level was an excellent tavern that catered to foreign travelers, adventurous locals with money to spend, and soldiers who had served under Daerahil, who were able to eat and drink at a discount. Wide arrays of exotic dishes were available, from the Plafs of the steppes of far Azhar to the fish stews of the river delta, to the curries of Shardan. Crisp, cold beer from Frostfields was offered along with good wine. The walls were simple white plaster over dark stones, with dark wooden beams forming the ceiling. Straw-filled tapestries had been placed between the beams to reduce the noise of the occupants. Wooden benches set with large tables filled most of the room, with some small round tables and wooden chairs for smaller groups of guests.

Many of the patrons were soldiers, either active or retired veterans. They showed the bronze disc that had their name and service number on it, and they enjoyed a hefty discount. Daerahil respected the men who had served under his command far too much to profit from them, and during the winter months, he even funded free food kitchens in the lower end of the Sixteenth district that served a simple fish stew with root vegetables and coarse bread to those soldiers and their families who had great need. Here in the tavern, there was one caveat: while officers and common soldiers were equally welcome, they had to leave rank outside the doors. Here a grizzled old corporal could rub elbows with a senior commander, and neither was publicly allowed to think anything of it. If officers did not like this custom, they were welcome to take their business elsewhere. Common soldiers needed a place to simply be men, just as much as their betters did, and the Dusty Cloak was such a place.

On the second level, however, it was an entirely different experience. A sophisticated private restaurant, the finest in Titania, served those who were allowed to drink and dine exclusively at Daerahil's discretion. Two excellent chefs, one Shardan, the other Eldoran, served exquisite food perfectly prepared to the fortunate. Many of the finest wines in all Nostraterra, from the sparkling wine of Chilton to the rich yet subtle wines of the North Vale, were served here. Robust wines from Shardan and triple refined spirits of Dorian from the sugar fields of the river delta were also on the list. The décor was significantly different from below. Private booths filled the three walls of the level, with sliding doors to ensure privacy. An expansive bar staffed with at least three servers provided seats for those who wanted to simply eat and drink without concern over their privacy. Other servers were discreetly arranged about the room.

* * *

Alfrahil arrived at the Dusty Cloak some hours later. As soon as he strode in, the manager asked after Alfrahil's needs with fawning obsequiousness. The prince ordered a bottle of Dwarven ale, which the manager imperiously instructed a server to bring without delay.

'I take it my brother is in his usual booth?' Alfrahil asked.

'Allow me to conduct you,' the manager said with a slight bow.

'I'll surprise him,' Alfrahil said. 'Just have that ale sent up.'

With that, he climbed the stairs, whose guard bowed and made way for him, and slid the door to Daerahil's booth open.

His brother, seated at a table facing the door, said nothing but raised his glass in greeting.

'You are very trusting,' Alfrahil commented. 'How did you know I was not an assassin?'

Daerahil laughed. 'Brother, no one walks like you in this world.' And he put his palms on the table and beat out a stumbling, shambling staccato. 'I recognized your steps as you climbed the stairs.'

Alfrahil felt himself blush. 'Is that really how I walk?'

'Perhaps I exaggerate slightly. Sit down and drink with me.'

Alfrahil slid the door closed and sat across from his brother in a luxurious leather chair. 'Well, brother, you certainly have done it this time.'

'Indeed? What happened at the Council after I left?'

Handing Daerahil Creon's scroll, Alfrahil said 'Our father was quite beside himself with anger. He has fined you five hundred gold pieces and revoked your annual leave this year, compelling you to remain on duty until you have redressed the grievance that you have caused. Furthermore, he has ordered that you are not to leave your inspection from the Out-Walls to return to the City until your reports have been reviewed and approved. You could be stuck there in the outer barracks for quite some time.'

'It is nothing that I did not expect,' said Daerahil with a shrug. 'At least I had the satisfaction of humiliating that vile serpent Mergin.'

'That you did,' said Alfrahil, 'but you and I both know that he is not going away. You might as well call a truce in your dealings with him before he can find another way to undermine you again.'

Daerahil's face moved into a darker shade of red, and Alfrahil knew that his brother was on the verge of another outburst.

'Peace, brother,' said Alfrahil. 'I do not disagree with your feelings, but you must learn to be more circumspect in your actions.'

'You do disagree with some of my feelings, brother. We disagree on how to end the rebellion and bring home our soldiers from abroad. You would have a series of fortifications built along the borders of Eldora and Shardan and keep our troops in Shardan only in large groups to suppress the most visible elements of the rebellion. You also do not approve of the sovereignty of the Shardan Trade Confederation.'

'Yes,' said Alfrahil. 'I believe that your methods, while effective, give too much power away to the rebels and would allow the rebellion to infiltrate all of Shardan and spread into Azhar and even into South Eldora. Clearly, your ideas of governance have already permeated the Trading cities, emboldening them enough to revolt against us here in Eldora. Additionally, there is no guarantee that the rebels in your pacified provinces or the Traders in their cities would not use their newfound wealth to continue the struggle to overthrow Eldora's rule.'

Daerahil leaned forward, eager to rehearse this argument yet again. 'I believe that the only way is to let Shardan rebuild itself from the ground up and establish warlords loyal to trade and to Eldora for supplying such trade. The people in the Trade Confederation are citizens not just of Eldora, but men from Kozak, Chilton, and other distant towns. Why, even a few Dwarves have moved there, renouncing their allegiance to the Bastion and helping set up the new alliance. There is little to be done to stop the Traders. We must forge commercial and then political alliances with them so that our northern borders are fortified with a strong buffer from any incursion from the South.'

'On this as on many issues, we must agree to disagree,' said Alfrahil. 'But I had hoped that we could agree at least on the necessity of creating a true Shardan front.'

'Front? What front?' snorted Daerahil derisively. 'Think of the history of our occupation and tell me how we can create a front with the situation as it currently is.'

A knock at the door silenced their argument.

'Enter,' called Daerahil.

The manager bowed himself in, carrying a platter bearing another glass of wine for Daerahil and a tankard of Dwarven ale for Alfrahil. He set this down on the table and inquired if he might bring anything else.

Daerahil waved him away. 'Just keep bringing the drinks. Oh, and some cheese and bread.'

The manager smiled and bowed himself out. Daerahil rose as if to follow him. 'Where are you going?' asked Alfrahil, surprised.

'Nature calls, brother,' said Daerahil, and he slipped past Alfrahil and out of the room.

Alone, Alfrahil sipped his Dwarven ale and brooded on the history of the Shardan rebellion. After the fall of Magnar, fighting had continued for nearly sixty years before the signing of the Great Treaty. In that treaty, the supremacy of the Lords of the West and North was acknowledged by all of Shardan, with local Lords given dominion in their own lands. A new charter was created, forging the Lords of Shardan into a new confederation, with the Lords being allowed one year to choose a king amongst them and to have their king send formal ambassadors to Eldora and to Kozak.

The Lords had fought and died for their chance to be king, and only after many had perished in brief but savage military encounters or individual combat challenges was a King of Shardan chosen. That king was Karban: a clever politician from an ancient Shardan family, he was the least offensive choice among other, more powerful warlords. While he had some autonomy, he could scarcely call his capital city of Harath his own, failing to bring stability to a country that desperately needed it. Still, he had maintained the peace for many years as Shardan had begun to rebuild itself with waterways and roads, farms and fields.

Fifty-two years ago, a minor but noisy noble, Lord Gronthin, had fomented rebellion against Eldora and Kozak, declaring war against the foreign invaders. Gronthin had been ordered to Harath to explain himself to King Karban, son of Karban, his Council, and the ambassadors of Kozak and Eldora.

He had come peacefully, with only a small guard, and was brought before the Council of Shardan Lords and King Karban seated at their ornate wooden table. Karban demanded an explanation, and Gronthin had repented, recanting his desire for war, saying, 'I do not know from where or why these thoughts came to me unbidden.'

Approaching the throne, he bowed and accepted King Karban's pardon, but rising, a great flush came over his face, his eyes rolled briefly back into his head, and he had to grip his knees for support. Suddenly he turned and screamed, 'Shardan will be free!' and plunged a small poisoned knife secreted in his sleeve into Karban's chest. Simultaneously, one of his guards hurled a similar blade into the throat of the Eldoran ambassador. Gronthin was wrestled down by the other guards and Lords as his entire guard detail was cut down.

King Karban and the Eldoran ambassador began to twitch and foam at the mouth, their faces mottling into terrible colors; their lives vanished even as healers from Eldora and Shardan burst into the room. When they died, so did the peace of Eldora. Civil war broke out within days; nobles slaying one another again, with each Lord occupying his own small demesne, refusing to agree about Karban's successor, united only in their hatred of Eldora and Kozak.

At his trial, Gronthin said he remembered nothing of the assassination, but only derisive laughter and jeers had come from the witnesses to the murders and he was swiftly convicted and sentenced to a horrible death in the desert wastes.

Alfrahil vividly remembered the tale of the terrible blue figure that had appeared during Gronthin's excruciation, slaying all the men immediately standing around the condemned man, save his father. Creon, drawing his sword, Caelestus, had entered into the circle of power put forth by the creature but was expelled a few moments later. Lightning flickered over his body as he lay unconscious on the ground, his sword dark and discolored. The King regained consciousness the following morning but would not speak of what he had endured.

Sunrise brought a unique spectacle to the King's eyes: a perfect, black circle two hundred yards across burned into the desert sands. There was no trace of Gronthin, but the bodies of the guards lay upon a large piece of stone made from the newly fused sands of the desert, covered in unknown characters. The bodies of the men were hideously disfigured with runes and symbols no one could decipher. The odor of corruption and death made the survivors retch and heave. The guardsmen from Shardan tried to throw sand and place stones to cover the dead, but the grains flew into the air when they were a few feet from the bodies, and the stones hurtled backward, injuring some of the men in the process.

Eventually, the King and the representatives from Eldora and Kozak left, the guardsmen of Shardan muttering under their breath at what they had seen. The bodies continued to decompose under the Shardan sun, adorning the odd stone sculpture with their bleached bones. No one, not even the wise men of

Eldora or the scholars of the Great Elves, could explain what had happened there. Only the legends of Shardan provided an answer, no matter how improbable it might be.

Rumors of blue devils that could melt the earth and air; transforming men and animals into hideous shapes, were an ancient legend in Shardan. Now, these mythical devils were held responsible for the conflagration that had struck this small corner of the desert. The tale grew in the retelling, and even today, as Alfrahil well know, there were rumors of horrible deaths and mysterious disappearances of the soldiers who patrolled the farthest reaches of Shardan, Hagar, and Azhar.

Creon refused to ever voice his opinion about what had happened, forbidding the topic of the 'Blue Vesper,' as the creature had come to be known, in his presence. The King was deeply affected by his experience, and it colored everything that he did and said regarding the South from that day forward.

Gronthin's presumed rescue from Creon inflamed the rebellion; nearly overnight, secret societies sprang up with '*Shardan shall be free*' as their rallying cry. Few Shardans, however, would exchange peace for war, despite the promise of independence, and the movement initially had little popular support.

Enraged over the death of his ambassador, Creon declared martial law in Shardan, summoning the army of Eldora and requesting aid from Kozak. Three months passed before the allied army, a hundred thousand strong could assemble and mass along the Shardan border. During that time, the diplomatic corps of Eldora and Shardan accomplished a miracle, despite the petty Shardan Lords who squabbled and fought over the succession to the Shardan Kingship.

A nephew of Karban, Barnag, was declared King of Shardan and escorted to the palace with great fanfare as the war was averted. Barnag's first proclamation pronounced peace. The Lords of the far southern province of Parnin, home to Gronthin, would be offered up as hostages along with half of their goods to

Eldora as recompense for Eldora's loss. This traditional manner historically settled great disputes in Shardan, and Creon's closest foreign advisors had counseled him to accept these terms. The Eldoran army would stay on alert, patrolling the Shardan border but not violating their territory.

Creon then made a fateful decision, confounding his advisors then and Alfrahil even today. The King rejected the terms, insisting upon the occupation of the principal cities of Shardan and demanding that the eldest sons of each Shardan Lord serve as hostages in Eldora. If any soldier of Eldora or Kozak died, these sons, even those of loyal Shardan lords, would be put to death. These terms were very harsh, harsher than any imposed upon Shardan since the days of Eldora's original primacy in Nostraterra.

The insistence upon occupation proved to be the stone that began an avalanche of rebellion that Eldora, Kozak, and even the Shardan Lords loyal to Eldora could not stem. The intended hostages fled into hiding as rebellion swept through Shardan, inflaming the countryside and moving swiftly into the cities, where the allied army sustained severe losses. Eventually, the Lords of Shardan began to return some semblance of order to Shardan, and the soldiers of Eldora patrolled the roads between the provinces, as the rebellion now returned to the countryside, whence it had begun.

The cost to the soldiers and the people of Shardan had been tremendous, and even today, hundreds of soldiers were killed while chasing rebels and over a thousand a year was injured, some so severely they could not return to war. While the Lords of Shardan all publicly decried the rebellion and ostensibly aided Eldora and Kozak in their quest for pacification, there were few, in or out of Shardan, who believed in their sincerity. The controversy over the occupation had stormed through Creon's Council chambers and briefly out into the streets of Titania. A report that over a hundred wounded soldiers on their way home to

Eldora had been captured and tortured, their mutilated corpses disfigured and desecrated in the foulest ways, ended the debate in Eldora, as the offices of the army were flooded with young volunteers.

It was at this moment that Alfrahil, sitting with his back to the closed door of Daerahil's private booth, was surprised by the sudden icy feel of a blade at his throat. He froze, not daring to move, not daring to breathe.

The keen edge lingered a moment, then lifted, accompanied by the laughter of Daerahil. 'You see, brother, some of us do not advertise our approach with the footsteps of a drunken ox!'

Alfrahil flushed but bit back his angry retort.

Daerahil took his former seat, still grinning. 'Look at you, so lost in a daydream that even facing the door you did not see me enter. A prince of Eldora cannot let his guard down. Not these days. What if I had been a Shardan assassin?'

Alfrahil sighed and took a sip of his Dwarven Ale. 'I have been thinking of that,' he said. 'Nearly sixty years have passed since the start of the rebellion, and little has changed. The war still rages on and on, and there is no end in sight.'

'I agree, brother, but you and I disagree as to how best to end the killing. Father will not listen to either of us, despite our personal experiences there.'

Daerahil had served with the army for over forty years, while Alfrahil had barely served for one. Daerahil had countless wounds, while Alfrahil had only seen combat once during his only disastrous mission leading a company of men in Shardan, his skin had never been pierced by a weapon. Alfrahil had little practical experience to draw upon, relying upon his military advisors to give him a sense of the war and the people of Shardan. Alfrahil's limited experience gave him only a shallow insight into the Shardans. He thought them an endless source of struggles and violence, foreign people who were truly too different to ever conform to the ways of Eldora. Still, he had no intrinsic dislike of Shardan or its peoples, and he privately hoped for another treaty that would bring the army home and end the war.

Daerahil, however, had roasted in the infernal sun of the plateau in summer and clutched his cloak against him during the cold winter nights in the high desert. Extensive experience had taught him respect for the Shardan people and the overwhelming difficulty of forcing a proud, stubborn, ancient race to accept foreign domination. But there were compensations, and he had found many things about Shardan he enjoyed: the food, the coffee, and especially the women.

Now, shaking his head, Alfrahil hoped for what seemed the hundredth time that his brother would curb his tongue about his solution to the southern war and simply allow their father more time to sort it out. He had little hope for his brother on this tangent, however. 'Brother, I suppose we must just agree to disagree on this topic,' he said again and raised his tankard of Dwarven brew as though in a toast.

'How can you drink that vile concoction?' asked Daerahil. 'It smells like a stable.'

'How can you remove three wine stewards from your private estate in the past two years, demanding that they learn their trade more deeply before meddling with your precious casks and bottles again?' retorted Alfrahil.

'Aye, brother,' said Daerahil with a dark smile. 'We both have our own vices, but really you should come to my apartments more often and let me teach you about food and wine.'

'And you, brother, should learn diplomacy from me and my advisors. You would not be in the constant trouble that you are in now if you followed my advice,' said Alfrahil.

The brothers smiled tiredly and shook their heads at each other's stubbornness in all aspects, not just foreign policy, and wine and beer.

'Regarding taxes and trade,' began Alfrahil, and their conversation continued along this line for a while. It then moved on to foreign relations with the Elves and Dwarves, where they were actually more in agreement than on anything else.

Finally, Daerahil said, 'Well, brother, someday these will all be your problems, and I will do my best to support you when you are king.'

'But you would wish to be king in my stead if the order of our births were reversed,' Alfrahil said with a sardonic smile. 'You believe that you could be a much better king than I. Don't deny it.'

Daerahil shrugged his shoulders. 'So rumor would convict me, but I have no desire to usurp your rightful place. Yes, if the kingship fell into my hands, I would not refuse it and would do my best to lead this country well. But our father has only one lawful heir, and that man is you.'

'Skillfully said, brother,' laughed Alfrahil, 'but I am glad that I can count on your help someday. Regarding help, another thing you should know from the Security Council meeting is that a leader must be chosen to attempt the return of a block of stone from the Blood Temple containing active strands of Dark Lightning. Do not push our father too hard, or you might find yourself leading that expedition.'

'Even our father would not waste my talents on such a vain task, but thank you, brother.'

Rising as if to go, Alfrahil leaned in and whispered, 'One last piece of advice, brother: end your relationship with your Shardan girl before Mergin reveals your secrets to our father and you are in a predicament far worse than you are in today.'

'My personal life is none of your business,' Daerahil rejoined sharply. 'How did you find out, and what have you said to anyone?'

'I have said nothing to anyone,' said Alfrahil. 'As to how I found out, there was a joke from Minister Zarthir a few weeks ago when he was throwing a dinner party, and he intimated that you and he were business partners, saying that he had helped you find new enthusiasm in "all things Shardan." It didn't take much digging for me to find out the truth. Luckily for you, the King is completely preoccupied with the rebellion and has not spent much time delving into your personal life, but beware: after today, you can expect Mergin to time this revelation much more closely, so keep things quiet until you are recalled from your new inspection tour and can end your relationship with her honorably and quietly. Also, Lord Mergin is quite suspicious of Minister Zarthir; there are too many rumors of corruption to ignore. I know you and he is good friends; eventually, Mergin's eye will fall on your friendship. If you are also business partners with Zarthir, keep that even quieter. In fact, it might be prudent to sever such ties. According to Mergin, Zarthir treads on the boundaries of corruption much of the time, and it is probably only a matter of time before he is formally investigated. Certainly, his foul personal habits are enough for me to distrust him regardless of any financial misdeeds.'

'Your loathing of Zarthir is on record, brother, as mine is of Mergin,' said Daerahil, 'but each of us has need of those that we can trust, and for some reason, you believe that you can trust Mergin, and I believe that I can trust Zarthir. Who knows if we can trust any man, even each other?'

Alfrahil felt his brother's anger wash over him, causing terrible pain in Alfrahil's temple. 'Peace, brother, you are hurting me.'

'Sorry, brother.' Daerahil relaxed the focus of his mental powers that he had inadvertently set loose on his brother. Rubbing his own temples, Daerahil said, 'It causes me discomfort, too, when I use my skills even by mistake. I am sorry for my loss of control. I did not mean to hurt you, brother.'

'I know it, and I know such skills can be a burden. Yet sometimes I wish I had inherited them. Try being as blind as the rest of us.'

'No, thank you, brother. My skills have come in useful before and will be useful in the future. But let us return to what you were saying.'

'I did not wish to make you angry,' said Alfrahil, 'but to warn you of making too many friends in the wrong places. Take heed of my words before you suffer yet banishment from the City or even worse at the hands of Mergin and our father.'

'And I would bid you return to the Citadel and curry more favor with Mergin and our father, for clearly, you will side with them against me as well,' said Daerahil angrily, though at the same time careful to keep his mental powers in check.

Alfrahil did not reply, but turned to leave, reaching for the door. But before he could open it, Daerahil spoke again. 'Peace, brother. I appreciate your advice and your fears for my future. I know you mean well, but I can take care of myself.'

Shaking his head sadly at his obstinate brother, Alfrahil left the tavern, heading out on foot to the royal stables where he kept his horse.

* * *

Daerahil waited a few more moments, finishing his fifth glass of wine. Swaying slightly, he turned and left several silver pieces on the table to cover the bill for both of them and headed down to the messenger stable to retrieve another horse before riding to the Fifteenth District, where his mistress, Hala, dwelt. Giving his horse to another messenger stable prior to completing his journey, he walked the last few blocks to the Hala's apartment building. Entering into a small foyer, he acknowledged the guard standing at the entrance to the stairs, giving him a silver coin in a fit of generosity. Daerahil climbed the stairs until he reached the third floor, where he knocked lightly. Almost at once Hala appeared. Short, slender, and dark, with a lovely brown complexion, she was willowy and graceful, something that never ceased to amaze Daerahil. Even now, as she closed the door behind him, he began to relax and accepted the glass of wine that she poured for him from his private stock.

Hala was barely five feet tall, with long dark hair sweeping down her back ending just above her firm buttocks. Her child-like face presented a stark contrast to her lush womanly curves. At twenty-three, she was in her physical prime, and her musky perfume wafted up from her slender frame. 'Tell me what is troubling you, Lord, and then let me bring you joy,' she said in a lilting Shardan accent.

Hala sat on the long divan and had Daerahil place his head in her lap. Daerahil took a look around the room decorated in the Shardan style, with soft cushions on the floor and a low dining table. The windows were closed, and the scents of Shardan food and incense filled his nostrils as Hala began a gentle massage to his face and neck. Soon his troubles were coaxed from his mind, and he enjoyed a hot bath, soothed and cleansed by Hala before she led him to her bed.

Waking early the next morning, he left Hala sleeping comfortably and slipped into his soiled clothes from the day before. Daerahil left the apartment quietly, again cursing the fact that he could not leave any evidence of his visits to Hala for any to find. He was taking enough of a chance by keeping some of his personal wine stock in the apartment for their mutual enjoyment.

Dawn was not yet breaking as Daerahil strode steadily up to his private apartments, not seeing or noticing that a Shadow had followed him the day before and now was following him home, soon to tell his tale to Mergin.

* * *

Daerahil strode into his apartments. Seeing the first of his servants rising, he bade the man prepare a bath and some breakfast. Marda, his head woman, was just emerging from her small room off of the great room in the middle of his dwelling. Dark haired and a bit plump, Marda had run Daerahil's household for twenty years. In her mid-fifties, she had never married, devoting herself to tending to Daerahil who she regarded as her own prodigal son. She approached him with a small bow and said, 'I hope your night was restful, Lord, after all the ruckus that you caused in the Council chamber yesterday.'

'Has rumor of those events spread that quickly?' asked Daerahil in surprise.

'Yes, my Lord. The entire City is abuzz with your insults to Lord Mergin, so be careful, Lord, I beseech you.'

'Even you, Marda? Now you sound just like that worrywart brother of mine.'

'You should listen to him, my Lord, for he is always in good odor with the King and his ministers, and I know that he cares for you and wishes you well. But speaking of odor, where were you last night?' She sniffed at his clothes with exaggerated dismay.

'You know very well where I was,' Daerahil replied. 'I was on official business. Let us say no more about it.'

'Yes, Lord. Come, your bath is ready.'

Daerahil bathed, breakfasted, and put on his mail, preparing for the first day of his new command.

Chapter Four

Random Convergence

Alfrahil left the Security Council meeting and spent the night in his royal chambers having a quiet dinner alone. He rose early the next day, determined to take a ride to the village of Amarant, located just past the Out-Walls, to clear his head and spend the night with his close friend Beldar, his former mentor now retired to his country estate.

Saddling his horse, he began a steady trot down to the Sixteenth District and across the plain of Sisera. His horse's hooves echoed underneath him as he crossed the bridge over the rock quarry through the Great Escarpment. After pausing for an early lunch and to water his horse at a nearby tavern, Alfrahil remounted, knowing he had another hour before he reached the Great Wall.

As he approached the wall, he heard and felt the metallic crunch of the shoe on his horse's left forefoot give way, causing a slight stumble in the animal's stride. Alighting from the saddle, he checked the hoof; seeing the shoe cracked straight through, he grumbled to himself. Luckily, the royal messenger stables were nearby. He walked his horse toward the buildings, determined to have him shod as quickly as possible so that he could enjoy a restful day in the country.

The sentries at the stables snapped to attention as he entered. Alfrahil was immediately overwhelmed by the stench of horse excrement, visible from the outer chamber, revealed in great piles from the little daylight coming in from the doorway. The acrid odor of stale urine, both human and equine, was equally revolting.

Alfrahil made his way to a high wooden counter behind which stood a sergeant of the guard busily filling out forms and grumbling under his breath as if the task were beneath him. When Alfrahil politely coughed, the sergeant, without looking up from his papers, said, 'Mind your tongue; I will speak with you once I am finished.'

Amazed at the man's temerity, Alfrahil spoke ringingly. 'Where is your captain, Sergeant?'

Starting and staring, the sergeant recognized the Crown Prince. After stammering out an apology, the sergeant said, 'Captain Dunner is indisposed and not to be disturbed, my lord. He left strict orders.'

'Did he indeed?' asked Alfrahil. 'Sergeant, are you now hoping for reassignment to the Azhar frontier for the next year? For it certainly seems that way.'

'No, sir,' the sergeant replied. 'I just… beg your pardon, sire. I'll take you to him right away.'

The sergeant bellowed to a nearby corporal to take over the stables until he returned. He then escorted Alfrahil out the door and down the main way, a short distance from the Great Gate, before turning into a series of smaller and smaller streets and plunging down a short stair into the musky dankness of a series of houses of ill repute. Few people were about except for some joy girls who had not found a customer the night before. Many of these, not recognizing the crown prince, made salacious offers. Men skulked nearby, watching with greedy ferret eyes glinting under hooded cloaks.

Alfrahil was angry that these houses were in existence again after Creon's strict orders to close them down had been issued last year, much less operating so boldly. Ignoring the stares of these vile denizens, Alfrahil wore a grim smile, following the sergeant through the door of one of the larger establishments, the Red Lantern.

Alfrahil noticed a small waiting room, with bawdy paintings on one wall and a bar of sorts along another. The smells of stale sweat and cheap perfume and other less savory odors came from the interior. Tawdry cloth-covered couches and worn wooden chairs were scattered over the floor. The mid-morning light seeped in through the open door as if wary of what it might find. Small lamps with feeble flames kept shadows moving in an endless dance around the room.

Two soldiers, sprawled on a couch, recognized Alfrahil and snapped to attention. Otherwise, the room was empty. Alfrahil ordered one of the soldiers to run back to the stables to fetch reinforcements and ordered the other soldier to guard his person.

The stable sergeant bellowed, 'Captain Dunner, you are needed downstairs immediately! There is no time for delay!'

Waiting for Dunner, Alfrahil saw nothing upon the counter, so he looked behind it. There, tucked under the bar, he saw what appeared to be a ledger of some kind. Upon opening it, he immediately saw the names of two of the King's most favored courtiers and one of his minor ministers.

His perusal of the ledger was interrupted by the jingle of chain mail and the cadence of well-drilled men marching at double time. Alfrahil looked up to see the soldier he had dispatched return with twenty men of the guard platoon. Closing the book and placing it upon the counter, Alfrahil addressed the platoon sergeant. 'Take five of your best men and go room to room until you find Captain Dunner of the messenger corps. Bring him to me immediately.'

While the sergeant selected his men and ascended the stairs, Alfrahil waited patiently. Soon a commotion started upstairs as room after room was emptied and women and their customers came down the stairs in various states of disarray. Their protests died when they saw Alfrahil standing with a platoon of guards. The men quickly slunk away, hoping not to be recognized.

Alfrahil was content to let them go ... for now. But he would not forget their faces or their names.

One man, however, he detained. 'I am surprised and disappointed to see you here, Minister Zarthir. While your personal reputation is vile and your tastes run to women of ill repute, this house would seem to be beneath even your questionable standards.'

'Alas, my Lord Prince, you find me at a great disadvantage. While our tastes in pleasures and comforts do not run in the same vein, you might try some of the pleasures of this particular house before you judge so quickly,' said Zarthir with an arrogant leer. 'At any rate, my reputation is what it is, but even you must acknowledge that I am tremendously valuable to our King and to the realm.'

'You craven worm,' replied Alfrahil. 'Capable in foreign trade and fabulously rich you may be, and my father may be stuck with your sneering face sitting around his Council table, but when he and other members of the Council hear my report, I suspect your seat at the table will be swiftly taken by another. Now you will accompany some of my men back to the Citadel and await my father's displeasure.'

'I am a full Minister,' replied Zarthir with overwhelming confidence on his handsome face. 'You cannot order me anywhere or to do anything, unless you actually see me commit a felony, and so far all you have seen is me standing here in a mild state of undress. Therefore, unless you have a Royal Warrant executed by the King and countersigned by Lord Mergin, as the law requires, I shall presume myself free to get dressed and take my leave. Do you have a warrant?'

'No, you are free to go.' said Alfrahil after a long pause through clenched teeth.

'Very well.' said Zarthir, giving Alfrahil a half-mocking bow. 'Until our next meeting, my Prince.'

'Do not get too comfortable, Zarthir,' said Alfrahil with a sudden inspiration. 'You are correct. I cannot order your confinement or arrest you now, but that is not the case for anyone else in this house. Sergeant, arrest the other occupants on suspicion of prostitution and bring me the madam of the house for questioning.'

Without another word, but with murder in his gaze, Zarthir marched back up the stairs to dress before leaving.

Next, Captain Dunner was brought forward under escort.

'Captain Dunner,' said Alfrahil, 'I require your services.'

'Services, my Lord?' stammered Dunner. 'Only tell me your desire, and I shall honor your command.'

Alfrahil's smile was wintry as he considered the fawning, terrified man standing before him. He was dressed and without female companionship, so he had obviously heard the commotion prior to eviction from one of the chambers upstairs. 'Well, Captain,' said Alfrahil, 'for that is still your rank. You can explain the reason for the overwhelming filth in your stables, along with the lack of discipline and insolence I encountered at your command post.'

'Filth, my Lord?' asked Captain Dunner. 'Insolence? I don't understand.'

Grimly, Alfrahil stated, 'Perhaps, Captain, you would care to escort me back to the stables and see the chaos firsthand?'

Smiling a little too quickly for a man in his position, Captain Dunner replied, 'With all due respect, my Lord, perhaps there was one idle soldier who irritated your grace. But overall, the stables should be in good working order, even if they are not quite fit for a parade inspection.'

Alfrahil held Dunner's eye. 'Captain, you have a choice to make. Either we can return to the stables for my formal inspection, or you can immediately volunteer to replace the Messenger Captain currently assigned to the Eastern Shardan command for the next year. If you volunteer and conclude your assignment satisfactorily, you may return and resume your duties within the City, and this business will be forgotten. If you fail the inspection, you will be dismissed from the army and left amongst other unemployed veterans. Choose now.'

Dunner paused for a moment, but then, swallowing hard, said, 'I volunteer for the assignment, my Lord.'

'Wise choice, Captain,' said Alfrahil approvingly. 'Why don't you run ahead and inform your senior lieutenant that we are on our way to return to the stables and that I will be choosing your successor presently.'

'Yes, my Lord Prince,' said the captain. 'At once, sir.'

As Dunner scurried away, Alfrahil called for the madam of the house to step forward.

A large, matronly woman dressed in expensive but gaudy clothing emerged from the crowd. With an oily obsequiousness and a gaze that did not quite reach the Crown Prince's eye, she inquired as to his needs and how she could best serve them. Her voluptuous frame had clearly gone to seed, but the hints of fading beauty were still evident in her face. Anyone could tell that she was one of the lucky women to rise from the ranks of common 'joy girls,' as women of ill repute were politely known, to oversee an entire house of younger desperate women.

'You can serve them, woman, by telling me who owns this house,' said Alfrahil.

'Well, Lord, I am not sure,' she temporized, rapidly trying to think a way out of this calamity. 'I believe this house is owned by different businessmen within the City.'

'Who is the man or men who control the activities of this house?' thundered Alfrahil.

'I don't know, my Lord,' she repeated. 'We work through different moneymen and brokers within the City, and I am not sure who actually the owner of this house is.'

'Silence, woman!' Alfrahil barked. 'I have had my fill today of sly looks and lack of candor. Your lying schemes have bought you a special reward today. You shall be sent forthwith to the Azhar frontier as a common serving wench.'

Stricken, the woman looked desperately into Alfrahil's face. 'My Lord,' she stammered. 'Perhaps you and I could withdraw privately to my room, where we could discuss this matter more comfortably?'

Alfrahil extended his hand in a gesture indicating that she should show him to her room and only one guard would follow them. She led Alfrahil and the soldier along a couple of back passageways until she entered a nondescript storage room. She touched a portion of the wall, and Alfrahil saw that the stone depressed inward an inch or so, revealing a hidden door, which she opened with the touch of another hidden switch. She stood aside and indicated that Alfrahil should precede her into the room thus revealed.

The prince shook his head and instead gestured for the soldier to enter. Then, taking the woman by the arm, Alfrahil guided her inside. The soft yellow light came from crystal light fixtures on the ceiling; he was astounded by the opulence that confronted him. Only the finest weavers could have created the tapestries that hung upon the walls, and the furniture was ornate and antique, worth a small fortune. A small abacus lay on a writing desk composed of the finest northern hardwoods. An odor of perfume filled the room, a scent that Alfrahil did not recognize. A beautifully painted screen of far Azhar separated the working room from private areas revealed only by dark shadows and a sense of greater space than what was actually visible. Clearly this woman, despite her flaws, had an appreciation of beauty.

The woman quickly asked the Prince to sit. 'Now, my Lord Prince,' she said, 'there has been a misunderstanding between us, and for that, I apologize. I will be happy to offer you a permanent gift of companionship in this house, valuable secrets many would kill for, along with fifty gold pieces per month. All I request in return is that this small matter is overlooked.'

Alfrahil said nothing, appearing to contemplate her offer for a moment. Then he invited the soldier closer for a brief whispered discussion, after which the soldier saluted smartly and left the room.

'Now,' said Alfrahil to the madam with a tight smile, 'you shall tell me the name of the owner of this house if you would escape my sentence of banishment.'

Thinking that this was only an opening gambit, the woman replied, 'Perhaps my secrets, one hundred gold pieces per month, and a quarter of my wealth can find their way to your coffers, my Lord, so that our dealings may operate more smoothly.'

Smiling, the Prince said politely, 'I am giving you one last opportunity to redeem yourself. Do not waste it on idle flattery or foolish attempts to bribe or seduce me.'

The woman said, 'A quarter of my current wealth is the best that I can do, but I can give you one hundred fifty gold pieces a month.'

Alfrahil said nothing and remained silent as the steady tread of booted feet came down the hall and through the empty false storeroom. The sergeant of the guard entered the room, his eyes darting everywhere at once as he observed the rich decorations.

'Sergeant,' stated Alfrahil, 'I order you to place this woman in your custody immediately. See that she is questioned by Lord Mergin and his men. Once Lord Mergin is done with her, she is to be dispatched to the Azhar frontier with the patrol that is leaving this week to take up their positions there. She is a new serving woman for the men, and should prove valuable to their needs and comfort.'

'My Lord, I beseech you,' the woman cried. 'You will never have such an opportunity again, for the documents that I have hidden could well make you one of the most powerful men in the realm.'

'Silence, wench of misfortune!' roared Alfrahil. 'I am already one of the most powerful men in the realm, or have you forgotten that you are speaking to your Crown Prince?'

Angrily and enigmatically the woman replied, 'You are now, my Lord Prince. You are now.'

Regarding her statement as the angry retort of a desperate woman, Alfrahil dismissed the implied threat. 'Sergeant,' he said, 'after you have taken this creature to her meeting with Lord Mergin, send a messenger to Lord Golbur, Dwarf Lord of Edelhohle, who is here on leave from his kingdom, requesting the services of Dwarven engineers to aid me in search of the secrets this room surely holds.'

As if suddenly stricken by the seriousness of her situation, the woman fell to her knees and cried out for mercy.

'You had your opportunity,' Alfrahil said with distaste in his tone. 'Now the Dwarves will uncover your secrets, and all of your wealth will be seized and given to the poor and the needy. Perhaps you will learn the meaning of honest labor as you cook and clean upon the distant frontier.'

One last wail came from the woman as she was wrenched back to her feet and escorted from the room.

Summoning the senior corporal, Alfrahil asked him to guard the room against entry until the Dwarven engineers arrived. He then returned to the main lobby of the house, where a few confused women were still gathered. He bade them to return to their rooms and retrieve their belongings before leaving the house forever.

'But this is our home,' one of the women protested.

'No longer,' he replied. 'This house will be cleaned and repaired and given to the families of honest people who have nowhere else to live.'

With luck, thought Alfrahil as all the women, weeping now, fled up the stairs, news of his intent would travel quickly and serve to bring the true owners of the establishment out from their hiding places.

Alfrahil spent the better part of an hour reviewing a detailed list of patrons discovered in a drawer of the madam's writing desk. Slowly, and with growing disgust, Alfrahil noted the names of prominent men in the City, government officials, merchants, even members of the army staff and the King's personal guard. Placing the list and the ledger he'd found earlier in the hands of the senior corporal, Alfrahil bade him bring it safely back to the Citadel.

While Alfrahil did not doubt the loyalty of his soldiers, he was concerned that once word spread of his actions and his discovery, an attempt to steal the book might be possible. Thinking further about what he might find here, he sent another soldier to bring down a detachment of his personal guards, his Guard Captain, Biramin, and a full company of soldiers. Once Biramin and his men arrived, Alfrahil would have him secure this house and the neighboring homes and streets against theft and fire that could damage the information Alfrahil was certain the house contained.

Biramin was the second son of the Duke of Anscomb. Unable to inherit as long as his brother lived, he had entered the military, which customarily took in the unlanded sons of nobility, giving them special training for military posts. The dark-haired and dark-eyed Biramin was a huge man, nearly seven feet tall, barrel-chested but without any fat upon him. In addition to his regular military training, he had spent three years with Shadows learning counter-intelligence, close-hand combat, and urban warfare as well as desert warfare, to become Alfrahil's personal guard captain. The two men had been lifelong friends ever since the day they had met, and Alfrahil trusted no one else as thoroughly as he did Biramin.

The Dwarven engineers—four in number—were the first to arrive, an hour after being summoned. Alfrahil led them back into the secret room, which one of the engineers laughingly derided as 'so crude a blind Man child could find it.'

'It is precisely because of your skill at finding things that I have asked you here,' said Alfrahil. 'I would request that you diligently employ all of your skills at finding secret doors, panels, and other hiding places. Please give any of the things you find there to this soldier of the guard.' He indicated the young corporal. 'He will remain here and provide any aid that you need. I will send one of my merchant account men to negotiate your fee, but please begin without delay.'

Emerging back into the common room, Alfrahil waited for another hour until a harried-looking Biramin entered the room. 'Biramin, I am sorry to disturb your rest, but there are important things to be done here today,' said Alfrahil.

'How may I serve, Lord?' the captain asked.

Taking Biramin aside, Alfrahil explained what he had found, and what he suspected might yet be found, within the house. He needed men whose loyalty was unquestionable to guard both the house and the Dwarves within it until the search could be completed.

'Yes, Lord,' said Biramin. 'I will dispatch twenty-five of my men to watch the company you have summoned. Nothing shall happen to this house or its contents; I will personally escort the madam to Lord Mergin.'

Feeling a sense of relief, Alfrahil ordered half of his guard to accompany him back to the stables so he could proceed with his long-postponed visit to Amarant.

Striding back toward the stables, he noted the modest crowd that had gathered around the brothel. By the time he had climbed out of the alley, a small throng of curious citizens was following at his heels. Alfrahil paused to address them.

'Good citizens of Titania,' he said. 'I have attended to a blight upon the bright reputation of our fair City. One joy house will no longer contribute to the degradation of Eldora and the corruption of its moral fiber. This house shall be assigned to the families of the veterans of the wars who find themselves in a serious plight and have nowhere else to live.'

Hearing the hoarse cheers of the local populace, especially the women, Alfrahil turned upon his heel and proceeded to the stables. Upon arriving there, Alfrahil was greeted smartly by two of the messenger guards in clean and shining uniforms. Entering the stables, Alfrahil was frankly astonished. While his eye could still see repair work that needed attending to, much of the rampant filth and malevolent odor had been dispelled. The remaining piles of excrement had been loaded onto what looked like dozens of carts. The dank stone walls had been scrubbed, along with the gray flagstone floor. The wooden rails had had their coating of manure and flies removed and showed the gleam of old polish under their newly scrubbed surfaces. Even the ceiling had lost most of its cobwebs and lint, and air circulated freely from deep-set windows that had been closed during his prior visit.

Suitably impressed, Alfrahil proceeded to the desk and dispatch area that had hitherto contained the unpleasant personage of the rude sergeant. Standing in his stead was a dark-haired man of about forty. Bearing the rank of a lieutenant, the man introduced himself as Caelus, son of Caelar.

'Please forgive the conditions of the stables, my Lord; they have fallen into neglect and disrepair. I have recently had the opportunity to begin cleaning and repairing them, and I hope to have them up to proper standards within a fortnight,' said Caelus.

'How long have you had your present post, Lieutenant?' asked Alfrahil. 'Barely four hours ago a surly; gray-haired sergeant was sitting where you now stand, and this building looked as if rude corsairs from the Shardan coast had been living here for generations.'

'I was off duty when I heard the guard captain was being sought for by the Crown Prince to explain the state of the stables. I hurried here to take command of the stables, as I am the first officer and hoped I could use this opportunity to bring the stables into some semblance of functionality so that when your Grace returned you would be able to complete your errand.'

Just then, two young guardsmen escorting a group of stone-masons hurried by with buckets and trowels laden with cement and began patching the damaged walls. Looking farther down the hallway, Alfrahil saw a journeyman stone-mason directing laborers with barrows of flagstones to place them in stacks along the floor where the apprentice stonemasons were already beginning to remove the broken and stained stones.

Alfrahil had rarely seen such industry in Eldora in recent days and remarked to Caelus, 'This sort of behavior might just land you a promotion.'

Not sensing Alfrahil's jest, Caelus replied shortly, 'Promotion is the furthest thing from my mind. I only hope to fulfill my duties.'

Seeing the rising color in Caelus' face, Alfrahil was suddenly struck by the thought that this man truly meant what he said and that he was trying to do his job with faith and honor. 'While these stables are in a shambles and you may have been less than diligent for not seeing to their upkeep before now, I cannot help but be impressed by your present attention to duty and detail. Therefore, from this day forward, Caelus, you are hereby promoted to Captain of the Messenger Stables and carry all of the honors and duties that your position entails. I give you free "rein" to choose your subordinate officers and sergeants so that you may continue your excellent work.' Seeing the astonished face of Caelus and hearing the man's stammering protests that he did not deserve such an honor, Alfrahil knew he had acted wisely. 'Now, Captain,' he added, 'I require two things of you: swift horses with a small honor guard and the recommendation of someone who can help me with a task requiring discretion and wisdom.'

'Can you tell me more of this task, my Lord?' asked Caelus. 'I could then perhaps recommend someone who could suit your needs.'

'No,' replied Alfrahil. But leaning in for a close whisper, he added, 'I need someone besides Biramin, who is performing an equally valuable service for me now, who I can trust implicitly, who would draw their sword, stand their ground, and defend me to the death. Who besides yourself would fit this duty?'

Without pause, Caelus said, 'My older brother would be the man you are looking for, my Lord.'

'Where is he and how is he known?' asked Alfrahil.

'Alcar, son of Caelar, my Lord. He was Captain of the Prince of Ackerlea's guard until politics got the better of him. Now he is a pikeman upon the outer wall. You can ask for him at the guard house north of the Great Gates, and they will tell you how to find him, sire.'

'Send one of your messengers to bring him to me while you choose ten horses for my guard and have my horse re-shod,' said Alfrahil.

Caelus bowed and departed.

At that moment, one of the soldiers of Alfrahil's company approached him and stated, 'There was an attempt to fire the house you recently visited, my Lord. A couple of the would-be arsonists have been apprehended.'

Alfrahil asked in alarm, 'Did the house burn?'

'No, my Lord,' replied the messenger. 'Captain Biramin had men with shovels and barrels of water stationed nearby, and they were able to extinguish the blaze before it spread.'

'What other news?' asked Alfrahil.

'Well, my Lord, the former madam of the house was walking with the guard detachment when an arrow came from a high rooftop and slew her where she stood,' the messenger reported.

'Slain!' cried Alfrahil. 'Slain, you say?'

'Yes, my Lord,' replied the messenger. 'She is dead.'

'What of the men that I entrusted to guard her?'

'My Lord,' replied the messenger, 'Captain Biramin tells me that his men were hand-picked and marched closely around her and that only an exceptionally fine archer could have attempted the shot, much less sent the arrow home.'

Swallowing down a curse, Alfrahil asked, 'Is there anything else?'

'No, my Lord,' said the messenger. 'Captain Biramin will be here shortly to update you on the status of his progress.'

'Thank you, messenger,' said Alfrahil. 'You may return to your post.'

Pondering this latest development, Alfrahil berated himself for failing to see that the woman had knowledge that men would literally kill to protect. He hoped the Dwarven engineers would have better fortune in searching the house.

Half an hour later, Biramin appeared but could add nothing to the information already reported. Alfrahil bade him wait until Caelus returned with his brother.

Soon, Caelus appeared and introduced his brother, Alcar, who looked like an older version of his brother. He saluted the Prince and asked how he could be of service. Seeing the look of command authority in Alcar's face, Alfrahil could readily believe that the man had once led the guard detachment for the prince of Ackerlea.

'Alcar, I have it on good authority that you were once a Captain of the guard of Ackerlea,' said Alfrahil.

'Yes, my Lord,' said Alcar. 'But I no longer hold that position. I have been banned from Nen Brynn and serve now as a pikeman upon the walls.'

'Why?'

'I tried to stop one of Zarthir's close companions from forcing himself on a young servant girl, not even twenty, sire, and I was wrongfully convicted of assault. Zarthir's lackey bribed several soldiers under my command to verify his story, and my Lord Paladir had no choice but to dismiss me from his service.'

Alfrahil took stock of this man for a moment, watching Alcar's face go red with shame and anger, soon replaced by a pale purple color consistent with betrayal and thoughts of revenge as he tried to regain his composure.

'Well,' said Alfrahil, 'after seeing the actions of your brother and hearing him vouch for you today, as well as hearing your own tale, I am going to offer you a task more worthy than propping a pike upon the wall. I want you and your brother to assemble ten horses for my honor guard, plus ten horses for guardsmen from the Citadel, plus a horse for yourself, and spare mounts prepared in case we encounter any problems along the way.'

'It shall be done, my Lord. Where are we going, so I can make certain the horses and men are properly prepared?'

'We leave on a short journey of a few days or less to Amarant. We need rations only for ourselves, not our horses, so lay in a supply of food and drink that will suffice for such a journey. Assemble pack animals and provisions as well. Here is some money. Bring me the receipt when you are ready.'

Hearing Alfrahil's plans, Biramin hastily took his prince aside. 'My lord, I must accompany you to Amarant; after the brazen assassination of the madam, I fear for your safety. In fact, better you forego your journey and return to the Citadel until this conspiracy can be unmasked.'

Smiling, Alfrahil told Biramin, 'I am currently next to the outer wall and near to the Great Gate; the chances of me being waylaid are actually higher if I return to the Citadel. I wish to consult my friend Beldar the scholar about these events. Go now and take this book and list to Mergin. Have him do his best to uncover the people and machinations behind these recent events. I will return in three days. Send word to me if there are any developments.'

'My Lord, that I will do and more, but please let me accompany you,' said Biramin.

Alfrahil reached forward and firmly grasped Biramin's shoulder. 'I need you to carry out these orders, for I can trust no other man with this news. Help Mergin and make certain there is a trustworthy guard around him and his quarters at all times. Look especially to the rooftops for hidden archers and to the surrounding buildings for arsonists. If they will risk so much to remove an ordinary proprietor of whores, they will risk much more once they determine that Mergin will start rooting them out.'

Reluctantly, Biramin said, 'It will be done, sire. Safe journey.'

Alfrahil bade Biramin farewell and mounted his horse. Quickly trotting out of the stables, he turned right, toward the Great Gates. The rest of the company followed.

Alfrahil's gaze became fixed upon the Great Gates. One hundred feet tall and fifty feet across lay each door, burnished steel overlaid with Platina wrought with Dwarven skill that presented a mirror few in Nostraterra could lay claim to own. In their surface was reflected back the images of all that moved among them, but by Dwarven art, the background of the City and the tower was always reflected and magnified, making travelers stare about them as if they caught within a portrait frozen by time. If a traveler were to stand long enough and fix his gaze upon a particular part of the gates, he could glimpse for a brief moment the Last Bastion, mountain home to the Dwarves at the farthest end of the Ice Mountains far to the north and east of Eldora. In the images from the Gates, the Last Bastion towered above the river below it, a granitic battlement surrounded by young but hale forests that had re-grown after the Great War.

A traveler might instead get a glimpse of the ancient lamps of the Dwarves as they hung in Nerea, long before the fall of the Dwarves and the coming of the Fire Demon. Others could see the wizened faces of the smiths who had wrought the doors, the creased lines in their stern faces belying the inner joy that they were making an artifact that would stand long after they and their progeny had turned to dust, buried in stone coffins in their mines as was the custom of Dwarves. Platina mixed with secret Dwarven metals; created a perfect surface immutable from stains or rust. This outer mirror overlay an inner core alloy of Platina and steel constructed in a honeycomb made the gates marvelously light but strong, intertwining all of the properties of the metals by the secret Dwarven smithing techniques.

Returning to the present, Alfrahil and his men took the road to the Southern-most gate of the Out-walls, bound for Amarant and a quiet evening. Alfrahil wondered if his brother had enjoyed such a remarkable day or if he was whiling away the hours in his tedious inspection tour.

* * *

Daerahil was indeed as bored as his brother could wish, having risen early and proceeded northward to the first forts along the Out-walls. There he inspected the men as quickly as he could and slowly proceeded to the next tower, noting that he was expected to spend at least a week examining these fortifications before riding to inspect the customs men and the border forts along the river. He regretted only having a light breakfast and was determined to enjoy lunch at an excellent inn a mile or so from the Out-walls, adjacent to the eastern road to the bridge at Estellius.

His meal was interrupted by a messenger bearing the markings of the Prince of Ackerlea, who presented a scroll for Daerahil's review. It proved to be a message from Prince Paladir asking him to secretly ride to meet with him in Ackerlea. The imprint of Paladir's signet ring was stamped into wax at the bottom of the scroll. Daerahil wrote a brief message to the King, informing him of what had happened, and handed it to a member of the messenger corps with orders to deliver it to the Citadel.

Rolling up the scroll, Daerahil tucked it into his shoulder bag and then finished his meal before mounting his horse and, in the company of his honor guard, galloping off to Nen Brynn.

Chapter Five

Anatomy of a Plot

Alfrahil arrived in Amarant in time for a luxurious late dinner with Beldar. It fascinated him that a man intelligent enough to be inducted into the Brotherhood of the Cold would insist on preparing their dinner himself. His servants prepped the meat and vegetables, but he did the cooking himself, making complex sauces with meat stocks and wines.

Beldar was tall and thin, with short grey hair and the sharp eyes of the academic that he was. Now, retired from the Brotherhood, he was content to enjoy a peaceful life, conducting research and problem-solving at his leisure while enjoying his favorite pastime, cooking. Anyone who wished to spend time with Beldar had to spend time in his kitchen, no matter the heat or the smoke. But any discomfort in this regard was more than made up for by the quality of the meals, at least in Alfrahil's opinion.

The two friends had met several years ago when Beldar was chief liaison between the Brotherhood and the King. Established over a millennia ago; the Brotherhood was the largest collection of scholars in the world of Men. They would solve nearly any problem for anyone who could afford their price. Their emotionless relentless dedication to problem-solving had earned them their nickname, as their only humane attribute lay in dedicating their profits to the needs of the poor, otherwise, they were ruthlessly logical. The Brotherhood supported many different charities that were in opposition to the will of Eldoran kings, but they were wholly independent, refusing to bow to any authority outside of their order. The Brotherhood was never violent, but they were loyal to each other, and if the sanctity of their world was jeopardized, they all stopped working, and no more clever solutions would be forthcoming from them.

Unique in all of Nostraterra, each brother took a vow of poverty when they entered into that world, surrendering their worldly possessions. Beldar was one of the few brothers who had ever left the order and returned to the world, as the brothers put it, seeming none the worse for wear. But Alfrahil knew that his friend had renounced his vows after a diplomatic crisis in Shardan, during which the influence of King Creon had, in Beldar's view, intruded impermissibly on the ancient perquisites of the Brotherhood. Beldar's wealth was the result of inheriting from his father's estate after he had left the Brotherhood. Eldoran law forbade the transfer of money and property not yet conferred upon a donor, so Beldar benefited by leaving the order prior to his father's demise.

Now Alfrahil sat upon a large patio that was covered with a cloth tarp against the late afternoon sun, enjoying the spectacular view of the river to his south and the city to his east. Beldar's mansion sprawled behind him. He had originally planned this visit to his old friend simply as a break from the stresses of his duties, a chance to enjoy a fine meal and fine conversation. But now that had changed. If his instincts were correct, what he had stumbled upon that morning was just the tip of the iceberg. Thus he gently asked his friend for help, knowing that while Beldar would not betray any confidence gained from his twenty years within the Brotherhood, he would listen and apply his accumulated wisdom when asked.

After listening to Alfrahil's description of the corruption and moral dry rot he had uncovered, Beldar chuckled. 'You, my friend, have probably not heard the ancient phrase that "abso-lute power corrupts absolutely¿"

'No, I have not. Can you clarify?'

'Now that Eldora has emerged as the greatest military and economic power in Nostraterra, there is little that can stand in her way. Therefore, the only competition to the King's au-thority must come from within rather than without. Eldora has conquered its dangerous competitors, such as Shardan, or made certain that the military powers of other Men and even the Dwarves are much smaller in scope and scale. Only the Lesser Elves could represent a possible threat to Eldora, and so long as their king, Albericus, and your father remain friends and al-lies, whose worlds do not overlap, Eldora has no real enemies anymore.'

'So you are saying that we must look exclusively inside our own realm for answers to my questions regarding corruption?'

'Not exclusively, Alf.' Only Beldar called Alfrahil by this nickname. 'You really must learn to order your thoughts more clearly and precisely. There very well maybe foreign parties in-volved in this corruption, profiting from it and encouraging it. These parties may include any and or all of the races, from any-where. I do not know, and as you know, now that I have left the Brotherhood, I have no more exclusive knowledge. But without betraying confidences from prior clients, I can say that the outer filaments of this web that you have stumbled upon are just the first strands of a vast interwoven maze of money, influence, and politics that very well may threaten the primacy of Eldora and the stability of your realm. As the one who has first decided to take on this coalition, you are in personal danger. Make certain that you get home to Eldora safely and have Mergin and the King spend more time worrying about internal enemies rather than focusing on the Shardan people they so openly despise.'

With those words still echoing in his mind, Alfrahil woke early the next day. It was difficult to regard the dark warning from Beldar as real and present in the soft, moist morning air. Alfrahil was uncertain as to whether or not he should stay an extra day to enjoy the quiet comforts of this country estate or return to the City and see if progress had been made regarding the conspiracy to murder the madam and burn her house of ill repute.

After he had refreshed himself and dressed, Alfrahil was enjoying a large breakfast served on the patio with Beldar, when Alcar presented himself. 'Two of the scouts that I dispatched at first light have returned, my Lord, with tidings for your ears alone'

'I will hear them,' said Alfrahil.

Alcar gestured, and Alfrahil saw the two guardsmen from his retinue approach in the company of Caelus and four guardsmen he did not know.

'Captain Caelus, I confess I am surprised to see you so far from your post,' Alfrahil said. 'Is there trouble at the gates?'

'No, My Lord,' answered Caelus. 'There is nothing unusual at the gates, but I bring a private message for your ears alone.' Glancing at Beldar, his friend nodded and rising from the table left Alfrahil with his men.

'Very well, but who are these guardsmen? I do not recognize them.'

'They are Shadows in disguise,' said Caelus. 'Dispatched on the personal orders of Lord Mergin to assure your safety.'

'Thank you, Captain. Which of you Shadows is the leader?' asked Alfrahil.

'I am, my lord Prince. My code name is Dark Mist.' said a nondescript man with blonde hair and cemetery eyes.

'Very well, Dark Mist, please take your place amongst my men. I will inform you when we are leaving.'

Then, addressing Caelus again: 'Come, Captain, you and I shall walk along the garden path, and you will tell me your news.'

'Yes, Lord.'

'Alcar, prepare for our departure,' said Alfrahil.

Alcar saluted smartly and strode off toward the stables.

Alfrahil drew Caelus into the garden. When they were alone, he asked, 'What news, Captain?'

'Biramin bade me ride to you and inform you that it would be safe to return today at the fourth hour afternoon. He guards the bridge over the Escarpment. And Lord Mergin gave me this sealed scroll for you to read.'

Alfrahil broke the seal and recognized Mergin's terse handwriting, outlining the route that Alfrahil and his escort should take through the city to the Citadel. The first part was rather circuitous, winding through neighborhoods in the Sixteenth District that travelers in a direct line would not take. From there it was a straightforward dash through the Escarpment back to the Citadel.

'Why the delay? Why should I not leave now?' asked Alfrahil.

'The delay is to afford Lord Mergin time to arrest all of the miscreants who stand ready to waylay your return home,' said Caelus.

Shocked by this news, as Alfrahil, despite Beldar's warning, had not thought there was a credible threat to his life, he stood quietly for a moment, trying to absorb it as stoically as possible. 'How many men does Lord Mergin suspect are involved?' asked Alfrahil at last.

'Twenty, at the least, my Lord; all at various choke points along your expected path back within the City and to the Citadel,' replied Caelus. 'Lord Mergin wanted to make certain that this information would only be revealed in person, to prevent his plans from being discovered were I killed or ambushed on my way here. That is why none of this is written in the scroll.'

'What else has Mergin learned?'

'Traps have been set for you in three separate congested areas in the Sixteenth District. There are archers stationed on rooftops and incendiary devices disguised as refuse. Lord Mergin asks that you betray no awareness of these traps. He asks that you ride close to the first and let the trap be sprung. Fear not—you will be in no danger. But this way, Lord Mergin's men will move in and seize the conspirators in the midst of their treason.'

'A well-ordered conspiracy, for so many men to be assembled in so short a time,' said Alfrahil. 'Are we certain that Lord Mergin has discovered them all?'

'No, my Lord, so far Lord Mergin has only discovered men in the Sixteenth District. He believes the Third and Second Districts are safe, along with the Citadel, and has seen no one upon the First Hill that seeks to waylay you.'

'Thank you, Caelus. You have done well.' Alfrahil then returned to the house, where he reviewed this new information with Beldar.

Beldar thought for several minutes and then disappeared briefly to consult a scroll in one of his libraries. When he returned, he shook his head and stated darkly, 'Things have changed a great deal in Eldora if there are men willing to assassinate the Crown Prince over the contents of a joy house and the embarrassment of a senior minister. There must be far more at stake for them to risk so much and move so openly against you. What that is, I cannot begin to fathom. Tell Lord Mergin that I am willing to aid him if I can, but I will need much more information on the current political state of the realm to be of any use. Perhaps he will consider contracting with the Brotherhood.'

'You know how much Mergin and my father distrust the Brotherhood,' Alfrahil said. 'Give me your best guess, Beldar. Who is behind this?'

'Zarthir is the most likely candidate for the ringleader of any general conspiracy, but he has no military experience, and I can't see how he would profit enough by your demise to make the risk worthwhile. He is not a risk taker politically, even if his personal life is tawdry. No, there are others involved, you may be sure of it. But who they may be, I cannot say.'

'Should I remain here, Beldar?'

'I have thought that through as well. This is a house, not a fortress. We are vulnerable here, isolated and remote as we are. If you remain, it would take hundreds of Men to safeguard your stay. No, the Citadel is the best place for you now. You need only reach it. As to that, I recommend following Mergin's plan rather than remaining here.'

'Very well, I am sure you are correct. I will not discover the answers here, at any rate. I shall return to the City according to the plan.'

* * *

An hour before noon, Alfrahil took his leave, thanking Beldar for his hospitality. He was too preoccupied to notice the beautiful day unfolding around him or how the breeze blew down off the mountains, cool and dry, refreshing and light. He did, however, take note of the Shadows, Mergin's messenger assassins disguised as ordinary guardsmen, and he took confidence in their constant vigilance.

The journey passed without incident, and soon the group was approaching the Great Gates. Alfrahil ordered his men to tighten up their formation.

Cantering through the Great Gates, Alfrahil received the salute of the guards and turned right to follow a road parallel to the main stone road through crowded market streets and streets lined with common homes. Gravel crunched under the horses' hooves. Within twenty minutes, they were beyond the buildings and out on a country lane of dirt riding through a barley field on their way to intersect with the great road just outside a small village, the last danger before more open country leading to the Escarpment. Seeing nothing unusual, Alfrahil was tempted to let his guard down but instead told his men to watch carefully for anything out of the ordinary. Joining the Great Road again, they came to a small merchant center filled with several two-story stone buildings, the businesses of merchants and traders.

The late afternoon sun cast deep shadows over the street, and Alfrahil saw unusual congestion of people before him, with many citizens craning their necks to see what it was that delayed their passage. At this time of day, most people would be in the market streets shopping for their evening meal. Here there were no shops, just the unremarkable offices of businesses; therefore the crowd of people was quite unusual. Alfrahil suddenly noticed sheen to the white granite under his horse's hooves that bespoke oil of some type having been spilled ahead. He asked a nearby citizen, who nearly choked when he saw his Crown Prince, what the delay was. The man replied that the cart of an oil seller had collided with the corner of a building and that the guards were trying to apply sand and ashes to the spill to absorb it before it ran all over the road to the gates.

As if the man's explanation was a signal, flaming arrows suddenly rained down on the milling crowd, and more flames, deep and smoky, erupted from the front of the crowd. Screams and cries of fear were heard as the street before them was turned into a billowing quagmire of smoke. Alfrahil heard Alcar cry to gather around the Prince, and he realized that despite all Mergin's assurances, things were not as well in hand as he had been led to expect. But now was not the time for such thoughts. Alfrahil ordered Alcar forward, crying, 'We must force our way through the people!'

Whinnying and neighing, their horses initially balked at their commands, but having faith in their riders, trotted along the road into the smoke. At first, all was gray, and Alfrahil's breath was choked by the smoke from the burning oil, but within a few moments, the smoke cleared, revealing a path forward.

Alfrahil and his men soon found themselves clear of the conflagration. Advising his men to tear strips from their garments as smoke filters for both themselves and their mounts, Alcar had them soak the strips in a nearby water barrel. Now prepared as best they could be, they cantered up the road again. Behind them, Alfrahil heard the cries of the people and the strident commands of the street guards trying to reestablish order.

Now the great road was open before them, their destination the Bridge over the quarry. Alfrahil knew that this was the natural chokepoint for anyone riding through Eldora unwilling to take the small roads that led around the massive granite feature. He knew that there was danger here, but he also knew that Biramin would be holding the bridge with over a hundred hand-picked guardsmen, with more guardsmen on either side of the bridge. Once safely across, Biramin and his entire guard contingent would escort Alfrahil back to the Citadel. Holding the bridge was paramount, and Biramin remained there because of the composition of the terrain immediately in front of the Escarpment: thin soil, full of rocks, only fit for the growing of herbs provided even less cover than the vegetable fields closer to the city walls. Alfrahil felt certain that if there was to be any more trouble, it would come at the Bridge. But the massive reinforcements there set his mind at ease.

Approaching the Escarpment, Alfrahil breathed a sigh of relief; once on the other side, he would be safe on his way to the Citadel. The gap in the Escarpment was stark. Great steel picks and wedges had split the massive edifice into two slightly uneven pieces, and the artificial walls of a canyon rose up around them as Alfrahil and his detachment rode into the first part of the rock wall. Just ahead, Biramin sat upon his horse. There were only fifty feet between them when Alfrahil shouted a greeting and Biramin called back in a loud and confident voice, 'You're safe now, sire. Let us get you home to your father.'

Arrows hissed and whined in a virtual cloud that cut down Biramin and his men. Their horses screamed as their flanks were pierced again and again. Appearing out of nowhere on each side of the canyon, twenty archers were shooting nearly straight down into the mass of men. The fire decimated Biramin's hand-picked guard force.

The men on the bridge itself and the reinforcements waiting on the other side responded, sending volley after volley against the archers, whose initial effectiveness was rapidly reduced as they took cover. After a moment of shock, Alfrahil urged his men forward. As they neared the bridge, a terrible rumbling broke out, shaking the very ground. This was accompanied by the shrieks and groans of massive timbers. Suddenly the bridge began to collapse in front of them. The guardsman just in front of Alfrahil, unable to stop his horse in time, toppled into the abyss.

'Retreat!' bellowed Dark Mist, assuming command from Alfrahil. Alfrahil and his men began the difficult task of turning around and reversing course in the narrow confines of the canyon. Shouting men, screaming horses, and the constant buzz of arrows filled Alfrahil's ears. As they turned, the archers on the edges of the quarry trained their deadly arrows upon them again. Now, with only the Shadows providing covering fire, these archers were much more deadly. Six more of Alfrahil's guards fell and three others were injured as Alfrahil gave way to panic and kicked at his horse to escape the deadly trap, caring for nothing but his personal safety. Galloping ahead, he was soon beyond the reach of the archers. His guardsmen rejoined him. Despite the losses of half of his regular guards, all of the Shadows were unharmed.

Alfrahil, despite his brief time in the military, had been very sheltered and had never seen another man die before, much less been so close to death himself. He spent several crucial minutes trying to recover his equilibrium, lost within himself and oblivious to the shouts of Dark Mist. When he had finally recovered somewhat from his fear, he saw that they were about two hundred fifty yards from the Escarpment. Archers were running rapidly across the Escarpment. Clearly, there was no way past the massive stone cliff: they would have to ride around it or proceed back to the relative safety of the guard barracks at the gates. But that route appeared closed to them, judging by the flames and thick smoke that could be seen rising into the sky.

'We must ride west, my lord,' cried Dark Mist. 'There is a passage known to only a few through the stone wall. We can penetrate it there before the archers can reach that position.'

'What about going around the Escarpment on the side roads?' asked a dazed Alfrahil.

'There are fruit orchards on either end of the Escarpment, offering much better cover for assassins than is present here. This trap was cunningly laid. Riding around the rock will have been anticipated.'

'Very well. Let us proceed.'

With that, they rode slowly through tilled fields, their horses trampling the herbs and sending fragrant odors upward. The late afternoon sun made vision difficult, but he could still see the archers that ran along the top of the rock, seeking to cut off their escape. But their progress on horseback was faster, and at last, they approached the narrow split in the rock.

Entering into this tiny natural ravine, Alfrahil saw that little had been done by the hand of Man to change the natural surroundings. Riding three abreast, they picked their way forward and upward, emerging into a small enclosure, just over a hundred feet deep and two hundred feet wide. Rude straw huts reinforced with mud greeted them. Thin lines of string linked the huts, and coarse peasant clothes hung from the strings, drying in the small amount of sunlight that penetrated the narrow opening. Flies buzzed over a fetid rubbish heap at the southern lower end of the village, but the huts were strangely empty. Only the wind, channeling through the small canyon, could be heard.

Dark Mist addressed the prince. 'A month ago, my lord, I was on a routine scouting mission, and this area was filled with over fifty peasants and a thriving community of artisans, the most industrious of them a blacksmith who turned out tools and horseshoes cheaply and efficiently. Now everyone is gone. We must move quickly.'

Spurring their horses to a gallop Alfrahil and his men passed by the blacksmith's shop, where a large iron cauldron, hung above a bed of red-hot coals; emitted a high-pitched whistling sound. Glancing at this strange contrivance, Alfrahil saw that the cauldron's lid had been welded to the red- hot metal bottom, with a large stone block, delicately balanced, covering what appeared to be a vent hole in the center. Small flames appeared and disappeared around the block as hissing and gasping blue tongues caressed the edges of it.

Dark Mist suddenly shouted to Alfrahil's escort to ride for their lives. Two seconds later, as Alfrahil and the first of his men were clearing the cauldron, arrows hissed out of the sky and knocked the heavy stone block aside, freeing the boiling oil inside of the cauldron. A great whooshing sound went up from the vent, and a column of flame twenty feet high erupted from the cauldron. More arrows sped downward, and the cauldron's ropes, which had begun to smolder, were shot through. The cauldron collapsed onto its side on the bed of coals. Instantly, burning oil spewed forth from the vent in a fountain of orange flame, setting the entire set of buildings ablaze and firing the rest of the street in seconds. Two more guardsmen went down in the terrible flames, but Alfrahil and the rest of his men sped on, singed but alive.

Alfrahil exited the Escarpment, led now by Dark Mist. As they approached the great road, they found it crowded with hundreds of people who were trying to get through the Escarpment and out of the city before the gates closed but did not know that the bridge was gone. There were no signs of any of the guardsmen that Alfrahil had expected to find, only the swirling masses of common folk.

'Time is the enemy now, my Lord,' said Dark Mist. 'The assassins have been a step ahead of us so far, but they cannot know we survived the last ambush. If we dash for the Citadel now, I believe we can make it safely.'

'Then let us be off at once,' Alfrahil commanded. Resuming their flight to the Citadel, they trotted their winded steeds toward the Third District and its gate. Alfrahil began to relax at last. He was surprised at the lack of activity, thinking that Mergin surely should have sent additional guards down to them, but then he realized that only thirty minutes had elapsed since the attack in the Escarpment, and they were only a few minutes behind schedule.

Glancing at the curious faces of the guards who had noticed the smoke and sweat on their faces and their lathered horses, Alfrahil realized that no word of the disasters that had befallen them had yet reached the Citadel.

As they rode up to the gate, the guard sergeant asked if they needed any aid.

'Do you have any spare mounts at hand?' asked Dark Mist.

'No, sir, the messenger stable is well up in the Second District. We have no horses here. I could send one of my men to fetch some if you like. It would only take half an hour or so.'

'We have no time,' said Dark Mist. 'The prince has been attacked by traitors. Guard the gate well and prepare for anything. We must press on but sound the alarm.'

Dark Mist led them up through the gates and into the Third District as the deep growling moan of an ancient brass horn reverberated behind them. Alfrahil was beginning to relax slightly as they passed through the Second District gate. Alerted by the alarm, the guardsman reported no unusual activity here, and Dark Mist moved them on at great speed towards the Citadel gates, ten minutes away now.

The circle of the hill was quite small, and the road turned completely back upon itself as it wound up to the First District gate and the Citadel beyond. They were in a small exclusive market district, with the usual crowd of servants from wealthy homes shopping for last-minute items for the evening meal. Small shops of one and two stories, made entirely of stone, with tiled roofs, lined the narrow street. The odors of roasting meats, rich spices, and frying vegetables from the market stalls seemed surreal to Alfrahil after nearly having been burned alive. The hum of the shoppers was all around him as the people dutifully made way.

Rounding a turn, they found themselves facing a column of young Shardan orphans, whose parents and entire villages had been laid waste by the army of Eldora. This was an all-too-regular scene these days in Eldora, as the 'unfortunates,' as they were called, were organized by charitable men and women to petition the King and his ministers for funds to aid themselves in providing the necessary food, shelter, medicines, and other goods the orphans needed to survive. No doubt, thought Alfrahil, having received alms from the King, they were now returning to their compound within the Fifteenth District. Some of the children might be claimed by distant relatives in Shardan. Others would be adopted into local families. The rest, less fortunate, would grow to adulthood within the orphan barracks or the refugee camp; a grim life, Alfrahil reflected, but better than perishing from disease or famine.

'Wait, Dark Mist,' said Alfrahil. 'Let the children pass. I am exhausted and must rest for a moment.'

'My Lord,' replied the Shadow, 'you can rest when we are in the Citadel. Another ten minutes, and you will be safe.'

The orphans, meanwhile, had recognized Alfrahil and began to call to him as they approached, beseeching his generosity and aid. An older boy, perhaps fourteen, his white teeth gleaming in a smile brighter still in contrast with his brown skin and black hair, came up to Alfrahil with his palm out and a smile on his face. Alfrahil smiled back and reached for his purse. Dark

Mist was abreast of the middle of the children, unconcerned with their plight when he saw Alfrahil's mind briefly re-engage with this innocent procession, reaching in a trance for his purse to give this child some coins. Dark Mist noticed distantly that only the child's mouth was smiling, the rest of his countenance was sent in fierce determination. Black obsidian chips were his eyes, reflecting desperation and anger rarely seen in someone so young. The dusky face was a fixed mask determined to reveal nothing until the ultimate moment arrived, maintaining his smile, and focusing upon Alfrahil. At that same instant, the youth reached under his robe and made a slight pulling gesture. Oil spurted from his tunic, dyed a bright shade of red. It poured down his limbs and pooled briefly around his feet before spreading rapidly downhill. An unusual pungent odor arose from this unique oil as Dark Mist recognized the smell of pine pitch intermingled with the oil of the great sea creatures that were sometimes captured by the fisherfolk. The cost of the oil of the sea creatures in such a vast quantity staggered the mind of Dark Mist, but chillingly he remembered how volatile and explosive the oil was and knew that his prince was in terrible danger.

Cursing his faith in Lord Mergin's security report, Dark Mist was the first to react. Ordering the men to gallop to the Citadel as quickly as possible, he reached out and pulled Alfrahil's horse, slapping its flank.

Alfrahil's horse plunged forward, scattering the remaining children. As the guardsmen began to react to the Shadow's orders, two other youths emerged from an alley ahead and similarly released a flood of oil upon the street. The Shadows reacted instantly, hurling poisoned knives to slay the children where they stood, the buzz of arrows followed almost at once.

One Shadow fell from his horse, impaled with arrows intended for Alfrahil. Another Shadow drew his sword and, in an incredible display, cut two arrows from the air before he was struck down by a third. But some arrows had been aimed at a different target: the oil. And these arrows were aflame.

In an instant, the street was on fire. Alfrahil, at the front of the column thanks to Dark Mist's quick thinking and quicker action, was able to get clear of the oil with mere seconds to spare. Feeling the flash of heat behind him, he turned and watched in horror as Dark Mist and most of his guardsmen vanished in a bright orange wall of flame. Before he could react, four horses leaped through those flames. One was riderless. Two carried soldiers of the guard. And the third bore a Shadow.

A great explosion filled the street behind them. Alfrahil saw debris from destroyed homes and shops along the street flung hundreds of feet skyward. The acrid stench of burning flesh filled his nostrils, and the screams of men and the higher pitched screams of horses filled his ears. Vague, glowing forms that could only be guessed to be the shapes of men and animals moved within the billowing orange flames, beneath the ghastly black plume of smoke rising from the street.

Unable to think clearly, in the grip of a renewed panic, Alfrahil stopped his horse and made as if to flee in a different direction. But the Shadow, seeing the absence of reason in Alfrahil's face, screamed, 'My Lord, there is nothing you can do. You must save yourself and ride with us to the Citadel, for no one and nothing can save those men.'

At that, a new buzzing was heard. One of the remaining guards toppled from his horse, an arrow embedded in his chest. A blinding pain crossed Alfrahil's forehead, and blood filled his eyes. His horse screamed and then bolted.

Alfrahil, realizing that an arrow must have laid open his scalp—how badly, he did not yet know—was able to grab a napkin from his saddlebag and staunch the flow of blood into his eyes even as he held on to the reins with his free hand. Finally regaining control of his horse, he felt around his saddle and found his canteen. Pouring the contents over his eyes, he, at last, was able to clear the blood from his face. Glancing over his shoulder, with his horse still in full gallop, Alfrahil saw the Shadow and the last guard hard on his heels.

The Shadow, who had an arrow protruding from his shoulder, cried, 'Fly, my Lord, for the enemy are still on the rooftops!'

Glancing up, Alfrahil saw that indeed there were men dressed in drab gray colors leaping from rooftop to rooftop, determined to finish what they had started. Alfrahil spurred his exhausted, terrified horse. He saw the Shadow firing his bow at their attackers with blinding speed. Then his horse rounded a corner, and he saw no more.

Knowing that expert bowmen would soon close the distance on the rooftops and could not be expected to miss at such close range, Alfrahil urged his exhausted horse to go even faster. The hum of an arrow passed so closely to his ear that Alfrahil was certain he had been hit until he heard a surprised, anguished cry from the rooftops behind him.

In front of Alfrahil, stood a small company of archers from the Citadel: it was one of their arrows he had felt flit by, to find its target among the traitors on the roofs. Their commander shouted something to Alfrahil, but he could not make out even a word of it. Then he saw another volley of arrows take flight. Agile forms raced past the archers, leaped upon the walls, and scaled them like monkeys: more Shadows on their way to attack and capture the archers.

A fresh escort, all horsed, surrounded him, and before he could ask a question or issue a command he was bound for the Citadel again. Consumed by shock and grief, Alfrahil scarcely noticed what was going on around him until he saw they were clattering up the last tunnel and emerging into the Citadel proper.

Dismounting, the guards helped Alfrahil and his sole surviving guardsman— grievously wounded—from their horses and half-carried them deeper within the protection of the ancient walls.

Mergin stood there with several guardsmen, the expression on his ashen face a mixture of wrath and relief. 'My Lord, inside quickly. A healer is standing by to aid you.'

Nodding, too weary to speak, Alfrahil allowed himself to be led indoors by two guards. Mergin followed as the men conducted Alfrahil to a nearby guardroom where a young healer was waiting. There Mergin took his leave, explaining that he would have food and wine sent, but that meanwhile, he had to oversee the defense of the Citadel.

As Alfrahil was pressed back onto a cot, he heard shouts from the hallway, and more guardsmen passed by the wooden door at a run. He struggled to rise, but the healer pushed him back easily. He was as weak as a newborn; he could be of no help to anyone now.

The healer was rinsing the blood from his forehead when the wine arrived. Raising a hand to the healer, who stepped back, Alfrahil grabbed a full goblet and drank it down without tasting it, then consumed another one before allowing the healer to resume his task.

As the man worked, Alfrahil regained his composure. His wits began to return, and he noticed a horrible stench of charred flesh, smoke, and stale sweat mixed with blood and urine. He suddenly became aware that he was the source of the latter and had pissed himself in his terror. For a moment he felt embarrassed but then anger flared through him at Mergin for allowing this debacle to happen. At that moment, as if on cue, a brief knock was heard, and Mergin entered the room flanked by two Shadows.

Before Alfrahil could say a word, Mergin said, 'My Lord, I cannot express my apologies deeply enough or my regret that I failed to keep you safe today. I have tendered my resignation to the King, but he has refused to allow me to quit my post.'

Struggling to rise from the cot, Alfrahil was suddenly terrified for his father's well-being. 'Where is he, Mergin? Is he safe?'

'Yes, my Lord. As soon as the initial plans of the ambush were known, I doubled his Majesty's guard, placing him within a remote part of the Citadel. He has heard of your plight and desires to see you as soon as it is safe and you are able. I have just come from him.'

'What in the name of the gods happened, Mergin?' demanded Alfrahil in a weak but angry voice. 'You are supposed to keep anything like this from ever being plotted, much less executed!'

'I do not know yet what happened, my Lord. I have dispatched riders and men afoot throughout the Second District in search of information. I hope to have some preliminary information by this evening.'

Satisfied that his father was safe, Alfrahil's thoughts turned in another direction. 'What of Daerahil, Mergin? He must be in great danger as well.'

'I do not know, my lord. I have one unconfirmed report that he suddenly left his post at the out-walls yesterday morning with his guard detachment at about the same time we were taking countermeasures against the ambush. His precipitous departure raises the question of whether or not he had any part in today's horrible events.'

Alfrahil's anger returned, albeit at a lesser pitch. 'Your dislike of my brother colors your judgment Mergin; Daerahil would never conspire against me, or against our father. He must have had a good reason for leaving his post if your report is even accurate in that respect. But what of my men; how are Biramin, Alcar, Dark Mist, and the rest of my guard detail?'

'Perhaps you should wait to hear the news, my Lord until you are better rested and have had your wounds tended.'

'Tell me now, Mergin. Nothing else could shock me further. Or must I go and see for myself?' He again tried to rise, but again the healer pushed him back as if he were an infant.

'Wait, my Lord,' said Mergin. 'Allow the healer to do his work. I will tell you what you wish to know.'

'Then do so,' replied Alfrahil.

'All of your men are presumed dead. The only survivor besides the one who brought you in is Alcar. He was burnt horribly, shot through with six arrows and is lying in the Healers' Hall now, close to death. We have had no news yet of Biramin. That is the extent of my knowledge, I'm afraid. If you will excuse me, my Lord, I will return in a few minutes after speaking with Gray Water, the Shadow leader, to see what more I can discover.'

'Do not tarry overlong, Mergin,' said Alfrahil. 'I wish to see my father.'

'As you command,' said Mergin. He bowed and left.

When they were alone, the healer offered Alfrahil a powerful potion. 'My Lord, this will allow you to sleep, sparing you additional pain so I can stitch your wound.'

'Sleep? Nay, healer, I need my wits about me this day. I cannot sleep until I learn the fate of my men.'

'As you wish, my Lord, this may sting a bit.' The healer touched a cloth to Alfrahil's cut brow, and a searing sensation flashed across the wound.

Gritting his teeth against the pain, Alfrahil was amazed when it receded as quickly as it had arrived, taking the rest of his pain with it. Now the healer was able to clean and stitch the wound. All the while, Alfrahil he felt nothing at all. 'How is this possible?' he asked the healer. The healer replied, 'A plant from the Great Forest has recently been rediscovered in the shadows of Tarin Nazar.'

'Tarin Nazar? Is this then a weed of evil?' asked a startled Alfrahil.

'No, Lord, it is an ancient healing herb that had thrived upon the stony heights below that ancient keep. It was feared lost forever once Magnar took the fortress from the Elves but hidden away in a few recesses, the plants managed to sustain themselves. It is only this year that the plants were plentiful enough to be harvested and their unguents traded to us by the Lesser Elves.

One last tug and the healer stepped back. 'I am done with stitching your wounds, but I am afraid you will bear a scar for the rest of your life. I will leave you now, lord. Try and rest until Lord Mergin returns.'

'Thank you, please have a bath prepared for me along with fresh clothes.' replied Alfrahil. He scarcely saw the healer leave preoccupied with memories of all the horrors he had witnessed and endured this day.

* * *

Thirty minutes later, a brief knock announced Mergin's return. The minister brought two of Alfrahil's servants with him to tend his needs.

Mergin, still pale from the day's events, saw the marks of terror and uncertainty on Alfrahil's face and wondered again if Alfrahil were too weak to one day serve as King. '*Still, better Alfrahil than his brother.*' What had horrified Mergin more than anything in the attacks was the knowledge that if Alfrahil had been slain, Daerahil would have stood next in line to the throne. '*Alfrahil, for all his faults, would at least be easier to manipulate. Not so the brilliant hot-headed Daerahil. If he should succeed King Creon, then my plan to rule the kingdom from behind the throne will vanish in the blink of an eye and the drop of my own head.*'

Covering his feelings, Mergin was grateful that Alfrahil did not have his brother's skills, and even more grateful that Creon in his rage had interrogated him only briefly with his mental powers in the wake of the attacks. The king had grown far too reliant on his abilities, believing that no one could hide anything from him. And that was a simple truth, Mergin knew. But he also knew that Creon was lazy and did not like to expend the effort necessary to probe beneath a powerful mind like Mergin's.

As they exited his room, Mergin said,

'We will go to see your father now.'

Alfrahil turned to Mergin and asked, 'What of my brother? Is there any additional word?'

'I received a message that he was visiting Prince Paladir; he claims he received an urgent message from Paladir to visit him in Ackerlea immediately. Apparently, he was about to return when he learned of the attempt on your life. He was then heard to comment that there was no need for both Princes of Eldora to be at risk.'

'Well, that's simply common sense. One of us must remain alive to ensure the succession of the realm. What of this statement?'

'He apparently uttered it prior to the attack upon you here in the City, before the first waft of smoke arose.'

Stopping in his tracks, Alfrahil looked about him and realized that besides guards fore and aft of their position, many paces away, that they were alone in a side corridor parallel to the main corridor of the Citadel.

'Yes, Lord, you heard me right,' said Mergin. It may be that your brother had prior knowledge of this afternoon's events, for how would he know, even after the first smoke went up, what it meant? How could he know that you were anywhere near the blaze, much less the intended target? This way he could have an ironclad excuse for any involvement, as he was far away from the City. Do you not find it strange that he chose this day to visit Paladir, a journey not on his schedule for at least another month? Besides, I doubt that there was a message from Paladir at all, and in addition to deserting his post, he placed himself away from the City and out of danger. More importantly, military protocol demands that when a senior commander, such as your brother leaves his post, he must send word to the King. Your father did not receive such a message.' Mergin smiled internally, as there had indeed been a message from Daerahil, but he had caused it to be destroyed, while the messenger who had brought it was sent on a long journey floating face-down on the river Aphon.

'Well,' Alfrahil said, 'we shall see what he has to say for himself when he returns. Now I must see my father.'

'Yes, my Lord,' replied Mergin. 'Let us go to him now.'

Moving through the eerily quiet halls, Alfrahil glanced about himself and at Mergin from the corner of his eye. 'Where is everyone?'

Murmuring so his voice did not carry too far down the corridor, Mergin answered, 'The usual servants and courtiers have been removed at my order. Only Citadel guards are allowed within the First District, along with a few trustworthy servants, all ex-soldiers and completely loyal to you and your family.'

'What of Minister Zarthir, Mergin?' asked Alfrahil. 'He and his cohorts must be the chief suspects in this conspiracy.'

'Yes, my Lord, they are indeed suspects,' said Mergin. 'Minister Zarthir returned directly to his apartments after you broke up the little party he was involved in at the joy house. He dressed in his apartments and was waiting along with other courtiers and Ministers in the foyer outside the Council room.'

'Was he there all day?' asked Alfrahil.

'Yes, my Lord, and he returned there until you returned, supremely arrogant and confident as ever, making his importance felt as usual,' said Mergin.

'Is he under watch, Mergin?'

'Yes, Lord. Once I learned that he was at the joy house where you confronted him, I had Shadows follow him and report back to me.'

'Did the Shadows notice anything unusual?'

'No, Lord. The day that you confronted him he returned to his home without incident. He apparently ate, drank, spent some time with a young serving wench, bathed, attired himself in his usual raiment, and left his home in a little over an hour.'

'Who else, Mergin? Who else could be behind this?' asked Alfrahil.

'We know not, my Lord. There are those that are of a similar disposition to Zarthir, including the head of the fishing guild and other wealthy merchants. We have also had the sons of the Shardan lords under close eye today, but they seem more interested in idling their time away with the other privileged youths of the Citadel.'

Alfrahil thought briefly of the Shardan lords who had pledged their loyalty to Eldora, giving their sons as hostages for their good behavior. Lately, the links between the Shardan nobility and the rebels had become more tenuous, at least publicly. The King had, therefore, decreed that the youths would serve for a year and a day as captives. They would then be replaced by new hostages and sent home. It was difficult but not inconceivable to imagine these idle lordlings involved in today's conspiracy.

'Yes, Mergin, they probably are more concerned with drinking and gaming than with fomenting rebellion, even at their fathers' request,'said Alfrahil. 'Please keep me informed of the results of your inquiries.'

Grimly Mergin nodded his silvered head. 'Yes, Lord, I will certainly do so.'

Seeing they were coming to an end of these disused corridors, Alfrahil asked, 'Is my father nearby?'

'Yes, Lord, in the base of the old astrologers' tower. Now that the astrologers have built themselves a watchtower on the farthest shoulder of the Great Peak, they only return here for their monthly meetings. Usually, their servants are present to keep the place dusted and prepared for their return. But I have had them dispatched on errands out of the City for the next few days.'

Entering the courtyard adjoining the astrologers' tower, Alfrahil looked around to see the King's guards. Startled to see nothing more than a pair of crows circling overhead, Alfrahil turned to Mergin with a questioning look.

'They are well hidden, my Lord, well hidden indeed,' said Mergin. 'Archers from Anscomb and Shadows. Anyone entering this courtyard beside me, you, or your brother, and the King himself, of course, serving as an escort, would be slain without warning. It will be tedious ferrying food, servants, and the like from this doorway to the tower yonder for the next few days, but we will all have to bear it.'

'Are there no others you trust?' asked Alfrahil.

'The other counselors that I know who are loyal are all older than I, and I have set them to discreetly aid me in my quest to find out who the conspirators are. Some of them are close enough to the suspected conspirators to prove useful. The rest will find out where the loyalties of their own families and servants lie. By the end of the week, we should have a reasonably good picture of whom we can count upon for certain.'

'What of Biramin and my guard detachment that was with him?' asked Alfrahil.

'Miraculously, Biramin is alive. He was just pulled from the ruins of the bridge an hour ago. There are a few of your regular guardsmen that survived, but the final count is as yet unknown.'

'Will he recover?'

'He shall, my Lord. The finest healers in the Hospice have tended him, and while it will be several weeks before he is hale again, his Dwarf mail served him well.'

'Dwarf mail? You mean he actually was wearing it today beneath his tunic?' asked an amazed Alfrahil. Smiling darkly, he continued, 'Truth is indeed stranger than fiction. Biramin routinely swore he had no need of such protection and that the mail was far too ostentatious and much too expensive to be worn. But tell me, Mergin; how is it that he survived the fall? Dwarf armor or no, it was nearly a hundred feet down to the stone floor of the quarry!'

'He was caught between the broken remnants of some of the beams of the bridge, one of only a handful of survivors there. I know of no more details at this time.'

Passing within the seemingly unguarded archway, Alfrahil saw a brief flash of steel in a nook to his left as a Shadow lowered a raised weapon and spoke from behind a tapestry covering an old doorway. 'I have confirmed that it is you, Lord Mergin, and you, my Lord Prince. You may enter.'

'Thank you, group leader. Please return to your duties,' replied Mergin.

Entering into the crowded main room of the astrologers' tower, Alfrahil saw a dozen guards on duty, with others taking their ease around hastily set up tables. The room itself contained the crude, comfortable furniture found in the haunts of academics. Various devices were on shelves scattered on the edges of the room: an astrolabe, a sextant, and several other odd bits of a metal unknown to Alfrahil but presumably used in astrology. An enormous map of the known constellations was on the far wall, depicting the night sky at midsummer. Desks had been hastily stacked upon one another, and a musty smell of books and scrolls filled the air.

Grim-faced men circled amongst the guards, distributing fresh fruits, dried meats, and cheeses and bread, for there could be no cooking fires if they were to continue their deception that the tower was unoccupied. The servants all had a military bearing. Most of them were middle-aged, and many had visible scars, and a few with altered gaits, limping across the room showing the sacrifices their bodies had made in the service of the King. Alfrahil noted that many of them had a distant look about them as if they were still reliving the struggles on some old battlefield.

It was the older men who eventually suffered the worst, having to live with what they had seen and done in the service of the realm. Too many comrades lost in distant lands, too many times coming within an inch of death. Many times they had prayed for death to visit them and spare them their continued existence. Alfrahil wondered if enough was being done to aid these men who had given so much to Eldora. His brother stated not nearly enough was being done, but Daerahil was often rash in his judgments. Still, shaking his head, Alfrahil didn't know, and he added it to his list of things to discover. The last thing that was needed was for these veterans to feel that they and their sacrifices were both unappreciated and unneeded.

As Alfrahil and Mergin stepped completely into the room, a quick command was given by the senior captain. Alfrahil returned their salute as crisply as his wounds would allow and bade them return to their former positions.

The senior guard captain strode forward to make his report. 'Prince Alfrahil, Lord Mergin, the King is within, and he is well if a little tired.'

'Excellent, Captain,' said Mergin. 'We shall now see the King ourselves.'

'Forgive me, my Lord,' said the captain. Turning to Alfrahil, he asked, 'My Lord, how are you and how is Captain Biramin? We are all anxious to hear.'

Noting that all of the faces had turned toward him to hear his news and that even the guards on duty were surreptitiously listening to him, Alfrahil replied with a heartiness he did not feel. 'Besides a scratch on my head and few bumps, I am fine. I owe my life to my guards.'

Flushing with pride, the captain stated, 'It was only our duty, sir. Were the archers any help?'

Before Alfrahil could reply, Mergin said, 'Once the Prince has seen his father, he may be able to answer a few questions if his time allows.'

'That's all right, Mergin. These men risked much to save me today.' Alfrahil spoke then to the guards: 'Captain, you asked of Biramin. He was indeed injured, and seriously. But I have been told he will make a full recovery, though it will be some time before he will be fit for duty—especially the duty that awaits him at home.'

The men chuckled and passed appreciative looks and grins back and forth, for Biramin's young wife was a resounding beauty from Kozak, a Valkyrja who had given up her lust for battle to be his. The Valkyrja were trained as the personal guard of Bernardus, King of Kozak. Their loyalty was a byword, and tales of their bravery were the stuff of legend. It was well known that any man who wed a Valkyrja must first impress his wife-to-be on the field of battle and on the field of the bed sheets, for the Valkyrja would only marry those they regarded as equals … and few men met that standard. Biramin obviously had been one of the few … if barely, at least to judge by the first month after his wedding, when, to the ribald taunts of his men, he had seemed more dead than alive each morning when he reviewed the troops outside their barracks.

Continuing now, Alfrahil said, 'Once I have attended the King, I will return and share a glass of ale and tell you my tale.'

Astonished looks spread around the room, including from Mergin. But then they were replaced with looks of the deepest respect. Alfrahil knew this was the right thing to do. While court protocol allowed the captain on duty to speak with him, no other common guardsman was supposed to speak to the Prince, the King, or any ministers without being spoken to first. Breaking protocol and letting his men know that he did indeed care for them was the best insurance policy that he could think of for now.

Striding forward, Alfrahil and Mergin approached an inner door. Two guards snapped a salute and opened the doors before them. Entering the inner chamber, Alfrahil saw a smaller meeting room with several tables close together, with cots lining the walls. The close proximity of so many bodies made the room warm and musty, and dank organic odors revealed too many chamber pots in use with too little changing. Hastily placed tapestries on crude wooden frames indicated small private areas while several of his father's courtiers and council members were all moving like a hive of bestirred bees.

His father immediately approached. 'My son,' said Creon with real warmth in his normally cold voice, 'it is good to see you well!'

In the flickering light of torches and candles, Alfrahil noted that his father's weariness was pronounced as if the weight of the years were lying more heavily upon his shoulders than usual. Lately, the King had appeared slightly haunted to Alfrahil's eyes, looking as if he were in a gilded cage and seeking a way out of his prison. While his smile was broad and welcoming, his eyes were penetrating and questioning, seeking answers in the very souls of men. An air of frustrated power emanated from his body as if a tiger that had roamed free had suddenly been confined.

Creon pulled Alfrahil into a great hug, kissing him on both cheeks. Alfrahil noted that there was the faintest quiver to his father's embrace, and a look of deep despair under the external layer of confidence his father habitually wore. Releasing his hold, at last, Creon greeted his chief minister with as much sincerity, if not as much warmth, and then turned back to Alfrahil. 'Tell me your tale, son,' he said impatiently.

As Alfrahil recalled the successive ambushes, he tried to hold back his emotions, but when relating the last desperate dash, when he had been saved from the assassins only by the timely intervention of the archers of Anscomb, his voice broke, and it was a moment before he could finish.

'Well, son, you have told me much, but I can see there are things that still need to be discussed,' said Creon. Then, looking at Mergin: 'Have you summoned Daerahil back to the city yet?'

'No, Lord. I wanted to make certain that all was well before I asked him to return,' said Mergin.

'Have him return in the morning if you think that will be safe.'

'It should be safe enough, Lord. But there is a slight problem.' Briefly, Mergin told the King what he had told to Alfrahil.

Creon's face darkened. 'This time he has gone too far. Disagreeing with me in Council and even in public was bad enough, but this is unconscionable. It's treason! Have him come home tomorrow, Mergin, and arrange an escort to bring him before me prior to his seeing anyone else in the City. Take no chances with his safety, but bring him directly to me with the highest security.'

'I will leave you now to send the message personally,' said Mergin. Turning to Alfrahil, he added, 'Your quarters are upstairs next to your father's; it would be wise to remain in the tower until the morrow. I should have a better idea then as to what is afoot, both with Prince Daerahil and with others who may have had something to do with this outrage.'

As Mergin left the room, he mentally shrugged. '*Another example of Alfrahil's poor leadership skills, distracted by the children when his first thought should have been to get to the Citadel as quickly as possible. Where shall I find the man to lead this kingdom when Creon is gone?*'

* * *

As he left the room to speak with Gray Water, leader of the Shadows, Mergin thought back to ten years ago, when the elite group of messenger assassins was first created following his meeting with an unusual Hagarian tribesman called Ichiro. Ichiro had petitioned Creon for protection from Hagarian nomads, offering an alliance with Eldora. Mergin agreed to meet with Ichiro instead of Creon, and as he approached a small conference room with his guards, Ichiro rose from a kneeling position. Two crystal oil lamps revealed Ichiro's unusual appearance. His head was mostly bald, only a long black queue hung down from the back of his head. He wore, long flowing clothes, resembling a dress, with two swords tucked into his soft cloth sash that ran around his middle. Mergin asked Ichiro, 'Would you please remove your weapons and hand them to my guards?'

'Certainly,' replied Ichiro. He bowed as he held his swords up in front of him before placing them in the hands of one of Mergin's guardsmen. He then bowed to Mergin who bade him enter into the meeting room. Walking behind his guest, Mergin, noticed that while Ichiro was short and squat, he gave the appearance of tremendous restrained power. He moved like water flowing over the floor, and despite the fact that he was unarmed Mergin found him both threatening and unsettling.

Mergin ordered his guards to stand post inside the room. A simple lunch was brought in, and Mergin listened to Ichiro with as much feigned sympathy as he could muster, his mind beginning to wander back to the sheaf of papers on his desk. Diplomatically, he said to Ichiro, 'I am sorry, Ichiro, but I cannot see that your people will bring anything of worth to Eldora, and while I would like to aid you against the raiders of which you speak, we have neither the time or the resources to commit to you.'

Ichiro appeared to think about that for a moment, before he pulled a long-tined serving fork from the food tray in front of him and, in a motion too swift for the eye to follow, threw the fork in the direction of the farthest guardsmen in the room. A hiss of pain followed the throw, and as other guardsmen rushed toward Ichiro, others went to the aid of their fellow. As the nearby guards drew their weapons, Mergin cried, 'Halt, bring the injured guard here.'

The young man cried that he was stuck and could not come to the First Minister. Glancing at the tribesman, Mergin rose to his feet and went to where the young man stood. Upon his arrival, Mergin saw that the fork had pierced the top of the guard's shoulder, penetrating through a small gap between his shoulder guard and his arm guard. Penetrating his flesh, the fork had slipped between the cracks in the building stone and had become solidly wedged in place. Grasping the fork, Mergin pulled it straight out, though with some effort, and looked over his shoulder at the tribesman, who had not moved since his throw. 'Thirty feet,' mused Mergin. 'Thirty feet with an unbalanced weapon into the most difficult target in the room, and through the target into the wall behind so the weapon would pin the man. Unbelievable.' Turning to the young guardsman, Mergin said, 'Take yourself to the healers and have this wound tended.'

Ichiro remained perfectly still as Mergin returned to the table and took his seat. 'Your throw was unbelievable,' he said, 'but an affront upon the King's guards is an offense that is punishable by death. Since you have disobeyed the ancient laws of heraldry by using violence within a foreign city, your life is forfeit.'

Smiling, Ichiro replied, 'I think not, my Lord, I think not.'

'What, you will defeat the eleven other guards along with myself to flee the Citadel and the City below alive, much less unscathed?' asked an amused yet skeptical Mergin.

Ichiro moved his hand amongst the fruit in a blur; Mergin became aware of screams behind him. He moved his hand to his knife, but before he could touch it, the tribesman reached out and touched his chest rhythmically for a fraction of a second. It was if a knife had cut his lungs. Suddenly Mergin had no air to breathe. Slumped in his chair, he watched helplessly as Ichiro turned and, with a few rapid movements, produced more screams before returning calmly to his seat. Studying Mergin for a moment, he reached toward him with his open hand.

Expecting a deathblow, Mergin instead felt the fingers of his attacker touch the side of his neck. Suddenly his lungs filled with air, and he could breathe again. Grasping the arm of his chair, he pulled himself back into an upright position. Gasping, he glanced around the room: four of his men were on the floor, writhing with pain, and the other seven were either doubled over clutching their stomachs or, like the first soldier, trying to pull free of the instrument that pinned them to the wall.

'Verily I can see you could have escaped,' muttered a raspy Mergin. 'Why are you still here?'

'As I said, my people need your help.'

'How did you dispatch my guards?

'I took down seven of them with the tableware in front of me. The other four have Date pits in their eyes.'

'Dates,' repeated an incredulous Mergin. 'You took down four of my best guards with Date pits?'

'If these are your best, I hesitate to see the support troops,' replied Ichiro wryly. 'But yes, Dates, Lord. Each of them has a Date pit in the eye, a pit they cannot remove without help. Before you react, Lord, no, they are not blinded—one of your healers can remove the pits and restore their sight, but it will take a few weeks of unguents and an eye patch before they are ready to resume their duties. Surely such skills as these have a value to you and your King.'

'In exchange for our protection, what do you offer us?' asked Mergin.

'I and some of my kinsman will teach a select group of your men the rudiments of our skills. Who knows? After fifteen to twenty years of intense training, some of them might actually become worth regarding.'

Thus they had struck their bargain: the tribesmen of Hagar would be allies of Eldora, training a select group of soldiers as phenomenal warriors in exchange for foodstuffs, cessation of hostilities, medicines, and trade.

Mergin asked, 'Why, with your superior skills, have you not simply eliminated the nomads yourselves?'

Ichiro answered, 'In all, we comprise barely six hundred people. The nomads have ten times our number. In open warfare, while we are unmatched as warriors, we cannot deflect or dodge all arrows and spears sent our way. When enough men attack us at a given point, even we cannot stand against great numbers.

Therefore, if soldiers of Eldora can protect the borders of our small land, we can honor our commitments.'

From that day forward, the legend of the Hagarian tribesmen had spread, and a full cavalry army of twenty Faris of Kozak protected the tribesman from the marauding nomads.

* * *

After Mergin's departure, Alfrahil turned back to his father. The shock and weariness he had noticed earlier were gone, replaced by signs of white-hot rage. Placing a restraining hand on his father's arm, Alfrahil said, 'Father, try to put aside your anger for a moment. These events could be a harbinger of worse to come. We may have only seen the length, to which these assassins can reach, not the depths to which they can descend. Nor do we know why these events transpired now. Mergin has his methods, I know, yet it seems to me that these mysteries will not be quickly or easily unraveled.'

'They tried to take your life! What could they hope to gain?'

'The obvious answer, Father, is that they would hope to have my brother in line for the throne instead of me. Or perhaps Frederic, Prince of Amadeus, if something was to befall Daerahil.'

'Your brother is rash and bold, but until today I placed no more credence than you in the rumors that he had designs on the throne,' said the King. 'If there is any truth to what Mergin's reported, then he has much to answer for. You and he disagree on many things, and while someday you will be King, I know that you do not desire the Kingship as Daerahil does. However, until today I believed that he would no more seek out your death than he would mine. In that, I thought I knew my son, but now I shall have to speak with him about these matters, perhaps even put him to the Question. His prior acts of defiance and sedition, flagrant disregard of me and my policies, along with his statements of today, will lead to a severe outcome this time, regardless of his actual participation in these direst events.'

'I do love my brother and have no desire to think ill of him,' answered Alfrahil. 'Please, Father, presume that Daerahil is innocent until you have spoken with him. Decisiveness is one of your strengths, yet it has failed you on occasion.'

Frowning slightly, Creon replied, 'Do not presume to lecture me, my son, regarding me or your brother, but I promise he will be treated as fairly as he deserves. There will be no special treatment for him. He will be treated as any other citizen of Eldora would be in similar circumstances.'

Alfrahil tried another tack. 'Frederic is the real benefactor if all of us were to be killed, Father. Perhaps that was what today was supposed to start.'

'Maybe,' mused Creon, 'and perhaps the real result that they want is for the Kingdom to be thrown into chaos, for if our family and your cousin Frederic were killed, that would leave Paladir as the rightful King. Paladir has never been popular, and I can see men of wealth and power rallying to the cause of one of your younger cousins, or even Frederic's son. Regardless, we cannot find out until we have more information. Let us go now, son, to our apartments above, for we might as well sleep in comfort and peace one more night before we see whither this evil and twisted path leads us.'

Departing the inner room, Creon strode through his guards proudly toward a small stone spiral staircase that Alfrahil had not noticed on entering into the tower and, turning, saw that Alfrahil had paused.

'Forgive me, Father, but I would like to sit here with the men for a moment and share a glass of ale,' said Alfrahil.

Murmuring and appreciative looks stole across the faces of these men as Alfrahil took a seat among them.

'You are welcome to join us, Father, in a glass.' Sensing the appealing looks amongst his men, Alfrahil hoped that just this once his father's infamous regard for court protocol would stand aside and allow him to sit among his men.

Creon's eyes flickered as if he were about to rebuke his son, but some inner voice told him, '*Not today, for their sacrifices, have been great, and they alone are responsible for the safety of both me and my son.*' Aloud he said, 'Nay, my son. I will retire to my chambers, and you may call upon me if you need me.' Turning to go, he paused and turned back to speak with the beginning of a scowl on his face. 'Ale, my son, did you say that you were drinking ale with these men? Are they not on duty?'

'Yes, Father,' said Alfrahil, quailing inwardly, 'they are drinking ale, and I will drink a glass with them. Of course, those on duty will abstain.'

'Ale,' muttered the King. 'No, I don't think that will do.'

Summoning his chief courtier, he looked as if he were about to have the ale confiscated from his men. Then, after a brief conversation, Creon said, 'It is not ale that the men who saved my son today should be drinking, but wine from the fields of Chilton. I have ordered a small barrel to be brought here. Please accept this as a token of my thanks, for while you men of the Citadel did nothing that was not your duty, I am grateful nonetheless.'

As an astonished cheer rang out, the King held up his hands for silence and said, with a wintry smile upon his face, 'Enjoy the wine, men, and let my son tell you his tale, but try to keep the noise low so that an old man can have his rest.'

'The cunning old fox,' thought Alfrahil. 'This tale will spread like wildfire, and the King will be more revered than ever by tomorrow.'

Turning to the guards, Alfrahil told a carefully edited tale, focusing on the bravery of his guardsmen and their individual accomplishments. By the time he reached the last ambush, Alfrahil's voice began to shake as the fear that he had kept at bay all evening began to overwhelm him. He felt a black silent wave of despair and grief, begin to overtake him. Silently it came as if he were trapped in a nightmare without end building higher and higher. Shrieks broke his internal silence, the screams of men and horses and the overwhelming odor of burning flesh. His glass suddenly fell from his hand, shattering upon the floor.

Startled out of his waking nightmare, Alfrahil glanced around him and, instead of scorn for his feelings, saw only pity and compassion. Alfrahil felt a hand on his shoulder and saw one of the oldest veteran servers standing next to him. Alfrahil looked up into the grizzled countenance of a man who looked old enough to be his grandsire.

'Peace, Lord,' said the retired soldier as he extended a fresh crystal goblet of the excellent Chilton wine. Momentarily, Alfrahil was lost in the deep plum color of the wine, of the odor of black cherries and leather that emanated from its surface. Taking a sip of the wine, Alfrahil noted the richness and feel of the wine, and it helped break his spell of despair.

'Aye, lad,' muttered the old soldier, 'now you can see what haunts us all, be it an ambush here in the City or one out in the desert wastes. I heard your tale and talked to those that saw the final ambush. There was nothing you could do once the trap was sprung but save yourself and as many of your men that you could, for it was cunningly laid.'

Alfrahil heard these honest words. In a louder voice than he thought he could manage, Alfrahil said, 'Thank you, soldier. What is your name?'

'I am Aradar, my Lord, servant of the King.'

'What rank did you hold in the army?'

'Army, Sire? Nay, I was a desert scout, Lord, leading a patrol of regular army when we were ambushed.'

'How did it happen, Aradar?'

'The young lieutenant wanted to go down a small wash, as he thought it would be easier to follow than to ride along the top of the river bank,' said Aradar.

'You disagreed, I take it,' said Alfrahil.

'Yes, Lord, for the banks were two fathoms high and broken with sand and stone. Once you are in there, you are not easily seen, it is true, but you cannot get out. I told him this, but as I was a scout and not regular army, he overruled my recommendation and insisted on taking his men in there. Several of his soldiers knew I spoke the truth and tried to speak to their lieutenant, but he bade them be silent and follow him.'

'What happened, Aradar?'

'Well, Lord, we were allowed to proceed about five leagues before the bandits struck. Suddenly there were arrows from all sides. Boulders rolled down in a narrow place fore and aft, and we were completely cut off. Some men tried to get their horses up the banks, but they were too steep. Others tried to jump the barriers. One succeeded and rode for help. The rest of us took cover under and behind the bodies of our horses, for none of them survived the first few minutes. Half the men were dead already, including that lieutenant.' Aradar coughed and spat into his handkerchief before continuing. 'He took an arrow through his eye. The rest were wounded. We fought as well as we could, dropping several of them, but there were fifty of them and only forty of us to start, and they had the high ground. When they charged in, we killed at least twenty, but our numbers steadily dwindled until only seven of us were left alive. They then used clubs to disarm the rest of us. I lay there, Lord, with three arrows in my body, praying for death. The bandits then began torturing the rest of the wounded. Their screams and pleas for mercy went on for hours, well through the night. Finally, Lord, I was the only one left alive, and they came for me. I had an arrow in the side of my chest, and one of the filthy scum grabbed the fletching and started wiggling it about. I am not ashamed to say that I screamed aloud, Lord, for the pain was unbearable.

'At that moment, the sounds of distant horses came as if in a dream. The bandits abandoned me and began scrambling up the bank, preparing to disappear into the wilderness. I heard later that it was a Kozaki that was in charge of the reinforcing company, and he led his cavalry along both sides of the wash, with only a small rear guard following behind. Proper formation, too, flanking the bandits and turning them back into the trap that had been set for us. That fool of a lieutenant knew nothing; just came from a rich family.'

Alfrahil was surprised at the venom in his voice, but Aradar seemed to collect himself and went on with his tale.

'None of the bandits escaped, Lord, and we left their bodies there to rot under the desert sun.'

'What happened to you afterward?' asked Alfrahil.

'I was returned more dead than alive to our camp, and the healers managed to staunch my wounds and bandage me well enough so I could be moved in a wagon with other wounded back to the oasis,' replied Aradar. 'When I returned I learned that I had to leave the scouts, as I was no longer fit for duty. But I had no job, Lord, no skills but soldiering, which I couldn't do no more. So, I was part of the veterans you see in the streets trying to find some kind of work, scrounging and begging when necessary, doing the scut work that others didn't want to do. Some nights I could barely walk home from the heavy labor to earn some bread and maybe a glass of beer.'

Again the flash of anger flitted across Aradar's face, but the mask of composure rapidly restored itself.

'It was then that the King's ministers opened up jobs for injured veterans to serve the King. Serving drinks, my Lord, I never would have guessed the like for me, but I am grateful for the chance to work,' he said with a bitter smile.

Hearing the murmurs of the other guardsmen, Alfrahil said, 'Well said, Aradar. I see that I am not alone in fighting my personal battles against the fear and memories that do not die easily. I hope that soon we can do more for you and for others who have made such great sacrifices.'

'Thank you, Lord, and forgive me for speaking out of turn, but you looked as if you were still out there even though you are safe in here,' said Aradar.

'I was,' said Alfrahil. 'I was.'

'Yes, Lord, and if you are like the rest of us, you will find your-self out there again and again, especially in your dreams. Try to make peace with it, Lord, before it gets a hold of you permanent like. I wish I had been able to make peace with my burdens, both then and now.' Turning to go on his way, he walked with the rolling, staggered gait of a man who had been wounded too deeply in body and spirit to move quickly.

Shortly afterward, Alfrahil bade the men goodnight and walked through the door to the stairwell of the tower, up to his room.

Chapter Six

Daerahil

Daerahil rode steadily across Sisera in the morning light. A cool wind from the north blew across the interior of Eldora, south toward the river. Lulled by the thud of hooves and the creaking of a worn leather saddle, Daerahil found himself contemplating his escort.

Accompanying him was his best friend, Hardacil, and an escort of ten guards. Hardacil was fifty years old, from the Delta region of Eldora. To escape a life of boring drudgery, he, like his father before him, had enlisted in the army at eighteen. Tall but thin from years of riding to foreign commands, his plain peasant face was deeply tanned from his time in the desert. A thin, constant stubble covered his face in clear violation of army regulations. Hardacil was not just a common soldier, though he had begun that way. He was Daerahil's aide-de-camp, the highest rank an enlisted soldier could achieve in the army.

The two men had been friends for years, ever since Hardacil, a sergeant with over ten years of service, had been forced to suffer under the command of Daerahil, a brand-new lieutenant fresh from officers' school.

Daerahil's first command had hardly been a glorious one: just a simple platoon of soldiers and a sergeant who vexed the prince severely. This sergeant, Hardacil, was a grizzled veteran in his early thirties who had been on the Shardan front or in occupied Shardan for over a dozen years. Seeing that his new commander was a brilliant shade of green as a new officer, he had offered what were meant to be helpful hints and thoughts. After the first few comments and suggestions, Daerahil had ordered him to keep silent. Shortly thereafter, Daerahil had blundered badly about the disposition of the men during the night, and two of them had been wounded when local skirmishers snuck close to their picket line. After that incident, Daerahil had privately apologized to Hardacil and asked him to speak freely and not keep silent in the future.

Over the next few months, he had found Hardacil to be indispensable, not only for his experience and advice but for his undying loyalty. Twice during the past twenty years, Daerahil had tried to promote him to an officer, but both times Hardacil had politely declined, stating that he only wanted to serve the Prince, and the burden of an officer's rank would take away from his duties. Compromising, Daerahil had made him an aide-de-camp, answerable only to Daerahil. And though he had been unable to promote Hardacil, he had ordered that Hardacil's father's official rank on the retired list be increased from corporal to senior sergeant, nearly doubling his retirement pay and giving him two acres of farmland in the Delta, making the elderly man's last few years of retirement much more comfortable. Now they rode together to Prince Paladir's realm as Daerahil pondered the nature of the emergency that Paladir had alluded to in his message.

Crossing the last of the outlands, Daerahil paid scant heed to the farms and houses that had sprung up in the past few years. The squalor of the squatter camps of various refugees, their families, and camp followers disturbed him, but there was little he could do. Sadly, Daerahil had long realized that while some men were meant to rule the world and dictate its course, others were meant to follow.

Daerahil's mind wandered to the past, six years ago, when on leave, and he remembered receiving the deed to a large estate from Zarthir and partial financial interest in a joy house in the Fifteenth District. Daerahil had first gone there with Zarthir, who had wanted to show Daerahil a nice time. After too many glasses of wine at the Dusty Cloak, they had taken their horses and ridden down to the Fifteenth District. There the party continued, and Daerahil had soon ascended the stairs with a Shardan lass. Hala was her name; just over eighteen but already quite talented, and Daerahil enjoyed her thoroughly.

Rising late in the morning, Daerahil noted the girl was gone and that his breakfast was waiting. Rapidly dressing and preparing to leave the house, he found Zarthir waiting downstairs, looking rather smug.

'My Lord Prince, how did you enjoy your night?' asked Zarthir.

Smiling despite his condition, he replied, 'It was quite satisfactory, Zarthir, but it is now time for me to depart.'

'Perhaps, Lord, I could call upon you at a later time, for I have a business proposition for you,' said Zarthir.

Agreeing hastily, Daerahil wanted to only leave, have a bath, and return to the Citadel, where he could keep an eye on his brother and his father's scheming ministers. But later that night, he found himself missing female companionship and reluctantly traveled to the joy house again. He went again the next night.

Zarthir found him there and, handing him a deed to a large farm area, said, 'It is yours, my Prince. I hope that you profit from it.'

'What do you want in exchange, Zarthir? I hope that you are not trying to bribe me.'

'No, Lord, I thought that this farm's profits could be used to aid the veterans groups, but this time the money will be transferred secretly to aid those men, without your father or Mergin's interference.'

Daerahil, thinking that he could do some good for the men and their families, acquiesced; telling Zarthir clearly that this was for the benefit of his men, not for himself. Zarthir agreed, and over the next several weeks made a concerted effort to win the Prince's favor, providing Daerahil with many other business opportunities, making certain that the Prince's profits reached his charity groups in a timely manner.

Zarthir also introduced him to other like-minded men of the City who wanted to worm their way into the counsel of the King and thereby acquire the necessary influence to make them, richer and more powerful. Over the next three and a half years, even when Daerahil was in Shardan this financial relationship expanded along with their friendship, for Zarthir was privy to secret information. Daerahil began to enjoy some of the profits directly, refusing to think of them as bribes but instead as well-deserved rewards for all the years he had spent in the desert, defending the kingdom.

Daerahil was only allowed two weeks leave out of every six months, and he spent much of the time with Zarthir during the day and with Hala at night, having as little as possible to do with his prissy brother and overbearing father. His enjoyment of Hala rapidly increased to the point where he no longer wished to have her shared by other men and arranged through Zarthir to buy out her contract, placing her in an apartment near the original joy house and employing retired soldiers to guard her around the clock. Eventually, he found that he could talk of things to Hala that he could discuss with no other. While she rarely understood all of the subtleties or conditions that went into his very existence and relations with others, she never judged him, listening patiently and occasionally offering some advice based in common sense rather than political skill. Within three years, Daerahil's heart was given to her totally and completely.

He knew that it was socially impossible for him to love her, but he did nonetheless, in passionate disregard of the reality of politics in the Citadel. Every time he thought of his father and what he would do if he found out that his son was in love with a Shardan prostitute, he shuddered and spent more money in bribes and favors to keep this relationship completely hidden. Wanting to help her as much as possible, he had even hired the best lawyer to smooth out Hala's path to becoming an Eldoran citizen. Now, fresh with the knowledge from his brother that Mergin was aware of Hala, Daerahil knew he must spend vast sums to have Hala's citizenship granted with great alacrity before Mergin could persecute her as a foreigner.

Many hours later, Daerahil saw the greens hills of Prince Paladir's fiefdom rising in front of him. The horses slowed their pace as they embarked upon the road that began to spiral above the woodlands, winding their way through the thick and verdant forest. Soon the fragrance of the flowers that clung to the river cliffs began to waft around them, faint at first and then greater as their loop of the road took them along the eastern side of the hills. Now over three hundred feet above the plain Daerahil saw the vale of Aphon laid out before him. While this view was quite impressive, it was not nearly as magnificent as the view from the Prince's keep. Daerahil, wanting to spare the mounts, slowed his horse to a walk and gestured for his guards to do the same. While it was not a long climb in terms of distance, the road rose steeply to its final height some twelve hundred feet above the river. Daerahil loved his horse and did not want him to become winded on the way up.

Hardacil remarked upon the view from the road. 'As many times as I have come here with you, Lord, I never tire of it.'

'Many times indeed,' replied Daerahil. 'How the years have passed.'

Daerahil remained silent as they rounded the final turn and rode to the open gates of the keep, which lay before them. Gardens for vegetables and fruit surrounded the keep, filling out the hilltop to its farthest edges. A small shed for chickens and milk cows was nearby, crowding next to the horse stables. The afternoon sun shone on the single tower of the keep rising sixty feet above the hilltop, completing the picture of a heavily fortified manor house rather than a traditional watchtower. Over a thousand years ago a small but important watchtower had been ensconced upon this hilltop, manned by the men of Eldora at the beginning of the realm. As the centuries passed, it had fallen into disrepair, essentially abandoned as the realm of Eldora spread far and wide. In later years the kings of Eldora had repaired part of it, as the tower had a commanding view of the river and of south Ackerlea. After the end of the Great War, the surviving watchtower was restored and enlarged, transforming it into a keep of modest size.

The battlements were only twenty feet high and would only withstand a modest assault, but still, it would hold out long enough to, hopefully, get a messenger to the City if attacked. The road and the defenses along the side of the road would deny almost any enemy for the better part of a day, perhaps two. Daerahil knew, as very few of the military men in Eldora did, that there were steep narrow trails laid into the eastern side of the hills that would swiftly allow messengers to descend to the forests of Ackerlea. He had heard tell that there was one dire path along the western cliffs that led to the marshes below. Daerahil mentally shuddered at the thought of descending those steep cliffs comprised of soft limestone that crumbled underfoot. Only fragrant flowers were at home there, spreading their beautiful scent upon the breeze.

Now, as he approached the keep, guards wearing the silver and white of the Prince of Ackerlea sprang to life before him.

'Hail, Lord Daerahil, Prince of the realm. Welcome to Nen Brynn,' said the sergeant of the guards formally.

'Hail and well met,' cried Daerahil. 'Where is Prince Paladir? I am here at his request.'

A slightly quizzical expression crossed the sergeant's face, and he told the fleetest of his men to find the Prince.

'Please enter, Lord, and let us stable your horses while you wait for my Lord Prince,' said the sergeant.

'Thank you, Sergeant,' replied Daerahil. 'Please see to their needs and have your groomsmen rub them down and victual them well, as they have had a hard day's journey here.'

Following a young servant, Daerahil and his ten men made to enter the grounds on foot as custom dictated. The ancient order of the Princes of Ackerlea required all men except the King's war messengers to enter on foot and their horses are stabled outside the walls. There were disused stables within the walls that could be readied in times of war, but it was Prince Paladir's order that the peace and beauty of the keep not be disturbed by the sights, sounds, and odors of horses clattering and neighing within the walls. Daerahil thought this was somewhat ironic given that Paladir surrounded himself with a breed of dogs, known as Seeing Hounds, that, though they barked little and moved with unusual grace, were noted for a peculiar odor.

One of these dogs began walking toward Daerahil, gently stepping on the white gravel pathway that led from the outer wall to the doors of the keep. Daerahil knew that these animals were found in far Hagar; legend had it that they were fleet enough to run down deer. While Daerahil had never seen them at the hunt, they were certainly bred for it: exceedingly tall, long in limb, but deep in chest, with an extended snout that pointed slightly downward. Their bright eyes were constantly scanning the horizon as if perpetually seeking their quarry. Daerahil paused momentarily, admiring the liquid grace that these fleetest of canines exhibited. Moving without a sound over the stones of the courtyard, the tan and white hound came to him with a pleasant if aloof look. Daerahil extended his hand palm up for the dog to sniff. Administering a brief lick, the dog wagged its tail and seemed about to wander off, when it froze suddenly, staring intently at Daerahil's throat.

For an instant, Daerahil thought the dog was going to spring for him and was about to reach for his sword. But before he could act, the hound, with a flash of motion too swift to be truly followed, lunged to Daerahil's right. He heard more than saw the click of sharp white teeth inches from his face.

Shaking its head, the dog spat a small object from its mouth. Whimpering and whining, it worked its tongue gingerly, as if in great pain.

Peering down, Daerahil saw a large, unfamiliar wasp with brown and yellow stripes; writhing its last on the gravel. Daerahil had not heard it, much less seen it, as it had buzzed toward his face. Realizing the dog had saved him from a nasty sting, he said to the young servant who was accompanying him and his men, 'Fetch the chief handler and give the dog something for his poor tongue.'

The dog's tongue even now was becoming swollen and purple from the sting of the wasp.

'The chief handler, my Lord?' said the servant. 'He is not here, but I will summon the healer as soon as we are inside.'

'Nay, lad, summon him straightaway, for this magnificent beast took the sting that was meant for me. I will be comfortable here while you are away. Hurry now!'

With an incredulous glance, the youth darted off into the side of the keep. Hearing the whimper of the hound, Daerahil gently patted its head, trying to reassure it that help was on the way. Hearing feet crunch upon the gravel, Daerahil turned and saw the young servant trotting breathlessly back toward him with an older man huffing and puffing alongside him. Two attendants followed a step behind, carrying satchels full of goods.

Not recognizing the older man, Daerahil was slightly con-fused when the man briefly acknowledged him with a half salute and immediately began tending to the dog at his feet. The animal's distress had increased. As the man pried the dog's jaws open, Daerahil saw over his shoulder that the animal's mouth and tongue had swelled substantially and were quite red. Rasping orders to his two attendants, the man began pouring a thin, greenish liquid down the dog's throat. Coughing and spluttering, the dog tried to spit it out, but most of it went down. The healer called for the attendants to begin mixing a salve as he remained focused on his canine patient.

The young servant finally caught his breath and said, 'My Lord, please follow me into the keep, where rooms are being prepared for you and your men.'

Pausing for a moment, Daerahil asked the old man how the dog was going to fare.

'She should live, my Lord Prince,' replied the man with a gravelly voice.

'Live? It was only a wasp! How could it cause this poor dog to have a brush with death?' asked Daerahil.

'Just a wasp, my Lord? Nay, this was no ordinary pest. It was a Banded Wasp; surely you have seen them before?'

'A Banded Wasp? I have heard them described, but I have thankfully never seen one,' replied Daerahil.

'You have now,' said the healer.

All men knew of these dreaded wasps. Living among the stunted copses high in the hills and mountains surrounding the Plaga Erebus, they were thought to be a changed form of wasp that had prospered when the Dark Lightning ran through that darkest of lands in the days of Magnar. They were ferocious in defending their nests, and woe befell the unfortunate Man, Dwarf, or Elf who stumbled upon them. Legend had it that once provoked, the wasps would sting until they were dead, and their stings were incredibly powerful. Just one would cause the recipient hours of convulsive agony and produce huge swollen areas. Two or three stings, quite common with these vicious insects, resulted in a coma lasting for days if not weeks. More than five stings were invariably fatal; hitherto there had been no known antidote for their venom. Daerahil looked back upon the dog and thought that such a sting in the mouth would surely cause the dog's throat to swell shut as he had seen.

Amazingly, the tongue was far less protuberant than it had been just moments ago, and some of the anxious slobberings had subsided. Breathing a sigh of relief, the healer said, 'Yes, I believe she will recover.'

'What was it that you gave her?' asked Daerahil.

'A tonic for insect stings, which thankfully works quite quickly.'

Amazed, Daerahil said, 'I thought there was no antidote for the vile wasps.'

'There wasn't, Lord, until quite recently. A young healer by the name of Findalas came up with this concoction two years ago, and all of us healers keep a phial handy.'

'Findalas?'

'Surely, Lord, you have heard the story of the woman who was given the title of master healer at the age of twenty, the youngest by thirty years?'

'Yes,' said Daerahil. He had heard some mention of it two years ago.

'Well, Lord, you have her to thank as much as me for saving this animal's life. But really, it is we who are in your debt.'

'How so?' asked Daerahil.

'This is no ordinary dog, my Lord,' the healer replied. 'This is Prince Paladir's favorite bitch, and we just found out she is to have pups from the finest stud hound that was recently brought in from Hagar. I would not want to have been the man to tell the Prince that his bitch had died and her brood been lost.'

'Well, then, healer, it was fortuitous that I arrived when I did, for who knows? She might have encountered the wasp without a witness to her travails. I trust you will notify the groundskeeper to begin a search for the wasp nest, or she will not be the last to feel their brutal stings.'

Straightening up from his charge, the healer had his apprentices gently lay the dog upon a cloth stretcher and bear her away toward the keep. Asking and receiving permission to leave, the healer and his charge left the courtyard, and Daerahil followed the lead of the young servant into the keep.

Striding through the huge wooden doors of the main building, Daerahil, now joined by Hardacil, saw high ceilings built to maximize the light from deep set windows. The ceiling beams were mostly hidden in the glow of candles and lamps lit to compensate for the failing daylight. Daerahil was escorted to the room where he customarily stayed. He noted that there were more Shardan-style furnishings than previously. Surprised at the political risk that Paladir had taken by decorating the room in this fashion, Daerahil was impressed that Paladir had the independence to do as he saw fit in his own realm and not concern himself overmuch with what his uncle Creon might think.

Daerahil found the room that had been prepared for him quite comfortable. He and Hardacil were refreshing themselves with some fresh fruits and wine when Paladir's Chief Counselor, Girnon, entered the room. Girnon was of middle height and years. Daerahil knew him to be an efficient administrator.

'How may I be of service?' the man asked.

Feeling slightly confused, Daerahil asked, 'I would like to see the Prince as soon as possible.'

'The Prince, my Lord? The Prince is not here,' said Girnon.

'Not here!' cried Daerahil. 'How dare he send a message to me and not be here?'

'There must be some mistake, Lord, for Lord Paladir has been gone for a week, hunting with his hounds, and is not due to return until tonight at the earliest,' said Girnon.

Rising to his feet, Daerahil produced the message, holding it out to the counselor. 'Clearly, you are mistaken, sir, for here is the Prince's message with his signet ring seal stamped in wax upon the bottom.'

'May I see that Lord?' asked Girnon.

'Certainly,' said Daerahil.

As the counselor examined the message, his face rapidly lost color.

'My Lord, this is a clever forgery, for while the signet insignia is indeed the Prince's, we stopped using this white wax two weeks ago, when beautiful silver wax arrived from the Bastion. The Prince is quite fond of it, as it preserves the details of the ring most admirably. What distresses me more is that someone was able to make excellent use of the Prince's ring, as it never leaves his hand, Lord, never.'

'Well, this is a pretty puzzle that we are set. You tell me the Prince is away and that the message is a forgery most cleverly done,' said Daerahil. 'Clearly, someone wanted me here at the keep. What is your readiness to repel invaders?'

'Repel invaders, my Lord?' asked Girnon.

'Yes. Stop talking as if you are one of those colorful birds that have become popular in the City which endlessly repeat what they have heard,' said Daerahil. 'I repeat, what is your readiness?'

'We have fifty guards here on duty, with ten more escorting Prince Paladir, but their military status is a matter for their guard captain, not myself,' said Girnon.

Turning to Hardacil, Daerahil said, 'Go and find Paladir's guard captain and place the keep on full alert. Close the gates and bring in the men and the horses, except for the scouts at their posts. Have them alerted to be on the lookout for intruders.'

'By whose authority are you usurping the power of Prince Paladir?' asked the startled and now angry Girnon.

'By the authority of the King,' replied Daerahil. 'As his son and a Prince of the realm, I take authority over all others except my father and brother, particularly in matters of security, when the local lord is absent.'

Pausing a moment before responding, Girnon stated, 'Yes, Lord, you are correct, but when my Lord Paladir returns, you may find yourself in conflict with his wishes.'

Daerahil knew that Girnon was correct, for even a royal Prince of Eldora could not supersede another Prince of Eldora in his own fiefdom unless the realm was in immediate danger.

'Well,' said Daerahil. 'We will cross that bridge when we come to it if we come to it at all.'

'If, Lord?' said Girnon. 'Prince Paladir should be here by daybreak with his hounds and his hunting party.'

'Think, man, think,' retorted Daerahil. 'You have a traitor in your midst; someone whom you say very cleverly falsified the Prince's signet ring and drew me here for some purpose unknown to us. Locate and question any and all men, servants, soldiers, wenches, and the like who could have had access to the Prince's ring.'

'But, Lord, I have told you that he never takes it off. His hand has grown in the years since he first put it on, and now there is no way to remove it; save to cut the ring or the finger.'

Musing for a moment, Daerahil stated, 'If no one could have borrowed it, then we are left with two choices. Either someone copied the ring from an impression in wax, or they used the ring as it lay on the Prince's hand.'

'Lord, you misunderstood me,' replied Girnon, 'for this is a near-perfect forgery. But for the change in the wax, I would have sworn it to be the Prince's own.'

'Certainly, someone could have used the signet mark on a different message to make a copy of the ring,' said Daerahil.

'Well, Lord, perhaps,' said Girnon, 'but this is so clear, with such fine details, that it is unlikely.'

'Then tell me how and when the Prince's hand would have been available for this forgery, presuming he did not send it himself.'

Girnon paused, and then stated, 'Ten days ago there was a great feast here, Lord, held by Zarthir in the Prince's honor. I am sad to say that the Prince, who can usually hold his wine with the best of men, became drunk quickly and had to be taken away early in the evening and left to sleep off the wine.'

'Who was with him that night?' asked Daerahil.

'Well, Lord, as you know, the Prince is betrothed to Amadren, daughter of the Duke of Anscomb, and no longer seeks out the company of wenches. But that night a young woman had been asked by Zarthir to see to the Prince's needs if he awoke in the night,' Girnon admitted.

'Can you describe her?' asked Daerahil.

'She was very pretty, Lord. A Shardan woman—small and slender, almost childlike. But Zarthir had three or four women of similar looks, Lord. I could not say which of them attended to Lord Paladir.'

Daerahil thought for a few moments. A tormenting recollection had come upon him. At the same time as this party, Hala had begged leave to depart in order to visit a sick relative in the refugee camps. Daerahil had granted the request. Hala had returned after three days. He had not thought of the matter since then, but now the connection to Zarthir, and the fact that Girnon's description of the woman, however cursory, fit Hala; gave him pause. True, many Shardan joy girls resembled Hala superficially. But even so...

'Clearly, one of these wenches brought the message and used his signet ring,' Daerahil said at last. 'The question is why; and why tonight of all nights, did someone wish to draw me here?'

'I do not know, Lord,' said Girnon. 'But I will question the soldiers and staff; as you ask.' He bowed and made to go, but Daerahil raised a hand.

'Hold a moment.' Fixing his gaze on Girnon's face, Daerahil gently pushed into the other's mind, looking for treachery or other strong emotions that would betray any plot. But he sensed only Girnon's fear for Paladir and his fear that he would lose his position. Daerahil released him after only a few moments. Girnon staggered, and Daerahil escorted him to a nearby chair, where Girnon began to color with anger.

'I am sorry that I needed to search your mind, but eliminating you as a traitor allows you to search for the truth. Once you are feeling better, please begin your search for anything unusual that would reveal how and why I was summoned here today. My men will aid you now.'

Now, Hardacil returned from alerting the keep and Daerahil bade him send two of Daerahil's personal guards who had trained as scouts, along with the Keep's guard captain with an escort of five more of Paladir's guards to go and find Paladir.

'Girnon, where was the Prince supposed to be hunting today?' asked Daerahil.

'Well, Lord, he should be along the south river road as we speak, due to return tomorrow,' said Girnon his voice tight with anger over being violated.

'Very well,' replied Daerahil. He instructed his men to find Paladir and bring him as hastily as possible back to the keep.

'My Lord,' asked Hardacil, 'shouldn't we depart for the City as quickly as possible for your own safety?'

'I have thought of that, Hardacil,' said Daerahil. 'I deem that I am safer within these walls than on a ride down the road with only a few men while passing through the squatter camps late at night. It may be that whoever caused this message to be sent wanted me to be distracted, dashing for the Citadel only to be caught in the twilight upon tired horses. No, I will stay here for tonight and return to the City on the morrow.'

* * *

Jerking awake from a troubled sleep, Daerahil rose from his bed. He glanced out the eastern window of the keep and saw the faintest hint of gray above the Southern Highlands. Another morning was about to break upon the realm of Eldora, and Daerahil was no happier for it. Once again, his sleep had been troubled by nightmares, though only disjointed flashes remained. He recalled his brother's gloating face somehow imposed upon the banner of Eldora, his father cursing him upon his deathbed, calling him craven and callow. His nightmares came when they saw fit, encroaching upon the day and denying him meaningful sleep when it was most needed. Daerahil had become accustomed to drinking himself to sleep, though the wine did not subdue the nocturnal horrors completely. Instead, they were less powerful, a blurred disquiet instead of the poignant and particular set of terrors they usually provided.

Rising quickly, he was about to put on his robe for his morning ablutions, when he heard feet running down the hall. Bleary-eyed from lack of sleep, he reached for his sword and had just drawn it from its scabbard when there was a hurried knock at his door. Lowering the sword slightly, as few assassins would knock before entering, Daerahil said, 'Come.'

Bounding in behind the opening door, Daerahil's two guards—veterans of the eastern campaigns—glanced at him and his sword with a frown, as if to say, '*No one could get past us, Lord, but that the whole keep would hear our cries.*'

Daerahil had done his best, against his father's wishes, to look after the families of the veterans who had served under his command. Ten years ago, he had quietly set up conservative investments whose income was directed to the struggling family members of the eastern armies. Mergin had discovered Daerahil's plans, revealing them to the king, who sent for him, demanding an explanation. In the Council chambers, Daerahil had his first public disagreement with his father.

'Not enough is being done to care for these men and their families who have sacrificed for the realm, father. You told me there were no funds in the public budget, and I have used my own money to redress this injustice.'

'These men and their families knew the risks. They gambled with their lives and lost. I have no sympathy for them, there has been no "injustice,"' responded Creon.

'Disregarding semantics, I wish to help these people. Since this money is my own, how and why are you be angered at my generosity?'

'Because, my rash son, your personal charity makes us look stingy by comparison,' said the King. 'If you solve their alleged needs, then the clamoring to stop the war will grow and the people will continue to grow restless. If instead, we protect the safety of Eldora and marginalize these worthless miscreants, we can all rest easier in our beds.'

'Worthless miscreants, Father! Worthless, do you say?' bellowed Daerahil. 'These families have spent the lives of their sons, fathers, and brothers in order to do your bidding. The realm of Eldora is larger and farther afield than ever it was back in the days of old, and it is only your arrogance that demands obeisance from every man south of Aphon—arrogance that exerts a toll upon our country and our people, and which we can ill afford to indulge. Let us instead come to terms with the peoples of the Shardan and the nomadic tribes of Hagar and Azhar, and bring our armies home.'

Rising to his feet, Creon spoke. 'You speak against your King and your Kingdom. For all here know that throughout the ages, whenever the vigilance of Eldora has waned, enemies through our neglect and in our very somnolence have always plotted and wormed their way ever closer to Eldora, biding their time until they are ready to strike.'

'Who, Father?' roared back Daerahil. 'Who can strike? Your father and yourself with the Kings of Kozak have annihilated most of the leadership of the southern lands, taken their children hostage, laid waste their towns and cities. For every enemy of Eldora that you kill, you make three more with your policies. Bring the army home and let our prosperity and generosity speak for us rather than our swords and arrows.'

'Enough, my son, for you have said things here today that would have a lesser man in chains,' said Creon. 'Begone from my presence and return not to me for a fortnight.'

When Daerahil had refused to inform Mergin of the names of those who had set up his investments for the families of the troops, he had been banished from the City for a month. He had spent the first week encamped outside Sisera in a furious sulk, angry with his father and also his brother for not coming to his aid. The following week, while riding in Ackerlea, he had been welcomed by Ferox, Elven Lord of Ackerlea and Prince of the North Forest. Ferox sympathized with Daerahil's plight, as he had a similarly contentious relationship with his uncle, King Albericus. Upon their parting, Daerahil discovered he had a new friend in Ferox, who offered him the hospitality of the Elven city of Ackerlea whenever he desired.

Shaking his head at the memories, Daerahil lowered his sword and returned it to his scabbard and asked, 'What is so urgent?'

'My Lord Prince, Prince Paladir has been found and is on his way here. Shall I order your breakfast?'

'Yes, and do not disturb Hardacil, as he was up later than I was last night. After breakfast have the baths prepared for me.'

A few minutes later, a brief knock at the door announced the arrival of his breakfast. The guards escorted in a young serving man from the kitchens. He bore a large platter of food, a small portable brazier to ward off the morning chill, and a large jug of coffee. Rapidly setting the meal before the Prince, he inquired if there was anything else.

'No, thank you,' replied Daerahil. Not feeling particularly hungry but knowing he needed to eat, Daerahil absently consumed the breakfast before him. Drinking the last of the coffee, he rose from his repast and strode out the door and down several corridors with his guards in tow. Soon, they were, joined by a tousled Hardacil, still bleary with sleep.

'My lord, why did you not summon me when you awoke?'

'My friend, there was nothing for you to do, and you were up well past the middle of the night reviewing security plans for the Keep. You deserved your rest. Besides, how did you know I was awake?'

Smiling, Hardacil said 'I always know where you are my lord, my job requires it.'

'Well, now go and get some breakfast, my friend.'

'I will have some sent to me outside the baths, so I can ensure your safety.'

Sighing, Daerahil knew it was fruitless to argue with Hardacil, and he continued on to the baths, followed by his guards and Hardacil.

Daerahil approached a large set of wooden doors, which a servant standing outside opened, announcing quietly to another servant in the room that Daerahil was present. Bowing, the interior servant knocked on a large wooden door leading from the antechamber into the bathing room, to alert the bathing attendant within. Daerahil bade his guards keep watch here in the antechamber, where the stone walls were unfinished and comfortable benches and tables allowed those waiting to bathe to enjoy refreshment brought to them. As there was only one entrance and exit from the baths, the guards gratefully agreed, and Hardacil ordered breakfast for himself and the rest of the guards.

'Hardacil, since you insist on accompanying me, you are of course in charge; I do not wish to be disturbed by anyone unless it is a true emergency,' said Daerahil.

'Yes, my lord.'

The inner door of the antechamber was opened by a matronly woman in a long bathrobe. 'My lord, if you would follow me.'

Daerahil entered a room similar in appearance to the antechamber; but here, large copper cauldrons of steaming water fired by small coal fires underneath filled the room with steam. Bidding Daerahil to strip naked, the serving wench began washing him with soap and a thick cloth from head to toe. The first time Daerahil had visited this keep as an adult, he had been shocked by the concept of washing before he got in the bath. But he had been told that dirt and sweat from his person would pollute the pristine waters of the hot spring.

At last, considered clean enough to enter the baths proper, Daerahil was given a plush bathrobe and a large soft towel. Then the bathing wench opened the door to the baths themselves, allowing him to enter alone into the empty bathing chamber.

The baths were quite large, ten by thirty feet, resembling a bent oval. Benches of natural stone had been installed in the ledges of the pool. Daerahil knew that the center of the pool was at least forty feet deep and that the hot water streamed up through small fissures in the bottom. Deep within the earth, steam had burrowed up beneath the hills, creating a natural hot spring, and the keep had been extended in this particular direction to make use of this wonderfully rare phenomenon. Thinking back to his first visit here, all of his objections had ebbed away once he first immersed himself in the lightly hissing waters and smelled the faintest hint of sulfur emanating from the still surface, testifying to its source deep in the earth.

Many different minerals were dissolved in these waters, and their properties were said to be unique to these springs. The powders left behind when the waters departed were highly regarded for their healing abilities and would have been sold at a high price but for Paladir's generosity. Those who could not journey here, yet were in great need, were able to use the powders to heal their ailments. Regardless of the reasons, the baths were renowned for their soothing and healing powers, and, once per month, the ill and infirm of Nen Brynn were scrubbed head to toe and allowed the otherwise unknown privilege of these baths, a gesture not lost on Paladir's subjects. The prince was loved by his people and his soldiers for this and other activities that promoted their well-being over his own purse or sense of place.

Steam rose thickly from the waters, swirling in drafts of cool air from the open windows. The soft morning light coming through those windows was diffused in the mists, making the room seem huge and endless. Obscured by clouds of steam, Daerahil heard the slow murmur of water trickling out from the far side of the pool drain into collecting ponds for the mineral powders prior to entering the sewers of the keep.

While he had not consumed more than his usual two bottles of wine the night before, he was still quite tired; a lethargy and malaise more of the spirit than of the mind and the body. With a grunt, he sat on a stone ledge and slid his legs into the pool.

Musing for several minutes, Daerahil tried to relax amid the silence of the pool, but nothing could shake the exhaustion he felt in every fiber of his being, or the residual dread left behind by his dreams. He closed his eyes and tried to let the tension slip away. He felt his breathing become deeper and his heart began to slow. Drifting on the edge of sleep, he was startled to hear a hoarse whisper in his ear.

'If you value your life, Prince, you will not return to the City until the morrow.'

His eyes sprang open, and he turned to see who had spoken. But Daerahil had forgotten that the ledge in front of his seat was narrow, and so he plunged into the deeper, hotter water that lay just in front of him. He caught only a glimpse of a cloaked form receding from the edge of the pool and vanishing into the swirling mists.

Caught unaware, he inadvertently breathed some water into his lungs. It was a moment before he was able to grab the bench upon which he had been seated. Coughing out the water, Daerahil glanced around, but there was no sign of the mysterious cloaked figure that had spoken its warning—or threat. But Daerahil gathered his bathing towel from a rack along the wall and rapidly circumnavigated the pool. There was no one else present, and Daerahil thought to himself that this joke had gone on long enough.

Bursting into the antechamber, Daerahil saw the same woman who had washed him look at him with a quizzical stare. 'Is there something you need, my Lord?'

'Who intruded upon my bath, woman?' asked Daerahil quietly, but there was no mistaking his intensity.

'Intruded, my Lord?' she replied. 'No one: you left strict orders that no one was to disturb you unless your guards deemed it necessary. I turned away the guard captain who normally bathes at this time and told him I would send a servant for him as soon as you were done.'

Striding quickly toward the woman, Daerahil grabbed the edges of her robe and, lowering his voice even further, stated, 'Don't toy with me, woman, as if I were a dullard or a child, for I am neither. Someone entered the pool and spoke with me, and I want to know who it was.' Extending his mind, he found only fear and confusion present in her feeble brain. Releasing her, she staggered back, fearfully stammering a repetition of her earlier statement. Roughly pushing her aside, Daerahil opened the antechamber where Hardacil and the guards were finishing their breakfast.

'Who entered the room after I did?' demanded Daerahil.

'No one, Lord,' replied a startled Hardacil.'

'No one? Are you quite sure?' asked Daerahil.

'Yes, Lord,' Hardacil said. 'We may not see as well as we did when we were young, but rest assured that no one got past this door this morning.'

Shocked, Daerahil said woodenly, 'Thank you Hardacil; I must have dozed off and imagined someone in the baths with me.'

Apologizing briefly to the still shaken bathing woman, he returned to the bath chamber and carefully looked around the room. He did not find anything amiss, except for one small wet shoeprint on the stone floor, pointing away from the pool toward one of the high windows at least fifteen feet off of the floor. *'Either I fell asleep and had a dream, or someone quite acrobatic was able to slip in and out by this window.'* With the keep on high alert, Daerahil knew that the intruder was either now caught or gone without a trace.

Shaking his head, he returned to the antechamber and dressed quickly, leaving with Hardacil to walk the battlements of the keep, trying to make sense of the morning's events. Battlements they might have been called out of tradition, but one watchtower with two guards that barely stood fifty feet above the hilltop could scarcely compare to other battlements throughout the realm. Measuring only a fifteen-foot diameter, the watchtower was surrounded by crenelments about four feet high with arrow slits carved into them. The soft morning light was filtered by the tall ash trees that grew to their east, the sun just beginning to crest the topmost branches. The rich and lush smell of flowers came to him on a soft breeze moistened slightly by the distant river.

Once atop the stairs, Daerahil asked his friend, 'Hardacil, how many years have we known each other?'

Raising an eyebrow, Hardacil responded, 'Over twenty, as you know, Lord.'

'Why are you not my guard captain?' asked Daerahil.

Smiling for the first time that morning, Hardacil said, 'Because you know I am not a leader of men, only a fighter of them. Therefore, remaining your aide-de-camp is all the honor and responsibility I need.'

Knowing that Hardacil had foiled two direct assassination attempts personally, disrupted a third, and regularly advised Daerahil's various guard captains, Daerahil knew his friend's worth.

Swearing him to secrecy, Daerahil gave him the message whispered to him in the baths. Hardacil was about to express his angry thoughts that anyone could get so close to the Prince when Daerahil, who knew this particular expression, stated, 'If the person wanted me dead, you would have found me floating in the pool.'

'Person, Lord? Why do you say a person and not a Man, my Lord?' asked Hardacil.

Daerahil responded, 'Either an incredibly silent and agile Man was involved, an acrobat or a Shadow, perhaps, or it was an Elf. I tend to think it was an Elf.'

'Why an Elf, Lord?' asked Hardacil.

'Because of the incredibly artistic way the deed was done,' said Daerahil. 'Someone scales fifteen feet of the wall outside a keep that has been placed on alert without making a sound or alerting a guard in the full sun of an early morning. They then enter a silent bathing room where they are able to contact me without alerting the inner guards, and then make their escape the same way within seconds and remain undetected. Either it was one of the Shadows that Mergin has trained with the help of his Hagarian allies, or it was an Elf.'

But you don't think it was a Shadow,' Hardacil said.

'No, it was not one of Mergin's assassins. If it had been, the man would have killed me, not warned me. No, it must have been an Elf … though I suppose it could have been a Hagarian tribesman. In any case, this was skillfully done.'

Quietly, he wondered if the Hagar tribesmen had trained others besides Mergin's men in their arts. They had promised loyalty, but not exclusivity. 'But why do they want me here,' he mused aloud, 'if their intent is not to harm me?'

Knowing that an Elf could have just as easily killed his Prince as a Man, a shaken Hardacil stated, 'Perhaps, Lord, they want you here because they do not want you somewhere else. Where would you be today and what would you be doing if you were not here?'

'I would be at my new post inspecting the Out-walls. Before the meeting of the Council two days ago, I would have ridden to Western Ackerlea, actually near to this keep, to speak with one of Zarthir's friends regarding the Fishing Guild, and perhaps I would have hunted in Ackerlea that afternoon prior to returning to the Citadel, for there was an important meeting of the Council of Ministers today I did not want to miss.'

'Therefore, Lord, if no one wanted you to necessarily be here, but rather not to be in the City or nearby, then that is why you are here,' concluded Hardacil.

'Well, Hardacil, we can talk about this all morning, but I fear we will learn little without more information,' said Daerahil. 'Please go below and see that the horses are saddled and ready to depart, for I do not wish to give these conspirators any further joy of my absence.'

Hardacil moved as if to descend to the stables but turned and said, 'Lord, if there is indeed a conspiracy, perhaps the mysterious messenger was telling the truth, and returning to the City is not advisable today.'

'Perhaps,' Daerahil replied, 'but you of all men should know that I do not turn up my nose at danger.' With that, Daerahil made a rarely used but significant gesture of dismissal, moving his right hand outward and downward, and Hardacil went below.

At that moment, Paladir arrived with Girnon. Daerahil greeted his fellow prince as the red-haired, broad-chested Paladir strode toward him. The prince's features proclaimed the unusual blend of Kozaki blood from his great-grandfather and Westmen blood from his great-grandmother. Paladir was shorter and stockier than most men of Eldora, and his mane of red hair, flowing down his back, and bright blue eyes were striking and disconcerting until one became used to them.

This morning, Paladir's countenance was drawn and pale. 'Girnon has informed me of the forged message, my Lord Daerahil. I have examined it closely, and it is indeed a forgery, though the signet impression is real. It was dated yesterday, but we started using the new silver wax from the Bastion over ten days ago.'

'Was this wax used inadvertently on this message?' asked Daerahil somewhat maliciously. Daerahil gently used his powers on Paladir, but sensed only the prince's fear and apprehension, coupled with astonishment, too raw and fresh to be rehearsed. He was fairly confident that Paladir was telling the truth.

'No, Lord, for the day that the silver wax was put into use, the white wax was sold to merchants who were quite pleased to receive such high-quality wax, and a message was quickly distributed throughout my fiefdom and throughout Eldora via the messenger corps that my wax had changed,' said Paladir.

'*It is so like Mergin to not inform me that a Prince of the realm changed his sealing wax,*' thought Daerahil. Regardless, feeling somewhat defeated, Daerahil did not quite know what to say.

'Lord, while I know we have not always seen eye to eye on many issues, let me take the first step in trying to bridge the gulf between us. I want to personally thank you for saving my beloved hound, Sammie, yesterday afternoon; I appreciate it more than words can say,' said Paladir with clear sincerity.

Looking at the man for the first time in a long time without rancor, Daerahil saw the expression of genuine friendship on his face and needed no mental powers to sense the pure intent behind it. He extended his hand. 'Well said, my Lord Paladir well said; it was no effort on my part. I owe your beautiful bitch a debt, and I am glad to repay it in some fashion. Let there be a new bond of friendship between us, and perhaps together we can solve this mystery.'

'Indeed, Lord, let me first say that I am sorry for whatever part, inadvertent though it might have been, that I have played in this affair,' said Paladir. 'I am deeply ashamed to admit, as honesty compels me to do, that it must have been the work of a wench whom, in my weakness, I allowed to escort me to my bedchamber on the night in question.' His face red with embarrassment, he recounted the events of that night, at least those of them that he could remember.

Daerahil listened sympathetically. 'We have all had such nights, Prince. Think no more of it. But the question is why was I directed here? What can anyone hope to gain from my presence? Did your scouts find anything unusual?'

'No, Lord Daerahil. They rode to the foot of the hill and along both the south and north roads until they encountered their first patrols. No one had anything unusual to report.'

'Well, then, I will leave you to investigate this matter on your end, and I shall investigate it on mine. Perhaps we shall uncover the mystery,' said Daerahil. 'I trust I can count on your full support in this matter?'

'Yes, you can. While you and I have not always agreed on policy, I don't believe it is stretching the truth to say that we have always respected each other's abilities. Today is a new beginning between us,' Paladir avowed.

'No, Paladir, it is not a stretch, and seeing as how we have both been practiced upon by others, we should certainly combine our resources and discover who is responsible and why this event has occurred. I am honored by our new beginning, and I will work hard to honor my words with deeds so that we can become closer friends and allies against those that would take advantage of us. I will take my leave of you now, Paladir.'

'Certainly, Lord Daerahil,' said Paladir. 'But you are more than welcome to spend the day here and leave tomorrow.'

Smiling, Daerahil said, 'Thank you indeed, Lord, for your keep is most refreshing, and I owe much to your Seeing Hound, but I shall depart. When challenged in this way, whether on the field of battle or in the council chambers, my nature compels me to respond aggressively. I cannot hide or hold back, no more than Sammie held back when she sighted the wasp.'

Paladir grinned. 'As you know, Sammie will soon bear her litter. Let me send you a brace when the pups are old enough as some measure of recompense for your inconvenience and as a gesture of our new friendship.'

'I thank you,' Daerahil replied. 'Heretofore I have been indifferent to the merits of dogs, but now I have learned something new. If it is not a great hardship, then a brace of these finest of coursing hounds would be greatly appreciated.'

The two men descended the stairs and made their way to the stables. There Daerahil was greeted by Hardacil, who had a dark expression on his face.

'My Lord Daerahil, all the saddles, and other tack have been cut. We cannot leave until they are repaired unless you wish to ride Elf fashion.'

'Whoever wanted me here is certainly determined to keep me here,' Daerahil stated in a tone of frustration mixed with grudging admiration.

'Again it seems I must apologize,' said Paladir, whose countenance had grown even darker than Hardacil's. 'How long does the chief groom say the repairs will take?'

Hardacil replied, 'Lord, he believes we can leave by late afternoon, which would allow us to descend the hill and make it to the first army encampment halfway to the bridge before nightfall.'

'This becomes more and more curious,' Daerahil said. 'The timing of this sequence of events is exquisite. There was no way I could have been permitted to be in the City today, but I am apparently allowed to return tomorrow. Well, let us take our leisure until we are ready. With your permission, Lord Paladir, I will become your guest for a while longer.'

'No, Lord, you are quite welcome. I will send my wine steward to you along with my chief cook; you should at least have a proper meal before you depart,' said Paladir. 'Now I must see to this additional breach of security.'

Daerahil nodded. 'That reminds me. I had meant to mention an earlier occurrence—another lapse of security.'

Paladir evinced astonishment when Daerahil informed him of the mysterious warning he had received in the baths.

'I shall have the keep and all in the surrounding area questioned, Lord Daerahil,' he said. 'It would seem that things are less secure than I had ever imagined possible.'

'The conspiracy must indeed be larger than any of us could have dreamed,' Daerahil agreed. 'Well, there is nothing to be done about it now. I shall remain in your demesne, drink your wine, eat your afternoon meal with you, and depart when the horses are ready. No doubt my brother will be most pleased, for I shall surely miss the Council meeting today, and he has been most unhappy of late with my words there. He is a good man, a patriot of Eldora, but too hidebound and cautious when it comes to military and political matters. Too willing to follow the lead of that vile serpent, Mergin, who pours his poisoned words into my father's ear. If only the order of our births had been reversed or my brother never born at all...'

'Lord Daerahil, that is both indiscreet and nearly treasonous to think, much less state aloud,' said Paladir with a shocked expression upon his face.

'I have been banished twice already, my Lord Paladir, and I am far from Eldora today. But I meant nothing treasonous. I love my brother and am loyal to my father, though I make no secret of my disagreements with their policies. Yet there is treason afoot; if they can get to me this easily, they can also get to Alfrahil. Eldora can scarcely afford to lose both its Princes on the same day. Let us send word by a messenger runner now, so that my father can have some idea as to what has occurred and can set extra guards to watch over my brother.'

'That is well-spoken, and wise counsel indeed,' said Paladir. 'A messenger shall be sent at once. But I pray you, sir, to compose its contents with more thought and circumspection than was evidenced in the words you just spoke to me, which I shall keep in confidence, knowing as I do that there was no ill-will behind them. Others, however, might be less fair in their assessments, so once again I counsel you, in friendship, to keep a closer guard upon your tongue, my lord, lest your own words are turned against you.'

'Now you sound like my brother,' said Daerahil, laughing. 'Very well, I know you speak in friendship, my Lord Paladir, and I shall heed your advice as best I am able.'

Chapter Seven

Confrontation

Daerahil spent the night at an army encampment, and soon after waking, a messenger arrived reporting the dire events that had taken place in the city.

'My brother,' Daerahil broke in impatiently. 'Is he all right?'

'Yes, Lord. He was wounded, but the healers believe he shall make a complete recovery,' said the messenger.

'Thank the Gods for that,' said Daerahil fervently. Turning to Hardacil, who had brought the messenger to him, he said, 'Prepare to depart.'

'Yes, Lord,' he replied.

Reaching the great bridge over the Aphon, he was not altogether surprised to see a *Faris*—a mounted company of one hundred Kozaki—waiting to escort him back to the City. Daerahil did not recognize the captain of the Faris, and while Daerahil greeted him warmly, he received only a flinty gaze through squinted eyes in return. The deeply tanned blond rider introduced himself,

'I am Hugon, Prince Daerahil. I have orders to escort you to the gates of Titania and protect you from harm.' Hugon presented Daerahil with a scroll confirming these orders, signed by Mergin, in the name of the king.

The sight of that signature, as much as the contents of the order itself stirred Daerahil's blood. 'Am I under arrest, Captain?'

'No, Lord,' replied the stoic rider.

'Why are not men of Eldora here instead of Kozaki?' asked an even angrier Daerahil.

'I do not know, Lord, except for the fact that we are far better horsemen than the men of Eldora. Let us proceed swiftly.'

Hugon then cried out in the rich tongue of Kozak, and the Faris turned as one, assuming a flattened wedge, with the archers on the periphery spreading out to over twelve hundred feet along an arc. Daerahil could see that no one could come within bowshot and that his safety was being taken most seriously.

Riding at a swift canter, nearly a gallop, the Faris quickly traversed the road to the City, where Daerahil saw smoke rising from several different locations. Black oily plumes drifted skyward, pushed eastward by a light breeze. Daerahil was truly shocked. His years in Shardan had accustomed him to such sights but never had he expected to see the same dreadful display above Eldora's capital.

Riding by his side, Hardacil murmured, 'Is this just a terrible dream, my lord?'

'I wish it were.' replied Daerahil. Nothing the messenger had told him the night before had prepared Daerahil for the scope of the tragedy. Hearing that there had been a fire set against his brother, he had assumed a tavern or stable had been set alight. Now it looked as if half the city was wrecked.

'Why are the fires still burning, Captain?' demanded Daerahil of Hugon.

'I do not know, lord, but rumor has it that it after the attacks on your brother, several assassins were caught in heavily populated areas of the city. They supposedly set additional fires, wishing to kill as many others as they could before they died.'

With that, Daerahil remained silent as they approached the Great Gates, where Daerahil was turned over to a Shadow and a company of Citadel guards. The Shadow was Gray Water. 'You will proceed with me to the Citadel, Prince Daerahil. There you will meet Lord Mergin. Do you wish to see my orders?'

Shaking his head, Daerahil presumed that these men were here to see him safely to the Citadel. Continuing along the main road from the gates to the Citadel, Daerahil knew there had not been this many cavalry within the City since the siege during the Great War. Passing near to the first attack in the Sixteenth District, Daerahil noted the stunned look on the common folk standing alongside the main road, forced to wait until Daerahil passed. As they approached the Escarpment, Daerahil saw that they were turning westward.

'Why are we not riding to the Great Bridge?' he inquired of Gray Water.

'The Great Bridge is in ruins,' answered the Shadow. 'They are still pulling up the bodies of the slain. It will be months before the wreckage is cleared and new construction can begin.'

'The bridge is destroyed?' asked an incredulous Daerahil. 'It has remained intact for over five hundred years. The base timbers were constructed of whole northern oak trees, nearly four feet thick. How was it demolished?'

'No one knows, lord. Even now the engineering corps is trying to fathom how this happened.'

Moving to their west, they passed close to the ravine where Alfrahil had nearly perished the day before. A sudden gust of wind blew grayish soot out from the small chasm, and as Daerahil distractedly wiped it away from his cloak, he realized that the tiny flakes had once been a man. The smell of burnt human flesh was unmistakable. Daerahil had smelled it during his campaigns too many times, but to smell it here at home was most horrifying.

Circling around the Escarpment, they returned to the main road and entered into the Third and Second districts. It was then that Daerahil saw smoke billowing from active fires, no longer the smolder of charred wood and ashes. The scope of the attack on his brother shocked Daerahil as much as the actual destruction wrought in the course of it. Dozens of men working for weeks if not months would have been required to secretly bring in enough oil, wood, and who knew what else to create this one conflagration, not to mention the destruction of the Bridge. Secrecy for one ambush, much less three, should have been impossible. Daerahil's face drained of what little color it had left as he realized that either Mergin had neglected his intelligence duties most shamefully, or he must have known of these attacks in advance. Neither conclusion made sense, as Mergin was most thorough in his security apparatus, and if there was even a hint of his complicity in these attacks, Mergin would right now be enjoying the dubious pleasures of his own torture pits after having had his mind drained by Creon for every bit of information. For the first time on a field of conflict, Daerahil was completely perplexed about what his next move should be.

Rounding a last turn in the narrow road, Daerahil was greeted by Mergin and another half company of men from the Citadel. Six Shadows attended Mergin as a personal escort. With a cold look upon his face, Mergin greeted Daerahil formally and announced, 'You will be taken before the King shortly. Hardacil and the rest of your personal escort will be detained until after the meeting with your sovereign.'

'Am I under arrest?' asked Daerahil impatiently. 'Or are all of these measures for my own security? What in the name of all the Gods happened here?'

'You will hear soon enough, from your father's lips. I am instructed to say no more.' Mergin answered even as he studied Daerahil closely. Bewilderment and fear were visible on the prince's usually haughty face.

'You say I am not under arrest, yet you refuse to tell me any-thing of these attacks, or even how my brother fares. You go too far, Mergin.'

'*Well,*' thought Mergin, '*he certainly did not plan or launch these attacks. Daerahil simply does not dissemble that well. He might have had an indirect hand in this disaster, perhaps through his money men or his close friends, but I don't believe he was di-rectly involved. More's the pity.*'

But though he acknowledged Daerahil's innocence privately, Mergin intended to use this tragedy to its greatest effect against the prince.

'My Lord Prince,' he said, 'you are not under arrest at this time, but you must go before the King.'

Daerahil blanched at the implied threat in Mergin's voice. Did his father intend to put him to the question? Swiftly passing into the Citadel, Daerahil was not terribly surprised that they were not ascending into the royal apartments or adjacent buildings. When he realized where he was being taken, though, he had to credit Mergin for this deception, for who would believe that the King and Crown Prince were ensconced within the drafty and disheveled astrologers' tower? Not seeing any visible guards, Daerahil knew they must be there somewhere and that nearby there must lurk at least a dozen Shadows. While they were not yet as skilled as their teachers, against any lesser foes they were truly lethal.

Regaining his equilibrium, Daerahil mentally prepared him-self for whatever awaited him. Yet instead of being immediately brought before the King, Daerahil was escorted to a room where he was allowed to breakfast properly and attend to his morning ablutions. Prior to closing the door where Daerahil's personal guards stood watch, Mergin said, 'As soon as you are ready, Lord Daerahil, send one of your guards into the hallway, and my men will bring your father the message.'

Daerahil said, 'I will be ready to see my father in half an hour.'

Mergin smiled his wintry smile. 'Your brother, Lord, may not yet be ready then. It is for him that we are actually waiting. Otherwise, Prince or no Prince, you would have been brought straight to your father.'

Cursing, Daerahil strode toward Mergin, his hand upon his sword. But before he had closed even half the distance between them, a darkly cloaked form dropped silently from the ceiling and planted himself between the first minister and the Prince. Daerahil stopped short. He knew there was nothing he or any of his men could do against a Shadow. In theory, of course, as a prince of Eldora, Daerahil had nothing to fear from this or any other Shadow. But it was not a theory he cared to put to the test. His father had erred badly in giving Mergin control of the Shadows. The man had built them into his own private army. Why was it that no one else, not even Alfrahil, saw the danger?

Fuming, Daerahil addressed the smirking Mergin. 'Presuming you survive my father's wrath for this incredible display of incompetence that nearly killed my brother, someday your time of worth to my father shall be over, and on that day I shall delight in wreaking my vengeance, your magic soldiers notwithstanding.'

Only by the glitter of his eyes did Mergin reveal his wrath. 'Be that day ever delayed, Lord Prince, for when you come, I shall be waiting. And I will not be alone.'

About to turn on his heel and leave, Mergin suddenly grabbed his temples, feeling as if a vise were pressing upon the sides of his head. Helpless to speak, he felt Daerahil's mind increase the pressure for a moment and then release.

Mergin staggered against the wall, his face contorted in fear and pain. Still unable to speak, he glanced with hate-filled eyes at Daerahil, who had remained motionless.

'Remember, little man, even with your tame killers by your side, I can still reach you,' said Daerahil. 'Be thankful that I am prohibited from causing you or any member of the Court permanent damage. Now be gone from my presence.'

Mergin glanced at Daerahil's calm countenance, but inwardly he felt the angry tension begin to touch his mind again. With the help of the Shadow, he lurched down the hall, fleeing a confrontation he could not win.

* * *

Nearly two hours passed before Daerahil was summoned to his father's presence. Entering into the meeting room of the astrologers' tower, he found his father there with his personal guard, supplemented by a dozen Shadows. Mergin stood to one side, his face expressionless.

'Hail and well met,' cried Creon formally.

'Hail and well met,' replied Daerahil, striding toward his father. He paused three paces away and slowly drew his sword, aware all the while of the Shadows' attention fixed upon him. He did not falter but knelt smoothly and held the sword out to his father, the blade resting on his open palms. 'This sword is ever at the service of the King, along with this unworthy servant. Command me as you will,' said Daerahil.

Instead of advancing toward Daerahil and taking the sword immediately, then handing it back to him as custom dictated, particularly when it was a Prince of the realm who was on one knee, Creon said, 'Rise, my son, but please hand your sword to my guard captain.'

Suppressing an angry retort, Daerahil knew that this morning of all mornings, with the attack on his brother and his own mental assault on Mergin, his father might just clap him in chains for any reason or no reason at all. Rising, Daerahil gave his sword to the guard captain and waited for his father to speak.

'You have heard of the attempt on your brother's life by now?' asked the King rhetorically.

'Yes, Lord,' said Daerahil, 'and I have seen the unbelievable destruction that the assassins unleashed upon the city. It grieves me most deeply. But where is my brother? Is he unhurt?'

'He is unscathed but for a few cuts and scrapes, and it is kind of you to ask,' replied Creon coldly.

'Kind, my Lord? *Kind*? He is my brother,' replied Daerahil indignantly, his tanned face going a light shade of umber as the temper and shock he had repressed all morning began to get the better of him. 'While he and I disagree on many things, I love him above all others—besides you, of course, Father.'

For reply, the king approached Daerahil and fixed his unblinking stare upon him, focusing his will upon his son. Only once before, when he was a very young child and played a prank that had damaging consequences, had Daerahil been subjected to what was coming. Daerahil fought to keep the King's mind from his own. Yet despite his maturity and strong mental powers, Daerahil felt his will begin to crumble beneath the King's relentless onslaught. Inexorably he felt his father's mind penetrate his own. The sensation was like hot irons piercing his flesh: his father was not being subtle or gentle. He was probing as he might probe an enemy, with no regard for Daerahil's comfort, much less his dignity, ripping his mental fibers asunder, leaving Daerahil's psyche tortured and quivering. Only with the greatest of effort, requiring strength of will that surprised him even as his defenses crumbled, was Daerahil able to keep a few thoughts shielded from his father's mind as it searched for the truth. And even then, had his father probed diligently, rather than like a burglar ransacking a room, he would have discovered those hidden thoughts.

Then Creon withdrew abruptly, leaving Daerahil's mind in painful tatters, gloating over his helpless son. Daerahil fell to the ground, his elbow landing painfully on the stone floor. He lay there for a moment, only half conscious. But slowly, rage and humiliation boiled up in him. 'So this is what it must feel like to be raped,' he thought. At that moment, had he the strength and the opportunity, he would have killed Creon in the blink of an eye. But he had neither.

Mergin, standing to the side, smiled inwardly. '*Good. That vile ingrate knows what it feels like to be attacked without a defense.*' he thought. '*But I have never seen the King have to bring so much power to bear. Anyone but Daerahil would have quailed and collapsed within a few seconds; he may be harder to dispose of than I thought.*'

Creon turned to his guard captain. 'Return the prince's sword and help him to his feet.'

Standing with assistance, and panting from the unsuccessful effort to deny his father entry into his mind, Daerahil looked at his father with smoldering rage. 'Now, Father, that you have taken from me by force what I would have willingly given you, had you but asked what will you have me do? For know now that I will hold you responsible for this violent assault upon me, and I shall seek vengeance unless you beg my forgiveness.'

Instead of replying directly, Creon commanded his soldiers, counselors, and even Mergin to leave the room. After they had gone, he said, 'You can come out now.'

Daerahil, amazed, saw his brother emerge from behind a tapestry and move somewhat stiffly into the room. 'Brother!' Daerahil cried. 'Glad am I to see you!' He made to embrace him.

But Creon said, 'Hold. You may make peace with your brother later, Daerahil, but for now, you will listen to me. You may hold me responsible for whatever you like, but as long as I am your father and sovereign, you will remember your place. I could just as easily have had Mergin take the truth from your flesh over one of his interrogation pits. Be thankful that I love you and that I would never subject you to such physical abuse. Remember that you are powerless in this land without my permission. Do not let your love for me fail!'

'Love! Peace? How can I love you after today? And why would I need to make peace with my brother? There is no conflict between Alfrahil and me. But the conflict between us two, Father, has reached a terrible point.'

As Daerahil spoke, he used his own powers to soothe his wounded mind. Already he had recovered sufficiently to sense the brooding anger and suspicion behind his father's face. The emotions he sensed from Alfrahil were more disturbing still. Though his brother's face showed only cold indifference, his mind projected faint suspicion and uncertainty.

'We have heard of your treasonous words in Nen Brynn, and but for the fact that I sensed no treachery in your thoughts, you would currently be under arrest,' said Creon. Creon knew that he had delved only partially into Daerahil's mind, as Daerahil's natural defenses were so strong that breaking through these barriers completely would have destroyed Daerahil's mind utterly. This was not something Creon was willing to do, for he still loved his son, no matter how misguided he had become. A small part of Creon's mind wondered, however, if he would have been strong enough to tear down the final walls of anger and defiance that Daerahil had erected against him. Creon felt some remorse for what he had done, but only fear could command respect, as history had taught him again and again, and he was determined to be feared and respected by everyone—including his own children.

'Treason?' asked Daerahil with equal parts rage and confusion. 'What treason?'

'Do you deny that you told Prince Paladir you wished you were Crown Prince instead of your brother? And that you wished you had been born first, or your brother not born at all? And that you stated your belief that Eldora would be better led by you than by your brother or even your own King?' thundered Creon.

Daerahil was astonished to hear his own words, which he had said in confidence to the prince, less than a full day ago, repeated back to him from his father's lips. But he did his best to hide his distress. 'I spoke out of frustration, Lord, for while I was not attacked as Alfrahil was, I, too, was the victim of a conspiracy—one that may well be related to that which so nearly took my brother's life. Perhaps I do wish that Alfrahil's burdens were mine to bear—that does not mean I wish him ill or am disloyal to the realm. That is the truth, Father, no matter what Mergin's messenger corps has told you.'

'How is it, then, on the day that he is attacked, you abandon your scheduled inspections and instead make for Nen Brynn, a part of the Kingdom you do not frequent and with whose Lord you do not generally associate?'

'What?' cried Daerahil, his face now a deep purple under his dark tan. 'Can you honestly believe I had anything to do with this atrocity? I love my brother, and I would gladly sacrifice my life for his, and before today for yours. Who dares accuse me of this outrage? Let him face me! Or is this just another fling of your ill will into my eye?'

Creon, feeling Daerahil's tremendous self-righteous anger fill the room, cast a mental shield between Alfrahil and his brother to keep his lesser mind from this fray as he battled against his son's attack and after a few moments forced it back into Daerahil's mind.

'Silence!' rasped Creon with hoarseness that revealed how much effort it had taken to protect one son while defeating the other. 'Silence, my son, for you stand in taint of high treason. Answer my question, if you please.'

'Verily, Lord, verily.' And Daerahil heatedly told the tale of his journey to his father, from the moment he had received the forged message purporting to be from Paladir.

Creon listened gravely. 'And Prince Paladir will bear out your tale, my son?'

'Yes, Father, he will, for he was as gravely concerned about the security breach as I was,' said Daerahil. 'His chief counselor, Girnon, will also tell you the truth of my words.'

Frowning for a moment, Creon asked, 'Do you have any questions, Alfrahil?'

'No, Lord,' replied a relieved-looking Alfrahil. 'While my brother is politically reckless as usual, I do not sense any malice in him, either. But the possible involvement of several of his friends, such as Zarthir, cannot be overlooked. I, therefore, make my peace with him and count myself reconciled.'

'Reconciled?' asked a furious Daerahil. 'What have I ever done to you in open or in secret that would cause such a rift between us, much less be a matter for reconciliation?'

'Your desire to take your brother's place,' responded Creon. 'That is enough for any Lord to ask for reconciliation.'

Laughing darkly, Daerahil said, 'You will outlive all of us Father, as your mother was Elven. Despite your hundred ninety-nine years, you look no older than a man mature but not yet declining into dotage. Neither my brother nor I will live half as long as you. I apologize for upsetting you, brother. You must believe that I would never take any steps to harm you or attempt to usurp your place in the Kingdom. Father's distrust no longer surprises me, but I am hurt and disappointed that you, too, would doubt me.'

A pained looked crossed Alfrahil's face, but he did not reply.

Creon said, 'Have you not given me reason for distrust, my son? You have defied me outright in open Council, where others who differed with me were content to speak to me later, in private. That is not something to be overlooked.'

'So, it comes down to pride,' said Daerahil scornfully. 'I am treated like a treacherous outlaw because the almighty King and my too righteous brother have thin skins.'

'I see that even these horrific events have not taught you to keep a civil tongue,' said Creon. 'You will return to your Command on the morrow and finish the inspection tour that you were assigned. You have leave to visit your apartment tonight in the City, but you may not seek out your brother or any of your friends until you return to me for judgment in three weeks' time. You are also forbidden to ride away from the Out Walls and have any contact with outsiders. Mergin will supply you with a complete list of your restrictions.'

'Judgment,' began Daerahil. 'What judgment? I have committed no crime!'

'Perhaps not,' said Creon. 'Now go from my presence, and let me see or hear nothing of you until three weeks have passed.'

Turning on his heel, Daerahil burst from the room. Hardacil and the rest of Daerahil's personal guards, who had apparently been waiting outside, sprang to attention as he emerged. Without a word, Daerahil gestured for them to follow him. But he had not taken more than two steps before a messenger in traditional gold and silver attire stepped into his path, bringing the prince to halt. As still and silent as a statue, the man stood with an outstretched hand. In that hand was a scroll.

'What is this?' Daerahil demanded.

'A list of restrictions imposed on your freedom, my lord,' replied the messenger, who looked as though he would rather be elsewhere. 'Beg your pardon, sir, but I have been commanded by your father and Lord Mergin to hand this to you personally.'

'Bah.' Daerahil snatched the scroll out of his hand and tore it in half without bothering to open it. Throwing the two halves onto the floor, he stormed off, followed by Hardacil and the guards.

Emerging from the base of the astrologers' tower, Daerahil dismissed his guards but had Hardacil accompany him as he looked for his horse. Finding no one but Citadel guards, he asked the nearest where his horse had been taken.

'Down to the stables, Lord, to be fed; I was to say that if you cared to wait until the third hour after nuncheon, another horse will be brought here for your convenience,' replied the guard.

Cursing under his breath, Daerahil strode out from the gate. He had expected to see guards from the Citadel along the road down to the plain but instead saw only a scattering of regular guards from the City present at their usual posts. The hundreds of guards who had secured the road earlier had been dismissed. Feeling fresh rage rising within him, Daerahil strode at his fastest pace toward the base of the City. 'Those men who escorted us were not there to protect me but instead to keep me from some insane course of action,' he remarked to Hardacil, who strode beside him. 'How could my father or my brother think I would harm either of them?'

'I do not know, Lord,' Hardacil replied. 'But clearly you must watch your step, and your voice, until you see your father again.'

Daerahil paused briefly and then resumed his rapid stride. 'You speak boldly, Hardacil, but correctly. I have spoken rashly already, but in truth, it is hard to hold my tongue when…' He mastered himself. 'No matter, perhaps I have not been wise after all in my business dealings and friendships. There is much I would ask Zarthir, but I am forbidden to see or speak with him.'

At a temporary messenger stable in the Third District, Daerahil requisitioned horses for himself and Hardacil. Without replying to Hardacil's questions as to their destination, he set off at a canter. Ever since he had stormed out of his father's presence, his only thought had been to escape to the one place in all the city that he felt free of suspicion and of the burdens imposed upon him by his father's malice. He would go to see his beloved Hala. He needed her loving look and soothing touch more than ever now.

Yet when he turned into the Lamplighter's street, he was astounded to see men of the Citadel standing guard on the corner of the small side street that would take him to his woman. Daerahil paused and saw there were more guards in front of the joy house and more still on the far corner. Raising his glance, he saw more guards and the unmistakable uniform of an Anscombian archer on the rooftop of his playhouse. '*What in the name of wonder is going on now?*' he thought. Approaching the nearest guardsman, a corporal, he asked, 'What are you and your men doing here?'

'Lord, our orders are to forbid all from entering or leaving this street without the express permission of the King, Prince Alfrahil, or Lord Mergin,' replied the guard.

'Well, stand aside, man, for I wish to proceed,' said Daerahil.

'No, Lord, for with all due respect, you are not one of the three men I named, and you may not pass,' said the guard.

Turning to move his horse around the young corporal, Daerahil was immediately confronted by three more guards, who politely but firmly told him he could not proceed without written permission. Momentarily thinking of using his mental powers to overwhelm these men, he saw that the Anscombian archer had been joined by another, and with that, reason supplanted rage and he knew that—for now at least—he had no choice but to back down.

Daerahil and Hardacil wheeled their horses around and retreated back the way they had come. He had not gone far when he heard his name whispered. Turning to the right, he saw one of Zarthir's closest advisers, Larissa, standing within the shade of a rundown tavern entrance. She beckoned him to join her.

'Quickly, Lord, before the Shadows see me,' she said.

Daerahil knew Larissa as Zarthir's trusted right hand, a lovely woman just leaving her youth behind her and entering maturity. Long red hair that would normally stand out like a beacon had been hidden under a somber scarf, the curves of her figure that would normally entice any man had also been reduced by the rather shapeless gown she wore. Few outside Zarthir's closest companions knew that she was anything other than a pleasure woman, and indeed she had begun her association with Zarthir as a beautiful plaything. But her agile mind and talent for cunning and politics had soon become evident, and Zarthir had added more and more duties to her list, until one day she was no longer his plaything but instead his chief of staff in all but name. Zarthir trusted her utterly, for who else in the Kingdom would give a woman from her background such honors and freedom?

Daerahil also knew how sensual she could be, having had the opportunity several years ago to enjoy all of her charms.

Tying their horses to an iron ring in the outside wall of the tavern Daerahil entered the tavern with Hardacil. The tavern was small; six crude tables and a tiny bar filled the interior, which was dimly lit by what little of the afternoon sunlight was able to pierce the grimy windows. The smell of stale cheap beer filled the room, but there were no other patrons, just a man behind the bar, who nodded at Larissa. She nodded back, and he walked into a back room, the dirty sawdust releasing its odors in the warmth of the day. There was an upper storage area, and though Daerahil could sense at least one man up there, he was content to believe that they were for all intents and purposes alone, but for Hardacil.

'The tavern has been cleared, Lord, so that we might meet for a few minutes privately, and so that I can remain hidden after you leave,' said Larissa.

'What is going on, Larissa?' Daerahil asked.

She seated herself at a table and gestured for him to do likewise. He took a seat, though Hardacil remained standing, one hand on the pommel of his sword.

'Minister Zarthir, his closest advisors, and other Council members friendly to you are being closely watched,' Larissa informed him in a low voice. 'I was lucky, Lord, in that Mergin does not know of my close involvement with Lord Zarthir and still believes I am no more than a pleasure girl. Thus, Mergin has set no Shadows to watch me as he has the others.'

'How do you know this?' asked Daerahil.

'Because, Lord, two of Zarthir's closest acquaintances tried to sneak out and were immediately waylaid by Shadows before being taken into custody for violating the King's orders. Since I am here, unless Mergin is the cleverest man to ever have existed, we are safe for a while... at least until the Shadows following you come to look for you. This is not an establishment with any known ties to Zarthir or his men, but it is conveniently close to where we thought you would go today.'

'Do you mean that if I had not chanced to enter this street, our meeting would not have occurred?' asked Daerahil.

'You would have been led here one way or another,' she answered. 'Mergin is not the only one with scouts and spies at his disposal.'

'Are you telling me,' hissed Daerahil, 'that there are Shadows not under Mergin's control?'

'No, Lord. But there are military scouts trained by Shadows and nearly as skilled who were dismissed from the army and now sell their services to the highest bidder. There are also Elves who disguise themselves as Men and use their particular skills to aid us in learning much that goes on in the Citadel.'

'Why then you must know who is responsible for this unconscionable attack upon my brother!' Daerahil exclaimed.

Larissa replied, 'There are those that would harm your brother. He is not good for business, trade, or the future of the realm, as you yourself have said. Obviously, someone took a chance yesterday. A chance that failed, but it was a well-laid plan.'

'So I have been led to believe,' Daerahil said. 'Tell me everything you know about this plot, Larissa, or your life is forfeit.'

'I think not, Lord, for before you or your friend here could so much as twitch a finger, you would both be dead, and I would take my chances with the Shadows. But calm yourself, Lord,' she said quickly, for Daerahil had begun to rise from his chair. 'We mean you no harm, and we did not have anything directly to do with the attempt on your brother's life. Indirectly, our actions may have aided the attackers, but we suspect that the plot, while long in the making, was executed at very short notice. Something happened yesterday to force his hand.'

'*His* hand?' asked Daerahil. 'Who is this he? Is it Zarthir of whom you speak? What are you talking about?'

'I do not know, and you do not need to know,' Larissa answered. 'Suffice it to say, Lord, that I have been told on good authority that "he" supports your claim to the realm and will aid you as best he can.'

'I do not want the realm,' replied Daerahil. 'I simply want to change some of the wayward policies that exist now.'

'Yes, Lord,' replied Larissa soothingly. 'Yes, that was impertinent of me. Zarthir will send you another messenger soon. Why don't you enjoy a mug of ale, and I will take my leave of you. As you return to the Citadel tonight, try and behave as normally as possible. One of us will be in contact with more information once we have it.'

Seeing his chance, Daerahil marshaled his powers and struck at her unguarded mind as quickly and brutally as his father, just hours earlier, had struck at his own. Sweat began to pour down her brow, and she tried to mouth words, perhaps call for help, but Daerahil silenced her with a single thought. He thrust more deeply into her mind, compelling her untrained psyche to respond to his questions.

Answers slowly spooled across the forefront of her mind. Yes, Zarthir and another person she did not know had known of the assassination plot against his brother, but she had not known herself until after the fact. Nor did she know anything of the messenger who had come to him in the baths at Nen Brynn. Having satisfied himself that he now knew all of the value that was known to her, Daerahil released his mental hold.

Larissa slumped back into her chair. But in the next instant, she sprang to her feet, a knife in her hand, surprising Daerahil with the speed of her recovery.

'I wouldn't do that if I were you,' he said softly, motioning meanwhile for Hardacil to stand down. 'I can leave you a helpless idiot in the blink of an eye with another mental probe before you can signal, move, or call for help.'

Larissa hesitated, anger and fear visible in her expression. Then resolve gained the upper hand, and she slid back into her seat, tucking the knife back up her sleeve.

'I'm glad to see you are as intelligent as ever,' Daerahil said. 'I will leave your mind intact this time but do not ever try to hide anything again from me, Larissa, no matter who tells you to keep it secret. And speaking of secrets, you will tell no one what has just passed between us, is that understood?'

'Yes, Lord,' she said.

'Good. I am afraid that your makeup has run down your face; you are showing your thirty-one years today. Now wipe your brow and go take a bath. The reek of your fear offends me.'

Larissa stood. Her hands were trembling, but her voice was strong, and she met Daerahil's gaze unblinking. 'Be wary, Daerahil, lest the son becomes worse than the father.'

He flushed at that, stung by the justice of it. 'Get out,' he said. 'And when we meet again, remember what will happen if you try to lie to me or manipulate me. I will take no pleasure in breaking a fine mind like yours, but do not doubt that I will do it if you give me cause.'

She seemed about to reply, then, as if thinking better of it, simply gave a terse nod and hurried out of the tavern.

A moment later, the barkeep returned to the room and brought Daerahil a mug of good Eldoran beer. But though Daerahil did not sense any danger from the man, neither did he trust him. After all, this tavern had been selected by Larissa and Zarthir … and the mysterious 'he,' no doubt.

'No thank you, good Barkeep,' he said, getting to his feet. 'Here is some silver for your trouble.'

'I thank your lordship,' said the man with a bow.

Outside, Daerahil continued on his way, with Hardacil riding beside him. 'Well, Hardacil,' he said. 'I can see you wish to ask me something. Go on.'

'What did you learn from Larissa's mind, Lord?'

'Little enough, I'm afraid.' Daerahil filled him in. 'What think you?'

'She is caught between two fires, Lord—Zarthir and yourself. She will have to dissemble well and take that bath you recommended before she can see her master again! But now you have an avenue into Zarthir's camp. I would suggest that, if possible, you put him to the question as you did Larissa. Clearly, he is involved in the events against your brother, and turning him over to your father and Mergin may do much to allay their unfounded suspicions of you.'

'Yes, but then I shall have no allies at all on the Council, and none of Zarthir's resources, financial and otherwise, would be at my disposal. Even if I could expose the entire plot, Mergin and my father would become suspicious that this information became available only after I had been indirectly accused of involvement. No, not until I can present them with the ringleader and proof that I had no prior knowledge of the attempts on my brother's life shall I be able to clear my name and petition a grateful father to return to my Shardan command. I must bide my time and gather more evidence before I betray my most powerful ally.'

Daerahil and Hardacil rode toward their apartments in the Third District. The City had begun to recover some of its emotional balance, and Daerahil sensed the stirrings of normalcy as the citizens went about their business. Still, he knew it would take weeks for them to recover their peace of mind and return to being the bored sheep that most of them were. Reaching the Third District gate, Daerahil and Hardacil dismounted, turning their horses over to the guards. Hardacil accompanied Daerahil to the entrance of Daerahil's apartment before departing for his own modest abode.

Entering his apartments, Daerahil was greeted by his servants and the matronly older woman, Marda, who ran his household.

Daerahil caught a familiar, enticing odor. 'Is that roast duck I smell?'

'I know you had a troublesome day, Lord,' said Marda. 'I thought you might appreciate your favorite meal.'

Thanking her, Daerahil quickly washed the dust and dirt away and then went to his dining room, where the food had already been set out. The room contained an antique table carved from one block of marble with straight upright chairs of dark northern hardwoods. Richly embroidered cushions of soft, thick silk covered the chairs. Antique silver graced the table, and delicate crystal held the wine.

Seating himself, Daerahil took a moment to savor the wonderful odors of duck with orange sauce. A servant appeared and silently, expertly, carved the bird. It was cooked to perfection, crackling brown skin outside, pink flesh within. Another servant poured him a glass of a particularly rare Frostfields vintage from his extensive wine cellars, the dark garnet color testifying to its depth and subtlety.

As he ate and drank, Daerahil felt his customary confidence return.

'Judgment, what judgment? What have I done to deserve this level of suspicion from my own father?' he thought petulantly. Feeling his anger begin to rise again, Daerahil forced such thoughts from his mind. Instead, his thoughts turned to Hala and how he wished that she were here now.

Rising from the table, he wiped his hands and mouth and, thanking Marda again for the wonderful meal, strode into his bath chamber, where he soaked himself and enjoyed another couple of glasses of wine before bed.

His bed had been turned down, and he slipped between the sheets, so overwhelmed with fatigue that he barely had the strength to douse the candle at his bedside. Yet he did not fall asleep at once. A familiar fragrance reached him in the dark, and he sat up in surprise. 'Hala?' he whispered for he had smelled her distinctive perfume. 'Are you here?'

There was no answer. He lit the candle, but its illumination revealed only an empty room. Daerahil sniffed again. The smell was coming from the bed. He reached beneath one of his pillows and drew forth a small envelope, bearing a note and a lace handkerchief. He recognized it as one of Hala's. He brought it to his nose and breathed deeply. There it was; her particular musky, spicy perfume. The effect on him was so profound that tears came to his eyes. The note said 'My lord, a red-haired woman wrote this for me, but the words are mine. I love you and have a wonderful secret to tell you when I see you again.' Daerahil could see the secret mark he had taught Hala to use instead of her name; the note was genuine.

Suddenly he recalled his parting words to Larissa and regretted them now. In smuggling this letter and handkerchief into his bedchamber, Larissa had clearly shown her loyalty. He reclined, the handkerchief still pressed to his nose, and with all the concentration of which he was capable, conjured up in his mind the source of that intoxicating perfume.

Chapter Eight

After the Ordeal

The previous night, Alfrahil had left the guardsmen in the common room of the astrologer's tower, where they continued drinking the wine his father had provided. He climbed one flight of tight spiral stairs and entered the room prepared for him. Space was cramped, with two small oil lamps and several candles on a small end table near a rustic cot adjacent upon a round dining table with two chairs. A short wardrobe with a small rude mirror on its surface lay on the far wall, next to a large cabinet bursting with parchments stuffed into a small corner. Heavy curtains screened off a small window, the air stale with candle smoke. Alfrahil was about to remove his armor when he heard a knock at the door.

'Enter.'

The door opened and a servant of the Healer hall entered, wearing the traditional white over tunic with a bunch of medicinal herbs embroidered on the upper left corner. This man was followed by a very comely woman, along with two of his household servants, Jayliss and Rafel.

The two servants bowed low to their lord. Replying to Alfrahil's inquiries as to their presence, Jayliss replied, 'Lord Mergin sent us, my lord, but we were blindfolded and do not know where we are.'

'That is of little importance. Be at ease, simply tend to your duties as usual, and I am sure that we will all be back where we belong soon enough,' said Alfrahil, turning his gaze to the stranger in the room. The woman's youthful face, illuminated by a dozen candles burning alongside four bright oil lamps, looked up at him expectantly. She was appealing to him: her thick, tawny hair, lightly tanned skin, and pretty, symmetrical face, with high cheekbones and large gray eyes, lit a spark of passion in him, and her slender yet curvaceous frame, combined with her height of just over five feet, made him want to possess her and protect her at the same time.

'I am Findalas, my lord, Senior Healer, here to tend your wounds,' the woman said.

'So you are Findalas, I have heard of you. But you look no more than a lass of twenty!' said Alfrahil, quite taken aback.

'Twenty-three, actually, Lord,' she replied with a smile. 'I had an early talent for healing, and I began tending the beasts of my father when I was five. The local healer recognized my gifts, and I was summoned to the Healers' School here in Titania when I was seven. I became their youngest graduate, and at twenty, I was a master healer.'

Findalas' professional demeanor hid romantic feelings toward Alfrahil that she had nurtured from childhood. 'All little girls want to grow up and marry a prince,' her mother used to gently tease her. 'But there aren't enough princes to go around. Don't be heartbroken if your dreams don't come true.' Findalas had banked the embers of her heart under medical studies, enjoying a few of her fellow students along the way. But she still nurtured her romantic, unrealistic dream.

Alfrahil's reputation was common knowledge: kind, loyal in word and deed, disliking conflict and believing the spoken word could solve nearly any problem. Abhorring violence, yet loyal to his ruthless father, Alfrahil was quite complex, next in line for the throne, but gentle compared to the reputation of his reckless brother. Alfrahil would rather compromise than dominate, respecting the positions of others, even commoners like herself; he was a man she could truly admire. Inwardly excited, her pulse racing, she might only have him now as a patient rather than a lover or husband, but even this encounter was more than she had ever believed possible.

Alfrahil protested that her personal care was not necessary but received such a stern glance in reply that he extended his arms with a sigh and motioned for his servants to undress him to the waist. Findalas approached and gently helped him pull his soft cotton undershirt over his head, her fingers making slight but definite contact. Was it his imagination, or was there more than the expert touch of a professional healer in the way her fingers seemed to caress his skin?

After guiding him to a wooden chair, Findalas examined his stitched wounds and applied some soothing unguents, her skilled, nimble hands helping Alfrahil's exhausted body to relax. Once again Alfrahil found himself wondering if her interest in him went beyond that of a professional healer. But he did not wish to shame himself or her by leaping to any conclusions. Here was a young woman who was justifiably proud of her professional accomplishments.

Last, of all, Findalas took some phials from her bag and poured them into a cup of water, which she then held out for him to drink.

Alfrahil took the cup and sniffed, recoiling at the bitter smell. 'Are you trying to poison me?' he joked.

'Merely ensuring that you have a restful night's sleep,' she answered without missing a beat. Smiling slightly trying to keep her desire in check, Findalas said, 'The potion is bitter to the taste, I admit, but it is a sweet salve to mind and body, as you shall see, provided you follow the directions of your healer and drink it down.'

'I can see that you are a stern mistress,' he said, only half jok-ing now, then drained the bitter brew in a single long swallow. 'Wine,' he gasped when he had finished. One of the servants quickly poured him a glass and handed it to him. He drank greedily, washing away the taste of the herbs.

'That was not so bad, was it?' Findalas asked with a sly smile.

'Compared to what?' he asked in turn.

'The draught will act quickly, Lord,' she said. 'You had best get to bed.'

Even as she spoke, Alfrahil felt the drugs begin to wash over him. Standing with difficulty, he let Findalas and the servants lead him into the bedchamber that had been prepared for him. There he was helped into soft nightclothes and, as though he were a child again, assisted into the firm, clean bed. Glanc-ing up at Findalas, he thought again how attractive she was: not just her looks, though of course, she was beautiful, for her other attributes: she was highly intelligent, compassionate, pre-cociously confident, and possessed apparently unprecedented healing skill. Alfrahil sincerely hoped that she would see him soon as a man rather than just a patient.

'Have a good night's rest, Lord,' said Findalas, smiling down at him in a way that struck him as both maternal and somehow wanton. 'I will have an apprentice from the Healer Hall on duty outside your door all night. If you have need of anything, they will summon me, and I shall tend to you.'

Alfrahil would have replied, but he was already deep in the coils of sleep.

* * *

With a start, Alfrahil awoke to see morning light streaming in a slender beam between the two heavy curtains draping the win-dow of the room. Momentarily, he was captivated by the slow dance of dust motes in that slant of the morning light. There was something peaceful about it, something soothing and harmonious as if he were watching a dance that governed not merely particles of dust but Men and Dwarves and Elves as well.

Suddenly fractured remnants of yesterday's terror broke upon him, and he bolted up in bed, shaking like a child awakened from a nightmare. Alfrahil tried to banish these dark memories, knowing that today would be long and stressful, and he would need his wits about him. Still, it was some time before he was able to fully master himself, and even then he was filled with a lingering sense of loss. Swinging his legs gingerly out of bed, he put his weight upon them with care, expecting that his bruises and wounds would pain him, but he felt a surprisingly little discomfort. It seemed that Findalas' reputation was well deserved.

Alfrahil strode to the window and peeked out between the curtains, wondering how late he had slept. The sun had just lifted itself above the edge of the city—had he not been in one of the tallest towers in all Titania, no light would have pierced the curtains to wake him. He considered returning to bed, but then a smell that had been lurking at the back of his awareness finally penetrated into consciousness.

His servant Jayliss entered, carrying a tray on which were plates of fried eggs, bacon and fresh toast with a pitcher of cold water, a ceramic mug along with a carafe of coffee, a small jug of cream and a bowl of sugar. Jayliss set the tray down on the small dining table and left, knowing Alfrahil's preference to eat alone and adjust his own coffee.

As he ate and sipped his sweet rich coffee—as piping hot as he could have wished—Alfrahil contemplated all that Mergin had told him of Daerahil's possible involvement in yesterday's events. He simply could not believe that his brother would willingly be a part of any treason, either against himself or against their father. Yet he knew Daerahil well enough to realize that there was a chance that his brother might be an unwitting accomplice to treason. He was a man who followed his heart and did not second-guess his first impressions, whether of people or situations. A strength upon the battlefield, but dangerous in politics, it was vulnerable to manipulation. He hoped that when he had a chance to confront Daerahil later today, his brother would have a plausible explanation for all that Mergin had reported.

Rising to his feet, he quickly began dressing, but feeling a stabbing pain in his shoulder, as well as the pain from the cuts on his face and body, he was forced to call for the apprentice healer and Jayliss. Briefly examining Alfrahil, the healer in training said, 'There is no serious structural damage, but all of the tissues in your shoulder have been pulled and it will be some time before they will knit and you will be pain-free.' Grimacing at this news, Alfrahil had Jayliss help him dress. Glancing into the small mirror that was set upon the dresser, Alfrahil noted his haggard appearance, his face lined with care and with sorrow.

Alfrahil insisted upon wearing his armor and sword, though their weight, never easy to bear, was rendered a greater burden by his injuries. Still, he did not dare leave himself vulnerable to another attack. He had escaped yesterday by pure luck. He would not make it easy for his enemies—whoever they were—to finish the job.

Escorted to the meeting room by a Shadow, he found Mergin and his father in the inner chamber waiting along with a plain-faced man; his tanned face recognizable to Alfrahil as Gray Water, chief of the Shadows. The man glanced at him, and Alfrahil was shocked, not by the intensity of the look, but by the complete absence of emotion. Once as a young child, Alfrahil had found himself staring into the eyes of a small harmless garden snake as it hunted in his mother's flowers. That same inhuman predatory gaze flicked up and down his tall frame, dismissing him as non-threatening to the King.

Creon bade him be seated around a small table with only four places. Fresh fruits and sweetmeats were offered to him, which he declined, while two servants remained against the far walls to attend to their needs.

Creon asked Gray Water to begin the meeting.

The man nodded and began. 'The fires are out all across the city, but it will take several days to clear the main road through the Second District. The Bridge over the quarry has been totally destroyed, and the small group of peasants who dwelt in the ravine in the escarpment will have to find new places to live; we will have to ride around it for months, if not years. The ambush near the Great Gate was small and did only minor damage. Regarding the attackers, there were at least forty to sixty men present as archers, with an unknown number who destroyed the bridge. The bodies of the slain archers are being searched along with their belongings, but so far all we know is that they appear to be veterans of the Shardan campaign.'

'How many did we capture alive?' asked Creon.

Blankly, Gray Water said, 'None sire.'

'None?' echoed a stunned Creon. 'How could they escape?'

'The surviving archers fled off the rooftops of the Second District and escaped on horseback. Apparently, they had seized control of the closest Messenger stable. We Shadows are fast—but cannot run down a galloping horse. We could not follow immediately, as the attackers took all the horses with them when they fled.'

'Were none of the archers wounded instead of killed?' asked Creon.

'Yes, Sire. Two. But they were able to take poison before they could be interrogated. We are clearly dealing with very dedicated men.'

'What of the archers at the Escarpment, or the men who destroyed the bridge?'

'The archers fled from the Escarpment and are possibly still in the City, but we have no leads yet to their location. I have increased security at the Great Gate and the gates that lead north out of the City, but it might be too late, and the enemy already is gone. However, the men who set the first ambush, along with the arsonists who tried to set the joy house on fire, are in custody. I gave them to Lord Mergin.'

Creon raised a questioning eyebrow, and Mergin took over for Gray Water. 'I questioned them rigorously for nearly a day. While they were stubborn at first, we broke them eventually. Unfortunately, they are simple criminals hired by an unknown man in a tavern. They were offered a large sum of gold if they would set their fires and even more gold if they succeeded. Little did they suspect that they would have been slain if they had completed their tasks and returned to their benefactor. As for the archer who slew the madam of that house, no sign of him has been found. Clearly, these conspirators are taking no chances.'

Alfrahil nodded grimly. 'If they are prepared to kill themselves, much less their mercenary cohorts, in order to avoid capture, we may be dealing with a political faction that we have not seen before. Are there any clues as to their origin?'

'Well, Lord,' replied Gray Water, 'the slain appeared to be an even mix of younger Shardan soldiers and older Eldoran men. One of the Eldorans bore the crossed swords tattoo of your brother's first personal guard regiment. However, all those men were retired years ago.'

'What of their clothing and weaponry?'

'Nothing remarkable there, I'm sorry to say. Their clothes were common, their weapons made by the Elves and traded to us in the ordinary course of business. This was a very well organized conspiracy, and we have learned little so far. Perhaps within a few days, we will learn more.'

'What of any news from outside Titania?' asked Alfrahil. 'Do the Dwarves and the Lesser Elves know anything that may help us?'

Mergin replied, 'The Dwarves have stated that they know nothing, but they will make further inquiries. We have not yet made contact with the Elves, but we hope to do so within a day or two. The local Kozaki Komandir knows nothing, but he has sped messages to Kozak to officially inquire if their King has heard of any plots against us or anything else that may aid us.'

'So we are completely baffled, it seems,' said Alfrahil in disgust.

'Not completely,' said Mergin. 'I have placed Minister Zarthir and his aides, along with several other important men who have expressed reservations about the King's policies, or engaged in other suspicious activities, under close watch and restricted their movements. Two of Zarthir's aides ignored this command. They are now in custody, and we are searching their homes and offices. Minister Zarthir has cooperated fully, however, and has retained one of the best counselors in the city, and I fear without some new evidence coming to light in the next few days, Zarthir and his aides will be free to move about the city again. As you are aware, Majesty, ancient Eldoran law regarding a Full Minister or a member of the nobility requires solid evidence to issue an arrest warrant, and so far there is only rumor and hearsay against Zarthir.'

'I cannot believe there is no evidence whatsoever,' said Alfrahil.

Mergin nodded. 'Two odd things were found on one of the rooftops. The first was an Elven cloak with significant magical properties of concealment. We have never seen it's like before. This would explain how and why the bowmen were able to elude our Shadows. We believe that the surviving archers are using these cloaks to hide. Also, a grapnel, incredibly small and, light, with long, thin tines like hair, was found connected to threadlike Elven ropes. The grapnel appears to be an alloy of Platina and other metals. Our best metalsmiths have examined it and pronounced it to be of Dwarven manufacture.'

'Dwarves and Elves,' muttered Alfrahil. 'Wonderful. Now in addition to looking inside Eldora, we must look outside as well.

I can see that it is none too soon to begin my diplomatic tour, Father. Before I make any official inquiries, I should start with Lord Golbur, who is currently in the city, and then proceed to speak with the Lesser Elves.'

'You may be correct, Son,' said the king. 'I understand that you have a good relationship with Lord Golbur?'

'Yes, Father. During my diplomatic posting for a year at the Bastion, I got on very well with Lord Golbur when he visited there.'

'Yes,' mused Creon. 'Why, now that I think on it, you actually learned a bit of their strange tongue, did you not?'

'It is strange to our ears, rough and unmusical, but there is a deep beauty in it,' said Alfrahil. 'Actually, Father, I am nearly fluent. The tongue of the Elves, which I also learned, is beautiful on the outside and within, like rich music that soothes the ears and captivates the mind.'

'I sometimes have wished that you had less of the diplomat and more of the soldier about you,' said Creon. 'But your talents will serve us well now. You will go to see Lord Golbur tomorrow and ask if there are any "unofficial" bits and pieces of news that he might share with us in light of the recent events here. I will have Shadows accompany you to your meeting with Golbur, and a company of knights to escort you from the city.'

'Father, while I understand the risks, Golbur will not likely be completely open with me if he believes I do not trust him. I must have the authority to command the Shadows that come with me. Since I was nearly killed here in the heart of the City, while under guard, it would seem that the assassins can reach anywhere. I feel that I would be safer if I keep moving, with as few people as possible knowing my whereabouts. Therefore, I must reject the escort you propose.'

'He is correct sire,' Mergin chimed in. 'Until we learn more, the Prince could be attacked again anywhere. It is a calculated risk, but he is right: staying mobile, with Shadows toward him from danger, will keep him safer than broadcasting his movements by assigning him a heavy guard. Besides, it will not do for the crown prince to disappear from view after what has happened. That is how rumors get started. No, he must show himself openly but at the same time carefully. A diplomatic mission, with a handful of Shadows, will be just the thing to restore the aura of invincibility of the royal family.'

'Very well,' said the King irritably. 'But I insist that the Shadows will have the final say as to whether or not any particular situation is safe, and you must abide by their judgment. Can you agree to that?'

'Willingly,' said Alfrahil.

'Good. Then go, my son, and prepare for your journey to the Dwarves.'

'What about the Elves, Father? Shall I meet with Prince Ferox, who is nearby in Ackerlea, after meeting with Golbur?'

'You will not see the lord of the North Forest under any circumstances,' said a stone-faced Creon. 'Nor any of his court. I am sure that there are some Lesser Elves from the Great Forest rather than the Northern Forest that you will be able to speak with.'

'What is wrong with going to see Ferox?' asked a confused Alfrahil.

'Do not mention his name again,' said Creon his face flushing with rage. 'I have enough difficulty these days without everyone questioning my every decision! Find a different Elf to answer your questions. Are we clear about this?'

'Perfectly, father,' said a perplexed Alfrahil.

'Finally, Lord Mergin shall continue his inquiries, and we will watch to see who comes and goes from the out-walls and communicates with your brother to gauge his involvement. When will Daerahil arrive, Lord Mergin?

'He should arrive about midday, my lord. When do you want to see him?'

'I will see him two hours after he arrives. I want you here as well, Alfrahil.'

'I am eager to see Daerahil and learn the truth of his involvement. I must tell you, Father, that I still find it impossible to believe.'

'Such loyalty does you credit, my son. But you shall hear and judge for yourself. There is a passage that leads to a small alcove behind that tapestry over there. Lord Mergin will conduct you there so that you may watch and listen unobserved as I put your brother to the question."

'I would prefer to face him openly,' said Alfrahil.

'What you prefer does not interest me,' snapped Creon with a trace of his former anger. 'This is my command.'

'I will obey, Father,' said Alfrahil, bowing his head.

* * *

Before proceeding to the Healer Hall, in the Third District, Alfrahil had a brief but firm argument with his six guardsmen. While there was a real danger if he wandered around the city, a quick gallop down-hill to the Healer Hall would be unexpected; there would be no time for assassins to plot, as only Alfrahil and his guards would know his intent. The guardsmen seemed unconvinced but could not disobey Alfrahil's direct command.

The journey was without incident, save for those citizens of Titania who, seeing their prince riding without fear and seemingly uninjured, spread the news excitedly, as Alfrahil had hoped. He nodded to their cheers and waves, though the guardsmen were clearly ill at ease.

Bidding his guards to wait outside the Healer Hall, Alfrahil entered. White-washed walls and an immaculately clean white flagstone floor greeted him. The strong smells of medicinal herbs and plants filled the main hall, where many wounded people lay. Some patients had family visiting them, and there was a low hum of conversation present. One old woman wept loudly at the bedside of an old man. Seeing how the common people had suffered in yesterday's events filled Alfrahil with fresh anger and determination to find and punish those responsible.

Seeing Findalas across the hall, he walked quietly toward her. She appeared just as beautiful as she had the night before, and he stared at her with a nearly rapt expression on his face until quietly calling her name.

She looked up, seemingly startled by the sound of her name, and then looking even more flustered as she realized who had spoken. 'My lord prince, I did not expect—'

'Calm yourself, Findalas. My visit is unofficial and informal. I wanted to see my friend Biramin and my guard captain, Alcar. Can you help me find them?'

'Certainly, my lord, but what of your wounds, how are you feeling? You should be in bed resting!' Her face wrinkled in concern.

'I am well enough,' he answered with a laugh, feigning a strength he did not really feel. 'I am stiff and sore, and yes, I probably should be resting, but I cannot be at ease until I learn about my friends.' Alfrahil paused and glanced about the Hall. 'Thank you again for coming to me last night and caring for me, but I feel guilty now, with so many injured here in the hall. Surely there were others in greater need of your services.'

Flushing, Findalas replied with steel in her voice. 'Lord, I saw to all of my seriously injured patients before I came to you. I assure you that none of them were neglected.'

'That is not what I meant, Findalas,' said a chagrined Alfrahil. 'I was trying to thank you for your personal care for me, but I was concerned for those less fortunate than I.'

'My lord...,' Findalas began hesitantly.

Seeing her confusion and anxiety, Alfrahil interrupted. 'No matter, Findalas. Just know that I am grateful. Now, what can you tell me of Biramin?'

Findalas seemed glad of the change of subject. 'He is in a separate room, my lord, as befits his rank and station. He has several arrow wounds, to his legs and arms, none of them truly worrisome. He was wearing the most marvelous coat of mail I have ever seen, light as silk but so strong that broken arrowheads were tangled in it. I have never seen the like.'

'You never will, for it is a coat of pure Platina. But will he recover?'

'Yes, lord. He has a broken left leg, which will heal in six to eight weeks and will cleanly knit. Otherwise, many muscles were pulled and strained, but he will make a full recovery. Alcar, however, was horribly burned; we have him wrapped in our finest healing herbs and are keeping him unconscious with the juice of poppies. I have little hope for him. I have sent an urgent message to Lord Mergin requesting an Elven healer, but I have not received a response.'

'I will ask Lord Mergin about your request upon return to the Citadel. Now, can you take me to Biramin?'

Nodding, she led him to a small private chamber. 'I will be just outside, Lord, if you need me,' Findalas said with a bow.

Alfrahil nodded and opened the door to the room. Inside, he saw a small bright oil lamp, and a very beautiful young Kozaki woman anxiously keeping watch by Biramin's bedside. This was Wynhyrra, Biramin's wife of two months. Her long blonde hair had been plaited back in one thick strand, worn up in the traditional Valkyrja style.

She raised, her clear blue eyes shining with unshed tears, as Alfrahil entered the room, shutting the door behind him. 'My Lord,' she said in a hushed voice. 'Glad am I to see you here. But you are also injured?' as she glanced at the sutures in the middle of his forehead.

'My wounds are nothing,' he said, gesturing to her absently, his eyes on Biramin, whose sleeping form was wrapped in bandages. 'Please, return to your seat, Wynhyrra. There is no need for ceremony between you and me. Tell me, how is Biramin?'

'Lord, thanks to the healers, and especially Findalas, he is much improved,' she replied, seating herself again. 'He was awake this morning for an hour or so and asked after you. After hearing you had a very narrow escape but were safe in the Citadel, he was able to sleep again.'

At that moment, Biramin awoke and in a dry voice asked, 'Is it my Prince before me?'

'Yes,' replied Alfrahil, moving alongside the bed. 'I am here, old friend. How are you feeling?' There was a pitcher of water and glass set on a small table near the bed, and now, as he spoke, he filled a glass and handed it to Biramin.

The man took the glass in a shaky hand and drank deeply. When he spoke, his voice seemed stronger. 'My pride is hurt worse than my body, lord. To think that I was caught in such an ambush! I failed my men, and I failed you, my prince.'

'Nay,' said Alfrahil. 'Speak not of shame or failure. The ambushes were cunningly laid and well planned. You and I are lucky to be alive.'

'Luck had little to do with it,' muttered Biramin. 'It was the shirt of mail your father gifted me with that saved my life. Had I not been wearing it, I would have suffered the same fate as so many of my men.'

'It would be foolish of me to tell you not to mourn your men, as I mourn mine. Long shall it be before the memory of these events grows dim,' said Alfrahil. 'But do not despair or blame yourself, Biramin. I have need of your valor as soon as you are fit to return to duty. You and I will unmask this conspiracy, and our vengeance shall be swift and merciless.'

'I will stand with you on that day, Lord. May it some soon!'

But Alfrahil could see that even this brief exchange had left Biramin exhausted. In another moment, the man was asleep again.

'Thank you, Lord, for seeing my husband,' said Wynhyrra in a whisper, reaching to take the empty glass from her husband's nerveless hand. 'It means a great deal to him—and to me.'

'Nay, it was my privilege, for he is not only my guard captain but my great friend,' said Alfrahil. 'How are you, Wynhyrra?'

Her stony countenance did not soften. 'I am fine. I sent messengers to my cousin Flynn, nephew to the King of Kozak, to ask for his help if needed, and to find the men who tried to take my husband from me.'

'We are working diligently to find the assassins and the men behind the plot, Wynhyrra. Do not trouble yourself, for the men of Eldora will avenge your husband,' said Alfrahil.

'With all due respect, Lord, it was the men of Eldora who put my husband into this bed instead of mine in the first place. I do not know who to trust in these dark times. Only the traditional riders of Kozak do I know and believe in. Brief has it been since I left my life upon the open plain, and always there was the chance of brigands attacking you or your camp, coming to steal your horses if you were not careful. The weather could also not be ignored, but these were known and predictable dangers, unlike these foul assassins that would try to kill my beloved husband. I do not believe the men of this City can be trusted, except for a few, like you, Lord. Even then, I fear you will always do what is best for your realm and not for those whom you should love and care for.'

Alfrahil saw the flash of steely will in her large eyes and knew instinctively that she possessed at least one hidden knife; deadly as she was beautiful. 'I understand your fears, Wynhyrra. Findalas has told me that Biramin will be well enough to return to you in a month or so. I have granted him two weeks leave from that point, so that you may both see to the final stages of his recovery and be joyful again. I have always tried to keep your husband safe, but his duty to me knows no bounds, and he would willingly die for me, as I for him. Trust is indeed very dear in these times, but know this: long ago I pledged myself to your husband's life if that means anything to you.'

'Yes, Lord, it does mean something to me, and I beg your apology for my anger. It was not directed at you, but at these scheming men who do not know the value of life and honor, the desire to grow old with your man and bounce his grandchildren on your knee. Thank you, Lord, for his upcoming leave,' she added with a smile. 'That was kind of you.'

'I will come back to check on him again as soon as I may,' Alfrahil promised. He decided not to mention that he would be leaving the city soon.

Though outwardly calm, Alfrahil was troubled by Wynhyrra's response regarding the trustworthiness of the men of Eldora, and his grief for his best friend threatened to overpower him. Leaving Biramin's chamber, he merely glanced at Findalas, who said nothing yet whose eyes seemed to shimmer with understanding and sympathy.

Alcar's chamber was smaller and less well-appointed than Biramin's. A terrible smell of festering wounds and burned flesh filled the close air, and it was this, as well as the dim light, that caused Alfrahil to pause a moment. Barely suppressing the urge to retch, he waited a moment as his eyes adjusted to the light that fell through a small curtained window; he slowly came to see a narrow bed in which there lay not a person but rather a collection of bandages in the shape of a person. Beside the bed was a bucket containing blood-soaked bandages and other fluids that Alfrahil could not recognize and did not want to inquire about. Now overcome with retching, Alfrahil turned and fled the room and its mephitic odor. Choking down the gorge rising in his throat, he asked Findalas,

'Is he awake?' asked Alfrahil, his voice a throaty husk.

'No, Lord,' replied Findalas with professional detachment. 'He has woken twice, and each time the pain of his wounds has caused him to cry out and scream, so we are keeping him asleep for the next week in hopes that the infection will respond to our treatment and he will begin to heal.'

'But you do not think he will recover,' Alfrahil stated.

'The odds are not good, Lord. Yet I cannot say. Certainly, with an Elven healer, he would have a better chance. I hope he will survive in any case, but even if he does, he was badly burned over most of his body and took two arrows in his back. Regaining the full use of his limbs is doubtful, and his burns will disfigure him hideously for the rest of his life. Alas, despite all our advances in the healing arts, there are still so many wounds and injuries to men that are beyond our powers, and burns are the worst of them.'

With that, the pain and guilt that had assailed Alfrahil even before he'd set foot in the Healers' Hall overwhelmed him. Staggering to the only chair in the hall, he slumped down upon it, his head buried in his hands. Sobbing quietly and then openly, he gave in to his feelings and the terrible memories of the ambushes that overwhelmed him again. He was transfixed by his feelings of helplessness and ineptness, knowing that he was responsible for the deaths of his men, for Biramin's injuries and this man's agony and disfigurement.

'I did nothing, nothing.' he gasped weakly through his sobs, speaking his thoughts aloud. 'I did not know what to do, and most of my men are dead, with Alcar next due to my cowardice and fear. I should have known what to do! I should have acted. I am incompetent to lead men on a parade through the city, much less into combat. My brother is correct—he should be king, not I. I do not have the knowledge, much less the stomach, to prevail in these situations. If I cannot escape a simple ambush, how can I protect the realm? Daerahil would be much better as King someday. Perhaps I should tell Father that I resign the inheritance in favor of my brother.'

With that, he subsided into silence, only choking out unintelligible sounds as grief and anger washed over him. So wrapped up was he in these feelings that he had entirely forgotten about Findalas' presence until she spoke, her voice soft but so unexpected that he started.

'Lord, I have heard from other soldiers who came to see Biramin and Alcar,' she said. 'They described an inferno straight out of hell. They assured me, as I now assure you, that a deadly mind planned the ambushes for months if not years. According to them, you made no poor decisions, escaping as best you could and preserving the succession of the realm, which was your primary duty. Your guardsmen do not condemn you; instead, they praise your determination and courage in escaping the attacks. I beseech you to raise your head with pride and go talk with your guardsmen; they will tell you the truth of my words. While Alcar may die from his wounds, Biramin will recover, the realm will continue, and you will live to be king someday.'

Alfrahil's head rose from his hands at her hopeful words. Letting them settle into his mind for a moment, he began to push the despair and horror back into the recesses of his mind. Several minutes passed as he stared at the wall, his psyche slowly repairing itself to the point where he could consciously think and function again.

'Thank you, Findalas,' he said at last. 'You have brought me back from the abyss. All I saw of myself was a weak man only concerned for his own safety, unfit to lead the realm. Now I can at least face the rest of the day. Perhaps someday I can learn to lead men into combat as well as lead the realm itself. Besides an Elven healer, is there anything you require of me, or of anyone else in the realm to aid Alcar his recovery?'

'Nay, Lord, all we can do is wait; see how he is tomorrow,' said Findalas. 'I spoke only the truth, Lord. You are a man of honor and respect who cares for those that he leads in any capacity. Go now with the assurance that you did all that you could yesterday, and that I and my fellow healers are doing all we can to take care of your men.'

Nodding, Alfrahil thanked her and exited the room. Still deeply shaken by what he had seen, yet also strangely refreshed and heartened by Findalas' words, he returned to the Astrology Tower. There he found Mergin waiting impatiently in the common room, a pained expression on his face and sweat stains on his clothes.

'Lord, we must hurry. Your brother is already here. We are delaying him, but, as you well know, he is not a man who brooks delay patiently.'

'I am ready, Lord Mergin,' he replied. 'Lead on.'

Mergin nodded then pushed aside a tapestry, revealing a hidden panel with a veneer of stones on a wooden surface. He lit a torch contained in a small niche from a candle he brought with him from a table, escorting him along a narrow curved passage, which ended in an alcove with another tapestry hanging in front of it. Here a pinhole had been cunningly placed to provide an observer an unhindered view of the room on the other side—where, placing his eye to the spot, Alfrahil saw his father standing with a frown he recognized all too well.

'Not a word my lord, not a sound until your father asks for you,' Mergin cautioned in a whisper, then turned on his heel and left, leaving Alfrahil alone in the dark.

'*How many secret passages are there in this city that Mergin knows and I do not?*' pondered Alfrahil. '*How many secrets does he keep, revealing them only when it suits his purpose?*'

A noise from the other side of the tapestry stirred Alfrahil from his musings, and he placed his eye back to the pinhole in time to see his brother swiftly enter the room, along with Mergin and a handful of guardsmen. 'He has no look of guile about his face, just fear, and anxiety,' thought Alfrahil. Placing a mental hold upon his sympathy for his beloved but misguided brother, he nearly gasped when he saw his father make contact with his brother's mind. Not because he was surprised that Creon would interrogate Daerahil, but because Daerahil resisted so successfully. No other man, Alfrahil included, had lasted more than a few seconds against Creon's will, but Daerahil held out for nearly a full minute before yielding. As his brother began to shriek and finally collapsed to the floor in impotent rage, Alfrahil was horrified by the level of cruelty his father exhibited. Creon offered no pity or help to Daerahil. He simply waited for him to rise from the floor.

At last, summoned by his father, Alfrahil emerged from behind the tapestry in a state of shock, wishing that these terrible events had not happened. Informing his brother that he held himself reconciled, he was surprised to hear the venomous tone of his brother's reply. Alfrahil tried to remain impassive, but he felt his brother's wounded psyche and bitter anger sweep the room, touching his own mind for a moment. As Daerahil strode from the chamber, Alfrahil was overcome by the thought that his father had gone too far, that his brother was clearly innocent, and this terrible demonstration had served only to humiliate him needlessly and blow upon the coals of rebellion already smoldering in his soul.

'That was too much, Father,' he said after Daerahil had gone. 'You hurt him terribly and embarrassed him. You could have done this more gently, and in private. Why do you hate him so?'

Creon said nothing for a few moments, his face fixed upon the doorway until at last, he turned. Only then did Alfrahil see the pain and confusion he had been hiding. 'Do not seek to rebuke me, my son. Your brother, his ideas, his very popularity, constitutes threats to my reign and to the supremacy of Eldora. I will hear no more. Now go.'

'So it is true what my brother said,' Alfrahil responded, though it took all his courage to do so. 'You are more concerned with your pride than with the truth.'

'I said go!' his father thundered. 'Or do you wish to suffer the same examination as your brother?'

'I will go, Father. There have been times when I have disagreed with you. Times I have been angry at you; even disappointed. But never until today have I felt ashamed of you.'

Creon did not reply but communicated his displeasure with a silent mental thrust that caused a sharp pain to bloom behind Alfrahil's eyes—pain that was but a promise of worse to come. Unable to suppress a cry, Alfrahil ran half-blindly for the door.

He returned in anger and humiliation to his temporary chambers in the tower, reflecting that at last, he understood something of what his brother felt. But he would have given much not to have gained his knowledge in this way. All he wanted now was some Dwarven ale, a light meal, and time to shake these last minutes from his mind.

Chapter Nine

Dwarves

Awakening the next day, Alfrahil proceeded down through the Astrology Tower and gingerly climbed into the saddle of a gentle gelding brought from the messenger stables. His own horse was still recovering from two arrow wounds. Trotting around the devastation in the Second District, he made his way to the great plain of the City and toward his meeting place. Only Shadows accompanied him, disguised as common merchants. Two days' stubble on Alfrahil's normally clean-shaven face, along with some charcoal under his eyes, disguised him from the people of the city, and he found himself unnoticed, carried with the gentle yet inexorable tide of city folk about their business.

Arriving within the Eleventh District, Alfrahil crossed many streets until in a dark and dank cul-de-sac; he came to an alehouse: the Hammer and Tongs. A message sent to the Dwarven mission the night before by Mergin had requested that Lord Golbur meet Alfrahil here, under conditions of strictest secrecy, and a reply had been received in the affirmative.

Signaling the Shadows still unobtrusively guarding him to stay back and keep hidden unless he called for them, Alfrahil strode to the entrance of the alehouse and entered. He had barely time enough to dodge a very tall man whose body was flying through the air directly toward him. He stepped aside with alacrity, and the man continued his journey out the door and into the street beyond.

'My mother would be ashamed to see me defeat such pitiful foes,' spoke a voice in Dwarvish.

Smiling inwardly, Alfrahil proceeded toward the bar, where a small group of men was clustered, keeping their heads down both literally and figuratively now that the strongest of them lay unconscious outside in the street. The rest of the alehouse was filled with Dwarves, who were muttering to themselves and casting dangerous looks toward him and toward the other men. It did not seem to Alfrahil that the tension had been defused by the emphatic exit of the tall man a moment earlier. Rather, it seemed like both sides were taking a pause in which to consider how best they might continue their fighting.

Catching the bartender's eye, Alfrahil called in Dwarvish for a glass of proper ale. The bartender showed no surprise at a man speaking Dwarvish but simply and carelessly slopped a battered, stained pewter mug upon the counter. Then, removing a bottle from under the counter, he removed the cork and poured half the contents into the mug, setting the bottle down with a soft thump when the mug was full.

Speaking in the common tongue now, Alfrahil asked, 'Is this authentic, unaltered Dwarvish ale?'

Yes,'the barkeep said in a surly tone. 'This is indeed true Dwarvish ale, brought all the way from the Bastion, but you drink it at your own risk, sir. There are not many men who can stomach it. That will be one silver piece.'

Alfrahil reached into his purse for the coin, and added another one, stating quietly, 'For your trouble.'

The barkeep actually looked at Alfrahil then, and his eyes slowly opened widely in recognition.

Alfrahil grabbed his hand, pulling him closer, whispering. 'Well met, barkeep. Let's keep my identity quiet for now, shall we?'

Nodding mutely, with an expression that seemed to indicate he expected nothing good would come of the prince's visit; the barkeep turned away and resumed his desultory cleaning.

As Alfrahil's eyes continued to adjust to the dim light, he noticed that he had drawn the attention of the Dwarves at the bar with his fluent use of their tongue. Little did they know that he had long ago studied their language with a scholar at the Bastion, and there were few words unknown to him.

Alfrahil addressed the bartender again. 'I would like a full dozen more bottles, barkeep. I feel my thirst catching up with me.'

At this, the Dwarvish muttering subsided slightly, and looks of alcoholic greed shone upon the faces of many of the nearby patrons. When the bottles had been delivered, Alfrahil turned to the Dwarves and, again speaking in their language, said, 'If there are any Dwarves of merit here who can handle good ale, they should come and take a glass.'

Several horny hands extended themselves, and Alfrahil had to order another dozen bottles before the Dwarves were satisfied with his generosity. The men in the bar, meanwhile, regarded him silently, taking a glass each, viewing this sudden purveyor of drinks with suspicion, but they smiled and drank their ale quietly. Alfrahil waited, sipping his potent brew, which was flavored with the honey of the Chilton men and the scents of the flowers of the vale of Aphon ... and also with the keen edge of iron and the tang of gold and silver. The taste of metal was in everything touched by the hands of the Dwarves.

After a moment, a hooded Dwarf approached on his right side. Leaning close, he whispered in Dwarvish, 'Hail and well met, Crown Prince. Golbur, son of Goldan, your faithful friend.'

'Your most obedient servant,' replied Alfrahil softly in the correct Dwarven fashion.

'It is encouraging to see the Prince of Men enjoying the simple pleasure of the Dwarves,' said Golbur, dropping his hood.

Hale and hardy, the only child of Goldan, Lord of the Caves, Golbur was of medium height and build for a Dwarf, yet his unremarkable stature detracted not a whit from the noble air he possessed not only by virtue of his proud heritage but by his position as Dwarf Lord of the Edelhohle. His beard was brown and thick, and only his horny hands betrayed his two hundred plus years. Golbur's knowledge was deep, his wisdom and judgment bywords among Dwarves and Men alike. Less passionate and obstinate than many of his kind, he fit the changing needs of his people better than any other Dwarf chieftain known to Alfrahil. It was precisely this flexible and affable nature, combined with the respect shown to Golbur by other Dwarves that he intended to rely upon today.

Responding to Golbur's statement, Alfrahil said with a smile, 'Simple? Perhaps not overly ornate, but little of the lives or the crafts of the Dwarves could be said to be simple.'

With a smile and a nod, Golbur replied, 'I see the courtesy of Men did not completely pass away with the end of the Great War.' Raising his mug of ale, he continued, 'I thank you for your generosity.'

'You are more than welcome,' said Alfrahil. 'While I hope that the courtesy of Men remains in Nostraterra, I know that you certainly taught the men of Farley new respect for the might of the Dwarves.'

'So you heard that tale?' said Golbur with a chuckle. 'It was overstated—a few young rowdies that were taught some manners, nothing more.'

'Nothing more?' replied Alfrahil. 'Ten men left unconscious for two days, and twelve others so badly bruised their mothers could not have recognized them. You call that overstated?'

'Aye,' replied Golbur with a gleam in his eye, 'it was a good tussle after our fashion. We gave them fair odds, after all. Only four of us participated in the affray.'

Wonderingly, Alfrahil asked, 'Were the Men that drunk, or are the Dwarves such fearsome warriors that they can toss soldiers of Farley about like a child's toys?'

'A little of both,' replied Golbur, and took another drink. 'But that incident is not what brings you here. How can I aid you?'

'I am looking for help in solving the mystery of yesterday's attacks upon me and my men,' Alfrahil said.

'I know nothing that I have not already passed on to your father's minister, Lord Mergin, so I don't see how I can help you, my Lord Prince,' said Golbur. 'I and all my people are heartily sorry for the loss of men and property, and glad in your escape.'

'I hoped that you would know more than you had told, or that new information might have come to you during the night. But no matter, we shall unmask this conspiracy ourselves. Still, as long as we are here, we might as well iron out that new trade agreement, don't you think, Lord Golbur?'

Casually, Golbur agreed. 'Not a bad idea, come to think of it; may my fellow Dwarves consume some more ale while you and I talk?'

'Of course,' replied Alfrahil. He placed several more silver pieces on the bar to keep the beer flowing and saw a relieved smile on the barkeep's face. It had become routine for officers of the City guard and army to take what they wanted from merchants instead of paying for their items. This custom was vehemently opposed by the King, his sons, and the Council, but it thrived anyway. Most people looked at it as a special tax and a form of insurance against criminal acts or costly accidents. Now, at the sound of Alfrahil's silver on the bar, the Dwarves let out a rough cheer and began calling for refills.

'My Lord, as ever, you have the touch of a diplomat,' said Golbur.

Alfrahil waved aside the praise. 'Let us speak frankly, Lord Golbur. We know each other's mettle and worth do we not?'

Golbur nodded. 'Fair enough, lad. But if we are to speak frankly, then let us go somewhere absolutely private, away from my Dwarves and your Shadows.'

'Do you have such a place in mind?'

'I do. We shall repair to a small private workshop that I own nearby.'

Golbur led him out of the tavern and down a narrow side street, where the only sounds were those of the forge, the whoosh of bellows, the clang of a hammer on metal and the hissing screech of glowing metal quenched in water. The smells of hot iron and burning coal were everywhere, and Alfrahil was relieved when he was led through a small shop where Dwarves were laboring over gold and silver. Golbur led him to a large wooden door at the back. The Dwarf Lord took out a long, ornate bright steel key and opened this door, gesturing for Alfrahil to descend the stairs in front of him, the way downlit by small smoky torches.

Alfrahil descended a dozen stairs, finding himself in a small workshop, cold and dusty.

Golbur came down the stairs behind him, lit two oil lamps, and, in the yellow glow, said, 'Now, lad, we can speak in private, where no one can overhear us.'

Alfrahil asked, 'What news do you have of the ambush Golbur; that you would not pass on to my father and his ministers?'

'Are you questioning my honor? Do you claim that I was less than forthright with my answers to Lord Mergin's questions?' demanded Golbur gruffly.

'No, Lord Golbur, just—'

'Peace, lad, I am only jesting. You are right. We did not report everything that we knew in our message to your father, but for good reason. I had the preliminary report from documents located in that joy house of yours. It seems your brother is one of the owners of that house, and that he has financial dealings with Minister Zarthir.'

'I did not realize Daerahil was part owner of the joy house, but, knowing his habits as I do, and his friendship with Zarthir, I cannot claim to be surprised. Anything else?'

'Lad, we also found receipts for goods purchased from Dwarves and Elves. Mostly clothing, but some bows and arrows from the Elves and a very expensive receipt for an item referred to as 'the curled steel,' which we believe to be Dwarven in nature. But we can't determine precisely what it is, save that it cost a fortune. Also, there are indications that other Dwarven engineers have been quietly contracted by Zarthir and some of his friends, though regarding what we do not know. Therefore, I have to look into my own people to see if some of them are doing things that they should not be doing. Also, I do not know which men on your father's Council to trust, and even the Elves might be involved with this mess. That is what I did not tell your father yesterday, and until I have confirmation of my suspicions, the official position of the Dwarves will remain that we are continuing to investigate. I will ask high and low amongst my people and see what else I can discover for you. Now, do you have any news of your own?'

Alfrahil did not reply, but reached into his cloak and retrieved the grapnel made of a Platina alloy. This he handed to Golbur.

Golbur looked at it momentarily without recognition. Then, testing the strength of the slender tines and weighing it in his hand, he said, 'Gods, lad, where did you find this?'

'One of the ambush sites, is it important?'

'I have only seen this design of grapnel once, larger and sturdier. It was used once and only once in aiding our realm from a terrible danger, but those grapnels were soon melted down. I do not know who would have made this smaller version, but clearly, this is Dwarven in origin. I will send secret messages to Nerea, the great Dwarf mines in the Icy Mountains, and to the Bastion. All I can say for now is that this was not forged in my realm of Edelhohle. Clearly, here is proof that some of my brethren were involved at least indirectly in the ambushes. For that, I am most sorry. They will pay, never fear.'

'I do not doubt you on either score, Golbur,' said Alfrahil. 'One more thing: our metalsmiths tell us that these grapnels could not have supported the weight of a Man without some kind of magical reinforcement. I do not ask for the secrets of the Dwarves, and I do not inquire into them, only inform you of what we have learned.'

'If true, that would be a most unfortunate circumstance,' said Golbur with a deep frown, returning the Grapnel to Alfrahil.

'Keep me informed of what you find,' said Alfrahil. 'But I will tell you now in confidence that there is also evidence of the involvement of the Lesser Elves.'

'What evidence?'

'A cloak of concealment, worked with Elven magic to make its wearer all but invisible. Some of the archers who attacked me were wearing them.'

'Elves and Dwarves, allied against Men—it makes no sense,' said Golbur, a perplexed expression on his face.

'That is why I wish to learn more. I would be grateful if you could find four Dwarves that you trust implicitly and send them to me. I may have a mission for them outside the City.'

'What kind of mission? Where will you send them?'

'I prefer not to say as yet. I must consult with my father first. But I sense that we may need their eyes and ears. I will let you know soon. But make certain that the Dwarves you choose have some skill on horseback and can get along with Elves.'

'Horseback!' cried Golbur. 'You know us Dwarves scorn the use of those cursed beasts and despise Elves!'

'Yes, but surely you know some trustworthy Dwarves who are open-minded about horses and Elves.'

'I could find a few such Dwarves, I suppose,' said Golbur. 'I confess I am more curious than ever about this mission of yours.'

'All in good time, Golbur,' said Alfrahil. 'I must speak to my father, as I said; and to the Elves as well.'

'Whom among the Elves will you seek out?'

'I had thought to approach Ferox, King Albericus' nephew, who is occupied with the cleansing of Ackerlea.' Despite his father's insistence that he not speak with Ferox, Alfrahil knew of no other Elf that would be senior enough to give him valuable, yet unofficial, information.

Golbur rolled his eyes scornfully. 'Ferox is much occupied with Ferox. He fancies himself the Elf Lord of Ackerlea and the future King of the Lesser Elves, should Albericus ever suffer a hunting accident.'

Shaking his head, Alfrahil stated, 'I never knew worldly ambitions plagued the other races of Nostraterra besides us unfortunate Men.'

Golbur snorted. 'Who would think the crown prince of Eldora could be so naïve? All races are plagued by worldly ambitions, lad. Let me tell you of the Dwarves and one of our lords, Tillo IV. Do you wish to speak of ambition? Why Tillo has set his...' Golbur trailed off in a sigh. 'The internal politics of the Dwarves are not really relevant to the subject at hand. But to answer your question, I recommend that you seek out Hilforas, grandson of Delfin, the King's uncle. He is the leader of the Elven scouts and rides frequently between Ackerlea and the Great Forest. I believe he is near to Estellius now, your ruined river city. Unlike Ferox, he is said to be honest and true, with no interest in petty politics.'

'I thank you, Golbur. I will seek him out. Now, tell me of you and your kin, for it is long since we two have spoken: how are things in Edelhohle?'

'Come and see for yourself, lad. Glad would I be to show you the wonders of my kingdom! There we mine gold and silver and tend the Rainbow Gardens of Stone. Ah, if you could see the great chamber there! It is filled with stalactites and stalagmites of stone, great crystals, purple and pink, from the palest to the darkest shades, found nowhere else in Nostraterra. Smaller chambers exist that contain still more exotic crystals. One winks back at our torches with all the hues of emeralds, another with the tinge of sapphire. But all we see are the merest reflections, for the chamber openings are too small to allow us access. Dwarven engineers on pilgrimages from all other Dwarven realms supplement my own miners as we work to safely enlarge the openings of these Chambers of Wonder, as they are known, so that one day, perhaps in my lifetime, we can enter into these most beautiful works of our creator. In great confidence, because of our friendship, I will tell you of our efforts in Nerea, if you promise to not breathe a word of it to anyone.'

Slightly puzzled, Alfrahil agreed, and Golbur went on with his tale.

'As all know, Nerea was once our greatest city, our deepest, richest mine and ancestral home. Probing ever deeper beneath the earth, Dwarven priests awakened a Fire Demon whose evil power brought my people low. Thus was Nerea lost to us. And even now, a hundred years after the fall of the Fire Demon, there remains much evil there.' Golbur shivered slightly at the racial memory that had haunted the Dwarves for thousands of years. 'Fell creatures yet stalk the unremitting dark. Yet we have returned—yes, just as you Men will one day return to Malius and reclaim that foul city, so have we now reclaimed our home. Slowly we are draining the deeps and opening the passages that have been closed for so long.'

'That is wonderful news.' said Alfrahil, clapping the Dwarf Lord on one shoulder.

'Why there are wonders yet to tell,' Golbur exclaimed with a laugh. 'We have found Platina, lad! Platina! A seam so rich it might never run dry. And what's more, we are beginning to mine Nerea for that most precious of metals for the first time in hundreds of years. Soon we will once again be exporting Platina to the free world—soon, but not yet, for we must first replenish our own stores and reacquaint ourselves with the properties of this wondrous metal. Should the darkness come again, it will be well to have weapons forged of Platina and walls made stronger by it—as are the gates of your fair city.'

'The darkness?' replied Alfrahil. 'The darkness was destroyed with Magnar.'

'Was it? Was it not darkness that nearly struck you down yesterday in the narrow, twisting streets of Titania?' Smiling grimly, Golbur went on. 'The oldest of Dwarvish legends states that the darkness will ever return, lad, until the day that Elves and Dwarves call each brother. And while I like many of the Lesser Elves that I have worked with over the years, there are few we would call brother today, especially since the Great Tragedy.'

'The mysterious Great Tragedy,' echoed Alfrahil. 'I know that something terrible happened a hundred years ago or so, but no Dwarf or Elf has ever spoken frankly to my father or to me about this all-but-mythical event.'

'It is no myth, lad.'

'My father has asked Dwarf Lords about it before, and Lesser Elves, too, and he has always been politely but firmly informed that it is none of his business.'

'Then I will share one more secret with you today, as a token of my sincere regret that any Dwarf may have been involved in yesterday's unpleasantness. Tell your father and Mergin if you must, but this must not become public knowledge. You must swear to it.'

'On my honor as the crown prince of Eldora.'

'Very good. Our troubles with the Elves began shortly after the fall of Magnar, at least according to the Priests of Parsifal.'

'Priests of Parsifal. I have heard of them, especially in the construction of the Great Gates, but I know little of them. How do they influence your realm?'

'The Priests of Parsifal are Dwarves who speak with the Flame Dancers, the magical fire spirits who give us our knowledge of metallurgy and of magic. Only the priests are ever allowed to see them, much less speak with them, if you can call it that.'

Alfrahil's listened avidly, saying nothing.

'Come, lad, didn't anyone tell you of the Flame Dancers or the Priests when you were studying at the Bastion?'

'I heard the name "Flame Dancers," Golbur, but I never met a priest, much less saw a Flame Dancer. There were certain areas of the mountain, particularly the lower levels, where I was not allowed to go. I simply assumed that there were treasuries there that the Dwarves did not want to reveal. Your secular scholars were the ones who taught me your language, and I was not allowed to mingle with other Dwarves without their supervision. No one told me anything about your mythology or sources of magic, though I asked many questions.'

'The damn teachers did their job too well,' Golbur said. 'Though you know our language passably well for a Man, you learned a history significantly altered from reality. Apparently, the Lord of the Bastion wanted to keep the divisions of the Dwarves quiet. He may have had priestly help as well in conspiring to keep this information from you. But see now where this has gotten us? Dwarfs involved in the quarrels of men. Bah! Listen well, lad. I'm going to give you a remedial lesson. This is a day it seems for the sharing of secrets.' He shook his head and chuckled, though there was little enough of mirth in the sound.

'According to myth, rumor, and the religion of the priests, the Bastion, the Sandy Hills, Nerea, and possibly the Ocean Range each has a great fire pit where molten rock from the heart of the earth bubbles to the surface. It was there at the dawn of our existence that we discovered the Flame Dancers, spirits of fire that come and dance amid the flames for a few moments and then return to the molten rock. Long ago, certain Dwarves learned

243

to communicate with the Flame Dancers, or so they claimed. It was these Dwarves, the predecessors to the priests of Parsifal; that gave us the first secret skills to work metals. Skills to work stone soon followed, and magic to extend our lives long past their normal span were also given us.'

'Why do you say "claimed" when referring to these Dwarves and their communication with the fiery spirits?'

'Because, lad, unless you are a priest, you never get to see the fire pits, much less a Flame Dancer. Not even I, the Lord of Edelhohle, have seen the fire pits or the Dancers. The priests claim that the Flame Dancers whisper secrets to them. How, when, and why they will not say. The priests keep these secrets quite close to their chests, but once in a great while some new secret concerning metals, gems, stonework, and the like is given to us by the Priests. Much of the time, they keep their knowledge to themselves in order to maintain their power in the realm. It is only when they can profit from the disclosure of their knowledge that they share it with the rest of us Dwarves.'

'You said that you do not trust them ... Why is that so?' asked Alfrahil.

'They preach and proselytize the superiority of Dwarves over the rest of the races of Nostraterra,' replied Golbur, 'demanding that we isolate ourselves from all others. Some of the priests are demanding that we stop trading with Men and Elves, and hide away in the mountains. They are growing more and more numerous and dangerous. I have banished them from my realm, and they have little influence in the Ocean Range, but they have become a power amongst the Dwarven people in Nerea, the Sandy Hills, and particularly within the Bastion. I fear that there will be conflict amongst my own people before the hills have grown much older.'

'Why have you not said anything about this to me or my father before today?' asked Alfrahil.

'Lad, your father may be the High King of Nostraterra, but his attitude toward Elves, Dwarves, and non Eldoran Men are difficult to endure sometimes. Many of us are concerned that he wants to take away the freedom and rights of the Dwarves. This is another reason that the Priests of Parsifal have become so powerful in playing on our fears.'

'That is absurd, Golbur! My father wants to pacify and control Shardan, Azhar, and parts of Hagar, but he has no designs on expanding the boundaries of our kingdom any farther than they were historically. Besides, we need the aid of the Dwarves too much, even if my father were so inclined, to risk alienating them. On this you have my word, both now and as the future king of Eldora.'

'Your word has always been good enough for me, lad, and it is a relief to know that these rumors of King Creon's thoughts are just that: rumors. I will send messengers to the other Dwarf Lords later today.'

'Were you really so concerned about my father's ambitions?' asked an incredulous Alfrahil.

'Aye, lad, to a degree. But now I suspect that the Priests are behind these rumors, seeking to cause further divisions in my people. Rest assured that I will expose this nonsense for what it is: nonsense.'

'But what has any of this to do with the Great Tragedy?'

'Listen and you will see. According to our ancient legends, a Great Fire Spirit lives far beneath the ground, providing the heat found below the earth. He causes the molten rock to spew from fiery mountains and springs of hot water to gush steam into the air. His children are said to be the Flame Dancers, and it was hundreds of years ago, long before Magnar came to power, that the priests of Nerea tried to control the Flame Dancers rather than just speak with them. They created a powerful spell and attempted to summon the great Fire Spirit himself. Instead, his most powerful child, a Flame Dancer was transformed into a Fire

Demon by the flawed magic of the summoning. Before you ask, I do not know how the priests could have had such power, but according to legend they did. Regardless, a terrible Fire Demon appeared from the fire pit, slaying all the priests within the sacred chamber. Soon, growing in strength, the Demon was able to do something that no other Flame Dancer had ever done: leave the fire pit for hours, even days. Swiftly the Demon slew the rest of the Dwarves in the deep mines, with the other Dwarves fleeing to other realms or wandering as refugees throughout Nostraterra.

'The Fire Demon, Baldur, enlarged the fire pit in Nerea and was able to prevent the Flame Dancers from visiting the fire pits in other Dwarven realms, keeping them under his control in Nerea.'

'How was the Fire Demon defeated?'

'For reasons known only to themselves, one hundred years after the fall of Magnar, the Lesser Elves sent their greatest Water Spirit, Pluvia, to the Mines of Nerea, and this Spirit descended into the Mines with her most loyal Elven followers. There the Water Spirit fought the Fire Demon and the Flame Dancers it had bent to its will. Eventually, the Demon was defeated, but the cost was the life of the Water Spirit.

'Once the rumors reached us of what had happened we began assembling scout teams to verify that it was safe to return. These teams were primarily composed of refugees from Nerea—Dwarven males, females, and even a few children—and they confirmed that the Fire Demon was indeed dead. It was then that the Lesser Elves of the North Forest interfered, demanding recompense for the loss of their Water Spirit. The Dwarves of Nerea refused, and conflict broke out immediately. Who actually started the fight is unknown, but the Elves overwhelmed the Dwarves, slaying all of the Males, most of the Females, and even some of the children. This atrocity was reported back to Edelhohle, and messengers were dispatched to the Bastion. Before we could dispatch an army to retake the mines, the Elves began looting the treasures of Nerea, and much gold and gems were taken back by the Lesser Elves to their Northern Forest. Thankfully, the armories containing Platina and our suits of enhanced mail were too deep to be discovered quickly. Once the Dwarven army arrived, more slaughter ensued, but now it was the Elves who were slain and driven out of the Mines.

'We have been in Nerea ever since. Today, relations are still poor between the Northern Forest and the Dwarves, but relatively recently Albericus, King of the Lesser Elves, who dwells in the Great Forest, commanded his nephew, Ferox, who instigated the Great Tragedy, to stop attacking Dwarves, as had been his habit since the Tragedy.'

'What, the same Ferox we spoke of earlier?'

'There could not be two such,' said Golbur grimly. 'Now you see why I advised against dealing with him. At any rate, when news of Albericus' unilateral gesture reached the Bastion, a similar command was issued by Tillo. Thus a sort of unofficial ceasefire was put into effect, and for five years now, no Dwarf has killed an Elf, and no Elf has slain a Dwarf. Still, the peace is an uneasy one, and Elves and Dwarves do not trust each other—or, for that matter, themselves—to mingle freely, afraid that some accidental insult or unintentional slight, to say nothing of insults and slights purposefully delivered, might reignite hostilities. It is my hope and belief that one day the Lesser Elves and Dwarves will be friends and allies again. Indeed, among my own people, I have encouraged low-level trade meetings with the Lesser Elves of the Great Forest. All strictly unofficial, of course, but the first step to improved relations, you might say. But such is not the desire of the Priests of Parsifal.'

'There is one more thing,' said Alfrahil. 'Is there any news or even rumors of threats upon the borders of your land?'

'Well,' mused Golbur, 'there was that troop of Dwarvish lads who came in from patrol in the Never Summer Mountains claiming they had seen a dragon.'

'A dragon!' cried Alfrahil. 'No dragon has been seen in Nostraterra since the Great War! Do you believe dragons have returned to Nostraterra?'

'Truthfully, I do not know,' Golbur replied to an astonished Alfrahil. 'The Never Summer Range is largely unexplored, due to the severe cold and the great snowfields. There is much there that is unknown to us. Only now are mining survey parties traversing those distant lands. Besides this unconfirmed report of a dragon, there is nothing I can place my finger upon, my Lord, but some of my kin who are more friendly to Albericus' folk have reported broken bits of conversation overheard during nights of revelry that allow me to think that the Elves might know more,'said Golbur. 'I will let you know what we find.'

* * *

After taking his leave of Golbur, Alfrahil rejoined his Shadows and rode to the outer messenger stables. Caelus was waiting there, in charge of the prince's guard detachment for the day with Alcar hovering near death in the Healer Hall and Biramin too ill to resume his duties. Biramin's second in command had died next to him during the ambush, and there was no one else who had as much experience available to act as Alfrahil's guard captain. Also waiting were one hundred guardsmen, provided by the king. Seeing this escort, Alfrahil sighed, for he had rejected Creon's offer of these men, not wanting his movements to be so conspicuous. But it seemed that the king, as he often did, had decided his own judgment trumped that of his son and Lord Mergin. Knowing there was nothing to be done; Alfrahil returned the salute of the escort captain and rode out toward the city gates.

Once through the gates, he and his men galloped along the road that traversed the outlands, passing tilled fields and ordered streams. Alfrahil and his men soon reached the south gate of the Out-Walls. Saluted by the outlier guard, Alfrahil exited through the outer gates. He noted that the walls appeared to be in excellent condition. While other buildings may have suffered neglect, the memory of the great siege was still powerful, and the City's engineers made certain that these defenses, at least, were properly maintained.

A mile later, the ruins of Estellius were clearly visible, with construction scaffolding blurring the outlines of taller buildings. At a smooth canter, it took Alfrahil's company two hours to reach the outskirts of the river city. Alfrahil saw construction work that was slowly but steadily restoring the ruined city to its former glory. Soon Estellius would be a thriving city again, contributing to the might of the country. But more work was being done here than mere renovation and rebuilding; more than civic pride.

King Creon had long desired to seek the lost Acies of Estellius, the master crystal set that would allow the user to see through all three other sets given to Men. Only the powers of the Greater Elves who had created the Acies could destroy them, so it was generally believed that the Acies must have survived the Great War. If found, they would be intact: their power as great as ever. Creon was determined to take that power for Eldora. The crystal set of Estellius was believed to be buried somewhere in the ruins of Estellius or beneath the bed of the River Aphon, along whose banks the city was set. The search was very much like looking for a needle in a haystack and Creon had made the project a small but still important priority.

Viewing Estellius now closely, Alfrahil was pleasantly surprised to see how much progress had been made. Indeed, parts of the northern outskirts of the city were already inhabited, settled by the families of the men working to reclaim the rest. Nor was it only workers and their families who had taken up residence in the reviving city. A number of farmers had settled there, taking advantage of Creon's policies encouraging cultivation of the old, abandoned farmsteads, and a few men of business, mostly merchants, kept houses there as well. Before too much longer, Alfrahil hoped, other settlers might move in—homeless veterans of the Shardan campaigns and their families as well as other honorable citizens of Titania who had fallen on hard times through no fault of their own.

The road to the Aphon Bridge had recently been repaired, and the great gray flagstones, shipped all the way from the hills of the Mala Brynn, echoed beneath the cantering hooves of the horses. Sparks from their iron shoes flashed against the small grains of Flint and Chert contained within the surface of the flagstones, adding an air of the supernatural about Alfrahil and his guard.

The bridge itself, though repaired, was narrow, forming a natural choke point for any foes seeking to cross the river. Secretly, after the Great War, the bridge supports were rigged with barrels of secret blasting fire created by the last Earth Spirit of Eldora. Triggered, the blasting fire could and would demolish the bridge, sending the graceful arches tumbling into Aphon. Alfrahil remembered his father declaring that all the great attacks upon Eldora always came from south of the river, honoring history but filled with a healthy dose of paranoia and personal hatred. This justified these rather drastic safety precautions in Creon's mind, though Alfrahil had his doubts that all those from Shardan were treacherous, bent upon destruction.

After the war, despite Creon's paranoia, trade routes were restored within and without the realm of Eldora, connecting Lesser Elves, Dwarves and Men from all over Nostraterra with one another. Few could afford the honey and jams of the Hermits of the Southwest Highlands, but those who could enjoyed a taste that encapsulated the wildflowers better than any other.

The Lesser Elves sent out bows and arrows, along with light boats that had no equal. Dwarven goods from the Bastion and the Sandy Hills and fine hops and barley from Chilton, along with preserved meats, for which the Chilton men had become famous, were also in high demand. From southwest along the river, the fisherfolk sent their catch, both fresh and dried, up-river, while the Men of Shardan sent their annual tribute of gold and elephant tusks.

All of this commerce was good for the economy of the City and paid for many of the public works projects, such as the investiture of Malius and the reconstruction of Estellius. But both Alfrahil and Mergin had grave doubts as to the accuracy of the taxes and duties that were collected. Far too few men had far too much wealth for there to be an equitable distribution of all these monies. Alfrahil mused that he might speak with his father about having Prince Paladir of Nen Brynn add the customs duties of Estellius to his supervision. While this might place too much power in the prince's hands, Paladir was nothing if not scrupulously honest.

Clattering over the bridge, Alfrahil admired the mighty Aphon below. The broad expanse of the river was dotted with boatmen and ferrymen moving their cargoes up and down its length, calling out to each other and singing as they went. Directly below he saw the sunken battlements and broken bridge pilings that had once supported the heart of the city of Estellius itself. Somewhere down there, mused Alfrahil, the master crystal set of all the Acies might still lie, covered in broken stone and decayed woods eaten by the river worms, slimy with algae. Other treasures were there for the finding: gold and silver both wrought and in coins, precious gems and ancient statues, and other valuable items lurked under the mud and silt of the river bottom. Not for nothing did the lesser sons of the fisherfolk dive into those perilous depths, fixing ropes and grapnels to the ancient ruins, risking their lives for a find that might bring them—even after the king had taken his half—more than they might otherwise earn in a lifetime of hard labor. What drew them, even more, was the reward that Creon had promised to anyone who should recover the lost Acies: the finder's weight in gold and precious stones. Alfrahil smiled, remembering a young man who had paid a crystal-maker in Titania an entire month's wages to make a counterfeit Acies, though no one in the kingdom, other than the king himself, actually knew what they looked like. The King had been so amused when the dripping youth had presented his crystal tubes that, instead of punishing him, he had given him command of a small company of divers, stating that such ingenuity, while misplaced, was not to be overlooked. Still, Alfrahil's heart quailed when he thought of the number of young men who died every year, trapped beneath the debris or bursting their lungs on one final dive late in the day. So many young men lost, seeking in the depths of the Aphon a treasure that might be somewhere else entirely.

'*And even if it is here*,' thought Alfrahil, '*what good will it do the King? How many Acies can be used to see at one time*?'

While Alfrahil knew the master crystal set was rumored to contain many qualities that the Acies of Titania, Amadeus, and Hiberius did not, what they specifically were only Creon knew: secrets that were useless until and if the master set was found. The Amadeus set was currently useless as Creon refused to teach Prince Frederick how to use it. Alfrahil knew that, as the heir to the throne, someday his father would teach him to use the Acies, but Creon seemed in no hurry to do so.

Alfrahil came out of his thoughts as they left the bridge and set foot on the southern shore. Here the only rebuilding that had yet occurred was to the defenses and earthworks. Seeing that the sun was already setting, Alfrahil decided to press no farther today. Quarters had been prepared for him on the southern edge of the city. There he inquired of the local guard detachment where the encampment of the Lesser Elves was to be found, and, on receiving the answer, dispatched a messenger inviting Hilforas to visit the next morning, after his inspection of the southern outworks. Afterward, he stripped off his armor and clothing, took a steaming hot bath, enjoyed a hearty dinner washed down with a mug of the Dwarven ale that he had developed a taste for while studying at the Bastion—a keg of which he brought with him whenever possible on long trips such as this—and fell into a deep and dreamless sleep.

Chapter Ten

Elves

Alfrahil arose early the next morning and breakfasted quickly, eager to meet with Hilforas and see what the Lesser Elves could tell him about the cloaks used in the ambush. An Elf messenger was conducted into his presence and told him that Hilforas had received his invitation and would ride down from Hiberius to meet with him later that afternoon. Alfrahil thanked the Elf, and then embarked on his inspection tour of the southern breast-works of Estellius.

Luncheon had been arranged at a nearby inn. Alfrahil walked there along the riverbank with Caelus and his other guards, enjoying the peaceful surroundings. There were no trees here, nor for ten leagues east and west within two furlongs of the river's edge. While willows and small fruit trees would grow most handily, ancient decrees denying cover for an attacking enemy-held to this day. Instead, vegetable gardens, vineyards, and patches of sun-loving herbs grew here, well-tended by the local farmers.

Alfrahil came across two young children fishing from the bank. The boys, who by appearance must have been brothers, the elder seeming to be about ten years old, the younger no more than five, scrambled to their feet at the sight of the prince and his retinue. They seemed about to run but then evidently thought better of it and stood close together, clutching to each other's hands, their fishing poles forgotten at their feet as they gazed fearfully at Alfrahil.

'Well met, boys,' said Alfrahil cheerfully. 'Is the fishing good here?'

The elder boy stammered an anxious reply in the thick accent of the local farmers. 'We meant no harm, sir. We wouldn't sell no fish; don't tell the Guild.'

'Guild?' asked Alfrahil. 'What guild are you talking about, child?'

'I can answer that, my Lord,' said Caelus. 'Recently a Fishing Guild of the river was created, whereby the fisher-folk of the Delta enjoy a monopoly on all fish caught from the island of Innis Mallow, here in the River Aphon, westward to the sea.'

'What has that do to with these boys spending a pleasant afternoon trying to catch their dinner?' asked Alfrahil.

'Well, my Lord, if the boys catch their own dinner, then they or their parents will not have to buy their fish from the Guild, so the Guild loses money,' said Caelus.

Not for the first time, it occurred to Alfrahil that all the hours spent in academic study had ill-prepared him for the realities of daily life. As had happened earlier, following the shock of the ambushes, Alfrahil felt rage boil up in him—rage against those who would spoil the world as it should have been: a world without injustice and greed.

'So,' he said to Caelus, 'the men of money would take away even the simple pleasures of innocent children. Well, do I recall the good times that Daerahil and I once shared fishing along this very bank in our childhood. Now, these two youngsters would be punished for simply exercising what should be the birthright of all Eldoran boys.'

The oldest boy, listening to this speech with mouth agape now broke in. 'Please, sir, don't whip my brother. The fault was all mine. Whip me, but let my brother go. He don't know nothing about the Guild.'

'Whipping!' cried Alfrahil in disbelief. 'Who would whip you and why?'

Caelus replied again for the boys. 'The Fishing Guild now routinely pays guardsmen who find people fishing in the river to whip them as an example of what happens to those who break the charter of the Guild.'

'Since when do the terms of a guild charter supersede the laws of Eldora?' demanded Alfrahil. 'The rivers of the realm have always been open to the use of common folk. How long has this monstrosity been going on?'

'The Guild received their monopoly last year from the Council of Merchants, but only recently have they began enforcing their codes upon the populace,' Caelus replied.

'Why has nothing been said in Council of this? Does my father know of these outrages? Why was I not advised?'

'Lord, little of the minutiae of the average lives of our citizens' pass into the Third District, much less into the Citadel,'said Caelus. 'What little does is certainly prevented from reaching the ears of the King, yourself, and most of the senior ministers by those who would stand to lose money if your grace were informed of the true state of events.'

'What of Mergin and my father's other counselors? Surely they would not have allowed this to go on?'

'Perhaps not, Lord had they known. But the Fishing Guild is one of many that pay handsomely into the coffers of the Council of Merchants, and the Council of Merchants, in turn, pays handsomely into the private coffers of the men who serve as ministers. These men do not inquire too deeply into the source of these funds, or question what they are told. They are eager to accommodate the interests of those who are so generous in their contributions.'

'This is treason,' said Alfrahil.

'No, Lord,' said Caelus calmly. 'It is merely politics as usual.'

'What of my brother? What is his part in all this? Is he also ignorant of these practices?'

Looking troubled, Caelus replied softly, 'I cannot speak for your brother, my Lord, but he does spend quite a bit of time being flattered and courted by the Merchants, Guilds, and their minions.'

Aghast at the state of things, Alfrahil spoke his thought aloud. 'How long has this been going on, and what can I do about it?'

'I don't know, Lord, for rumor has corruption reaching the highest levels within the City, and there are those who would not take kindly to any efforts that would reduce their profits.'

Humiliated at his complete ignorance of these events, and chiding himself inwardly for living so long with closed eyes, Alfrahil replied bitterly. 'Profit before honor, greed instead of noble purpose, complacency before deeds: so does vice and apathy cloak itself in virtue throughout Eldora. Thank you, Caelus, for sharing this with me. I see more clearly now how a man of your ability and honesty ran afoul of vested interests.'

Turning to one of his other guards, he bade the man summon the local River Guard Watch Commander to meet him at the inn.

Then Alfrahil bent and picked up one of the willow poles and handed it to the elder boy. 'Return to your fishing, lad,' he said kindly. 'I am Alfrahil, your prince, and by my command, no one shall trouble you again for fishing here or anywhere in the realm. The bounty of Aphon belongs equally to all loyal citizens of Eldora.'

The boy nodded but seemed otherwise not to understand what was happening. His younger brother could not even manage a nod, gazing at Alfrahil with an awestruck expression, as if he were not merely a prince but a god.

Leaning close, Alfrahil pressed several silver coins into the elder boy's hand. 'If you fail to catch your family's dinner, then you can at least buy good fish for a few months from the market.'

'Th-thank you, your lordship.'

Tousling the boy's hair, Alfrahil moved swiftly along the path to the inn, where he settled down to a meal of fried fish and cool wine. '*How many other organizations exist that have wormed their way into the bureaucrats that feed into the Council of Ministers?*' he wondered to himself as he ate. '*Are they all involved in this conspiracy against me, or are most of them disinterested men who only seek an easy way to turn a quick profit?*'

At last the commander of the river guard arrived and was brought before Alfrahil. The various guard companies of Eldora wore distinct colors to signify their areas of command. The guards of the Citadel were clothed in silver and black; the regular army men had gray tunics with silver borders; the guards of Sisera wore silver and orange, and the distant border guards wore silver and green. The colors of the river watch were silver and blue, and it was in these colors that the local watch commander approached him now, looking both harried and perplexed. Alfrahil took note of his sad, grizzled face, with lines of care and worry embedded in the tanned skin. The man saluted with rigid formality and asked, 'How can I serve you, my Lord?'

'You can tell me of men under your command who assault little boys fishing for their dinner, and whether or not you knew of this custom,' said Alfrahil.

Alfrahil watched the blood drain from the man's tanned, tired face. 'Perhaps I could speak with you privately, my Lord?'

Alfrahil took a mental breath and dismissed the rest of his men, with the exception of Caelus. 'After the ambush, I am no longer content to be alone, watch commander,' he said. 'Your name please?'

'Cerlon, my Lord, I have heard of this evil practice and have tried to put a stop to it, but one of my lieutenants is the nephew of the Outlier Guard Commander. Thus, I have been given orders to look the other way and allow my men to regulate fishing along the river.'

'Why have you not tried to communicate this matter to higher authorities, for sure not all men of the City are corrupt?' Alfrahil demanded.

Smiling nervously, Cerlon said, 'My Lord, you know to whom the Outlier Commander reports, and it is rumored he approves of these measures.'

Alfrahil's angry countenance darkened even more. 'Certainly, I know. He reports to the King, or, if the King is unavailable, to the First Minister. Do you dare to suggest that either my father or Lord Mergin would tolerate this corruption for a moment?'

Caelus quietly spoke up. 'My Lord, the Outlier Commander was replaced about six months ago with a more pliable man, and the Council of Ministers gave the supervision of the Outlier Companies to your brother, Prince Daerahil, as it seemed a duty too onerous for either the King, Lord Mergin, or yourself to handle.'

'Are you telling me that all of the guards outside the City report to Daerahil?' said Alfrahil incredulously.

'Yes, my Lord, they report to him,' said Caelus.

'What of the guards inside the City?' asked Alfrahil.

'They still report to you, my Lord, but there has been talk in Council that only the Citadel guards should still report to you or the King directly,' said Caelus.

'So,' he said, 'are all the guards and their men subject to corruption?'

'No, my Lord, only those whose duty it is to come into contact with monetary situations, and then only the most craven,' said Caelus. 'For example, your border guards are essentially honest, but the customs men that sit along the roads are a different matter. It can be said that even your border scouts have been known to assist a merchant in finding his way around the various toll positions, but for the most part, the merchants pay their tariffs for the protection of the men of Eldora gladly. It is only recently that such commercial unions like the Fishing Guild have been bold enough to try and expand their license into a tyrannical monopoly.'

'Thank you, Caelus, for again you help to open my eyes,' said Alfrahil. He turned his attention back to the Watch Commander. 'Well, Cerlon, if this one lieutenant is dealt with, will the problem subside?'

'No,' replied Cerlon heavily, 'it will not subside. The Outlier Commander would simply replace the lieutenant with another of his cohort, and I would be even less effective in my duties.'

'Your duties,' echoed Alfrahil. 'You seem sadly remiss in your duties. You should have brought this matter to me personally.'

'My Lord, I beg you, how could I have known you would have reacted any differently than your brother?' asked Cerlon desperately.

Caelus said, 'He has a point, my Lord, for, until today, I was not sure of your thoughts in this matter, though the rumor of the land has you as virtuous as your father in all things. I see now that I should have raised the issue myself as soon as I entered directly into your service. I beg your forgiveness.'

'I can chastise no man here present more than I do myself, for my ignorance of these matters is equally inexcusable. I still cannot believe Daerahil knows that little boys are being whipped for fishing in the river.'

'I doubt, Lord, that he knows the sordid details,' replied Caelus.

After pausing for a few moments in thought, Alfrahil spoke. 'Cerlon, you shall list the men that you know or suspect are involved in this corruption, both those under your command and those who sit above you in the chain of command, and have their names mentioned in a duty report praising them for their particularly good behavior. This way, as the report passes through your captain's hands, he will think nothing of it, and you will be able to give me the information without placing yourself in danger. Thank you. You may go.'

Cerlon bowed. 'Thank you, my Lord. I will see to it at once.'

After Cerlon had departed, Alfrahil glanced inquiringly at Caelus, who shook his head. 'No, Lord, he is honest, if weak, and his voice rings true when he says there is nothing he can do. If you want to get to the heart of this matter and the other corruption, then the Outlier Captain is the logical choice, but you must take care, as he reports to very powerful men in the City.'

'So, summoning the head of the Fishing Guild would not avail me tonight?' asked Alfrahil.

'No, Lord, for the head of the Guild would tell you that he is shocked to hear of these rumors,' replied Caelus. 'He would swear to you that he would get to the bottom of the problem, and then, when you tried to follow up, you would be delayed repeatedly, until your patience ran out and eventually some low-level merchants and Guardsmen would be named as the culprits. Then, after they were dealt with, the Guild would keep a lower profile, until you were no longer watching them so closely. No, Lord, only by working from the top down can you hope to make significant changes in the way that business is done in Eldora today.'

'This requires much forethought and planning,' Alfrahil responded. 'We will speak more of this later, Caelus. But now we shall return to the inspection. There, at least, I can be assured of finding no unpleasant surprises.'

The schedule for the afternoon began with an artillery demonstration to be observed from atop the battlements, and there Alfrahil repaired now, accompanied by Caelus and his personal guard.

The over-commander, Dresden, was a puffed-up popinjay removed for too long from active command of soldiers in combat. His vast bulk sagged over his trousers, and his armor revealed great gaps between the metal plates where the underlying chain mail was strained to the breaking point.

Alfrahil quietly admired the defenses that had been created with the help of the Dwarves. Even if a host as large as Magnus' army during the Great War flung itself against these breastworks, they would break upon the defenses as a wave upon the shore; unless, of course, they possessed the ancient evil power of Magnar. But that was beyond unlikely. Magnar had been unique, the only person ever to live who could trace his heritage back to all of the races, allowing him to use the magic of each race. In addition, his hybrid blood had given him physical and magical powers far beyond those of ordinary Men, Dwarves, and Elves. Knowledge of the secrets of Magnar was considered a state secret in Eldora, and little if any of the information gleaned about that terrible dark magic had been conveyed to either the Elves or the Dwarves. Alfrahil suspected this policy was enforced within the other races as well, and they, too, had secrets from those days that they had not shared with Men.

Returning to the present, Alfrahil surveyed the defenses of the river. Level upon level, barrier upon barrier, the defenses were not necessarily designed to stop an army at a single point, but to allow them to slowly infiltrate the defensive perimeter a fathom at a time. At every two fathoms there were slightly different obstacles, funneling the would-be attackers through a web of objects that would expose them to direct fire, plunging fire, and enfilading fire simultaneously, protecting the defenders from actual assault. The Dwarven engineers who had designed the system had estimated that a ten-to-one advantage would be required to breach these defenses and Alfrahil saw no reason to quarrel with that assessment.

Alfrahil saw that catapults and ballistae had been set up to subject any invading army to long-range boulder and javelin attacks that would shatter enemy siege towers and wagons, and play havoc with their military formations. One of the newer ballistae was being attended to now by several soldiers. It fired four smaller javelins at the same distance as a larger javelin and was designed to attack enemy troops rather than fortified positions. The ballista was sitting on a wheeled dais so that it could be rotated toward its targets.

Dresden told him, 'The artillery is routinely cleaned, oiled, and tested to make certain that it is ready for action at any time. You can see hand-picked soldiers about to demonstrate the accuracy and range of our newest invention, the four-shot ballista. Look there, my Lord.'

Alfrahil looked out and saw several men attending an artillery piece. Bright white targets with a small red target the size of a human head were ranged from fifty to three hundred yards away. Knowing that he must begin to prepare for his military tour of Shardan, he paid close attention, and the first series of bolts shot away toward the closest targets fifty yards distant. The artillery was reloaded and the sighting mechanisms adjusted with each successive firing, until, after ten volleys, all of the shafts had struck their targets.

'Well,' said Alfrahil, 'I can see your artillery men know their business. What will they do now?'

'They will finalize their ranging data and readjust for the next set of targets at one hundred yards. I have arranged for a cavalry demonstration for you now, my Lord, unless you wish to continue to observe the artillery.'

'No, Commander, let us proceed with your demonstration.' Taking one last glance at the artillery, Alfrahil saw the apparatus rapidly spin to the right and point toward the battlements.

'Commander?' asked a perplexed Alfrahil.

'What in the name of wonder is going on down there?' demanded Dresden angrily of no one in particular. 'There should be no possibility that those artillery pieces can point back toward the battlements! They should only point away from us so that if they are ever taken in combat, they cannot be used against us! Excuse me, my lord.' And turning to his second in command, he ordered the man to descend to the field below and determine what was going on.

Alfrahil was about to suggest that they move on to the cavalry maneuvers when a slight gleam of light caught the corner of his eye. In the next instant, he was thrown to the ground. A shout rose up from one of the Shadows, a horrible, high-pitched screaming that rapidly died away.

Alfrahil felt a heavy weight pressing him down onto the stones. He struggled against it, and then suddenly felt the pressure leave. He was pulled to his feet by a Shadow, shaken but unscathed.

Dresden had not been as fortunate. He lay before Alfrahil, a confident popinjay no longer, holding his bleeding arm and moaning. A javelin had opened it to the bone. Near him was the body of a Shadow, who had taken a javelin directly to the head. Brains and blood were scattered across the battlements, trickling down Alfrahil's his neck in sickening sticky gobs.

Caelus exclaimed, 'Are you hurt, my Lord?'

'No,' said Alfrahil with disbelief. The ballista's two other javelins had claimed two more of his guardsmen. Once again death's cold hand had let Alfrahil's life slip through its fingers. Too shocked to take command of the situation, he asked, 'What happened?'

'The closest ballista suddenly turned toward us and fired.' Turning to a nearby sergeant, Caelus shouted, 'Get down there and find out what happened. Bring the entire ballista crew to me alive, so that they can be interrogated by Lord Mergin.'

As the sergeant left them, Caelus quietly called for guardsmen to take Bufus to the infirmary and helped a shocked Alfrahil into an inner room and called for some spirits of Dorian, liquor from the delta region of Eldora.

Moments later, servants arrived with the alcohol, still sealed against tampering, that Caelus requested. He poured a large measure for Alfrahil and firmly bade him drink it down.

Alfrahil complied in a daze. But the strong spirits restored his wits. Suddenly aware that he was drenched in blood and gore, he set down the empty goblet. He wanted nothing more at that moment than to tear off his ruined clothes and have servants scrub his body clean. But just then, Commander Dresden' adjutant entered the room.

The man, pale of visage, saluted and addressed the prince. 'Lord, I must deliver Commander Dresden' report, as he is with the military healers, but I have a preliminary report from the ballista crew. The normal crews of four men assigned to the ballista were replaced today, on orders from their captain, with a special detachment of four veterans from the Shardan campaign. These men were supposed to be preparing a demonstration of how the new ballista could be used for greater effect. When they saw you on the battlements, they turned their weapon toward you and with great precision fired the javelins.'

'Where are they now?' Alfrahil demanded. 'Surely they can tell us why and how they were able to launch such an attack.'

'I am sorry, Lord, but none of them are alive. Two drew their weapons and chose to fight. They were slain before they could be disarmed. The other two, seeing that they were going to be captured, stabbed each other through the throat. Each died within seconds. I have ordered a search of their barracks, clothing, and horses.'

'Send messages to Mergin, my father, and to the Shadow commander, Gray Water,' ordered Alfrahil. 'Get replacements for my guardsmen down here as soon as possible. That will be all.' The adjutant, the shame upon his face clear, saluted again and bolted from the room.

'My meeting with Hilforas has just taken on fresh urgency,' Alfrahil observed to Caelus.

'Lord, if you will take my advice, you will cancel your meeting with the Elf and proceed back to the Citadel immediately.'

Shaking his head, Alfrahil replied weakly, 'I have just been attacked at the center of the strongest fortifications in the kingdom by my own troops. If the conspirators can reach me here, they can penetrate even into the Citadel. I cannot spend the rest of my life in seclusion, and Hilforas may have information that may allow us to make progress in the investigation.'

'Then, Lord, I would suggest returning to the inn where you had lunch. I will send Shadows and some guardsmen ahead to make it secure. We can bring Hilforas there.'

'Very well,' said Alfrahil with resignation. 'I will first bathe and change into fresh clothes and leave my armor here to be cleaned and oiled. I will then meet with Hilforas while awaiting Mergin's message as to when it will be safe to return to the City.'

'Sire, you will be vulnerable without your armor. I beg you to put it on, bloody or no.'

'Both the ambushes employed weapons that would penetrate my armor, so wearing it would be useless. Besides, it's filthy, heavy, and hot. A thick leather jerkin will be sufficient. Now send word to prepare my bath.'

* * *

Alfrahil arrived at the inn, escorted by two Shadows where he nearly fell from his horse as the fear and fatigue from the attack caught up with him. Two more Shadows stood guard outside the inn, as Caelus gave Alfrahil a critical look as he as he helped him to stand, Caelus said, 'I do not think you were injured in your body, my lord.'

'No, just my mind, Caelus, I have avoided death in all its forms my entire life, and now, within a few days, it has reached out take me. But for happenstance, I would be a shade today.' Shaking, he barely walked into the inn under his own strength.

'Lord, neither ambush was your fault; you acquitted yourself nobly each time by escaping. Please rest quietly in the back room. I will have a carafe of wine brought to you while you take your ease. There are more than two hours before we are supposed to meet Hilforas.'

A Shadow escorted a serving woman bearing a large goblet of local wine towards Alfrahil, who sat on a simple overstuffed couch looking at both his shaking hands. Caelus moved to taste the wine first for poison, but the Shadow said, 'The Inn has been thoroughly searched, the food and wine tasted for poison, the Prince is safe.' Alfrahil gratefully removed his jerkin and relaxed upon the couch, quaffing two more glasses, and felt sleep wash over him.

Awakened by Caelus, he put on his jerkin again and exited the inn. Outside, he stood listening to the sound of the river. Then horsemen came into view, riding along the river pathway toward them and bearing the flags of the Elves of Ackerlea.

There were twenty, led by a tall Elf whose long dark hair streamed behind him. The Elf's horse whinnied gladly at the sight of so many of its brethren. As the riders approached, the leader cried out, 'Hail, and well met, Prince Alfrahil. I am Hilforas, chief scout and errand-rider to Ferox, Elf Lord of Ackerlea; Lord of the North Forest.'

'Elf Lord of Ackerlea?' asked a weary Alfrahil. 'I was unaware that Ackerlea had been turned over to the Elves by the Men of Eldora, or has Ferox decided to take what he so clearly covets?'

Smiling tightly, Hilforas said, 'This is the current title that Ferox uses, and I am required to use it, though it is not a title Albericus has or ever would convey upon the young upstart. Indeed, what better manners can you expect of someone who is only one thousand years old?'

'What manners indeed?' replied a relieved Alfrahil. 'Surely, though, Ferox does not lay claim to Ackerlea over the claims of Eldora?'

'Nay, Lord, he simply states he is the 'Elf Lord of Ackerlea', not its' actual Lord. While he is besotted with his own self-importance, even he recognizes he has neither the legitimate claim nor the strength to claim Ackerlea for his own,' said Hilforas.

'Well and good,' replied Alfrahil dryly. 'I would hate to think of recalling the army from the Shardan frontier, or summoning the Kozaki to honor their ancient obligations.'

'Never fear, Lord, for all who dwell in Ackerlea acknowledge the Lordship of Eldora. But now that this misunderstanding has been redressed, how can I be of service?' asked Hilforas.

'Can you speak openly with my men here?'

'No, your grace: too many ears and too little security. I can take you to a place where we can speak in complete confidence.'

Glancing at Caelus, he ordered horses to be saddled. Mounting a compliant steed, Alfrahil ordered twenty guardsmen along with his Shadows to accompany him, and move out.

Swiftly, Hilforas turned his fellow scouts around, cantering quickly away from the southern shore and leading Alfrahil and his guards south and east away from the river along a small game path through the dense forest and undergrowth where the horses were required to follow single file. Over an hour passed, with Estellius far behind them, before, leaving the paths along the river, Hilforas led them into wild country that existed between the river and the ancient north road farther to their east. Passing into a large clearing, Hilforas turned his horse around and approached the Prince. 'Will this suffice for our meeting, my Lord?'

'So long as we are alone.'

'If you are concerned for your safety, my Lord Prince, how do you know that you can trust me?'

'You were vouched for by Lord Golbur. Plus, you are from the Great Forest, compelled to scout for the Elves of the North Forest. Therefore you must be completely trustworthy as far as the Lesser Elves are concerned. Besides, if you and your escort wanted to kill me and my men, you could have done so by now. Therefore you are either playing an incredibly deep game against me, or you are trustworthy. Which is the truth?'

Smiling, Hilforas said, 'Your logic is flawless. I am trustworthy. Now, please follow me, your grace.' Hilforas dismounted and Alfrahil copied him, handing the reins of his horse to a protesting Shadow. 'Silence.' Said Alfrahil, 'I will go with Hilforas, you and the others get turned around and be prepared to leave the minute I return.' Quickly and stealthily, Hilforas led Alfrahil along another narrow forest path that quickly winded its way up a small but steep knoll which, from a distance, had not appeared to be as tall as it was. Coming to the summit where a cluster of limestone rocks offered a crude but natural seat, Hilforas bade Alfrahil sit amongst the small ferns that grew out of the limestone, where they provided shelter from the sun so that mosses could thrive under their cool shade. Gazing about, Alfrahil could only see other trees and a few open groves within the surrounding Ackerlea forests. For the hardy trees that had survived the domination of Magnar had responded to his fall from power with a resurgent strength, requiring the men of Eldora and their Elven allies to prune and trim their new growth so that the great north-south road and the eastern road to Hiberius remained open. Alfrahil could only hear the distant murmur of the great river and the sigh of the wind through the branches; the sounds of their escorts were completely lost to them.

Alfrahil spoke with Hilforas, telling him the personal details of the ambush in the City and the ambush that had nearly claimed his life today. 'Hilforas, I ask much of you personally. My father, Lord Mergin, and I believe that this conspiracy to kill me is not completely domestic in origin. We have found evidence that other races may have been involved.'

'That is indeed dire news,' said Hilforas. 'But surely you are not referring to the Elves.'

'I'm afraid I am. The archers who waylaid me from the city rooftops were wearing these.' He drew out the Elven cloak from under his own cloak and handed it to Hilforas.

'I have never seen one of these cloaks outside of our forest realm, except under specific circumstances and only given to specific Elves. Even our soldiers assigned to the Allied brigade were never allowed to take our magical cloaks with them.' Hilforas turned the garment over in his hands, examining it closely. 'I do not know what to say, my Lord, except please accept my apologies on behalf of the Elves for the aid that this cloak gave your would-be assassins. I will make inquiries regarding how this cloak could have left our realm.'

'We need accurate information, and rather quickly at that, not the sanitized nonsense that will come through official diplomatic channels.'

'How may I be of assistance?' Hilforas asked.

'I need trustworthy scouts to take these tidings to your distant kindred that wander Nostraterra, to all the realms of Dwarves and Elves, asking all they encounter if they have any information regarding what has happened here in Eldora, no matter how remote the possibility. Dwarves will allow you Elves access to their realms, as Elves will allow Dwarves into yours. I suspect that there are elements of all races that want to destroy the peace in Nostraterra. Will you help me?'

Hilforas remained quietly in thought for several minutes before responding. 'Prince Alfrahil, I will certainly lend you what aid I can, and several of these missions can be sent forth in the guise of normal communications, but taking Dwarves along is not something many of my kindred will tolerate. It would be sure to draw attention and invite rumor and speculation. While the Lesser Elves of the Great Forest and the Dwarves are closer now than at any time in our history, the cease-fire between the Lesser Elves of the North Forest and the Dwarves is nothing more than that.'

'Why is there a cease-fire in the first place?' asked Alfrahil. 'Neither I nor my father has heard anything official from the Elves regarding this matter.'

'That is a question with a long answer,' said Hilforas. 'When the Great War ended, Elves and Dwarves fought and died in the mines of Nerea in what both races refer to as the Great Tragedy.'

'Yes, I have heard rumors of the story, but I have never heard the Elven perspective. Will you tell me now?'

'Yes, after Elven involvement in your attack, I feel honor bound to tell you what I can. First I must tell you of Elven history of which you are not aware. When Magnar first attacked the Dwarves and the Lesser Elves, you men of Eldora initially hoped to sit out the war and profit from the spoils by attacking the victor, who would have been significantly weakened despite their success. When Magnar attacked our Great Forest, our lesser Water Spirits stayed his advance, using their magic to sustain our wounded, healing them and the forest from his assault. Our Water Spirits were never able to attack directly; they exist to give and sustain life, not take life. Only in sacrificing themselves could they stop a foe from attacking our realm. One by one, they gave up their existence, stemming the tide of Magnar, but he was too strong. Finally, he penetrated to our Great Spring, which Magnar personally attacked; but even he could not destroy it utterly. Our Great Water Spirit, Pluvia, denied him the advantage. It was then that Magnar unleashed a terrible personal weapon. Bolts of lightning came from his staff, causing nearby boulders to collapse across the spring, melting then hardening over it and cutting off Pluvia from her life's waters.

'After Magnar was destroyed, Pluvia realized that her powers were waning, as all of our efforts to break open the stone barrier were repulsed. Worse, the Great Fire spirit began to heat our surviving Elf wells from below, killing the fish and plants that depended upon cool forest water for their survival. The forest as a whole soon began to suffer, as some lesser Elf Wells began to boil. Jets of steam killed trees and animals, threatening to turn the entire forest into a vast heated swamp. Pluvia realized that the only way to stop the Great Fire spirit was to stop his son, who, according to rumors from surviving Dwarves, had become the Fire Demon in Nerea. According to the Dwarves, the Fire Demon received nearly a third of the Fire Spirit's magic, so if the Fire Demon was destroyed, the power of the Great Fire Spirit would be curtailed, the danger to our forest ended. Pluvia went there and gave up her life, destroying the Fire Demon and lessening the strength of the Fire Spirit by destroying his most powerful child.

'There are many Lesser Elves today who hold the Dwarves responsible for the loss of our greatest magical ally. If only the Dwarves had restrained their arrogance, the Fire Demon would never have destroyed and occupied the mightiest of Dwarf realms. If Nerea had remained inhabited and strong, Magnar would never have launched his wars of conquest, and we would not have sustained the losses that we did. Therefore, my Lord Prince, many Elves blame the Dwarves for allowing Magnar to launch his armies against the world.

'When Pluvia left, there was no actual word from Nerea, so in the ensuing confusion as to whether or not she had been successful; Ferox presented the Dwarves of Nerea with a demand for recompense at the loss of our Water Spirit. The Dwarves refused, starting a brief but terrible series of atrocities, where Dwarf and Elf slew each other. This memory is quite sharp in our minds since only by the sacrifice of our Great Water spirit was the realm of Nerea cleansed of the Fire Demon. The fact that we were attacked soon after helping the Dwarves is even more galling to most Elves. It will take much to overcome the death of Elves at the hands of the Dwarves and move the relations between our peoples forward.

'Now you know of the antipathy of many of my people toward the Dwarves. Regardless of history, I do know of four of my scouts who like a good glass of Dwarven Ale. They could be persuaded to carry Dwarves home to the Bastion and to their other realms, and even beyond their borders if need be. However, Lord Ferox would never countenance such a mission. Both I and my fellow Elves would suffer if it were known that I have agreed to help you. Only with direct permission from Albericus will my fellow scouts be able to go anywhere with Dwarves. I will send an urgent message if you like.'

'Why would Lord Ferox not countenance such a mission? It seems that it would stand both our peoples well to look into the involvement of Men, Dwarves, and even Elves in such a fiendish plot. If these conspirators can attack me, then certainly they can attack a Dwarf Lord or a member of the Elven royal family as well.'

Pausing for several minutes before speaking, Hilforas replied. 'Perhaps, Lord, you are familiar with the enmity that exists between Lord Ferox and your King?'

'Yes, I have noticed my father's refusal to speak with Ferox over the years, but yesterday was the first time I saw an implacable opposition to Ferox, though I do not know the cause,' said Alfrahil.

'Clearly, Lord, you are in the dark about on old sordid business. Perhaps I should not tell you of it now.'

'No, please go on. It seems that there are more and more secrets each day that I am privy to, and this will only prepare me better for the kingship someday.'

'Very well, my Lord. Your father, after assuming the throne with the passing of his father, fell in love with Adaril, sister to Ferox, niece of King Albericus, and asked for her hand in marriage. Her father had fallen in battle during the Great War, and both Ferox and Albericus assumed their care of her, though Adaril despised her brother and his hatred of Men. I do not pretend to guess at the cause of this hatred, but it exists, I assure you. Adaril and your father met at his coronation and apparently secretly thereafter a few times over the next couple of years. She returned your father's love and gave her consent in marriage freely. Ferox was enraged that his sister should plight her troth with a mortal, and was unwilling to countenance such a match, even with the High King of Men.'

'Even so,' said Alfrahil, 'she was a free woman, and she could have chosen to ignore her brother, or seek consent from King Albericus himself.'

'By our customs, with her father dead, it fell to Ferox to give his consent, though of course, Albericus would have the final decision. But as you suggest, she did have the right to seek the consent of Albericus directly, and this she did or rather attempted to do. Ferox, however, rather than laying her petition before the king, broke Elven law and locked Adaril away. When your father heard of this from Elves sympathetic to his cause, he was enraged and assembled his army, sending scouts ahead to prepare the way for an armed invasion. News soon reached Adaril that a great battle was brewing between Elves and Men on her account, and she fell into deep despair. She had no wish to be the cause of such a war and feared greatly for her people and for your father's safety. Thus she took her own life.

'Three days later, the armies met east of the Crossroads. There was a parley prior to the battle, where your father demanded that Adaril be released from prison and King Albericus be consulted regarding his consent forthwith. A final letter from Adaril to your father was given over to him then, as Ferox well knew that his small army of one thousand Elves could not withstand the ten thousand men your father had with him that day. Your father, after reading the letter, was in a great rage, crying out that Ferox had slain the woman he loved. Moving forward on his horse, he drew his sword and lashed out at Ferox, cutting his cheek, a scar that he bears to this day. Violating the parley was something shocking to both armies, and immediately after that moment, the King was led away in his madness by his own counselors and told that there was no longer a cause for war.

'Later that day, riders bearing messages from Albericus expressed their deepest apologies to the King, stating that Adaril's death was Ferox's personal fault and that the Elven King would have given his niece freely in marriage to your father. Ferox was immediately recalled and set to the task of cleaning the ruins of Tarin Nazar, the fortress Magnar constructed in the Great Forest at the height of his power. This task was turned over to another thirty years ago, at which point Ferox returned here, to Ackerlea. Though much time had passed by mortal measure, your father still wanted his vengeance, but his ministers persuaded him that he should bide his time against Ferox personally, and not assault the Elves. In this, the King eventually agreed, and this is the reason that no Men are allowed into the Elven city of Verdantia in Ackerlea, except under the tightest security, and the reason that Ferox has never set foot inside lands controlled by Eldora. Even when he rides out from Ackerlea to return to our forests, it is only with a large Elven cavalry formation. He has survived at least three assassination attempts, most likely by Shadows, since Adaril took her own life.'

Nodding his head, Alfrahil said, 'Well, I can certainly see why my father has no love for the Elves, and why Ferox's name has never been spoken aloud by him. This explains much in the relations of the Lesser Elves and Men here in Eldora and Ackerlea. It supports my suspicion that there is not only a foreign basis for this conspiracy, but that other races are probably involved.'

'Yes, Lord, and you should be aware that Ferox and Albericus still hate one another. It is only Ferox's political connections and wealth that have allowed him to return to his former post. That and the fact that I believe Albericus would gladly look the other way if the Shadows were successful someday; this I believe he has told your father indirectly. Keeping Ferox in Ackerlea allows this possibility while keeping Ferox and Albericus far apart from each other.'

'It seems that Ferox is capable of treachery, possessed as he is with a hatred of my father. But do you really think he would go so far as to help the conspirators?' asked a startled Alfrahil.

'Possibly Lord; but if the conspirators were successful, then your brother Daerahil would be next in line for the throne of Eldora, and, forgive me, but Ferox has stated that you are weaker than your brother and that a strong King of Men is not in the best interest of the Elves. Therefore while he would rejoice at the death of your father, it would make much more sense to target your brother, leaving you on the throne eventually.'

'Well, we must gather more information and hope that Albericus gives his consent and that Ferox remains in the dark about our plans. Besides money, I can also aid your messengers with relief mounts between Ackerlea and the Great Forest. Can you get a message to Celefin, Lord of the Greater Elves in Phoenicia?

'Yes. I will tell Ferox that I am sending messengers to Phoenicia to inform them of our mighty progress here. It will be both somewhat truthful and appeal to his vanity at the same time. I will also send messenger scouts home to the Great Forest, to seek out the King's permission, a routine activity that should not pique Ferox' interest. Assuming Albericus issues these orders, have the Dwarves wait for my scouts at the next full moon on the north bank of the Aphon directly opposite Innis Mallow. Our scouts will gather the Dwarves along with spare horses and they shall set out with no other Elf the wiser. You must supply food and money for their travels, plus compensate each scout for his time. This will not be a small sum, the supplies and money must be ready within ten days, as the next full moon is seventeen days away.'

'Do not worry, Hilforas. Money is the least of my concerns, there shall be plenty and to spare,' said Alfrahil. 'When the supplies and money are ready, I will alert you via a discreet message.

Please have your scouts take the time to speak with the peoples they meet on their way, and have one of your scouts head even to the distant southwest highlands, where they can speak with the Hermits who dwell there. I am glad that the tension between our peoples does not extend to us personally; for I would have only harmony between us.'

'I know that well, Prince Alfrahil, and that, along with my desire to answer these troubling questions, is why I aid you today. I also hope that this joint mission of cooperation will show at least some of us Elves directly and more of us, indirectly, that cooperation between all the races is still in our best interests, even after the fall of Magnar. Are there any other specifics, my Lord? My people rode these lands long before you were born and my scouts do know how to ask questions of fellow travelers.'

'My pardon, Hilforas,' said Alfrahil. 'You have seen the status of much of the realm of Eldora; sloth and greed have superseded honor and duty in many corners of the realm.'

'That is true,' replied Hilforas. 'Unfortunately, this tendency is not just confined to Men, but to Elves as well, particularly Ferox. Never fear; the scouts that go will speak with other scouts they encounter, and I should guess that within the next three months you should have answers to your questions, though whether those answers satisfy you or merely lead to other questions, I do not venture to predict.'

'Three months,' muttered Alfrahil. 'Much may happen in three months.'

'Yes, my Lord, but if there is any truth to your suspicions, then my people and the Dwarves must be diligent and look into the hidden crevices of their realms that otherwise might escape attention,' said Hilforas.

With that, they walked back down to their guardsmen. Determined to distract any who would spread tales, Alfrahil said, 'Thank you, Hilforas, for listening to my thoughts pertaining to the duty shifts of our work details and patrols along the Malius road. I hope before much longer to see the progress that our people have made within that accursed vale.'

'You are welcome for our meeting. Together our efforts shall succeed where one would fail,' said Hilforas with a small smile, and the Elven cavalry and the Eldoran escort cantered back to their meeting point. There Alfrahil thanked Hilforas again and returned to the inn to think about what he had been told.

Alfrahil then walked into the cool back room and, sitting down upon the couch, slaked his thirst with a cool glass of rough Ackerlea wine. Waiting for a messenger from Mergin that he was sure was coming after the terrible events in Estellius, he had some light refreshments while considering Hilforas' tale. Deep in thought over the events of the day, he looked up only when a messenger entered the inn, telling him that Mergin said it was safe now to return to Titania, and that he had given specific instructions as to their pathway back into the city for the Prince's safety.

'Well, it is high time I return to the city to conduct my investigation of all I have learned today,' thought Alfrahil. Then, speaking aloud: 'Caelus, let us depart.'

Hastening to the men who were taking their ease in the shade of the inn, Caelus cried, 'Guards! Assemble and make ready to depart.'

The men swiftly climbed into the saddle, forming a moving ring around the Prince and Caelus; an ancient custom adopted from the Kozaki. A moving ring of men, while providing instant mobilization in any direction, also provided a moving screen around the occupants of the ring so they could mount with safety and be protected so long as they did not want the ring to move too fast. They set out northward for the bridge, their hooves clattering along the flagstones of the road until they reached the larger stones of the bridge apron. Swiftly crossing the river, the soldiers cantered back toward the city.

Chapter Eleven

Undercurrents

Alfrahil rode back with his escort into Titania just as the sun was setting behind the mountains. Taking the roundabout way required by the destruction caused by the ambushes, he didn't reach the Citadel until it was full dark. Dismissing his escort but for a Shadow, he left his horse at the messenger stables and was shown into a small, cramped meeting room adjacent to the main chamber of the astrology tower, where an ashen-faced Mergin rose to greet him. An old round wooden table with three chairs was in the center of the room, and oil lamps hung above their heads. The Shadow took his place just behind Alfrahil, quietly keeping watch. Only one servant was present, Aradar, the former desert scout who had comforted Alfrahil the night of the first ambush.

'Hail, my Lord Prince, it is good to see you alive and well. We are closely investigating the events that nearly took your life today,' said Mergin. His haggard appearance was full of anger and frustration.

'Mergin, what concerns me most at the moment is that your vaunted intelligence network failed again,' said Alfrahil heatedly. 'Is there anywhere in the realm where I am safe?'

'My apologies, lord. I tendered my resignation to the King, but again he bids me continue as First Minister. Please, won't you have some food with me? Your father is resting quietly, and I for one am famished.'

Alfrahil, despite his anger and fatigue, also realized he was hungry. 'Yes, Mergin, let us eat together. You can brief me on your investigation.'

Mergin nodded to Aradar, who departed, returning in a moment with a cool crisp white wine favored by both men. Pouring the wine, Aradar said, 'My lord Mergin, we have a fish soup available as a first course with roasted beef and vegetables as the main plate and a light cake for dessert. Will that be alright?'

'Fine, servant, fine.' said Mergin dismissively. 'Just something filling and hot.'

Alfrahil saw a flash of anger wash over Aradar's face, but he turned on his heel to fetch the soup.

Pausing to marshal his thoughts while sipping his wine, Mergin said after a few moments, 'I am investigating as quickly and thoroughly as I can, but nearly everywhere I turn, the men who attack you are soon dead, and there are few leads to follow. Meanwhile, I have fresh news you should hear—so fresh, in fact, that even your father has not yet heard it. I have received a report from the Dwarven engineers you recruited to investigate the joy house, as well as a preliminary report from the Shadows assigned to investigate the ambushes.'

Before Alfrahil could speak, Aradar brought in a large serving bowl fragrant with fish, accompanied by a servant Alfrahil did not know to bear smaller bowls and a basket of fresh bread. Eating their soup for several moments, both men felt the sharpness of their hunger fade. Alfrahil asked, 'Well, Mergin, what did they find?'

'Books, my Lord. Primarily, the Dwarves found books, besides a fair cache of gold and silver,' said Mergin.

'What did these books contain?' asked Alfrahil with mounting exasperation.

'We are still going over them, my Lord, but it seems clear they hold records of many of the more important customers of the house,' said Mergin.

'That is old news, Mergin. I myself discovered a ledger full of such names.'

'Yes, Lord, but that ledger did not contain the name of your brother, Daerahil,' said Mergin.

'Well, what of it? Since we are speaking in privacy, in my younger days, though I never ventured into the joy houses, I was no stranger to the courtesans of the city.' After witnessing his brother's debasement before their father, Alfrahil found himself inclined to be more forgiving of Daerahil than usual, though inwardly Mergin's news had distressed him.

Mergin continued in the same bland tone. 'Well, Lord, it seems that he was a regular customer of a Shardan joy-girl called Hala, who was originally Zarthir's favorite plaything. Four months ago, your brother purchased her contract from the madam of the house, installing her in a private apartment so that she would be exclusively his. My reports tell me he is actually in love with the woman if such disgusting tales can be believed.'

Finishing his soup, Alfrahil glanced at Aradar, indicating he was finished, and said, 'Thank you, Aradar. Would you bring in the main dish now?'

'Yes, my prince. Thank you for remembering my name.' Clearing Mergin's bowl, which was empty as well, Aradar left the room with his fellow servant.

'Mergin, it has been an extremely long day, and you are not telling me anything that I don't know already. What does any of this have to do with the attacks on me?'

'There were also financial documents in the books,' Mergin said, 'showing links between Minister Zarthir and Southmen suspected of fomenting revolt in Shardan. The financier of these dubious dealings is a banker named Fafnir, who has also invested your brother's money to see to the needs of the Shardan veterans.'

Feeling the blood drain from his face, Alfrahil whispered, 'Is there any direct link between my brother's donations and this Fafnir's potentially treacherous finances?'

'No, Lord, not yet. Many of the documents are written in a coded form of Shardan text unfamiliar to my experts. In time, perhaps, we will be able to decipher the actual meaning, but perhaps not. The link I can prove is tenuous, I admit; your brother invested with Fafnir to help his favorite charity, the veterans, and Fafnir gave money to Shardans that are the leading suspects in the organized rebellion against Eldora.'

'So what you are telling me is that you have the definite possibility of a maybe that my brother is guilty of supporting these rebels. Worse, you expect me to believe that I was attacked with overwhelming force in a series of complicated ambushes within a few hours of raiding a random joy-house? This makes no sense, Mergin. But for my horse throwing a shoe, I would never have tracked Captain Dunner to the joy house, much less employed Dwarves to search it. There must be other reasons that I have been attacked.'

Aradar returned at that moment, bearing a silver platter with crusted roast beef, new potatoes, and asparagus, accompanied by a thick mushroom and cream sauce. His fellow servant brought in a folding table and a wicker basket containing plates, napkins and clean utensils. Both men attacked the food with gusto. A rich red wine was served in silver goblets, and Aradar withdrew to a place near the door. Eating rapidly, Alfrahil finished his meal and asked Mergin, 'What reports of the Shadows that you mentioned?'

'Additional searches found a second Elven cloak, under which was a unique bow,' Mergin said. 'Much stronger and longer than even the bows of our Shadows, of a type unknown to the quartermaster captain for the Army. This was not a weapon that the Lesser Elves sell to outsiders. In fact, it may not be Elven at all, though its style is certainly Elven in appearance. They also found a small climbing ladder topped with another Platina-infused grappling hook.

'Regarding weapons, my code breakers found a receipt from the joy house listing special Elf weapons, a Dwarf ladder, and other items. This receipt appears to have your brother's signature scrawled across the bottom of it. Before you say it, yes, this sort of circumstantial evidence has led to the imprisonment, trial, and execution of others over the years. Guilt by association, I agree, but wise men keep clear of such entanglements.'

'Yes,' said Alfrahil, 'wise men, but we all know that my brother is not wise. For all we know, he is completely innocent except for bad taste in wenches and companions. Please, for my sake and for my brother's, do not add any undue emphasis about what you have discovered. I know you and Daerahil are less than friends, but if he is innocent, inflaming the King against him will serve no purpose. If he is guilty, then he shall reveal himself in more obvious ways and can then be dealt with justly.'

'Lord, I must interpret this information as I see fit, and I for one am not nearly so trusting of your brother as you are. As far as I am concerned, he is a traitor to Eldora and its wise policies simply by opposing them in thought, let alone in deed. In this, you and I will have to agree to disagree,' said Mergin.

A flash of anger crossed Alfrahil's face as he said, 'Do not presume to lecture me, old man, for while I count you as one of my friends and trusted advisors, and value you as my father's closest counselor, it is my brother of whom we are speaking. Do not do anything that will make you regret your actions at a later date.'

Drawing closer, Mergin asked, 'Are you threatening me, my Lord? For that would be most unwise.'

'No, I am not threatening you,' replied Alfrahil with an uncharacteristically firm voice. 'I am instead promising you that if your aim with verbal slings and arrows is not very precise, then you shall have me to answer to either now or later when my father has less need of you. My brother may be reckless and careless, but I believe he loves both me and my father still. More important, I believe he loves Eldora.'

'Very well, Lord, I will be extraordinarily careful, but judging from your father's mood recently where your brother is concerned, little emphasis will be needed to get him to see the meaning behind this information.' said Mergin falsely placating the prince.

Alfrahil glared at Mergin, feeling that the man had overstepped his bounds but not quite knowing what to do about it. Mergin met his gaze with what seemed to Alfrahil a look of smug confidence. Then, before Alfrahil could speak, Mergin lowered his eyes.

'Come, Lord,' he said. 'I mean your brother no harm in this matter unless his behavior is indeed treasonous, and only your father can make that decision. If Daerahil is found guilty of treason or sedition, then I shall have the task of designing an appropriate punishment for him and his companions in crime. Such is my duty as First Minister, as even you must admit.'

'Fair enough,' said Alfrahil warily, 'so long as I have made my point. There is an alternative, however, Mergin.'

'What might that be?'

'Have you considered that this entire matter is a foreign-based conspiracy? The Elf weapons, Dwarf tools, and foreign money filtered through this Fafnir person all suggest such an explanation. Please tell me that you are investigating this avenue as well.'

'I am, Lord. Rest assured that regardless of who is involved in this plot, I will get to the bottom of it,' said Mergin. 'I will follow the path of guilt wherever it leads. But at the same time, I will not allow personal feelings to blind me to innocence. Now, if you will excuse me, my lord, I must attend to the latest messages

I suspect are waiting for me. The King left instructions to be awakened in two hours. Please get some rest until then.'

Alfrahil returned to his temporary quarters in the tower. There, as he sipped a glass of wine and nibbled an apple, Alfrahil felt the fatigue of the last several days wash over him. He lay down and dozed until he was gently shaken awake by Aradar, escorted by a Shadow. The two men conducted him to the main chamber of the astrology tower, where the king was waiting.

'Shocking,' said Creon, with absolute disbelief filling his face, 'absolutely shocking! That our own troops would attempt to kill you, my son—it is nearly beyond belief!'

'Well, Father, we are not yet certain that the men responsible were actually Eldoran. They may have been Shardans or outcasts that smuggled themselves into position.'

'No, my son. Lord Mergin's preliminary report from the army arrived an hour ago and clearly states that these men were exactly who they say they were: veterans of the Shardan campaigns. Veterans, moreover, who served under your brother's command and had been personally commended by him for valor on several occasions. The captain in charge of the ballista claims the four men who attacked you had transfer orders signed by your brother appointing them to operate ballistae at Estellius.'

'Why did they not go up the usual chain of command, through the Artillery Commander?' asked a perplexed Alfrahil.

'They claim that they were part of your brother's personal guard in Shardan and that they visited him at his command on the Out-Walls.'

'Does my brother confirm their stories?'

'Yes,' replied Mergin instead of the King, 'but that means little if he is trying to deceive us and using these men to do so.'

'Is there any evidence that he is being deceptive, Mergin?' asked Alfrahil.

'No, my Lord. It may be a coincidence that on the very day you are assaulted again, and by Shardan veterans formerly under your brother's command, your brother should receive several visits from other Shardan veterans formerly under his command. But I, for one, do not believe in coincidences.'

'Father, you probed his mind. Did you find any evidence of deceit?'

Pausing for a moment, Creon was forced to admit, 'No, my son, but your brother's mind is incredibly strong, nearly as strong as mine; I could not search all of the nooks and crannies in his head, or he would have been left a drooling idiot. He may have been able to keep the orders for his men secret from me.'

'Before we focus on my brother, Lord Mergin, how many men knew where I was going on this last visit?' asked Alfrahil.

'Your journey to Estellius was originally known only to the Security Council, but word of your quick inspection of the river defenses was available to some Council Ministers and to Dresden, Over-Commander of Estellius. It would seem, however, that these assassins were already in place, waiting for their opportunity. The plot against you seems more and more complex and layered the deeper we dig through the people and events surrounding you. I can trust no one in this city completely beside the three of us to investigate this matter. It will be slow going even with my Shadows and messenger corps aiding us.'

'Are there any people outside the city that we can trust, Mergin?' asked Creon.

'No, lord,' began Mergin, but he was interrupted by Alfrahil.

'There are others you can trust, Father.' And Alfrahil summarized his conversations with Golbur, Cerlon, Caelus, and Hilforas.

'Renegade Dwarves, foreign money, corruption at the highest levels in Titania, and the possible involvement of "him," ' raged Creon. 'Whom do you trust implicitly, son?'

'Implicitly, no one, but none of them has any ties to anyone who would wish me harm, Cerlon least of all,' said Alfrahil. 'Having him work with the other Out-Captains to ascertain their loyalties and the state of the realm would be prudent. He seemed to possess a sad lament about his person as if the state of the realm was really troubling to him.'

'Indeed,' replied Mergin. 'Well, I will send Cerlon a discreet message to begin circulating amongst the other Outlier Captains. Publicly, I will have him reprimanded for allowing his men to be used by the merchants. Privately I shall increase his salary and award him a small commendation for loyalty to the realm, with further increases and awards to follow with proven success. This should allow the pretense of wounded feelings to provide him with ample cover to work while providing a reward for his honesty and motivation for future effort.'

Shaking his head at Mergin's ability to think two steps ahead of most men, Alfrahil stated, 'Golbur should also be consulted.'

'Are Dwarves really necessary?' asked Creon. 'I would prefer to keep this matter solely amongst Men, and as few of them as possible.'

'Sire, after the madam was taken away, I briefly searched her room and found nothing, which led me to believe that anything useful must be cunningly hidden,' replied Alfrahil. 'The Dwarven engineers found the documents we are now trying to decipher; it is unlikely that our engineers would have found them. Besides, the Dwarven engineers have no interest in the affairs of our tawdry citizens; they only wish to trade their goods and serve those who can afford their services. We will also need their help in determining how the Bridge was destroyed, and how and when it can be repaired. Lord Golbur will favor us with Dwarven scouts who, alongside Elves, will proceed to the Dwarven and Elven realms to ask for news and any hints about these matters that may exist outside of Eldora. With the evidence of corruption seemingly everywhere, we must rely upon those who are known to be above reproach. Frankly, we need any trustworthy help we can get.'

'Very well,' said Creon after giving the matter some thought. 'But the comings and goings of Dwarves and especially Elves will reveal their aid to those conspirators we cannot yet find.'

'Not if you have some of the Dwarves and Elves here to set up temporary consulates while we are planning to build them both a new one,' said Alfrahil. 'Who would think anything odd in that?'

'What new consulates?' asked Mergin. 'We aren't building them new consulates.'

'As of today we are, both to reward the Dwarves and Elves for their efforts on our behalf and as a perfect cover for my father to stay here in the Astrology Tower, as the noise from new construction in the Citadel would be disruptive. This way he can stay here until it is safe for him to be seen in public again,' said Alfrahil.

'Mergin has taught you well, lad;' said the king, chuckling. 'I should have thought of it myself.'

'This way, who would notice various Dwarven and Elven messengers coming and going from the Citadel? And even if they did, it would be assumed that they were taking terms and contracts back and forth between here and their realms.'

Grimly, Mergin nodded his assent. 'I see you have given this much thought.'

'Why should that surprise you, Lord Mergin?' asked Alfrahil.

'It doesn't. But the last trade agreement, three years ago, caused much consternation amongst our merchants if you recall,' stated Mergin.

'Indeed I do,' replied Alfrahil sardonically. 'And as our merchants seem to be the most likely suspects in this plot, let us put some wolves amongst the sheep, perhaps letting rumors fly that those merchants less cooperative with the King and his policies are less likely to be happy with the outcome of the agreement.'

Creon laughed richly and said, 'Yes, indeed, my son. You will make a fine King someday when I am gone. Well, Lord Mergin, why don't you leave me and my son to our own devices as you get some well-needed rest.'

'Yes, my Lord, I think that I shall turn in, but I shall rise at dawn and continue this investigation.' With a bow to the king and Alfrahil, Mergin took his leave.

'Well, my son,' said the king after Mergin had departed, 'you have certainly had a full day, but there is one last item I wish to discuss. A messenger arrived from Kozak early today bearing a message that Priscus, strongest of the Magi, would like to speak with either me or one of my two sons. As your brother is already under watch, sending him is out of the question. And I, of course, am needed here. Thus it would be best that you go to him. Perhaps Priscus has information that would help us, though I doubt he knows anything of our most recent troubles. Besides, if you leave the City and ride hard to Kozak, you may be in less danger than you seem to be in here in Eldora, as terrible as that is for me to say.'

Alfrahil pondered his father's words for a few moments before nodding. 'Yes, that is well, Father. Perhaps when I return, you and Mergin will have rounded up the guilty so that all of us may return to regular life again. Besides, I have always wanted to meet the Magi. I have heard so many legends about those ancient Forest Spirits. It will be interesting to see the truth.'

The Magi were Forest Spirits who, according to myth, created the Emerald Vale in remote Kozak to preserve the wondrous creatures and plants that lived there and to use their magic to probe the future and the present for answers to questions addressed to them by pilgrims.

Chuckling darkly, Creon said, 'I do not think that you will be disappointed in meeting Priscus, my son. But tread lightly while in his realm and remember that he is both proud and ancient. Too such as he, even Eldoran royalty are but upstarts. Do not let your temper get the better of you.'

'When have I ever?" asked Alfrahil.

Again Creon laughed. 'Perhaps you have not yet been sufficiently provoked.'

'Now I am more intrigued than ever father, very well. After breakfast tomorrow I shall assemble my guards and take five Shadows with me to ease your mind.'

'Very good, my son. Now go and rest, I have one last task to perform before I retire. I will see you upon your return.'

Alfrahil rose and, bowing, left his father alone in the meeting room with his thoughts.

* * *

After a few moments, Creon rose, his weary mind demanding more answers prior to submitting to a restful sleep. The First District was awash with guardsmen and over thirty Shadows, but Creon, wary of the breaches in security, changed into the uniform of a common guardsman, with a large helmet to conceal his face. Bidding two Shadows to change into similar attire, Creon felt reasonably safe as he walked out into the dark First District. Oil lamps in great glass globes were placed at regular intervals, providing a flickering yellow light bright enough for Creon to see his way. Stopping at the edge of the battlements, he gazed down upon the lights below and across the City plain. The evening sounds of the City came up occasionally to him: faint laughter and the horses trotting upon the streets. A gentle waft of odors from a distant kitchen reminded him that there were benefits to being a simple citizen, free of the overwhelming burdens of leading the kingdom.

Creon pushed his tall frame back from the battlements and walked toward the Tower of Anicetus and its tall dark spire. Soaring above the highest point in the city, the bright white granite stones were muted as the moon had set early and the yellow lights of the lamps did not extend very far. Tonight of all nights he was weary and did not relish the climb ahead of him, but he knew there was no other way to speed his message as far and fast as it needed to go.

His Shadow escort opened the small iron door set into the north-facing the wall at the base of the tower. Passing into the marbled foyer, Creon removed his helmet, surprising the guards on duty, who jumped to attention.

'At ease, men,' he told them. 'Anything unusual to report?'

'No, your highness,' replied the guard on Creon's left. 'We relieved the day guards, and we shall be relieved shortly after midnight by the dawn watch.'

'Very well,' said Creon. Looking ahead, he saw the tower stairs, dark basalt set into a regular pattern, disappearing into the dark. Creon ordered one of the guards to bring him an oil lantern; then, gesturing to his Shadows to remain below, he mounted the stairs. Dust rose from beneath his feet in the feeble light. Every four flights there was a small rest area, with a bench and a covered pitcher of water, and Creon took advantage of each one. Even so, his legs were cramping by the time he reached the top of the tower and the black iron door that was locked fast against all save the King.

Removing a key of Platina from around his neck, Creon inserted it into the ancient lock and entered the room of the Acies. One chair there was, with windows all around the small room atop the tower. The King permitted no visitors here and had shown the room to each of his sons but once, upon the day that they reached the age of their majority. Even Mergin had never been permitted entrance.

Many months had elapsed since Creon's last visit. He sat in the chair and pondered the crystals before him. A collection of crystal pipes hung from the ceiling on a strong chain, crisscrossing and turning in dozens of different directions. The set was a rough cube about three feet on a side, but there was the odd pipe that protruded in an asymmetric fashion as if brass instruments had been welded together by a drunken smith. Now the set was obscured by the feeble light of Creon's oil lamp, but he knew that in the daytime the crystals reflected and refracted sunlight, sending a rainbow cascade across the room.

At last, he rose and opened all the windows in the small chamber. Creon knew that no matter his thoughts and his rightful claim to use the Acies much depended upon the wind blowing through this tower top. He had no idea how and why the crystals functioned only when air blew through them. Many times, he had come to use the Acies, only to find that there was a breeze from the wrong quarter or too weak a wind to generate more than feeble sounds, washed-out colors, and indistinct forms and figures. But when the wind was right, the pipes uttered different tones, some deep, others shrill, and emitted lights and colors that coalesced into a small sphere of light, two feet in diameter and centered four feet above the floor. It was in that sphere that the visions appeared.

Tonight he was quite fortunate: the wind blew from many different directions, swirling around the tower and drawing images from all points of the compass, and from the past, present, and possibly even the future. The lost Acies under the river Aphon was reputed to have valves that enabled the user to control which images manifested themselves; from which different times could be discerned, but this set lacked any such mechanism, leaving Creon dependent upon the winds to direct the focus of the Acies. The Greater Elves had denied Creon's requests over the years to share the secrets of controlling the Acies, despite their mutual alliance. If the lost Acies were recovered, Creon would have a much more useful tool to see what far events transpired in Nostraterra.

As the night breezes coursed through the crystal pipes, Creon fixed his mind upon the small sphere of color that appeared below the set. When the images were clear, he focused upon them, unable to control the magic of the Crystals themselves, except that with great mental effort he could bid them show him specific places albeit briefly. Using the Crystals required tremendous strength and patience, as they would usually show random images of places and people near and far. However, when the wind was relatively constant Creon might stare at one small scene set in a forest somewhere for many minutes, and, just as his mind lost focus, the crystals would shift to show something very important. Creon suspected that the magic flowing through the crystals was somehow alive, perhaps even sentient, but again any questions directed at the Greater Elves were never answered.

As always when using the Acies, Creon marveled at the magic of the Elves, thanks to which he was able to see people and places farther than his fastest scouts could reach in months, to say nothing of events dredged from the past or from days not yet dawned. Tonight, the scenes flickered too fast for him to make sense of at first, but gradually he was able to focus his mind and slow the kaleidoscope of fragments into a cohesive whole. Yet though he desperately wanted answers about the attempt on his son's life, only one glimpse did the set give him: that of the preparations made before the attack, when the assassins practiced with their Elven weapons and Dwarven ladders on a deserted city street in a light too dim to allow him the chance to identify any of the men's features.

At last, he felt a sharp, stabbing pain in his mind and the beginning of a terrible headache—such was always the case when he wrestled for long with the Acies. Suddenly he heard a strange sound coming from the many windows, a mournful howl like he had never heard before. The breezes changed direction in sequence, from east to south to west to north to east again, proceeding in this clockwise order for a few moments.

All at once, a new and much larger sphere appeared beneath the set, tinged with blue. Creon had never seen before a vision associated with this blue coloring, and he hoped that finally, he was gaining mental mastery over the set. But though he tried to glimpse into Shardan, the Acies instead took him with dizzying speed south over the sea to what could only have been Elvalon, that fabled city of the Greater Elves. There he saw Elves arrayed for battle, led by Aradia the legendary Elf queen who had left Nostraterra after the defeat of Magnar. She was speaking to a vast host of soldiers who stood at attention, her face resolute and angry. Behind the soldiers, Creon saw a harbor filled with an armada of ships ready for sailing.

A last plaintive sound came from the wind, and then the vision was gone.

'*Was this some future moment, an Elven Army assembled and ready to depart to who knows where?*' wondered Creon. '*If so, there could only be one possible destination for such an army: Nostraterra.*'

Deeply troubled, Creon used the last of his mental strength and exercised the only specific command he was empowered to give this particular Acies, one that the Greater Elves had woven into its magic. His vision blurred, briefly, before clearing, and he beheld a familiar Elven face—that of one of the keepers of the Acies in Phoenicia, the last stronghold of the Greater Elves in Nostraterra, gateway to the Immortal Lands.

'King Creon, this is indeed an honor. How may we help you?'

Creon swiftly related all that had recently transpired in Eldora. He kept his voice even, his tone polite, though in truth it galled him deeply to be compelled by circumstances to approach the Greater Elves as if on bended knee, as though he were an ordinary supplicant and not the High King of Men.

'I would ask the aid of the Elves of Phoenicia in unmasking those behind this murderous plot and bringing them to justice,' he said. 'I would also request that Lord Celefin himself be informed of the situation and be consulted on our behalf, as befits two royal allies.'

'Verily, your highness. These are dire tidings. I will speak with Celefin when he is awake on the morrow. We shall respond as quickly as possible,' said the Elf.

'No,' said Creon. 'Have him speak to me personally, for there are matters I wish to discuss that are for no other ears but his.'

'It shall be done, King Creon. In two days' time, Lord Celefin of Phoenicia will sit here at this same time and respond to your request.'

Creon withdrew his contact, sagging physically and mentally in weariness. After a moment, he rose from the stiff-backed chair. It was nearly dawn. He must hurry back to the Astrology Tower if he did not wish the daylight to reveal him to any who might be watching this tower and questioning the strange play of lights that had come from within.

Chapter Twelve

Warnings

Just after daybreak, Alfrahil assembled his guards, led by Caelus, in the courtyard of the Citadel with sixty Citadel guards and thirty knights of Kelsea, along with five Shadows. The knights were legendary cavalry, from the duchy of Kelsea, one of the six royal principalities that comprised the interior of Eldora. Alfrahil rode forth in full ceremonial armor, with a large plumed helmet that hid much of his face. His escort was likewise accoutered, while the Shadows wore their traditional camouflage garb. It was a short ride to the Healer Hall, down through the ruined Second District to the Third, where the horses were stabled at a messenger stable while Alfrahil and his Shadows entered the hall.

Clanking into the hall in royal regalia and dress mail, Alfrahil felt ridiculous in this outfit. Moreover, as he entered the hall, he strode into the common ward and saw the hurtful, angry glances of the families of the wounded. It did not take all of Alfrahil's political acumen to realize that these common folk thought he was posturing in his dress armor, only pretending to care for the wounded while looking princely for political reasons. Nothing could have been further from the truth, but Alfrahil knew that he must continue this charade no matter how uncomfortable.

Findalas quickly appeared, wiping the last crumbs from her morning breakfast from her face. She appeared stunned by his appearance.

'My prince, how can I be of service?' she asked, with a hint of anger in her voice and dark red splotches on her face, as if affronted by the bald-faced political nature of Alfrahil's garb.

'You can show me to my friend Biramin's room, Healer Findalas, and then Captain Alcar's room,' said Alfrahil emotionlessly.

Findalas flushed even more darkly before saying through clenched teeth, 'Certainly, my Lord. I think you know the way.'

Sending two Shadows ahead, and leaving the other three on the lower level, Alfrahil clanked up the stairs to the private ward on the second floor. Oil lamps in globes were in the stairway provided light, and Alfrahil saw a broom closet offset into the stairwell wall on the first landing above the main floor. Opening the closet door, Alfrahil told his two Shadows to proceed upstairs without him. Reaching up and pulling the oil lamp out of its bracket, Alfrahil propelled Findalas none too gently into the closet. Before she could voice any objection, he placed his mail-clad fingers against her mouth as gently as he could.

'Findalas please do not be angry with me. I am here for three reasons today. First, to see to my friends, the next second to continue a complex subterfuge created by Lord Mergin, and the third to see you again. This ludicrous outfit has its purpose. This is not political posturing, but a disguise.'

Confused and still angry, Findalas replied, 'You wanted to see me again. Why?'

Suddenly awkward, Alfrahil stuttered, 'Because you are beautiful and kind and an accomplished healer, I would like to see you again under less formal circumstances.'

Blushing even in the yellow light of the lamp, Findalas was momentarily speechless but then found her voice. 'Perhaps I can come to visit you in the Citadel tomorrow if you like?'

'That will not be possible, for I will be abroad tomorrow and the next few weeks, but as soon as I return, I would like it above all things. Now, however, I need your help. I will see my friends in this ludicrous getup, but then I must descend these stairs and change out of this armor into the clothing of a leper. Do you have such clothes?'

'Yes, lord,' said Findalas. 'But why…?'

'I need to get out of Titania unseen and unsuspected. If I ride out plainly, I will simply be a target again. A guardsman of my build will come here to put on my armor and leave the Healer Hall in my place, and I will sneak out with my Shadows through the tradesman entrance at the back of the hall.'

To this, Findalas readily agreed. They left the closet and hastened to Biramin's room. Alfrahil opened the door quietly and saw Biramin fast asleep, with Wynhyrra sleeping in a neighboring cot. Not wanting to wake his friend, Alfrahil withdrew and whispered to Findalas once the door was closed, 'How is he?'

'Better, Lord. He is mending well and will be fit to return to duty in a month or so.'

'Very well. Let me see Alcar and I will be away on my mission.' Not saying anything else, Alfrahil lumbered toward Alcar's room for several steps before he realized Findalas was not keeping pace with him any longer. Turning, he glanced back quizzically and saw Findalas standing there with a stricken expression on her face. When their gazes met, she shook her head softly. Realizing that Alcar was dead, Alfrahil tried his best to maintain his composure and succeeded after a few moments of shaking in despair.

Findalas approached and said, 'It was best that he died quickly, even the Elven healer could not stop the infection. There was nothing we could do.'

Pulling himself together, Alfrahil said, 'Very well, I must change now.'

'This way, lord,' said Findalas, pulling him down a service corridor.

* * *

Twenty minutes later, finally free from the cumbersome armor, Alfrahil, dressed in the dark blue robes of a leper, slipped down the rear stairs in the company of Findalas. Pausing in a darkened foyer that led into the small rear courtyard, he turned and gave Findalas' hands a gentle squeeze. 'I hope to see you on my return, Findalas.'

'You will, my prince. Send word when you return and I will come when you are available.'

Alfrahil then bade her return upstairs and emerged into the roughly cobbled courtyard, where he was joined by his Shadows, who had already removed their traditional garb and wore the ordinary tunics of common laborers. A long covered wagon, bearing the black skull of the dead on its tattered cloth roof, clattered into the courtyard with two of Alfrahil's guardsmen disguised in the somber black cloaks of funeral drivers. Alfrahil climbed into the back of the wagon and lay down on his back, pretending to be a dead leper. The Five Shadows climbed with him into the back of the wagon and joined the "bodies" made of straw-stuffed clothes, with painted cloth faces, laid out in tidy rows. Alfrahil remembered that Mergin thought his best chance of leaving the city undetected was in a corpse wagon, with all of his guardsmen driving other wagons in a long funeral procession. With all of the hundreds of dead from the ambush in the city, another long train of the dead being taken to gravesites outside the city wall should draw little attention. Still, Alfrahil was disguised as a leper so that in the unlikely event anyone looked into the back of the wagon, they would be put off seeing the diseased body.

Taking the rest of the day to reach the city gates, the wagon train exited Titania and two hours later entered a small valley, where they could secretly remove the black skull banners through rents in the cloth of each wagon, and the drivers changed places with guardsmen who were now wearing ordinary clothes. Within minutes what had been a long funeral procession now appeared to be a common merchant caravan. The wagons pulled into a warehouse district outside the city walls and parked in a common lot filled with sand and debris.

Feeble torchlight allowed Alfrahil to see. He climbed stiffly out of the wagon and walked into the closest warehouse, which was empty of people but for his guardsmen, who were slowly emerging from their wagons as well. All of the horses ridden by Alfrahil and his escort were there, having been ridden down during the day by other guardsmen in ordinary clothes, and spare horses were assembled, along with pack horses carrying dried food, medicines, camping equipment, and spare clothes.

Finishing their preparations by torchlight was not easy, but soon Alfrahil's escort was ready. Alfrahil personally knew each member of the company, and he considered it impossible that any of these men should be assassins or traitors. Traveling fast and light would permit Alfrahil to remain ahead of any rumor of his departure from the city, allowing him to reach the Vale quietly and safely … he hoped.

The next two days of hard riding left Alfrahil stiff and sore and reeking of horse sweat. Each night they pitched camp and ate like soldiers on campaign, rising early the next morning to press on. The stone road from Eldora ended at the Kozak border, transitioning to a sandy track thirty feet wide. This was maintained by the riders of Kozak and had a pliable surface that was gentle on horses' hooves. Just past the border, the track split in two. The straighter path penetrated a small old-growth forest of oaks and maples. It was a narrow way, so only three horses could ride abreast. The other track kept its original width but ran south and then back north nearly twenty miles, crossing a small river that was low and swampy. Caelus chose the southern track, knowing that the half day of additional travel was much safer, as the flat grasslands would offer few places for assassins to lie in wait. A full Faris of Kozaki riders greeted them after a short delay at the border, escorting them through their realm.

Leaving the grasses behind, Alfrahil and his men rode through shallow watery sands and mire before encountering the first of several low bridges designed to float upon the marshes and water. Despite the low height of the first bridge, Alfrahil repressed a sudden bitter memory of the Great Bridge collapsing in Titania. Though he knew objectively that if this bridge collapsed, he would be uncomfortable rather than dead, he breathed a sigh of relief when they crossed the third and last bridge and gently rode up a grassy slope out of the river valley.

Alfrahil's company and escort rode over eighty leagues first west-northwest and then north, curving around the Encircling Mountains through the realm of Eldora, before arriving at Mostyn, the Kozaki capital, eleven days after leaving Titania.

Upon his arrival, Alfrahil received the formal salute of the guards of Bernardus and was greeted warmly by Bernardus, King of Kozak. Tall and blond, like many Kozaki, Bernardus showed the youthful exuberance of a man recently come of age, though he would not see forty years again. Bernardus was thirty years younger than Alfrahil, but, lacking Elven blood, he appeared to be at least ten years older, with strands of gray visible in his long blond hair. His face was tanned from decades spent in the sun, and he had the blue-gray eyes that were so common amongst the Kozaki. Bernardus walked with the rolling gait common to men who spent more of their lives in a saddle than out of one, but his cheerful countenance and air of command suited him well. Alfrahil reflected that Kozak had a good man for a king. The country had prospered since Bernardus' ascension to the throne three years ago.

Bernardus escorted Alfrahil to a private tent, prepared for the Eldoran prince, with a fresh steaming bath. Bernardus said in the casual custom of Kozak, 'Alfrahil, you arrive unannounced and unexpected, but you are always welcome; come and join me at my table when you are finished washing from your long journey.'

'Thank you, Bernardus,' Alfrahil replied. 'A bath would be most welcome.'

Feeling safe in the great Kozaki tent city of Mostyn, Alfrahil gratefully relaxed in a portable hip bath made of animal hides coated with wax. It leaked slowly, and the strong scent of leather rose around him, but Alfrahil was clean for the first time in over a week and felt the soreness in his hips begin to fade away. The cut on his face, from the arrow wound during the first ambush, was nearly healed, as well as the other wounds suffered in both ambushes. He gratefully sipped a glass of tepid ale as he soaked; glad the first leg of his journey was over.

A breeze flapped against the side of the tent, and despite many layers, a soft draft blew the clean air of the grasses of Kozak through the tent, bearing the ever-present odors of horses and wood smoke and wafting the fragrant smells of roasting meats gently to his nose. The constant murmur of thousands of men coming and going from the caravan city blended into a blurred cacophony with the sharper sounds of a metal pan dropped onto a grate over a fire close by. Once again Alfrahil wondered at the Kozaki, their vast tent caravan spreading for over a mile, often struck down and packed onto horses and wagons each day and then erected each night again. History had taught the Kozaki that permanent structures were dangerous traps, allowing your enemies to approach and fire wooden buildings, slaying you and your kin within. A mobile city, however, was safe; there were tents that could burn, but the scouts moving around the great city each day and night kept their enemies at bay. Not having the experience of stone working, nor comfortable with its restrictions upon horses, the Kozaki had opted for tents and mobility over woodwork and solidity. It was only in the last hundred years or so, after the defeat of Magnar, that the Kozaki had constructed their first permanent stone buildings, and these were occupied by men of Kozak who were merchants rather than horsemen, trusting in granite and limestone rather than cloth to keep their goods and money safe.

* * *

That night at the high table in Mostyn, Bernardus and Alfrahil exchanged many toasts to their kingdoms, their people, and their hope for peace. The hall was an amazing sight to a man like Alfrahil, used to the solid buildings of Titania: thick beams rose from central pillars of dark wood, supported by chains and stakes driven into the ground. In turn, wooden beams formed support for a thick yet light thatched roof, covering the hall and its occupants. Even the great tables that filled the hall came apart easily and quickly, along with the padded benches, but once the room was occupied, you would only know that you were in a tent by the lack of stone. Pausing before he left for his tent, Alfrahil briefly explained his mission to Bernardus, who agreed to meet Alfrahil just after first light.

Retiring to his tent after the festivities, Alfrahil found sleep elusive. He tossed and turned as his mind churned the terrible events of the past weeks. But at last, he fell into a fitful sleep.

* * *

The sounds of a cock crowing the dawn wrenched Alfrahil from his slumber, drawing him from the worlds of dreams once more into the world of Men.

Hearing a polite cough from one of his guardsmen, Alfrahil said, 'Enter.'

Bernardus strode into the tent. He stared at Alfrahil's haggard countenance quizzically but politely said nothing. 'Good morning, Alfrahil. Come and break your fast with me. I know I cannot persuade you to tarry here on your journey to the Emerald Vale, nor tempt you to go hunting with me over the plains, but at least you and I shall drink a parting cup before you go about your errands. I may not be here upon your return; there have been rumors of a small band of Dark Elves lurking along the hills of the Shale Mountains, and I shall lead a great company to investigate and hunt the trespassers down if they are there.'

Startled, Alfrahil said, 'Dark Elves? Do you mean to tell me that there are Dark Elves in your lands again? Why did you not speak of this last night?'

'The report arrived only this morning,' said Bernardus, 'brought by a rider with a terrified shepherd at his back, wide-eyed with fear. It will be several days before I and my men will arrive at the remote encampment where the shepherd claims to have seen the Dark Elves. Most likely he got drunk and saw shadows moving in the dark by his fire; an overactive imagination and fear of the unknown did the rest. However, tracking a potential party of Dark Elves is certainly more sporting than chasing deer across the land.'

'It has been over two hundred years since the last of their kind was seen in Eldora, though it is said that numbers of them may still be found in the wastes of the east,' said Alfrahil. 'I wonder what could have drawn them back after so many years?'

'Perhaps a death wish,' answered Bernardus with a smile. 'For if they have come indeed, then death is all they will find here.'

'Well,' said Alfrahil. 'I must tarry no longer. Come, let us break our fast as you suggested, and then I am off to the Emerald Vale.'

* * *

After leaving Mostyn, Alfrahil and his men rode two days and nights, crossing the plains of Kozak and fording the river Wyryn. Now, as the third day wore on, the troop followed the

Wyryn north and east up toward the mountains that surrounded Eldora for several leagues.

The road wound up from the river valley below, clinging precariously to the mountainside of the northwest face of the valley. Already they were a thousand feet above the river, and their road, if it could be called a road, was a small grass track that continued without interruption between the lush cliff to their left and the sheer drop to their right. The vale was wide at the bottom but steadily narrowed as it rose over many miles until it reached the boundary of the Thunder Falls.

The falls fell from a height of over five hundred fathoms, and while there were falls above them that plunged even farther, no other cataract was as powerful. The roar of the river Wyryn coursing over its precipice could be heard for dozens of miles, and the ground itself trembled ceaselessly under the onslaught. The mist that rose from the falls produced spectacular vistas, especially when played upon by the rising or setting sun. The vale faced southwest at such an angle, that the prevailing upper winds steered moisture and storms up this valley. As the warm moist air from the humid southern plains was forced up through the valley, the air cooled as it rose, losing its ability to hold moisture and depositing it as rain at lower elevations and snow on the peaks themselves. The Emerald Vale itself lay within a spectacular oval amidst the highest peaks of the Encircling Mountains—the tallest in Nostraterra, towering nearly two leagues above the plains. Framing the narrow, incredibly deep upper vale within their icy confines, they provided the snows and rains that swelled the river Wyryn into the great torrent that it was. The snows of the lower slopes of the crystal peaks melted and fed rings of terraced stones that grew larger down the mountainsides. The lowest terrace was still nearly five hundred feet from the floor of the upper vale, and the waterfalls that cascaded from above combined with the deep moisture rising from the lower valley to produce the only known cloud forest in Nostraterra.

Too warm for snow, the upper vale was a riot of color and verdant shrubs and trees. Flowers grew there that grew nowhere else in Nostraterra, and fragrances found nowhere else ensnared the senses and beguiled the mind, distracting those that proceeded so far. As Alfrahil climbed, saplings of green trees he could not name appeared; the silver and gray-gold of their leaves shimmering like coins in the bright light.

The air became sweet and warm as if Alfrahil had somehow wandered back in time, to when the world was young. So much did he feel these sensations that Alfrahil expected Elves to drift gracefully downstream, lilting with their beautiful voices about forgotten beauties of the ancient world. For Alfrahil this was a waking dream, the first he had received in Nostraterra. His mind was enraptured by the senses of life and the dreams of forgotten creatures that drank deeply of the earth and for whom the seasons were as but the brief passing of clouds before the moon upon a night of swift wind.

Alfrahil and his companions soon found themselves riding in a dream of green and gold, where all motion continued and all movement ceased. Briefly, Alfrahil realized through a small rent in the clouds and mist that a glorious sunset had fallen, a scarlet conflagration that overshadowed all the colors of the day that had gone before with hues of salmon and vermillion, mauve and cerulean. As dusk fell upon the vale, he noticed that his horse and those of his comrades had stopped walking. He dimly understood that he and his men were under an unknown irresistible spell, and he and his men dismounted and lay upon the soft grass. Never had he felt so deeply at peace with the world. Was he asleep or awake? The distinction now seemed meaningless.

* * *

Alfrahil woke with a start as a brief rain shower passed overhead. The sun had set and all was dark gray, with the moon trying to come through gaps in the clouds aloft. Wondering how much time had passed, he drowsily pulled himself up from the fragrant turf as, around him, the rest of the party did likewise. All was mist, swirling like impudent wraiths upon the breath of the breeze.

A deep voice rose from Alfrahil's left, answered by an even deeper voice to his right. A dark shadow appeared, coursing through the mist like some leviathan of the ocean cutting through the waves. Alfrahil understood that he and his company were surrounded by the Magi, mystical creatures older than the very hills.

Alfrahil's fear of attack pushed aside by the wonders of the Vale, now returned full force, and it was with great difficulty that he did not order a retreat. 'Wait, and unsheathe no weapon,' he cried to his men. 'The Magi mean us no harm. Stand firm; endure what fate brings with grace and fortitude.'

Yet though the men exchanged nervous glances and whispers, keeping their hands close to their weapons, the horses of the company showed no alarm whatsoever but peacefully cropped the verdant grass as if this vale were their accustomed pasture.

The melodic voices sounded again, much closer, but as if from deep within the earth. Alfrahil stood enraptured by the wonder that such entities still existed out of song. While he had been told the tale of the Magi as a child and had dutifully repeated the lines to his teacher, he had not quite believed in their existence. Alfrahil recalled hearing of how Earth Spirits had blended their powers with Water Spirits to create the Forest Spirits when the world was young. These spirits moved to a remote mountain valley, transforming it into the Emerald Vale. There they created a garden of unequaled beauty in Nostraterra, vowing to protect the lives of trees and animals, and barring all from entering their valley uninvited.

The Magi were known as great Oracles, as they had the vast memory of immortals coupled with tremendous magical foresight. Many of their predictions were delivered in riddles. Some were spoken in sentences that ran in obscure order, while others were sung as songs. But the Magi could not be compelled to answer the questions put to them; indeed, there was little discernible rhyme or reason to why they would ignore some questions of great importance but answer seemingly minor questions instead. Sometimes they said nothing at all. At other times they would answer questions that had not yet been spoken.

Over time, the Magi had taken to ignoring almost all questions, instead issuing proclamations concerning the future at irregular intervals. It might take years or decades for their prophecies to come true, or for circumstances to, as it were, translate their more cryptic utterances into sense, but sooner or later they did come to pass. Now, for reasons unknown to Alfrahil, the greatest of all the Magi, Priscus, had summoned him to the Emerald Vale. Alfrahil was curious to learn those reasons, but he had every intention of posing questions of his own.

Alfrahil and his men were consumed in a thick, cloyingly fragrant mist that obscured their sight. All they heard was the soft drip of moisture and the distant roar of fast-moving water. Then the mist began to wane, and Alfrahil glimpsed ancient boughs clothed in lichens and moss that seemed to go hurtling by like starlings at twilight. The great melodic voices broke forth again, and a soft glow came from the dissolving mist, of many different colors. Alfrahil found himself gazing into whirling clouds of chartreuse smoke that seethed and roiled as if boiling with immense heat. Yet he felt no heat.

'Who are you, and why have you come?' asked a voice that seemed to come from out of those clouds.

The prince replied, 'Alfrahil am I, son of Creon, High King of Eldora and all the Westmen, who honors the promise of Men that all these lands within the Vale belong to the Magi in perpetuity. I have come in answer to the summons of Priscus, and to beg for your help regarding certain dire circumstances that have recently come to pass in our land.'

'I am Priscus, Prince of Eldora,' replied the voice with a mellifluous sigh, and suddenly Alfrahil realized that the chartreuse clouds before him were in actuality a pair of immense eyes. 'Many years of Men and the leaves of many seasons have passed since I last spoke with your father. Are you honest and true as he, or craven, carrying falsehood and treachery in your heart?'

At this, Alfrahil felt anger overcome his fear. His heart blazed within him, feeding off the murmurs of his men, and he said, 'I am the Crown Prince of Eldora! If I am to be treated with disrespect, my men and I shall go home, and you shall find no help from Men if you need it in the future.' Bristling with indignation, Alfrahil turned to mount his horse, but those amazing chartreuse eyes reappeared in front of him, revealing brief warmth, like a glint of distant sunlight on an overcast afternoon.

A tone of such purity and resonance came forth from behind those eyes that it seemed to Alfrahil his skull must surely shatter. Yet the pain vanished in an instant. In fact, he was not sure it had been a pain, simply a sensation he had never felt before, pitched too high for normal senses to register. He felt Priscus' mind enter his own. But this was no rough, uncaring intrusion such as he had experienced in the past from his father's mental investigations. He felt as if tiny invisible fingers were gently probing his thoughts, asking wordless questions yet also focusing on his fear and despair, and repairing many of Alfrahil's ragged mental fibers. Then Alfrahil felt the presence withdraw.

Priscus spoke again. 'You do indeed possess some of the good qualities of your father, but without many of his flaws. You are welcome here, Alfrahil, son of Creon. Let us withdraw now to the upper meadows of the Emerald Vale, where you and I may speak more privately. You shall have no need of any escort,

Prince Alfrahil. Your men can wait here, outside the Vale proper. They will be safe and comfortable.'

'Gladly will I accompany you, Priscus,' said Alfrahil. Then, to his men: "Wait here for my return. Do nothing to denigrate the hospitality of the Magi.'

'But my Lord,' said Caelus. 'If your father knew we had allowed you to travel unprotected..."

'I feel sure that Priscus is all the protection I shall require. Of course, you may take the matter up with him, Caelus, if you wish it.'

'N-no, Lord,' stammered Caelus, turning pale. 'We will abide until your return.'

Alfrahil made to mount his horse, but Priscus said, 'You must come on foot, Prince Alfrahil. And take care to keep to the path, lest you unwittingly damage or destroy any living thing.'

'I shall,' Alfrahil answered.

To be invited deep within the vale by the Magi was unheard of, and Alfrahil followed the chartreuse eyes with a great deal of wonder and curiosity, his mind much clearer and stronger than before, thanks to Priscus' mental intervention. Slowly he proceeded across a small sandy, muddy track amid lush meadows, only visible within a few feet as the mist surrounding him allowed him to see his feet and the ground before him, toward the far end of the Vale. Now, the mist of the Magi disappeared, remaining as a barrier to his men that they could not see through, but the natural mists of the valley diffused the light of the full moon into a gentle glow, allowing Alfrahil to dimly see. Thick leaves and flowers brushed his shoulders as Alfrahil wiped the moisture from his face. He felt that he was truly walking within a cloud; and that with a brief concentrated effort he could drift up with the mist, ascending to the great snowy peaks above, where he would meet the sun in its great fierceness, before gently settling down toward the verdant slopes below. Alfrahil felt the power of the Magi and of the forest grow, surrounding him he made his way through the shadowed mists. Shivering for a moment, Alfrahil looked quickly about, and could see only shadowy ripples ahead and alongside himself that he presumed were Priscus and the other Magi. Suddenly, while still walking across the meadow, Alfrahil heard the whisper of wind through the boughs of ancient branches. Not seeing any trees, the soft moonlight revealed only a dark gray barrier form around him.

But then he realized he must be hearing the sounds of Vespre, or Ghosts of the Forests, as they were also known, lesser, wilder forest spirits, incapable of or unwilling to speak with Men, Dwarves, or even Elves. More numerous than the Magi, they often assumed the forms of animals and trees slain unjustly. They patrolled the entire valley, both upper and lower, and ignored all intruders so long as they did not harm the plants, trees, or creatures that dwelt here. But if anyone should cause harm to anything that lived in the valley, then the Vespre would exact a terrible revenge. The Vespre could not be bargained with, and they were unfettered by pity or remorse. Not for naught did the Kozaki and other Men enter but rarely into the Vale, making certain to leave the trees and the creatures that dwelt there alone, and allowing no horse to graze. No wonder that Priscus had cautioned him to remain on the path.

A cool dry wind suddenly blew down from the sides of the valley and at last, Alfrahil could see the mountain walls that cupped the vale and its surrounding forests within their stony arms, as if someday they would fill the valley with rock; as if all that living hands, both mortal and immortal, had built would perish before their inexorable will. Alfrahil looked ahead and saw a wooden wall forming a great curve that reached from one narrow side of the valley to the other. The wind had pushed the mist up above the valley floor, hiding the tops of the wall completely. Alfrahil followed the path toward the wall, determined to show only wonder rather than fear to Priscus when he arrived at his unknown destination.

Priscus, like all the Magi, greeted present times with deep sadness, for his knowledge of the future had long revealed to him the coming of the dominion of Men. The Magi had known loss and hardship prior to the arrival of the Elves, and now Men were felling the forests of Nostraterra at a great pace, replacing trees with farms, ancient grasslands, with tilled earth. Many of the Magi were reluctant to speak with any creatures but those that dwelt within the forest, though they regarded the Elves more highly than most. Few of them wanted anything to do with Men, but Priscus felt differently. He hoped to turn Men away from their destructive pathways and preserve the forests, for without the forests, without the wild, natural places of Nostraterra, the Magi had no purpose and would retreat into the earth again from whence they came.

Now, sensing the mood of antipathy toward mortals from nearby Magi and Vespre, Priscus led Alfrahil deeper into the Vale, to the northeast end, where he took physical form. Rather than appearing as a disembodied, shimmering spirit, he was now part tree, part man-shaped, with two long arms, covered in leaves and bark, and hands with long, thin branches for fingers. His lower body was hidden in shadow, but his eyes glowed fifteen feet high off the ground. Other Magi were nearby, shimmering faintly in the soft fall of moonlight. One was a column of water twelve feet high that rippled and danced. Another was a dark ruby pillar of light; smoky particles moved through it, as if the light from a burning forest were present, ever-changing constantly in flux. A nearby pile of boulders rumbled as the individual stones moved upon and across one another, growing taller and then wider, taking a brief humanoid form before returning to a pile of rocks.

Priscus bent slightly to speak with Alfrahil. Instead of asking him what his questions were, or issuing some obscure pronouncement, Priscus did something unrecorded in the history of Men: he conversed.

'I have sensed many things of late in the air and from the rains and mist and water. A disquiet grows within the back of my mind, pushing ever forward to reach my waking thoughts,' he said. 'I sense that things are changing more rapidly than I would like and that great evil is about to be awakened once more within the world. This time, however, I do not believe that we Magi shall remain unchanged or even unscathed.'

'What do you foresee?' asked Alfrahil.

'Little good,' replied Priscus. 'The recent events in Eldora may be the first sign of what I fear may come to pass. If you and your father were slain, the realm of Eldora would descend into chaos, forcing your brother to win over the hearts and minds of powerful Men who do not love him.'

'How do you know of the inner workings of Eldora?' asked Alfrahil incredulously.

'There is little that can evade my thoughts, and I have many messengers that bring word to me from all parts of Nostraterra,' Priscus said. 'Besides, there is one other; a great power who still exists in this world: one who loves the trees and the wild creatures as much as I. It is he that provides me with many messengers, and I give him my counsel from afar.'

'To whom are you referring?' asked Alfrahil.

'This is not important now; suffice to say that most of what occurs in the outside world is known to me, either through the reports I receive or my own visions of the future. Yet I had no forewarning of the attempt on your life, young prince. That was news I pulled directly from your mind. Which is quite troubling, I must say. It seems that evil has spread farther and faster than I had thought possible.'

'What evil?' asked Alfrahil. 'And how does this relate to the attempts on my life?'

Priscus paused a moment. 'In our visions, we Magi have seen Dark Elves gathering in the East and South aided by terrible blue creatures such as we have never beheld: creatures whose magic is equally unique. We have seen the lands of all races seething with discontent and conflicts hidden beneath a placid surface erupting into wars amongst each race and then between the races. Chaos and terror will threaten all that live in Nostraterra—trees, animals, and sentient beings—with darkness greater than that brought by Magnar. These dark visions change from one day to the next, indicating that the future is not yet fixed in the books of fate. Individual choices by those in power in their lands, Elf, Dwarf, and Man, will ultimately determine the future of all Nostraterra.'

'These are indeed grave, if vague, tidings,' said Alfrahil. 'What can I do to avert this danger to Nostraterra?'

'I looked most closely into your mind to see what troubles you and to judge your character, but I did not probe all of your memories. What have you heard and seen in your realm that might lend support to the visions I have just related? It is for this reason that I sent my message to your father.'

'Besides the attacks upon me, nothing comes to mind. Of course, there are the usual grumblings from the Shardan front, as the insurrection continues, but it has been thus for many a year now. I have heard of internal difficulties in the realms of the Dwarves and the Lesser Elves, but nothing specifically dark or dangerous, just normal disagreements over politics and religion.'

'Has your father seen anything in his tower-top?' asked Priscus. 'Using the Acies there, he can see much.'

'My father does not use the Acies often, and whatever he does or does not see there is not relayed to me or to my brother, Daerahil. I will ask my father what he has seen on my return to Eldora. Currently, he and his counselors are concerned with unearthing the plot and conspiracy against me, and we would ask your help in rooting out the cause, as well as any other aid you can give.'

'Aid?' replied Priscus with a gleam in his eye. 'You shall come with me soon to receive such aid as I can give. But you must promise to aid the Magi in turn. I would ask you to dispatch scouts and riders, trustworthy Men, who will not easily yield to temptation, to the far corners of your realm and beyond to search for proof that the Dark Elves are arising again and that these mysterious blue creatures and their terrible magic exist. Persuade your allies amongst the Lesser Elves and the Dwarves to also send scouts through their lands. Once you know more, return to me here and give me your tidings.'

'I have already arranged for the aid of Dwarves and Elves in our search for these evil plotters,' Alfrahil replied.

'Excellent,' said Priscus. 'Now let me give you the aid I spoke of.'

Alfrahil saw the wooden wall before him, disappearing into the mists. Dappled shadows lay along the barrier until he drew close enough and found that it was comprised of huge trees, nearly twenty feet across, with dark spaces between them that no light penetrated. The tinkling sound of water came from the spaces between the trees, but overall there was a constant hiss and roar of smaller cataracts plunging from a great height somewhere close at hand. A small but deep stream lay before his feet, collecting itself from seven smaller streams emerging from the gaps between the trees. A faint hint of color flashed up from this water, appearing and disappearing as quickly as it was seen, and he shook his head at this most unusual occurrence.

Passing through the wall of giant trees, Alfrahil was astonished to see that they were in an enormous ring of trees, each over forty feet in diameter, with the trees rising above them nearly to the tops of the first terraced layers of stone. The mist surrounded Alfrahil departed, and he was able to look upon a sky that he had never seen before and would never see again.

The air had grown incredibly thin and cold; Alfrahil had a difficult time catching his breath. But not for that reason alone. Gazing up at the stars, he was amazed at their brilliance and colors. No longer plain white dots seen from mortal lands, these stars flashed and pulsed in myriad hues, and a mist of lesser stars ran across the sky like spilled silver dust. Here, Alfrahil thought, were the true sentinels of the world, and they would not care what course the mortals that basked in their eternal light might take. Clearly, the stars would remain and Men would swiftly disappear, without the stars taking notice or acknowledging the existence of Men. The thin air made Alfrahil swoon. The sounds of the cascading water from above blended with his heartbeat, and he staggered, nearly falling. At that moment, the mists returned, and Alfrahil was brought back within the actual world, though the memory of what he had seen would never leave him.

'You have seen what no other mortal has ever seen,' said Priscus. 'We have allowed you to experience what the universe is like for us. Even if you climbed to the very top of the Encircling Peaks, you would not see such a vision again. Cherish it well.'

'I will,' replied an awestruck Alfrahil.

'Now let us look upon where we are today.'

As Priscus spoke, the mists cleared again, revealing the mountain peaks and stars as before … only less incandescent. Now the stars twinkled down upon the Magi and the enormous trees of this end of the valley. The waterfalls cascading from the sheer cliffs above splashed and danced upon the stone terraces, and their droplets added to the mist that came from the vale, coating the trees and descending in a dense cloud of fog. The Magi began their song, and soon colors appeared within the mist, fleeting yet pervasive, and great shapes and shifts of color emerged and disappeared. Alfrahil knew instinctively that these colors were the basis for the visions seen by the Magi and that he was observing their true powers in action.

Long was their song, and Alfrahil saw that the colors were created by the trees, that the water that danced at their crowns trickled down their trunks and branches, sending small bits of color out along each branch and leaf. These colors grew in strength and in scope as they traveled down the trunk, and Alfrahil saw that on several branches large spheres were present, where the colors did not flow but instead proceeded down the trunks to where the Magi stood. A huge prismatic shape appeared in the center of the chanting Magi, and it changed form as rapidly as it changed color. At the feet of the Magi was a small but deep pool that gathered the magic. Colors and streamers billowed up from its surface back to the amorphous form of light that floated above them.

Through all of this, the Magi changed their song in pitch and tone, slower than faster, then faster again before becoming so slow that each note held for several minutes. Alfrahil knew that the Magi were controlling each strand of color in a thaumaturgic dance that was well beyond his skill at interpreting, and it was only toward the end of the song that the colored mist moved, covering Alfrahil within its confines. Alfrahil saw colors and forms that he had never seen before; nor was the effect limited to sight alone, but all of his senses—hearing, smell, taste, and touch—were stimulated. Unbelievably, Alfrahil tasted the color red, touched the color blue, and smelled the sound of rain tinkling off the leaves of the trees.

Suddenly, Alfrahil's spirit left its body. He saw himself standing suspended within the circle as a look of total incredulity consumed his face. His spirit floated rapidly, and he soared over the tops of the trees, penetrating the mist and clouds overhead. Emerging above the cloud tops, he was amazed to see the moon shining brightly down upon the clouds and the mountain peaks that protruded from them like islands from a milky sea.

He felt a force compelling his spirit downward, and he gazed down through the clouds at the vale below. How he was able to see so clearly he could not comprehend, but he did. Nor did his sight simply extend in front of him. It flew simultaneously in all directions, piercing the veil of distance and even, or so it seemed to him for a moment, that of time itself, as if, like the Magi, he were able to glimpse into the future. But his mortal mind recoiled from these immensities. He felt as if his head would shatter with the chaotic onslaught of images and sensations he lacked the ability to understand or control.

Then, just as it seemed he could withstand no more, the song of the Magi faded away. The colored cloud drifted upward and away from Alfrahil, and he felt both a tremendous loss and an enormous relief as his spirit returned to his exhausted body.

'Now you know something of our magic, young prince,' said Priscus. 'Use this gift well.'

Only then did Alfrahil realize that he had been as one with the powers of the Magi. And something of that exposure had stayed with him. He found that he could now sense emotion, and it seemed to him that, with practice and time, he might even learn to influence the emotions of others. It came to him that his mind had been expanded in ways that he had never dreamed of. For better or worse, his thought processes had been irrevocably changed. As he considered the burden that had been laid upon him with the Magi's influence and song, he was not certain if he had been given a great gift or a terrible curse.

'You have received aid of the Magi that none of your kind has ever received,' said Priscus.

'I am grateful,' said Alfrahil. 'But why me?'

'Do not forget that I have seen your thoughts, young prince. I have plumbed the depths of your heart. It is a true heart, and stouter than you know. We Magi will need a firm ally amongst Men, one who will not betray our trust. This magic will aid you to feel perceptions that no other Men can feel. Moreover, you will be able to sense the feelings and emotions of others, and determine the truth of their words, but not their actual thoughts without detection. This is something that your father and your brother cannot do.'

'How is this different from the abilities of my father and brother?'

'Their ability comes from the unique mingling of Elven blood they carry in a fashion unknown even to me. This talent is not given to either the Greater or Lesser Elves, so your father and brother are the only corporeal beings who have this ability. Despite the fact that you carry the same blood, for reasons unknown to me their skills did not pass to you. These new abilities we have given you derive from an older and purer source than the magic of Elves. It will take you many years, if not decades, to master the powers you now possess. You must practice when and where you can. And you must keep what has passed between us here a secret from all others, for an unsuspecting mind is much easier to read and influence than one that is forewarned. I hope you have a sense of the enormity of the gift that we have given you. Use it well, young prince. If your loyalty to us ever wavers, however, this gift will be withdrawn, and you will be a mere mortal again.'

'I will use it well indeed, and as for my loyalty, insofar as it does not conflict with my duty to king and country, I will be a firm and faithful ally to the Magi.'

'That is all we can ask,' said Priscus, who seemed pleased with this response.

'What else can I do to aid you beyond what you have already asked of me?' inquired Alfrahil.

'As I have said, once you have learned more, return here. But if you want to aid us further, have your father command that Men stop the felling of trees and the tilling of natural grasslands. Be content with the lands already altered by Men and let the wild things grow in peace.'

'I will do what I can,' said Alfrahil. 'In frankness, I must tell you that I doubt my words will have the effect you desire. As the numbers of Men increase, they seek new land to live upon, to plant their crops and build their homes. It is only natural.'

'Man is not all of nature, young prince,' said Priscus. 'Your kind would do well to remember that. The way of harmony with nature is the best way, as the Elves have long understood.'

'Men are not Elves, either,' said Alfrahil. 'But I will do my best to make your wishes in this matter known.'

'Good,' said Priscus, his form dissolving back into the mists, until only the whirling chartreuse orbs of his eyes were visible. 'Return now to your men, young prince; rest within the Vale this night as our guests. But you must depart at first light from our land.'

As Alfrahil left the grove of trees, he felt his mind and his spirit strengthened, his sense of purpose reinforced. His doubt and fear remained, but it was tempered by hope as he now had a tool that no other had to rely upon, and he was eager to learn the extent and nature of his new abilities.

* * *

Emerging from the glade, Alfrahil strode toward Caelus and the rest of his guard, who were busy laying out their bed-rolls and passing around leather flasks of wine and cold dried food. 'Lord, are you all right?' asked an anxious Caelus.

'Indeed I am,' said Alfrahil.

'What happened, my Lord?' asked Caelus.

Alfrahil felt the wonder and fear of the guards, combined with their respect. He could not yet distinguish individual emotions, but even so, the raw flood of sensations he was experiencing threatened to overwhelm him. Yet just as the Magi had gifted him with this enhanced sensitivity to the thoughts and emotions of Men, so, too, it seemed, had they given him the means to control it, for as if by instinct, a kind of mental barrier slipped into place, muting the onslaught to a bearable level. Only then was he able to answer Caelus. 'I received the aid of the Magi,' he said. 'That is what happened.'

'What aid?' Caelus persisted.

'I cannot say,' Alfrahil responded. 'And that is all I will ever answer on this matter.'

'But are you sure you are well, Lord?'

'I have never felt better,' replied Alfrahil. 'Rarely have my days seemed so clear of purpose, especially after these recent events in Eldora.' Knowing the origin of his newfound clarity, Alfrahil wondered for a moment if he was now a puppet of the Magi rather than a free man. But he quickly dismissed the idea. He knew instinctively that whatever the Magi had done to him, their gift had not changed who he was. Rather, he felt more confident in himself than ever, and he was eager to resume his search for the hidden enemies who sought to destroy Eldora and bring evil back to Nostraterra.

Chapter Thirteen

Soulless

Alfrahil and his company were riding back the way that they had come, along the Encircling Mountains, when they encountered errand-riders of Kozak coming toward them along the sandy track.

'Hail, Prince Alfrahil,' cried the leading rider. 'We bear news that one of the bridges over the marshes has come loose, drifting downstream.'

Alfrahil asked how the bridge had come loose.

'We are not sure, Lord. Some of the anchoring ropes appear to have been chewed through by the water moles infesting the swamp, and one of the pontoons under the bridge filled with water, straining the remaining ropes until they broke. The only way to return eastward is through the forest. If you take that route, you should meet a patrol from Shardan returning to Mostyn.'

'Is there no alternative?' asked Alfrahil.

'We have scouted the first two fords over the river, but with the snowmelt from the mountains, they are too deep to cross. Perhaps one of the southern fords above the Great River is usable, but we have not heard from our scouts sent to investigate. If you like, you can return to Mostyn until we know if you can proceed home without going through the forest.'

Pausing as if in thought; Alfrahil slowly opened his mind to his new powers. He sensed the minds of his men digesting the news brought by the Kozaki riders. He then extended his powers toward the Kozaki. His control was crude, but he sensed no subterfuge in them.

'We will go by the forest route,' he said.

'Very well, Lord,' said the Kozaki rider. 'We must press on. Safe travels to you.'

'And to you,' replied Alfrahil.

* * *

An hour later, Alfrahil and his men entered the forest. The bright light that had characterized the grasslands was now dappled in hints of green and gold, and the brisk west wind was reduced to a gentle wafting. The rich forest loam emanated a verdant smell of life and fertility.

Alfrahil extended his new senses several times as they rode, searching for treachery or other negative emotions, but his mind became increasingly weary with each attempt until finally, he could not summon sufficient strength any longer. He knew that practice would bring greater proficiency and stamina, but for now, he must use his new powers sparingly, and only at need. Yet a moment came when he felt a dark and bitter intrusion of emotion come into his mind, strong enough to register without an active search. Not sure what this meant, if anything, and recalling Priscus' warning to keep his powers secret, he said nothing. But he became more alert than ever, wishing that he had held some of his strength back instead of wasting his mental energies in a fruitless exercise.

The feeling soon ebbed, however, leaving Alfrahil uncertain if he had imagined it. But then he felt something sharp bounce off of his shoulder and heard something heavy hit the ground near his horse's hindquarters. The animal whinnied and shied, holding its rear leg off the ground and causing Alfrahil to lurch forward in his saddle, nearly falling to the ground. Meanwhile, a rain of objects fell from the tree branches overhead. Other horses shied, and several riders fell from their mounts. In another moment, it was over.

Alfrahil dismounted and, lifting his horse's rear leg, found a caltrop embedded in its hoof. Nor was his horse the only one thus afflicted.

'Be ready, men,' Alfrahil called out, drawing his sword. 'We've stumbled into a trap!'

No sooner had he spoken then he heard a cry from behind him. Turning, he saw several masked men, wearing heavy boots against the caltrops, charge toward the horses, waving torches and shouting. The spooked horses bolted, running onto the rest of the caltrops, which only served to further unnerve them. Whinnying and neighing, they plunged blindly, and many riders who had not fallen in the first wave of the attack were now thrown from their horses.

Suddenly more torches appeared in front of them, and the horses and their riders were forced back into a confused mass in the road. Dozens of small, dark, lithe forms dropped from the trees, squirming as they fell. One of these shapes fell onto Caelus, and Alfrahil was horrified to see that it was a Stone Asp, the deadliest snake in the world.

Mottled in dark shades of gray and brown, the small but terribly toxic snake flared a small hood from behind its neck, its black eyes staring remorselessly at its victim. There was no known antidote for the poison of a Stone Asp. If bitten, even a strong man could expect to last no more than fifteen or twenty minutes, and most victims succumbed even sooner.

Swiftly, the snake struck the neck of Caelus. He cried out, clutching his throat as the snake slid off onto the ground, where it struck the near foreleg of Caelus' horse. The horse, screaming in pain, threw Caelus to the ground, where more snakes were writhing. Alfrahil saw another asp strike Caelus repeatedly as he lunged blindly amongst the horses and men, gasping his final breath.

Alfrahil felt a cold, slick surface moving momentarily along his exposed neck, but before the asp could strike, a Shadow flung it off of him. Turning to the men that had not yet fallen victim to the snakes, Alfrahil cried for them to form two defensive lines.

The masked men who had caused the horses to bolt now resumed their attack. Arrows skipped off the armor of the knights, though some found their mark. The Shadows counterattacked, their curved Hagarian swords flicking and flashing as they darted in and out of the masked men. There were ten attackers in the rear and fifteen in the front, and while Alfrahil's company numbered ninety-five men, forty at least had fallen victim to the snakes, and another ten had mounts that charged wildly into the group of front attackers, where they were swiftly slain. But the five Shadows turned the tide of battle, aided by the Knights of Kelsea, though one Shadow went down from a poisoned blade.

The attackers pelted the company with more arrows. As the horses would not go past the hissing snakes, the company was forced to retreat back down the road. But they had not gotten far before a new batch of snakes was dropped onto the road behind them. Men hidden in the branches of the trees slid down ropes and began to fire arrows into the trapped men. The only way out was through the trees, and Alfrahil knew with certainty, extending his last mental energy, that there were more men hidden along the road's edges waiting for them to do so.

At that moment, when all hope seemed lost, a deep horn was heard. Looking down the road toward the east, Alfrahil saw a large troop of Kozaki riding toward them at speed, lances held ready. This charge caught the attackers unaware, and many of them were slain before they were able to retreat through the trees. The rear-most villains, seeing that their moment was gone, sped their final shafts, all aimed at Alfrahil, but alert Shadows plucked the arrows out of the air before they could strike home. The attackers then retreated into the forest as the Kozaki horsemen stopped just before the first group of asps in the road. The snakes coiled and hissed, striking at any man or beast that drew too near.

Using their lances, the riders slashed and crushed the snakes into the dirt, freeing the road for Alfrahil, who, weary and shocked at yet another attempt on his life, slumped forward to the ground next to his horse. The Kozaki captain stood in his saddle, ordering half of his men to pursue the brigands and report back. Alfrahil tried to rise and speak coherently when the terror he had been fighting against since the attack began overcame him and he distantly heard himself mumble over and over again. A firm hand at his shoulder pulled him upright and a Shadow hissed, 'My lord, you must rise for the respect of our realm!'

As he was pulled into an upright position, Alfrahil heard the Shadow say, 'Captain, this is our crown prince, Alfrahil. He was struck by a mace hurled by a brigand. Do you have any wine that might revive him? Above all, we thank you for your bravery and for saving our lives.'

'My name is Trystan, leader of this *Faris*. You are welcome, Prince Alfrahil,' said the Kozaki leader to a semi-coherent Alfrahil. Glancing around him for a moment, Trystan did not see any mace or another weapon; indeed, the prince looked physically intact. Handing over a small silver flask with spirits of Dorian to the man aiding Alfrahil, Trystan watched the man have a quick drink, checking for poison. Much of the flask was then poured into Alfrahil, who choked and sputtered before trying to sit up straight again, this time succeeding.

'Prince Alfrahil, we were returning from a patrol in Shardan and were advised that the southern route was closed. Hearing the sounds of battle, we rushed to your aid. It was fortunate that we were nearby, or I fear that Eldora would have lost a prince today.'

Alfrahil began to focus again and said, 'Thank you, Trystan, for your timely aid. I must see to my men.'

Trystan saw Alfrahil begin to turn towards his men, but the soldier aiding him instead gently turned Alfrahil's shoulders until they pointed towards a saddled horse of the Kozaki away from the dead and the dying, and glanced meaningfully at Trystan. Nodding to the soldier, Trystan said, 'Let us get you to safety. I will leave ten of my riders behind, along with enough spare horses to help your men to safety.'

'I cannot leave my men behind, as they may be in great danger still,' said Alfrahil weakly.

'Lord, if the stories from Eldora are to be believed, this trap was set for you and you alone. The sooner you are away from your men, the safer they will be,' replied Trystan.

Seeing the wisdom in this, Alfrahil agreed and was too weary to search the man's mind for treachery.

'We will escort you a mile east from these woods for your safety while we wait until my men return to make certain we are not pursued.'

Alfrahil looked at the tanned cavalry rider closely for the first time, noting that he was shorter in stature than the typical Kozaki, and had dark brown hair. Grimly Alfrahil nodded, not knowing what else to say. Once again he had led men into a catastrophe, most of them perishing and had barely escaped with his own life again. He heard the screams of the dead and dying, along with shouts of fighting rapidly fading away, and the terror and grief pushed aside by the liquor returned nearly as strong as before, but he clamped down on his feelings.

Now Alfrahil mounted the fresh horse, glancing around and seeing that nearly all of the Eldoran horses were down. Looking at his beautiful stallion, Helfaloth, Alfrahil saw that he was limping from two caltrops that had punctured his hooves. Spare horses from the Kozaki were quickly lent to the Shadows, and escorting Alfrahil they galloped eastward with Trystan until they cleared the edge of the forest.

Alfrahil heard Trystan call a halt, and seeing that he was safe for now, Alfrahil ordered one of the Shadows to return and take charge of the remnants of Alfrahil's guards, sending those strong enough to ride to rendezvous with Alfrahil here.

'Yes my lord.' The Shadow turned and galloped back into the forest as Alfrahil waited with Trystan for his men to return. Alfrahil tried to feel the thoughts of Trystan, but many men with strong emotions were too close for Alfrahil's exhausted, grief-stricken mind to perceive anything but general anger and confusion, with a faint wash of the deep foreboding he had sensed earlier. Cursing under his breath, he wished that he had been able to spend more time with Priscus, learning how to use this new power.

* * *

Two hours later, Alfrahil had recovered much of his composure when the riders chasing the brigands returned and spoke to Trystan, while the Shadow who accompanied them approached Alfrahil.

'Only eleven men survived,' the Shadow reported, 'and three of those are so wounded that they may not survive this day. They are too injured to move, but the Kozaki have agreed to tend to them in place until a healer from Titania can arrive. Of the remaining eight, two knights of Kelsea, along with six ordinary guardsmen, are ready to ride, and they were lent spare mounts.'

'Thank you, Shadow. Trystan, what of your men?

'I lost ten men searching for the attackers, but we slew twenty-three and are pursuing the rest. Do not worry: we shall have them dead or alive.'

'I would prefer alive. Could you not have captured any of the twenty-three for questioning?'

'We tried, Lord. But they took their own lives before we could do so.'

'I meant no criticism. It was the same as the men who attacked me in the city. They are a determined lot.'

'Fanatics, no doubt.'

'Perhaps. In any case, Trystan, thank you for all of your efforts on my behalf and on behalf of my men. Eldora owes you a debt that will be difficult to repay.'

'We are happy to honor our obligations, your grace. Leave the accounting to the bankers. All we ask is that you remember your debt of honor and that you repay it if ever you can aid Kozak.'

The entire party then moved eastward. By the end of the day, they had passed from the edge of the forest and made their way to a small fortress that lay along the border between Kozak and Eldora. Entering, Alfrahil had Helfaloth examined and tended to by the horse healer and laid his head down on a rustic cot provided for him by the soldiers of the fortress.

Alfrahil and his escort moved slowly eastward over the next few days, confident that reinforcements were on the way. Thankfully, small stone barracks with stables were set along this section of the road every twenty miles, so each night Alfrahil and his men had some security and were sheltered from the weather.

Rising at dawn the fourth day after the ambush, Alfrahil enjoyed a brief walk before returning to his men for breakfast. After a short, simple meal, he walked out to the stables and found that Helfaloth was well enough to stand but not to carry him on his journey. A messenger rider, a Shadow escort, and six spare horses clothed in silver and gold streaked past westward, most likely bound for Mostyn, but Alfrahil was shocked that the man did not speak with him. Five minutes later, however, as Alfrahil and his men were getting ready to ride out again, they were joined by an impressive escort and another messenger.

The messenger approached Alfrahil and handed him a sealed glass cylinder so that Alfrahil knew the message was genuine. Snapping the glass in his hands, he removed the message and saw that it was a terse note from Mergin instructing him to return with these guards by the most expedient means possible. Two hundred Citadel guards, with ten Shadows disguised as guardsmen, were waiting outside the fortress to escort him back to the City. While Alfrahil did not know the men's faces, Mergin's letter told him that each man would have two deep scuff marks on the outside of each boot, clever enough to look like an accident, but enough to tell Alfrahil where his special guards were. Alfrahil, checking the men and seeing the coded signs, thanked Trystan and asked him to accompany Alfrahil and his Eldoran escort for Titania.

* * *

Five days later, Alfrahil and his escort entered the City; passing the gleaming doors of Platina and steel, where he was joined by a dozen fresh Shadows. Alfrahil paused, thanking the riders for their aid, indicating a cavalry captain who would escort Trystan and his riders to their temporary quarters. Alfrahil tried to dismiss the rest of his escort, save the Shadows, but all two hundred guards were under strict orders from Mergin to escort Alfrahil through the city to the gates of the Citadel, where the Shadows would escort him inside.

Arriving at the Citadel without mishap, Alfrahil dismounted and handed his horse to a groomsman, then strode toward the astrology tower. But a Shadow redirected him to the Royal chambers instead, where he saw Mergin waiting for him.

'Your father asked for you to report to me while he sleeps,' said Mergin. 'Please follow me to my study.'

Alfrahil extended his new senses but found no emotions from Mergin besides fear and frustration. After a few seconds, his control lost focus, and he was bombarded with the feelings of the guardsmen on the stairs and the Shadows that were with him still. Closing off his extraordinary powers, he followed Mergin to his study.

Alfrahil knew few men had ever been invited into Mergin's inner sanctum, as the minister wished to preserve his privacy by meeting outside of his study at all costs. Alfrahil had never had reason enough to enter these rooms before today.

He expected to see the opulence that had become the style in Titania, with courtiers outdoing each other to show their wealth and power. Instead, he observed a neat but rather sparse main room, with closed doors leading off to two other rooms. A roomy desk piled with papers, journals, logs, and maps occupied one side of the room, with an empty brazier for cold mornings set in front of the desk. Alongside the desk stood two plain wooden chairs decorated with ancient leather trimmings. Bureaus and cabinets adorned the walls, with only one fair painting of Kelsea to break up the utilitarian nature of the room. Daylight streamed in from the one narrow window, illuminating dust motes that drifted in the stuffy air.

Mergin stood behind his desk and bade Alfrahil be seated. Alfrahil did so and was about to speak when Aradar entered with two other servants carrying trays laden with fruit, cheese, sweetmeats, coffee, and a flagon of crisp white wine. Aradar remained in attendance after the other servants had departed, and Alfrahil was able to sense only general anger from him. This did not disturb or surprise him; knowing the man's history, Alfrahil assumed that he was always angry and bitter about the life fate had bestowed upon him.

Both men ate for a few minutes in silence before Mergin asked Alfrahil about his journey and the attempt on his life, bidding him to begin at the beginning.

Alfrahil told him briefly what had transpired; leaving his encounter with Priscus vague and stating only that Priscus' visions indicated they should look abroad for enemies. His voice shook when he described the ambush of the Stone Asps, and he shuddered at the memory of how one snake had touched him briefly. Recovering his composure, he spent half an hour answering Mergin's questions.

'Why don't you go get some sleep, my lord,' Mergin said at last. 'It's nearly midday, and you must be exhausted after your long ride. I will send word to you when your father is awake and ready to speak with you. It is not safe for you and your father to appear together outside the Citadel, so one or both of you will have to remain here until I can make further progress regarding this plot. I do not believe that the King is any safer than you, but the conspirators are actively pursuing you for now, for reasons I don't yet understand.'

* * *

Watching Alfrahil go, Mergin was more determined than ever to choose Creon's successor. As a normal mortal, there was little likelihood he would out-live Creon, so Mergin had taken extraordinary steps to extend his life. Entering into his bedchamber, he barred the door after telling the Shadows to keep everyone out of the Royal corridor for the next two hours, as he would be resting.

Going to his desk, he opened the innermost secret cabinet and withdrew a Fire Opal of the Dwarves. This he dissolved into pungent sharp liquor that accompanied it. He drank the bitter mixture with a shudder and collapsed onto his couch. His body convulsed as the ancient Dwarven magic coursed through his veins, extending his lifespan.

Fire Opals were fabulously expensive, and Mergin could not afford them on his salary, but he was wise enough to siphon off some of the corruption that came through the land and use it to buy these stones from time to time.

'*So much for the honor of the Dwarves,*' he thought. '*Selling me their precious opals as long as the price is right. Clearly, anyone and everyone can be bought; everyone but me.*'

Drifting off to sleep, Mergin began planning anew for the royal succession. No doubt Creon still had many years to reign. But with these latest assassination attempts, nothing could be taken for granted. The fate of the realm might well depend on the decisions Mergin came to now.

* * *

Alfrahil returned to his own chamber in the Astrology tower and spent several hours napping, awakening in the mid-afternoon. He rose, put on a soft leather jerkin along with leather pants, and soft shoes rather than heavy boots. He returned to the Council chambers, expecting to see his father.

'Lord your father is still asleep,' said Mergin, who was waiting there. 'Shall I wake him?'

'No, Mergin, my father needs his rest. Do you have any news for me?'

'Yes, Lord. Here are the intelligence reports we have gathered since the initial ambush. Please review them while I attend to other matters. Would you like some food?'

'Yes, Mergin, just a cold collation, some toasted cheese, and some white wine. I can see there is plenty here for me to read.'

Mergin departed, and after fifteen minutes or so, while Alfrahil was deep into the intelligence report, Aradar appeared; gray and distant, bearing another tray, while a different servant bore wine, napkins, and cutlery. After placing the food and wine on the table, the other servant withdrew, leaving Aradar to care for Alfrahil.

'Aradar, it is good to see you again.'

'My Lord, I am grateful that you escaped this last terrible ambush alive; I watched a friend die from a Stone Asp bite once—he lasted only half an hour or so,' said Aradar with another flash of bitter anger on his lined face.

'How did you know about the Stone Asps, Aradar? I was the only survivor familiar with their description. None of my guards had seen one before.'

Aradar blanched briefly before replying. 'Lord, I heard Minister Mergin muttering about Stone Asps a day or so ago when the latest reports came in. I keep such news to myself, never fear, my Lord.'

'I hope that you are discretion itself,' said Alfrahil, and he now used his powers to search for Aradar's emotions. A deep well of anger lay there, but overall was a concern for his prince's well-being, and Alfrahil did not sense any treachery.

'Well, Aradar, please get some rest. I can pour my own wine.'

'Very well my lord,' said Aradar and left the room.

Two hours after sunset, Alfrahil stretched and, after marking his place in the intelligence reports, emerged into the hallway and addressed the nearest Shadow. 'Take these reports to Lord Mergin. I will return to my apartments now.'

Walking back to his apartments, Alfrahil saw the guards and Shadows stationed outside his door, and, nodding to them, he entered his chambers.

To his surprise, no servant was waiting for him. In fact, none of his servants seemed to be present. Only the knowledge that his guards stood just outside, kept Alfrahil from drawing his sword.

Entering the cooking area, Alfrahil noticed a small silver bucket upon a table as bright moonlight streamed in from the kitchen window. Approaching, he saw ice and water surrounding a bottle of sparkling wine: a rare delicacy from the eastern slopes of Alton Hill in Amadeus. Hearing the rustle of fabric, Alfrahil supposed that Mergin or one of the other ministers had provided him with an interesting diversion for the evening. Turning, he saw the slender yet curvy silhouette of a short woman clad in dark silk, wearing a mask that covered her features. Alfrahil presumed this was a girl for hire, sent by Mergin, and was excited: it had been over a year since he had last enjoyed such a diversion, and, knowing the tastes of the First Minister, she would be beautiful and talented, perhaps even talented enough to make him forget his grief. 'Well, after all, I have been through, I suppose I deserve a little companionship and an enjoyable evening,' he thought.

Fetching two crystal goblets from a shelf, he moved to the wine. Wrapping the wet bottle in a towel, he began the delicate task of removing the cork. Slowly but steadily, he eased the cork from the bottle, and, hearing a slight hiss from the unique air contained within, Alfrahil smelled the yeasty odors and fruit emerge, along with the sharp but subtle hint of alcohol. Truly it was an exceptional bottle, and he anticipated its complexity and flavors with great desire.

Sensing the woman's approach from behind him, Alfrahil wanted to turn and have a better look at her, but a soft voice whispered, 'No, my prince, not yet.'

Alfrahil searched briefly with his mind and felt only lust and, surprisingly, love before his mental concentration was distracted by the strong yet delicate hands that caressed his neck from behind, gently sliding down his back to remove the straps holding his leather jerkin in place. Swiftly, the leather leggings he wore were also undone, leaving his long linen pants as the only lower barrier.

Now all that remained upon his chest was his soft undershirt. He was enjoying the art of being undressed by someone unknown; there was a delectable tension in having layer upon layer stripped away by a complete stranger. The fragrance of the sparkling wine filled the room, along with the musky heat of his body. A soft feminine scent was also there, wafting gently from behind and below him as his companion continued to remove the outer trappings from his torso. Now his shirt was lifted over his head. Playfully turning to his right, all Alfrahil saw was a lithe form gracefully but quickly moving to his left, with the whispers again at the back of his neck bidding him to be still. Feeling himself rapidly rising to the sensual advances of this mysterious stranger, he willfully complied.

Sudden kisses upon the back of his neck startled him but added to his general sensation of pleasurable anticipation.

'She is very talented indeed,' he thought, 'to have me so ready for play and to have done nothing out of the ordinary yet in such an extraordinary way.'

Now her warm hands were upon his chest, probing his muscles, touching points under his flesh he didn't know existed. Groaning softly, he felt her hands rise up to his nipples, gently caressing at first but then insistently pulling at them, causing Alfrahil to nearly collapsing on knees that had mysteriously weakened beneath her sensual onslaught. Completely occupied with her very talented fingers, he suddenly felt the warmth of her body press against his back. He felt her own hardened nipples through the fine silk against his back and the heat from between her hips, and he knew that she was as aroused as he was.

Finally turning, he saw her more clearly. The thin silk she wore in no way detracted from her feminine curves. Slight, firm hips were revealed along with a strikingly slender waist that rose into the firm breasts that had touched his back. Her face was hidden in shadow the mask removed, but he bent to kiss her lips and felt the ardent need contained within her kiss. Kissing her back with increased fervor, Alfrahil felt his breath coming in shorter and shorter gasps. He moved his lips down her throat, kissing it again and again. Hearing her gasp and feeling her yield within his arms, Alfrahil finally broke off the embrace.

Turning, he poured the wine into the two goblets. Then, guiding the mystery girl into his bedroom, he saw a small candle carefully covered to give only the barest of light. He took a long appreciative sip from his goblet, savoring the tart fruitiness of the wine upon his tongue. Under the fruit, however, was the sophisticated structure his brother was always going on about. Turning, he brought the shadowed young woman to the bed. Watching her take a healthy drink from her crystal goblet, Alfrahil moved his hands along her back, feeling the silk between his fingers. Searching for the ties he knew must be there, his hands instead found nothing. He groaned in frustration, moving his hands to her waist. Giggling slightly, she reached down and slowly slid the garment up and over her head, falling to the floor. As he was bending forward to kiss her, a small insect flew into the candle. In the brief flash of its corporeal disintegration, he saw the flushed, beautiful face of Findalas.

'Findalas!' he gasped. 'How? Why?'

'Hush, Lord. Yes, it is me—but I come to you as a woman, not a healer. Finish your wine, my Lord, so that we can continue what we have begun.'

He began to reply, but she placed a delicate finger to his lips.

'Say nothing, Lord, for we have tonight to ourselves. No one knows I am here; your guards saw only a veiled young woman carrying a pass of the highest level enter and dismiss your servants. Relax, and let us bring joy to one another.'

Still stunned, Alfrahil did a thing he rarely did when beautiful women were concerned: he stopped speaking, asked no further questions, and placed his mouth where it was most needed.

* * *

Late the next morning, Alfrahil awoke with a great smile upon his face. Rolling over in his bed, he saw that Findalas had slipped away sometime during the night. He was sorry she had not lingered, yet as he recalled the wonderful events of the night before, he felt truly happy and relaxed for the first time in years.

'She is a wonderful woman, and I shall enjoy spending many more nights with her,' he thought.

Rising from his bed, he slipped on a robe and approached his bedroom door. The servant on duty, alert to his footsteps, opened the door from without and inquired if he would like some breakfast or perhaps an early lunch.

'A hearty breakfast would be most welcome,' Alfrahil said. 'Bring coffee, lots and lots of coffee.'

* * *

Alfrahil spent the rest of the day ensconced in a meeting in the Council Chambers, where it seemed that nothing new would be said. While Alfrahil did not mistrust Mergin; somehow, some way, most secret information was leaking from the Citadel, and after three assassination attempts, he was determined to keep the information he found between his father and himself. He was grateful when the meeting finally came to a close.

After everyone else, including Mergin, had left, the king spoke. 'My son, will you join me atop the Astrology tower one hour before midnight? There will be time for us to discuss your journey in complete security.'

'Yes, Father. If you don't mind, I will take my leave and attend to some personal matters until then.'

Nodding his agreement, the King rose, and they both returned to their quarters.

Alfrahil found Findalas waiting for him in his bed, two small candles flickering to reveal her more clearly than the night before. He eagerly undressed to join her.

An hour later, rolling onto his back and gasping for air, Alfrahil was astonished at Findalas' stamina and skill. Recovering, they began speaking, with Findalas telling Alfrahil that she loved him and hoped they could spend as much of the future together as possible.

'Findalas, while I care deeply for you, I do not love you yet. As you are aware, I may only marry a woman of royal descent under my father's decree, so I am afraid to love you when I cannot keep you. Court protocol forbids us even to be seen together in public, much less to wed someday.'

'Love me as much as you can, Lord,' she answered. 'I will always be with you, even if you are forced into a political marriage by these ridiculous protocols.'

Feeling her anger and frustration wash over him, Alfrahil knew that it was directed at his father; indeed, he shared those feelings. Findalas' purely Eldoran origins and high education would make her a formidable queen, were she allowed. He decided in an instant that he would try, gradually, over time, to convince his father to change the protocol, but he said nothing of this to Findalas.

At last, it came time for him to meet with his father at the Astrology tower. Kissing Findalas good-bye, he said, 'Findalas you are welcome to stay tonight and every night thereafter.'

'I must arise before dawn, lord, for I have my patients to attend. Perhaps I will return tomorrow night,' she said with a laugh. Her ready acquiescence, with no attempt to cling to him, as other women had done in the past, made him desire her all the more.

He dressed quickly and left his chambers. When he arrived at the top of the tower, he saw his father there already, surprisingly alone.

'Tell me of your meeting with Priscus,' said the king without preamble.

Briefly, Alfrahil described his journey and arrival at the Vale. He then relayed much of Priscus' message, stating that scouts must be assembled and sent out to search the realms of not only Men but Dwarves and both Lesser and Greater Elves. Alfrahil knew that he could tell no one, not even the king, about his personal encounter with Priscus, so, finishing with the fact that Priscus had asked for the King's help, Alfrahil waited for his father's response.

'Well, what did you think of the most ancient of beings?'

'I am ashamed to say, Father, that I did not believe your stories about the Magi. Their sheer power astounded me.'

'They are astounding. It is good to hear that they will aid us.' Pausing for a moment, Creon changed subjects. 'It is good to see that you have recovered from your wounds so quickly. It must be that pretty healer who has taken such a personal interest in your recovery.'

Startled again, Alfrahil began stammering an explanation.

'Nay, lad,' his father said, cutting him off. 'Do not fear that I will react to your consorting with a master healer of the realm who is pure Eldoran, though of common birth, the same way I will act regarding your brother's most recent playmate. While marriage to Findalas is out of the question, her racial purity, position, skill, and merit are sufficient to allow her the privilege of being seen with you in the Citadel, if you desire to bestow that honor upon her.'

'Thank you, Father. Your generosity surprises me,' said Alfrahil happily, hoping this news would make Findalas content for the time being.

'Not at all, my son. We all must make allowances in these difficult times. Now, what other news do you have?'

Alfrahil told him what Golbur and Hilforas had said about the internal dissent in their respective realms.

'Sadly, this does not surprise me,' said Creon, 'but the fact that there are such severe factions amongst the Elves and Dwarves is troubling. During the Great War, the Men of Eldora and Kozak were united with Elves and Dwarves against Magnar's forces. This unity died with Magnar, and now all races in Nostraterra have divided once again. Men of Eldora, we must balance our relationships with other races while looking for opportunities to exploit them when and where we can.' Smiling at Alfrahil's confusion, Creon added, 'A King must seek the advantage in any situation, no matter how dire. Always remember that.'

'Yes, Father,' replied Alfrahil, unhappy that his father meant to use deception and lies for Eldora's own good with races that were their friends.

'Now, between what the scouts can find abroad and what Lord Mergin will surely find here at home, I am certain we will get to the bottom of this mess sooner rather than later. While you were gone, messages arrived from Hilforas and Golbur. Four Dwarf and Elf teams have assembled to consult with the Elven and Dwarven realms to learn what they can. Now that Priscus has provided his warning, we shall ask them to look into the concerns of the Magi as well.'

'One thing worries me much, Father,' Alfrahil said. 'When Priscus described the magical creatures who pose such a dire threat to Nostraterra, I could not help but think of the Blue Vesper you faced in years gone by.'

'Do not speak of such a thing!' said Creon angrily. 'Even if that foul creature still exists after more than a hundred years, there is no evidence that it has returned to plague us.' Failing to suppress a shudder, the King returned in memory to that terrible day in the Shardan wastes, where he had walked into the maelstrom cloud of the Blue Vesper. Raising his sword to strike, he had been struck by many filaments of lightning, paralyzed within the grip of the creature's magic. Rapid questions concerning the defenses of Eldora and of the political stability of Men had come from the figure, its' will completely dominating Creon's mind, blanketing him in deep fear and despair. Forced to answer the Vesper's insistent questions, Creon had never felt as frightened or as helpless as he had at that moment. Suddenly he was wrenched out of the blue cloud and found himself lying prone at the feet of his guards, three of whom had ventured in and were never seen again.

Alfrahil felt a rush of terror and insecurity from his father's mind before it was blotted out by a blast of anger. Though worried that his father was turning a blind eye to a real threat, Alfrahil changed the subject. 'What of you, Father? What have you learned in my absence, perhaps by using the Acies?'

'I have seen little in the Acies atop the tower, only flashes and glimpses of evil stirring in the world, much of it in the places you would suspect—the east and south, particularly Jelani. I glimpsed Dark Elves in the Shale Mountains. If the Acies is not showing me an ancient vision, as it is apt to do from time to time, then the King of Kozak will have a new adventure with which to dispose of his riders,' said Creon. 'Further, I saw a singular vision wreathed in glimmering blue, something the Acies has never done before. Possibly it was a premonition rather than a vision of the present or the past.'

'What did you see, Father?'

'I saw what appeared to be current visions of Elvalon. The Greater Elves across the sea are alive and well. Their numbers have grown throughout the ages. In the brief moment allotted me, I saw that some of the Greater Elves were speaking of coming to Nostraterra, that there was great debate amongst the Elves over whether this should or should not be allowed.'

'How do we know Father; if your vision is current or from the past or even the future?'

'A good question, son. I do not know, and the uncertainty is unsettling.'

'Why, then, is this so grave a secret? The great joy you should have to see Elvalon in its glory, even if for but a moment.'

'Yes, son, great joy I had and have, but also fear, for the vision has put in my mind the possibility that a great host of Elven Princes might one day cross the seas to conquer Nostraterra. Where then would be the glory of Men?'

'I do not know,' Alfrahil answered. 'We might ask Priscus and the other Magi, for surely this would be in any future that they might glimpse. But I am more concerned about the present evils here in Nostraterra. What have you discovered regarding the ambushes, for you seem to be in fear, though you are hiding it well? Though you refuse to speak his name and change the subject, I must ask again: is the Blue Vesper involved, as the visions of Priscus would seem to indicate?'

'You presume much, my son. Suffice it to say that I have seen hints of its presence somewhere to the east, but whether past or present is impossible to tell. Perhaps it is indeed manipulating men or others into these atrocious actions, but for now, we shall concentrate our efforts on Eldora and what we can see and control.

'On another note, the documents in the joy house clearly indicate that your brother had financial dealings with the same money men as those that aided suspected rebels and Shardan sympathizers. But even if that were not enough, there was another set of documents found only a couple of days ago that implicates your brother in these attacks upon you.'

'What documents are these?' asked Alfrahil.

'All in good time, my son. Suffice it to say that I believe that your brother is guilty of sedition and conspiracy, and he will be given his sentence soon.'

'What about a trial, Father? Every Eldoran noble is entitled to one, even if the charge is treason.'

'He shall have his trial,' said the King, 'but the results will be the same. There is no excuse or explanation for what we found that would absolve him of guilt in my mind, or in the mind of the High Council. There may be those on the Council that will require additional persuasion, but you and I shall sit in judgment, and he shall be found guilty. In fact, the trial should be over swiftly, as your brother has refused to receive one of the top counselors in the land, who offered to represent him at trial. Even now his arrogance is scarce to be believed, and perhaps he does not perceive how much trouble he is really in. Regardless, my son, what shall we do with your brother?'

'You yourself have said that you sensed no malice in Daerahil. I would give Daerahil an opportunity to reflect upon his errors away from the tumult of the City,' said Alfrahil. 'Presuming he is found guilty, I believe the latest change for the garrison of the Plaga Erebus is about to depart and that the army captain stationed at the entrance to the dark land is overdue for rotation home.'

Laughing with pure pleasure for the first time in days, Creon stated, 'Yes, my son, I think your brother should replace the captain, but I shall forbid him to come more than fifteen leagues out from the gates to that land, making certain he has no contact with Shardan or their allies. Allowing him to have contact or, worse, go back south while his sympathies are so clearly torn, would be asking for trouble. He shall escort the engineering expedition that will go and begin the first exploration and survey of the ruins of the Blood Temple. Three months in the Land of Wounded Darkness should remind him what our ancestors fought against. When he returns to the north, perhaps he shall have a greater appreciation of Eldora and give up some of his unhealthy fascination with the south.' At this, Creon's voice hardened. 'Still, I want to make certain that he understands how he has dishonored our family by his disgusting taste in companions particularly that Shardan whore. I have a special punishment in mind for her, and for your brother's other less reputable companions.'

'Father, Daerahil has not yet been found guilty. I will vote my conscience and not predispose my brother's guilt. If you disagree, then I shall refuse to participate, and you will not have a legal quorum to proceed with only two royal princes rather than the minimum of three.'

Creon's anger flared, and Alfrahil felt his wrath, but using his powers for the first time defensively, he found he could dull the reception of emotion as well as seek it out, and after a few moments, his father regained control and said, 'Very well, my son.'

'Also, Father, Daerahil's woman is indeed a low-born joy girl, but her only crime is to be a member of an illegal yet common profession. Do not strike at my brother through her. Leave her alone.'

'She has affronted the entire establishment of Eldora for daring to consort with your brother,' Creon stated flatly. 'I barely tolerate craven Eldoran women who consort with men for profit, but for a Shardan prostitute to set her cap for your foolish brother is reprehensible. She and all of her kind and her race shall be reminded of their proper place at the bottom, where they have always dwelt. If she was Shardan royalty she would simply be fined and sent home, but a joy-girl? No, everyone from your brother to the lowest stable boy needs reminding of what is and is not permissible in this land.'

Striding quickly to the tower door, Creon gestured that Alfrahil should precede him down the stairs. After descending, the king bid his son good night.

Alfrahil returned to his own chambers, wondering about what punishment Creon would inflict on Daerahil's wench, and how that would only further inflame his brother against the cruelty of their father.

Chapter Fourteen

The Trial

The next morning, Alfrahil was informed that his brother's trial would begin the next day. According to Eldoran law, only the High Council could judge a Lord or Prince of the realm accused of a high crime. The High Council consisted of the King, Prince Alfrahil, Prince Daerahil, Paladir, Prince of Ackerlea, Prince Frederick of Amadeus, and finally Jasper, Prince of the Delta, each of them having one vote in the verdict. The lesser nobility of Eldora was represented as well: the dukes of Amarant and Anscomb, the earls of Pyry Valley and Galenas, and the two barons of Camden were known as the Six Lords of Eldora and had one collective vote in the verdict. Thus, though the High Council had twelve members, those members combined for a total of only seven votes.

In the present case, with Daerahil himself standing accused, and for that reason precluded from casting a vote, the total was reduced to six. In addition, Prince Frederic had not received the summons in time to journey to Eldora for the trial, and his vote would be cast by the King, acting as the prince's proxy and only in the event of a tie on the first ballot. Only a majority of votes could sustain a guilty verdict, with a tie going to the benefit of the accused. As any of the Council members could abstain from voting, a tie was theoretically possible even with an odd number of potential votes, so Alfrahil knew there was a chance that his father would have an opportunity to wield Frederick's proxy. And he had no doubt but that his father would use it in support of a guilty verdict.

After breakfast, Alfrahil went to see his brother, who was confined to his own apartments until the trial. Alfrahil was shown in by Marda, who said, 'Perhaps you can talk some sense into him, my lord. He stayed up late last night reviewing piles of papers for his trial. He spurned the services of an attorney, as you know, and insists upon handling everything himself.'

'I will do my best to stress the seriousness of the situation.'

Marda bowed outside the doors to Daerahil's study and took her leave.

Taking a moment to steel himself, Alfrahil opened the door and entered.

Daerahil looked up at Alfrahil from behind a large sheaf of papers and books. The only light in the room was what streamed in from several open windows. A fireplace stood cold and gray with ash; as it was a warm morning, no fire had been lit. Cups of coffee and scraps of food lay on dishes on a nearby end table. Alfrahil thought his brother looked unusually haggard.

Daerahil greeted him warmly, though it seemed to Alfrahil that his brother's smile lay in a face lined with stress and tension. Coffee was brought by Marda, and each of them sipped their brew, waiting for the other to begin.

'How are you, brother?' asked Alfrahil at last.

'As fine as can be expected,' said Daerahil in a clipped voice. 'I want this farce of a trial to be over so that I can resume my tedious inspection tour and petition our father for an opportunity to do something useful. How are you, brother? We have not been allowed to speak privately since you returned from the Vale.'

Alfrahil, meanwhile, extended his new powers, but he felt only raging anger directed outward: though not toward him.

The strength of his brother's mind began to give Alfrahil a headache. He pulled back his secret powers with a sigh.

'I am as well as can be expected,' he said. 'The journey back from the Vale was terrible. Once again I was the target of a well-planned assassination attempt, as you have doubtless heard.'

'Yes. I am glad to see you in one piece. But who is behind these attacks? No one will give me any information about them. It is most annoying.'

'No one yet knows who is behind them. Mergin has not had any luck looking here in Titania or in Eldora proper. Father and I are now searching for answers abroad, where our friends amongst the Elves and Dwarves are helping us.'

'You are lucky indeed to be alive, brother. I thank the gods that you were spared again. I only wish that these ridiculous charges would be dismissed so that I might aid in the search for the conspirators.'

'This trial is not a farce, nor are the charges ridiculous,' cautioned Alfrahil. 'I have looked at the charging documents, and there may be enough evidence to convict you of sedition. You should know that our father is in deadly earnest to have you found guilty. Mergin speaks for the prosecution in this matter and will show no mercy, as you well know.'

'My god, a pox on Mergin and his anger; it is one thing to simply despise one another personally, but quite another to influence the realm and attack me publicly again and again. Why won't he let the past be in the past? I did everything I could to save his son! It's not my fault that the lad was killed; he volunteered to lead the rearguard that day and was the most experienced man under my command.'

Alfrahil knew that Daerahil was referring to what was known in royal circles as "Daerahil's folly." Nearly fifteen years ago, Daerahil had commanded a small host in the deserts of Shardan. Refugees had come to Daerahil, begging him to protect them against a band of brigands that was marauding from village to village. Daerahil, in defiance of his orders to retreat directly to the great Oasis of Zanza, asked for volunteers to form a reinforced company of one hundred fifty cavalrymen in order to aid the village. Relying upon poor intelligence, Daerahil led his men rashly into battle, where he was attacked by over five hundred Shardan brigands. Driven from the village, Daerahil retreated with his wounded soldiers toward Zanza, where reinforcements were waiting. But it soon became clear that the decimated troop would not make it to the oasis. A difficult decision had to be made. As night fell, Daerahil requested volunteers to occupy a small, narrow pass controlling the road to Zanza. A small group of archers positioned there could hold the pursuers for hours—with any luck, until morning, when Daerahil would return with reinforcements. Mergin's only son, Kellen, a brilliant young officer experienced in small unit tactics, volunteered to lead the defense.

That night, as Daerahil assembled the relief force at Zanza, a sudden sandstorm descended, delaying their departure by several hours. As dawn broke, so did the weather; Daerahil led over two hundred cavalrymen over the sand to relieve Kellen and his men. Three hours later, as they neared the pass, Daerahil was stricken to see dozens of vultures circling overhead. He found only desecrated bodies, stripped naked and mutilated, Kellen's among them.

When news of this disaster reached Eldora, Daerahil was relieved of his command and sent back to Eldora to explain his decisions. No matter that Kellen had volunteered and had slain fifty of the brigands, Mergin never forgave Daerahil and from that day forward used every avenue at his disposal to undermine and humiliate Daerahil.

'No, brother,' Alfrahil responded now. 'Mergin will not forget, much less forgive. I have told you to be careful where he is concerned, for he will stop at nothing that does not blatantly violate our father's orders or the laws of Eldora to take his revenge. That being the case, and since he will be prosecuting the case against you, I must ask whether it is true that you have refused to retain counsel.'

'Yes, it's true.'

'May I ask why?'

'I do not need the mealy-mouthed mutterings of some lawyer, no matter how esteemed his reputation. The rules for the trial of a prince are clear: Mergin shall have his say and present his witnesses, as well as documents to be considered by the Council. I shall then present my witnesses and documents on my behalf. Mergin will present his argument against me, and I shall present my argument for myself. The Council will then retire and vote, but I have little fear as to the outcome.'

'Why do you say that, brother?'

'Because the chief evidence against me consists of my mis-interpreted statements here and in Ackerlea, the documents from the joy house, and finally my actions in Shardan, where I usurped the authority of the royal governor. All of these are easily explained.'

'You may be correct, brother,' said Alfrahil, 'but still, you should let another speak for you. I beg you to accept the service of Renfrew, the finest lawyer in the realm. He is waiting even now for your invitation to meet him. You are not an expert in the subtle nuances of the law, and there may be surprises both in the interpretation of the law and in the evidence that is presented against you. I need not remind you that the king serves as judge regarding the testimony, the admission of evidence, and, finally, what leeway each side may be granted regarding their actions at trial.'

'Enough brother!' cried Daerahil, slapping his knee with the palm of one hand. 'While I appreciate your concern, I am more than capable of responding to Mergin's jibes and verbal tricks without the need for a lawyer. I can count upon the votes of the lords, Paladir, and yourself. My exoneration is assured.'

'I hope so,' Alfrahil said.

Daerahil laughed. 'Why, I trust I may at least be assured of your vote, brother!'

'You may be assured of my love,' said Alfrahil, not wanting to tell Daerahil that his vote for acquittal would depend not on what lay in his heart but rather on what evidence was presented.

Alfrahil soon left his brother's quarters and took a long walk upon the Citadel's battlements. He knew that his brother was too confident by half and despite everything did not take Mergin's cunning and animosity seriously enough.

Retiring early, for he was weary of worrying about his brother, he returned to his apartments and found a note from Findalas. An urgent case in the Healer Hall would prevent her from visiting him as they had planned. Fuming slightly that he would be deprived of her company, Alfrahil ate his meal and drank more wine than usual so he could sleep.

* * *

Early the next morning, Alfrahil rose and changed into his magnificent silver and vermillion ceremonial robes. Then, accompanied by his guards, Alfrahil made his way to the royal throne room. The room was enormous, a hundred feet long and forty feet wide, with the ceiling fifty feet high. White granite covered the floor and white marble the walls. Normally the room was sparsely furnished, but now hundreds of chairs had been placed upon the floor for the witnesses to the trial, with still more chairs added to the upper balcony at the rear of the room. The banners of each province of Eldora hung down the walls, their colors stark and resplendent upon the pale background.

Voices echoed and reverberated coldly in the chamber as Alfrahil entered and took his seat at the high table reserved for the Princes of the Realm. His father was there in the center with Jasper, the Prince of the Delta, on his left; Alfrahil sat at his father's right hand, and next to him was Paladir of Ackerlea.

Making the requisite verbal courtesies, Creon tapped the ancient scepter of Alba three times, calling for the entrance of the Six Lords of Eldora. They filed in wearing robes less splendid, though still quite formal. In unison, the Lords took their seats on the lower benches, immediately below the King and the Princes of the realm. Finally, the King tapped his scepter twice, and the doors opened to admit Daerahil. He strode forward in the dark blue somber robes of an accused, followed by two servants holding sheaves of documents that they placed on a small dark table, next to an uncomfortable rigidly upright chair, inside a small railed area, where the accused were placed.

* * *

Daerahil bowed low to the assembled nobles and begged the King's pardon for forcing this trial to occur. Glancing over at the witness box, he saw that his finance manager, Fafnir, was there along with other witnesses that Daerahil could only presume were witnesses for the prosecution. A Dwarf and a man that Daerahil recognized as a code writer for the messenger corps would be the witnesses for the prosecution for the documents from the joy house. Another man in the livery of the governor of Shardan would speak about Daerahil's actions on behalf of the governor himself.

'Well, and good,' thought Daerahil. 'Nothing unexpected there, but who are those men to the far right of the witness box?'

A captain of the Western Army of Eldora was present, along with a Shadow in his formal robes of pure white, indicating undying loyalty to the King and to Eldora. 'Why are they here?' wondered Daerahil. 'What could they tell the Council that I do not know?'

For the first time, he began to have second thoughts about not having accepted Renfrew's offer of representation.

Tapping the scepter once more, the king waited until all conversation had quieted and then said, 'I hereby declare this court in session. You may all be seated. In the matter of the Crown versus Prince Alfrahil, Lord Mergin will act for the crown, as a prosecutor. Are you ready to proceed, Lord Mergin?'

Mergin rose to his feet, bowed to the bench, and then, turning toward Daerahil, asked in a condescending tone of voice, 'My Lord Prince, will you insist upon on a trial, or will you admit your guilt to this Court? If you do so, the King shall be merciful, and your punishment much lighter than you deserve.'

Daerahil stood. 'I will not,' he said. 'I am innocent of these charges. Smirk as much as you like, little man.' At this last comment, a gentle chuckle was heard from the gallery, where the remaining nobility of Eldora was gathered as public witnesses to the trial.

'You will address the prosecutor as Lord Mergin!' thundered the king. 'One more such outburst and I shall hold you in contempt.'

Daerahil glowered angrily but managed to hold his tongue. He gave a terse nod and seated himself again.

'Lord Mergin?' said the king, and gestured with his scepter.

'Very well, My Lord,' said Mergin implacably. 'I shall proceed.'

Mergin first called the Dwarf named Otto to the small raised platform that allowed the witnesses to be seen by everyone in the courtroom. Otto was of medium height and middle years; only a bit of gray showed in his dark brown beard. His brown eyes were piercing in their stare at Mergin, a quality that apparently served him well in finding out secrets. He proudly wore a studded leather jerkin, though his ax had to remain outside the courtroom as no weapons were permitted inside. Mergin spoke. 'Will you tell only the truth in your testimony under penalty of death?'

Otto replied, 'Yes.'

'Please tell us your name and occupation,' said Mergin.

'My name is Otto. I am a security engineer assigned to the City of Titania. Golbur, Lord of Edelhohle, sent me here, to help prince Alfrahil search a room in a joy house here in Titania.'

'Did you find anything in your investigation?'

'Yes, I discovered certain documents hidden in a secret compartment under the floor of the room where the madam of the house kept her accounts. I gave them to you personally, my Lord. What happened to them afterward, I do not know.'

'Are these the same documents that are before you today?' asked Mergin, striding forward and handing him a sheaf of parchments.

'They appear to be, Lord Mergin. They are in the original binding, and the writing looks the same.'

'Does the accused have any questions of this witness?' asked the king.

'No, my Lord.'

'Very well, Otto, you are excused,' replied Creon. 'Call your next witness, Lord Mergin.'

'I call Hemnar of the messenger corps.'

Hemnar was called to the witness stand and sworn in, and asked to give his name and profession by Mergin.

'I am Hemnar, a senior code breaker of the messenger corps.'

'Do you recognize these documents that Otto has just identified?

'Yes, you gave me those documents the same day that Otto found them; I spent several days translating them.'

'What do the documents say?' asked Mergin.

'The documents are financial records showing that monies paid by Prince Daerahil were given to one Fafnir, who is present here in the courtroom. Fafnir is a well-known banker and moneylender and is mentioned throughout these documents.'

'What else do these documents say, Hemnar?' asked Lord Mergin.

'The rest of the documents show that Fafnir has been financing known rebel groups in Shardan and that it is likely, though not certain, that some of Prince Daerahil's money was used to aid these rebels.'

'Thank you, Hemnar,' said Mergin. 'I have no further questions.'

Again the king asked if Daerahil cared to question the witness, and again Daerahil declined. Hemnar was then excused.

At Daerahil's refusal, there rose a distinct murmuring from the assembled ministers and other wealthy members of the gallery, and even the lesser lords of Eldora whispered amongst themselves.

'Your majesty,' said Mergin, 'I have here an open warrant for the arrest of Fafnir for conspiracy to commit treason, a charge supported by Hemnar in this Chamber today. As this is the highest charge in the land, I would ask that he be immediately taken under guard to a cell, there to wait for his day in Court.'

Daerahil leaped to his feet. 'I protest, your Majesty! Fafnir must be allowed to testify on my behalf, as he is the author of these documents and can clearly demonstrate my innocence where these books are concerned.'

The king paused for a moment before responding. 'The law of Eldora is clear. Once charges of treason have been brought, the accused shall be immediately isolated, so that his treason may not spread. I am sorry, Prince Daerahil, but Fafnir must be removed at once. You may have some additional time to familiarize yourself with the documents in question; however, so that you may present us with any testimony Fafnir might have otherwise given.'

Daerahil blanched at this. The documents were in a code he did not know and could not hope to translate even if he had weeks and not mere moments to do so. He sank back into his chair.

Next Mergin called the army captain to the stand and bade him state his name and rank.

'Kerer, my Lord, Captain of the army assigned to the defense of Estellius.'

'What can you tell us of the men who tried to slay Prince Alfrahil on that day?' asked Mergin.

'They were eastern veterans who had travel and reassignment orders allowing them to replace a normal crew on a ballista,' said Kerer.

'Was there anything out of the ordinary about their orders?' asked Mergin.

'Yes,' replied the captain. 'They were signed by Prince Daerahil himself.'

'I signed no such orders,' said Daerahil vehemently as he rose to his feet. 'I demand to be shown these documents!'

'Alas,' said the captain, 'the documents were stolen from my office by one of the cohorts of the assassins. He set them ablaze and then took his own life when we tried to capture him.'

'How convenient. So you have no evidence to present before this Council, just unsubstantiated allegations,' observed Daerahil scornfully. 'My Lord King, I urge you to strike the testimony of this witness, as there is no evidence to support his claims.'

'The truth of the witness' testimony is a question for all of the Judges in this Court to determine, but I will instruct the Judges to discount his testimony as to the contents of the orders if you can show bias or deceit. Do you have any questions of this witness?'

Daerahil was not about to make the same mistake twice. 'Captain Kerer, do you have any personal disagreements with me or any reason to speak falsely about me today? Were you not indeed under my brother's command? Is your first loyalty not to him?'

'No, my Lord Prince, I actually served under your command faithfully, and I have only the greatest respect for you and for what you have done for the veterans under your command. It is with great reluctance that I am here today, but I must tell the truth as I know it.'

Defeated again, Daerahil sat down but first asked that the guard captain remain in case he should want to recall him for further testimony.

'We now turn to the actions of Prince Daerahil in Ackerlea,' said Mergin, and called one of the guardsmen from Ackerlea to the stand.

'Who are you and what is your position?'

'My name is Elard. I am a sergeant of the guard of Ackerlea.'

'Did you see the accused on his most recent visit to Ackerlea?'

'Yes.'

'Did he say anything surprising in your presence?'

'Yes. He said that the two princes of Eldora should not be at risk on the same day and that he wished he had been born before his brother.'

There was more murmuring at this information, but Daerahil knew that he could refute this evidence quite easily, as Hardacil, his aide de camp, was present in the courtroom and had heard the statements and would testify that they had been made in jest. Therefore he did not ask any question of the guardsman.

Next, Mergin called the messenger from the governor of Shardan, who testified that Daerahil had usurped the powers of the governor and his men, forcing the governor's men to retreat to their barracks as Daerahil assumed command of the province. Again, the facts were not in dispute, only the reasons behind them. As Daerahil planned to develop those reasons later in his defense, he did not ask any questions of the messenger.

'Finally, my Lord King,' said Mergin, 'I would ask that this court take notice of Prince Daerahil's formal reprimand for supplying aid to veterans' groups in direct contradiction of the King's will. With that, I rest my case in chief against the accused.

Thank you, my Lords, for listening to the evidence presented today.'

Taking his seat, Mergin smiled malevolently at Daerahil, who now rose and stated, 'I cannot translate the documents from the joy house, but the translations of Fafnir are here at hand, and I would ask that they be admitted into evidence, my Lord King.'

'Gladly, Prince Daerahil,' said the king, 'but first you must have someone testify that the documents are authentic as to their content. Can you provide any such authentication?'

'Father, you know I cannot, and it was for this very purpose that my witness was taken from this chamber earlier today.'

'Silence, Prince Daerahil,' thundered Creon. 'You will address me as my Lord or my King. As to this matter, if you are so foolish to rely upon accused traitors in your defense, then you deserve to face the consequences of such reckless behavior. Perhaps there is another legal argument you care to make?'

Daerahil now cursed the fact that he did not have legal counsel, for he was so angry at the unfairness of these proceedings that he could not think straight and was forced to say, 'No, my Lord.'

'Then proceed with your next evidence or witness,' said the King.

'I shall first testify on my own behalf,' said Daerahil. 'My Lords, I can but swear to you that while Fafnir did indeed invest my money and gave some portions of it to the Veterans of Eldora, I am unaware of any link between Fafnir and rebels in Shardan.'

'I trust you can provide documentation of that,' said Creon.

'I have no documents to support my claim,' Daerahil admitted. 'But I speak as a prince of the realm.'

'A prince on trial for sedition,' Mergin interjected.

'Continue, Prince Daerahil,' said the king before Daerahil could respond to Mergin.

Daerahil called Captain Kerer back to the stand. 'What evidence do you have to support your claims that the assassins in Estellius were connected with me in any way?'

Stammering for a moment, the captain responded, 'I only know that I saw the orders with my own eyes, Prince Daerahil.'

'You claim to have seen my signature on the conveniently missing orders. Had you ever seen my signature before that day?'

'No, my Lord,' replied the captain.

'Have you seen it since that day?"

'No, my Lord.'

'Then for all you know, it was a forgery, similar to the one on the message calling me to Ackerlea. I now ask Prince Paladir to examine this message that I present and ask him to tell what he knows.'

Prince Paladir rose and, glancing down at the message bidding Daerahil to Ackerlea, told the tribunal that he had been drugged and his signet ring used on a message directing Daerahil to Ackerlea.

'Why is this relevant?' objected Mergin.

'Because if someone could gain access to the signet ring of a Prince of Eldora to authenticate a false message, then it is even more likely that someone gained access to the simple offices of a guard Captain of Eldora,' Daerahil said. 'Furthermore, it is highly likely that these same people were responsible for the message that the captain claims I signed.'

Muttering broke out from the assembled members of the court, and Daerahil saw several of the Lords of Eldora nodding their heads in agreement. Daerahil knew he had struck the first real blow against the evidence presented that day.

'If you have no further questions of the captain, then he is excused,' said the king stonily.

'I have no further questions of him, my Lord,' replied Daerahil. 'I admit I said those words about wishing that I had been born before my brother, but they were uttered in jest, as rumor would have me actually wanting to usurp my brother's place. Finally, that day in Ackerlea, when the first rumor of strife went up about the vile attack on my brother, what I said in all seriousness was: 'Eldora cannot afford to have both of its princes at risk.' May the gods protect my brother and my father from harm, but I must put my duty to Eldora and its people over even their safety. This is what I meant, and by no means did I wish my brother any ill.

'Finally, I admit to overreaching my bounds within Shardan and taking command from the provincial governor, but his troops were ransacking and looting the province. My Lords, I have brought documents supporting the condition of the provinces before and after I took over, and if I have committed sedition in this action, I must admit my guilt. I ask that these documents be admitted for consideration.'

Since Daerahil was there to authenticate the origin of the documents and that they were written in plain text, the King had no choice but to admit them into evidence. There was great muttering in the courtroom, and Mergin looked quite pleased with having this admission until Daerahil continued speaking.

'The documents also state that at the time of my actions, I caused an announcement to be made throughout the land that I was doing this only in the interests of Eldora and that I was fulfilling my orders to pacify the province as required by the king. I believe that the success of my actions and my restoration of order to the province far outweigh my breach of protocol in this matter.'

At this, a ragged cheer went up from Daerahil's supporters, and the king frowned as if in disbelief that the trial was not going as expected.

Daerahil now said, 'I deny any and all of these charges of sedition. I had no knowledge whatsoever of the attempts on my brother's life, and there has been no evidence presented here today to convict me of such charges. As such, my Lords, I end my defense in chief.'

Sitting down, Daerahil exhaled slowly, knowing he had explained away all but the financial documents taken from the joy house. Yet he did not doubt that the King would vote for his guilt, along with Prince Jasper of the Delta. Jasper had recently been promised vast estates in Shardan if he voted with the King, but this was only a rumor brought to Daerahil by Larissa; there was nothing that could actually be used to impeach Jasper's credibility. His brother smiled at him and nodded, confirming his suspicions that Alfrahil would vote for innocence, as would the Lords of Eldora, for many of them were openly nodding their heads in agreement at Daerahil's testimony. Thus, Daerahil told himself, it would all come down to Paladir and his vote, and Daerahil believed that Paladir was no more convinced by this weak evidence than anyone else would be who did not personally bear Daerahil ill will.

Mergin rose and seemed about to begin his summation, but surprisingly called Daerahil to the witness stand instead.

'I protest your Majesty,' said Daerahil. 'Lord Mergin presented his case against me and formally ended it before I began my defense.'

'There is a precedent, my Lord King: that of rebutting the testimony of a witness to prove the witness false. I have evidence to prove Prince Daerahil's testimony false and to show that he did indeed have knowledge of the attempt on Prince Alfrahil's life prior to the ambushes.'

'I will allow this line of questioning only to ascertain the accused's veracity, not to admit any evidence or documents at this stage of the trial,' said the King after a moment's consideration.

Mergin retrieved a small number of rough parchments from his table and approached Daerahil. 'Thank you, my Lord. Prince Daerahil, can you identify these documents before you?'

Daerahil looked down and saw a simple purchase order for thirty horses, another one for fifty bows and quivers of arrows, and smaller purchase orders for food and clothing. His signature was clearly marked on the orders for the horses and weapons, and his buying agent had signed for the rest.

'Yes, these are receipts for horses and weapons for a hunting party I planned to lead before the horrible events happened in this Kingdom. The other receipts are for clothing and food for a veterans group. What of them?'

'So, my Lord Prince, this is your signature on the documents?'

'Yes, Mergin, what of it?'

Ignoring Daerahil, Mergin asked, 'Finally, can you tell me what this document is?'

One final piece of paper was shown to Daerahil.

'It is a release from combat service order for the fifty men whose names are written here. It is also an order for an honorable discharge for all of them for services displayed in combat,' said Daerahil.

'Why did you personally write these orders?'

'I wrote them because these men were personally responsible for repelling the last attack upon me and my staff when we were separated during a dust storm in Shardan. There is nothing improper about these orders at all. My brother and I signed many such orders during our military commands,' responded Daerahil.

'Thank you, Prince Daerahil, you are excused. I now call the Shadow known as Gray Water to the stand.'

The Shadow rose and, after acknowledging his code name, responded to Mergin's questions.

'How do you come to be in this Chamber today?'

'You placed me in charge of investigating the assassination attempts on Prince Alfrahil. I gathered these documents and brought them to you.'

'Where did you find these receipts for the weapons and the clothes and food?'

'On one of the bodies of the assassins who were slain on the rooftops of the Second District, where Prince Alfrahil was attacked.'

'Did you identify who that man was?'

'Yes, my Lord. He was one of the men on the discharge orders signed by Prince Daerahil.'

'And where did you find the receipt for horses and the military orders?'

'The receipt for the horses was found in a saddle bag on a horse tied to a tree in the border forest, and the military orders were found on the body of one of the men who tried to kill Prince Alfrahil in the forest,' replied the Shadow.

'So all of these documents signed by Prince Daerahil or his proxy were found on the bodies of the slain assassins, and some of these same assassins were listed in the Prince's discharge orders?'

'Yes, my Lord, that is correct.' The Chamber erupted in noise at this statement. Mergin dismissed the Shadow and recalled Daerahil to the stand.

'Do you deny now that you did indeed aid the conspirators in their attempts on your brother's life?'

'Vehemently,' responded Daerahil. 'The military orders were written three months ago. The receipts for the horses and weapons were in the care of my proxy. Anyone could have taken them from his office and given them to your Shadow. After all, this Shadow is not an impartial witness but sworn to your allegiance personally. For all we know, he placed this evidence on the bodies himself. Where is an independent witness to hold me accountable for any actions against my brother? It is plain that you have gathered these receipts in a vain effort to substantiate these false charges against me.'

'I don't think we need any mysterious agents placing evidence, my Prince. Clearly you are linked to the attempts on your brother's life, and clearly, you have lied before this Council as to both your knowledge of these events and your complicity in them. I now do indeed rest my case.'

The chamber erupted in noise again, and it was several moments before quiet and order could be restored.

Mergin then completed his summation of the evidence and asked that the prince be found guilty.

Daerahil then rose and with great composure refuted these claims, arguing that the evidence was merely circumstantial and that he loved his brother and his father and would do nothing to harm either of them or defy their will. As Daerahil was about to sit, he looked up and caught his brother staring at him with anger and fear, as if wondering whether or not Daerahil was indeed guilty of these charges.

'The Council will now retire and deliberate,' said the king. 'We shall return with our vote. We will stand adjourned until after the evening meal when the verdict shall be read.'

Daerahil was escorted out of the courtroom and given a fine meal with wine as he waited for the trial to reconvene. Shortly before the eighth hour afternoon, the guards knocked on Daerahil's door and escorted him back to the courtroom.

'Prince Daerahil, approach and hear the verdict of this tribunal,' said the King. 'First, what say the Lords of Eldora?'

The Duke of Amarant rose and said, 'My lords, by a vote of four to two, the Lords find Prince Daerahil innocent of the charges against him. But as the most senior Lord let me make my personal statement: I believe the prince guilty and that only his reputation for success in combat has swayed the other members of the Lords. Still, our official vote is one of innocence.'

'I will now ask the Princes of the Realm to state their votes. Prince Jasper of the Delta, what do you say?'

'I vote for conviction, my Lord,' said Jasper. 'There are too many pieces of evidence that the prince has tried to explain away, particularly those of the financial records in the joy house. I believe when there is this much smoke, there must be a fire indeed.'

'Very well. Prince Paladir of Ackerlea, what say you?' asked the king.

'I have grave concerns regarding the prince's reckless behavior, and I fear that some of his money may indeed have gone to aid the rebels in Shardan, but I believe it was done without his knowledge. Having been a victim of a conspiracy in the message that was sent to the Prince, I believe him when he says that the purchase receipts were innocently bought. Furthermore, if the conspirators who arranged these attempts upon Prince Alfrahil were skillful enough to penetrate all of Lord Mergin's security measures in Eldora and my own measures in Ackerlea, then it is highly likely that these conspirators are to blame for this evidence, not the prince. I vote for his innocence.'

At this Daerahil looked to his brother, knowing that one more vote for innocence would clear him and restore his rank and title in the land.

'Prince Alfrahil, what do you say?' asked the king.

Alfrahil rose, his face one of conflicted emotion. The extension of his powers during the trial had been too unfocused to perceive Daerahil separately from the crowd. His examination of Daerahil in his chambers had revealed nothing, so Alfrahil found himself accepting the evidence presented with no clear insight into his brother's state of mind. 'I do not know what to say, my Lord. While I am not convinced my brother tried to aid those who attempted to kill me, I cannot overlook the evidence presented today. Furthermore, though I do not know what he believes in his heart, it is clear that even in jest my brother does wish that he was crown prince. For these reasons, I must abstain from voting.'

'That is your right,' said the King. 'I now cast my vote for guilt, as Prince Daerahil has clearly committed sedition against my will and the will of the Council of Ministers by his actions in Shardan, his statements about the royal succession, and his involvement, no matter how nebulous, in the conspiracy to assassinate Prince Alfrahil. The Council has come to a draw. Therefore, in accordance with ancient law, I cast the proxy vote of Prince Frederic of Amadeus as I see fit, and it is one for guilt. Prince Daerahil, you are found guilty of sedition. May the gods have mercy upon you.'

At this, complete pandemonium broke out in the court, and Daerahil was immediately surrounded by the guards of the King.

'Prince Daerahil, you will be taken back to your confinement, and you shall hear the judgment of the King tomorrow,' said Mergin, a look of triumph upon his face. Alfrahil saw the stunned disbelief cloud Daerahil's face as he cried out, 'I am innocent, innocent I tell you. Brother, I beseech you to change your vote before the official record is written.'

Alfrahil saw Daerahil dragged from the courtroom, feeling a terrible weight of despair at his brother's fate.

* * *

The next morning, Alfrahil was walking with his guards toward the Citadel. Numerous reports had come to the Citadel of angry soldiers shouting in the streets, a small mob of them actually marched to the Citadel demanding to see Daerahil before being dispelled by blunt arrows shot from the Citadel guards. Several prominent merchants had sent official protests to the King, claiming that Daerahil's rights to a counselor had been breached and that he must have a new trial. Worse, the general citizenry who had rallied behind their king and Alfrahil now openly called for Daerahil's freedom, and dozens of banners flown by Daerahil during his campaign in Shardan were flown from buildings all across the city.

Entering into the base of the tower of Anicetus, Alfrahil proceeded to the Council Chambers and, upon entering, was welcomed by Mergin and his father, who looked as though they had not slept much the past several weeks.

Mergin began the meeting with a summary of all that was known to date about those behind the assassination attempts.

'At this time,' he said in summing up, 'we can state with some confidence that the conspiracy was foreign-born, though implemented with local assistance. The scoundrel Fafnir certainly aided the conspirators, and so, it seems, did Prince Daerahil himself.'

Alfrahil rose. 'Let us not place the blame upon foreigners so easily, for even with local assistance, no foreigner could have set events in motion as quickly as was the case here, when it was my chance discovery of the joy house that triggered almost immediate attempts on my life. No one outside the City could have assembled the necessary men and the oil traps that were used so effectively in the first attack. Not in so short a time.'

'Though I believe we will ultimately discover the conspiracy to be of foreign origin,' said Mergin, 'I agree that we must leave no stone unturned here at home.'

'Perhaps, Lord Mergin, you are correct,' said the King, 'but the final blame must lie to the south. Only there is the true motivation and hatred to attack the realm of Eldora to be found.'

Not wishing to disagree with his father openly, Alfrahil remained silent with downcast eyes, knowing that his father's irrational hatred of all things Southern was once again in full bloom. 'Have I made a horrible mistake?' he asked himself silently. 'Should I have voted for innocence? It seems so unlike my brother to wish me harm, but the evidence from the Shadow was quite compelling. I only hope he can forgive me someday, but I had to abstain from voting, as I still cannot decide what is true and what is false.'

Hearing a polite cough from his right, Alfrahil saw Mergin staring at him. As he turned to face his father, Creon said sternly, 'Now that we have your attention again, my son, let us adjourn to the Throne Room and summon your brother so we may tell him of his fate.'

The members of the Council of Ministers adjourned first to take their seats in the Chamber as word was quickly sent to the Princes of the Realm and the Lords of Eldora that the Judgment was now at hand.

After the men had left the Council Chamber, Alfrahil approached his father.

'Father, wouldn't it be more prudent to tell my brother of his punishment in private? You know how proud he is. Condemning him to Plaga Erebus for three months will be hard enough to bear without the public humiliation.'

Sardonically, Creon replied, 'Perhaps you think his punishment too harsh, my son? Perhaps we should instead overlook all of these events and allow Daerahil to attend to his normal duties within the land?'

'No, Father. I just thought it might be easier on everyone to do this discreetly so that we do not inflame an already tense situation.'

Raising his chin arrogantly, Creon stated, 'Such public distress may very well force the conspirators out in the open where we can deal with them. Besides, I intended to make this trial as humiliating as possible for your brother. Perhaps that way he will learn some respect for me during his exile.'

As they entered the throne room, Alfrahil saw the richest and powerful men in the realm packed upon benches on both levels. Expectant whispers and murmurs flowed quickly back and forth as they speculated upon the Prince's punishment.

At the knock of the Citadel guards, Mergin cried 'Enter,' and Daerahil and his guards marched into the room. Filing up toward the counsel table, Daerahil had placed a rigid mask upon his face, seeming to accept whatever fate his father had in store for him.

'Daerahil, Prince of Eldora, you are found guilty of Sedition for wishing to usurp your brother's place and by your actions in Shardan Do you have anything to say in your defense before sentence is passed?' asked Mergin formally.

Ignoring Mergin, Daerahil turned toward his father and said, 'My Lord, I again pledge my undying loyalty to you, my brother, and the realm. Please forgive me for my rash and reckless speech, for I meant no evil to you or to any others in the realm. As for my actions, Lord, I only wanted to aid those soldiers who were in desperate need, and I did not mean to defy your authority. I would ask you to show me mercy and allow me to make redress for my transgressions.'

Alfrahil was amazed at his brother's restraint; he had expected him to erupt in anger again the minute the Sentencing hearing commenced. Someone must have been counseling him most closely, preparing him for today. Hoping that his father would likewise practice restraint, Alfrahil waited with anxious expectations.

Rising and facing his son, Creon said, 'Verily will I show you mercy, Prince Daerahil. The fact that you are my son has allowed me to be too lenient regarding your prior actions. I believe that the folly of youth, along with your exuberant pride and incredibly poor taste in counselors and social companions, has led you to your present predicament. I did not raise you to behave in such a fashion, and, but for your prior service to the realm, the love of your brother, and your lack of malice, your punishment would be far greater. Here is the sentence of the King. You are hereby exiled from the realm of Eldora for three months and commanded to serve as the garrison captain at Ianus Malus. Your rank of prince is suspended during your exile, and all privileges of that rank are forfeit. You are removed from command of the southern army of Eldora and are demoted to a simple captain in the general army. You will leave under guard on the morrow and proceed without delay to your new command. You are forbidden to leave the realm of Plaga Erebus and its immediate confines until your term is complete. Do you understand this decree?'

Daerahil tried to speak twice before he managed to reply in a strangled voice. 'Yes, Lord. I hear and obey, and with your leave, I shall prepare for my new command.'

'One moment,' said Mergin. 'I believe there was another matter, my Lord King?'

A wintry smile passed over Creon's face. 'Ah, yes, thank you, Lord Mergin. Captain Daerahil, you will find that your companion, Minister Zarthir, has been arrested for conspiracy to commit treason along with two of his closest counselors, who I believe is also known to you. The funds you have invested against our wishes for your own political ends have been confiscated and returned to the treasury. Upon your return, you will be watched quite closely to make certain you do not attempt to thwart our will again.'

Daerahil came to a rigid posture of attention. After saluting his father, he was about to turn and leave when Mergin again spoke. 'Captain, there is one more matter that should be addressed before you leave.'

Mergin gestured, and a pair of guards dragged a woman into the Throne Room. Daerahil gasped and flinched as if forcibly struck.

Loud murmurs and exclamations went up on all sides, and Alfrahil felt a mounting sense of pity and disgust in his heart. The woman was his brother's Shardan mistress, Hala. She had been brutally beaten and was able to stand only because of the two guardsmen gripping her arms, one on either side. She seemed unconscious, though her face was so battered that Alfrahil could not tell whether her eyes were open or not.

'Hala!' howled Daerahil in apparent agony.

Mergin continued with palpable venom in his voice, 'This Shardan whore was also involved in Zarthir's conspiracy and stands guilty as well of violating the racial purity laws of Eldora. While you, Captain Daerahil, cannot be punished for her actions, she certainly shall be. She shall be exiled to her homeland, where she shall serve as a general whore to the patrol that leaves for Shardan today.'

With a cry of rage, Daerahil leaped toward the smirking Mergin, knocking his two escorting guards out of the way. Reaching Mergin, he raised his fist and was about to strike when two Shadows grabbed him by the arms and him dragged away. Daerahil then brought his mental powers to bear, delving into Mergin's mind to cause as much pain and damage as possible, but he was thwarted by his father's mental powers, which deflected Daerahil's blow up into the gallery above. A shriek and a thump were distantly heard by Daerahil as a minor nobleman toppled onto the crowd below, provoking complete pandemonium.

Mergin hissed, 'Your little brown friend will pay for your sins in your stead; Captain. I just thought you should know her fate before you left.'

Daerahil slumped in the arms of the Shadows, and Mergin, drawn by this apparent weakness, came in close to gloat. As he did, Daerahil lashed out with one foot. His heel struck the inside of Mergin's right knee, causing it to snap like a twig. As Mergin stumbled forward, Daerahil brought up his other foot, which impacted squarely between the minister's legs. Screaming and collapsing into a retching heap on the floor, Mergin was suddenly no longer smiling.

One of the Shadows drew a knife, and Daerahil knew his life was measured in seconds. Using his mental abilities to confuse the Shadow, Daerahil looked for an escape, but before he could act, Creon's voice thundered, 'Hold!'

Striding down from his throne, the King ordered that Mergin be carried to the Healer Hall. He then ordered everyone but his sons and the Shadows to clear the room.

Approaching Daerahil, Creon struck his son across the face with the back of his hand. 'I cannot believe that after all of the leniency shown to you today, you would violate the sanctity of this trial. Your exile is a fitting punishment for your actions. Your treacherous companions, including this whore, deserve their fate.'

Daerahil cried out, 'Sanctity, Father? Sanctity? You bring me here and publicly humiliate me in front of the entire realm, arrest good and honest men for simply associating with me, and violently desecrate and sentence the woman I love to a fate worse than death. Sanctity? The only thing you hold holy is your insufferable self-love. If your father were alive today, he would deny that you were ever his son, for no ruler of Eldora has ever treated its citizens as foully as you have this day.'

'Silence,' thundered Creon, 'or your punishment will be far greater than it already is.'

'Greater?' cried Daerahil. 'What then would you do, burn my servants alive in front of me before you place my head upon a spike on the outer wall for all to see? Perhaps murder random innocent children and claim them to be seditious, too? Your hatred of all things Southern has unbalanced your mind! You still have not reconciled the death of my mother from a Southern plague. She was only trying to help them, Father! The unfortunate families that your policies have brought to such a state! But for your wars of madness and love of conquest, the refugee camps would never have been created in the first place. The overwhelming poverty would never have existed, compelling Mother to try and help them in any way she could. If you had provided them some basic comforts, then the filth and garbage that piles up there would never have spawned that deadly plague that killed most of the refugees, my mother, and so many others. Release your hatred, Father, for my sake, the sake of the soldiers, the realm, and, most importantly, for yourself. Release it before it is too late.'

Responding in a guttural whisper of rage, Creon said, 'I will pretend that your actions and your words are triggered only by the fate of your brown woman, that you were so besotted by her filthy charms you cannot think clearly. Never discuss your mother in my presence again, for her death was caused by those foul people who did not have the good sense to be loyal to Eldora. It is only my own mercy that keeps me from driving them into the deep desert to perish from hunger and thirst. Perhaps after your time in Plaga Erebus, you will begin to appreciate the North a little more. Speak no more words, or your exile shall be permanent.

Speaking to the Shadows, Creon said, 'Take him to his apartments and see that he stays there with no visitors until the morrow. At first, light, have him escorted out of the City with the new guard company until he reaches the river.'

Gesturing disdainfully and turning his back upon his son as the Shadows dragged him from the room, Creon addressed Alfrahil. 'Alfrahil, return to the Citadel and resume your normal duties tomorrow, but speak not to me of what has happened here. Now go—I wish to be alone.'

Seeing that there was nothing that he could do, Alfrahil bowed and left the chamber, following his father's will to the last. Once in the hallway, revulsion overwhelmed him and sent him staggering into the small room he had occupied the day before. Calling for wine and food, Alfrahil sat in shocked silence.

His brother was certainly impolitic in his dealings, particularly with his assault upon Mergin, but the enormity and indignity of the punishment of his brother astounded him. Banishment was the traditional punishment for royal family members who were convicted of Sedition. But the stripping of his rank and authority went well beyond tradition. The arrest of Minister Zarthir and Fafnir on the merest suspicion that they were bound up in this mess was even more startling.

Finally, what had been done to that poor girl, a beautiful but harmless joy-girl, was unforgivable. He had once seen her at a party thrown by Zarthir to which he had been invited. Indeed she had been lovely, moving with sensuality and an intriguing smile that hinted at her considerable charms. To see her reduced to a shattered hulk in an act of petty vengeance struck him as a crime more deserving of punishment than anything Daerahil had done.

'My father has gone too far,' he thought. 'Whether he likes it or not, I will mention it to him the next time we speak. And I will try to get a letter to my brother stating my greatest apologies and offering what aid I can. At least I can supplement the food supplies he will receive in Plaga Erebus. And perhaps I can do something for that poor girl.'

Chapter Fifteen

Exile

Daerahil spent the rest of the afternoon and evening within his private apartments, with guards and Shadows keeping watch outside the door. Inside, all was kept as normal as possible by his servants, but they had been told that they were to remain in the City during his exile and prepare for his eventual return. Realizing that this was his last night with good food, excellent wine and a soft bed, Daerahil made the most of it, enjoying roasted beef with an excellent wine sauce, the last of the spring vegetables, new potatoes, and a cheese course. Then he quite purposely got drunk on some of the finest wine in his cellar. Dark thoughts overwhelmed him and he mentally raged against his cowardly brother. His only smile came when he thought of Mergin. Daerahil had trained long and hard with the Shadows during his years in Shardan and he knew exactly how and where to place his feet. If Mergin ever walked without a limp on his broken knee, Daerahil would be surprised. Moreover, after crushing his manhood with his other foot, Daerahil would be shocked if Mergin could ever function as a man again. The minister would not soon forget the results of his last attempt to spite the prince.

Blackly, he thought of poor Hala and her fate, raging at his inability to do anything to save her. Once again he ran the variables over in his mind, but he could think of no way to escape from his rooms, much less rescue her from the departing troops dispatched to Shardan. He could only hope that she could find a way to end her life before she endured more of the horrible abuse that had already been heaped upon her. Yet at the same time, he wanted her to live, so that one day he could be with her again. The grief and anger were too much to bear, and he slumped down at the edge of the table, tears of helpless rage streaming down his face.

Now all he could do was go to bed, as the wine had made him very unsteady on his feet. While it had given him no joy, it had at least brought oblivion a step nearer. Rising, he stumbled toward his bedchamber.

* * *

A loud banging on the outer door was answered by the loud banging of a Dwarven gong within his head. Daerahil rolled to the edge of his bed and was violently sick all over the floor, even as Marda entered the room and told him that he had ten minutes to dress for his journey. On any other day she would have admonished him for his lack of control; today she simply held out a vial of brown liquid and a large glass of water. Holding his nose and downing the hangover remedy with a grimace, Daerahil immediately consumed the water as well.

'Once your Lordship is dressed, I have persuaded the guard sergeant to allow you a few minutes for breakfast,' Marda said softly.

Muttering that he had no appetite, Daerahil quickly dressed in the captain's tunic that had been provided for him and slipped the simple coat of rings over his head. Seeing there was fresh orange juice and fruit, he consumed them quickly to ease his transition from screaming misery to grumpy headache and mild nausea by noontime.

He thanked Marda for making his journey already a little easier.

'You will find everything in order upon your return, my Lord,' said Marda, wiping a tear from her eye.

Alfrahil was too overcome with emotion to do more than nod stiffly. He turned to the door, which was opened for him by another servant. He strode out and instructed the army guards who stood there alongside the Citadel guards to grab his gear and his baggage and have it placed upon the pack horses. Pausing as if to disobey the prince, the guard sergeant ordered his three men to grab the luggage and proceed to the road.

The sergeant's face was one of thinly veiled contempt, and, seeing that he might as well address this issue now before it became too widespread to control, Daerahil beckoned the sergeant over and said to him in a voice that all present could hear, 'While we both know that I am demoted to guard captain and no longer have my princely authority, rest assured that I will have my rank and privileges back three months from today, and if you have any desire to avoid a permanent reassignment to the Azhar frontier as a latrine orderly, then you had best wipe that smirk off your face and follow my orders as if the king himself were standing here in front of you.'

The color drained from the sergeant's face, and he stammered out, 'Y-yes, Lord Prince. My apologies, I simply thought—'

'Yes, you thought, which was your first mistake, acting upon it was your second. Leave thinking, much less acting upon thoughts, for your betters, or next time I won't be so lenient,' said Daerahil.

Marching with as much dignity as he could muster, he approached the blindingly bright light of a late spring morning in Eldora. A troop of horses was drawn up in front of his house; he was astonished to see Hardacil among them, who pursed his lips, offering only a long wink. Decimated by alcohol, Daerahil retained just enough sense to remain silent, knowing he would find out the truth from Hardacil later. Gingerly settling into the saddle of the handsome bay horse provided for him, Daerahil led the mounted soldiers down the streets of the City. Arriving at the great gates of the City, Daerahil was confronted by the Gate Captain, who unrolled a scroll with formal red handles and gold parchment and read in a loud voice.

'Prince Daerahil, your exile is permanent; but after three months you may petition the King for permission to return. You must surrender your purse to me, enjoying only things a guard captain may afford, and live on official rations. Fail to obey and you will be brought back to Eldora in chains. Do you understand?'

'They have taken my rank, not my wits,' grumbled Daerahil. 'Of course, I understand.'

Extending his hand for the purse, the captain said, 'Do not fear, Captain. You shall have this money back upon your return.'

With a sigh, Daerahil handed over his purse heavy with gold and silver coins. In return, he was given a much smaller purse that he suspected contained mostly copper coins. As he rode under the great arch, cheers erupted, sparsely at first, but rapidly growing from the tops of the wall as the soldiers of the City snapped their spears to their sides and removed their helmets, cheering their former prince. Many of them were Southern veterans who had rotated back home for a rest from combat. Daerahil paused and, drawing his sword, saluted the soldiers of the walls as he saw their officers frantically trying to get them to be quiet.

* * *

The company arrived at Estellius just after noon, where Daerahil ordered an hour's pause to eat and rest. Then they were off again.

As the afternoon wore on, Daerahil saw a small group of Elven horsemen riding toward them as they approached the

Crossroads. Keeping his men to the right side of the road, Daerahil snapped a salute as the Lesser Elves drew close enough to be recognized.

Returning the salute, the Lesser Elves did not pass but stopped their horses. The leader of the group, a tall Elf whose dark hair streamed nearly to his waist, said, 'Hail, Daerahil, Prince of Eldora. I am Hilforas. I have urgent news for you.'

Daerahil replied, 'I no longer have the rank of prince. I have been stripped of my royal title, privileges, and authority and am now but an ordinary army captain.'

'My message is indeed for you, Prince Daerahil, no matter your current rank. Please ride ahead with me to receive the news.'

Knowing the Elven predilection for secrecy in the simplest of things, Daerahil rode a furlong ahead of his men with the messenger and said, 'Is this far enough, or should we ride all the way to the Northern forest?'

'No, Lord, this is far enough. I am bid to tell you that you are invited to a meeting with Lord Ferox, Elf-lord of Ackerlea, tonight and that he greatly desires to see you again.'

'My duty prohibits me from tarrying on my way,' Daerahil said.

Smiling, Hilforas said, 'Why don't you and your friend Hardacil take two horses out through the east gate after sunset? I believe that even a simple captain of the army has the right to come and go as he pleases. I will escort you to our nearby encampment to take you to Ferox, and we will have you back long before dawn so that none of your soldiers or the men of the Crossroads will be the wiser that you have feasted with us.'

Normally, Men did not shy at traveling on the roads after nightfall, but in East Ackerlea, with Plaga Erebus and its ancient memories and terrors so near, it was a brave or desperate man who traveled the roads at night. Shapes could still be seen moving on moonlit nights in the foothills of the Odina Maura, and men, both singly and in small groups, had been taken from the road, never to be seen again. Even large companies had scouts or stragglers taken at night, and all of them had vanished without a trace. Legends said that Mountain Giants, Werewolves, or other unnamed horrors were responsible. Many times since the end of the Great War, Men, Dwarves, and even Elves had sought out these nocturnal predators. Each time they had found nothing besides moonbeams and harmless shadows. But always there was the lurking presence of evil, just out of reach and out of sight, on what was known as the "Haunted Road." Regardless, Daerahil knew that he was fated to take this road, and he was curious to see if the legends were true. Now, after accepting the invitation of Hilforas, he returned to his men and led them toward the Crossroads, where they would spend the night.

Chapter Sixteen

Shadows of Shadows

Daerahil arrived at the Crossroads an hour before sunset and had his sergeant see to the quartering of the men. Once, long ago, the Crossroads had been just that: a meeting of two roads surrounded by woods. Today the Crossroads had grown into a vast encampment of soldiers' barracks, guardhouses, merchant quarters, taverns, and the like. The Crossroads were surrounded by a high wall and a dike with guarded gates at the four entrances. The barracks were laid out against the inside circumference of the walls. Quarters and small stables for officers were stationed halfway between each quarter circle, so that what peace and quiet existed within the walls would not be disturbed by road traffic. Inside the ring of barracks were the inns, taverns, merchant shops, warehouses, granaries, and other buildings not directly concerned with the maintenance and supply of the troops that either passed through or were stationed there.

While two soldiers bore his gear to a nearby officer's barracks, Daerahil sent Hardacil to arrange for two additional pack animals to carry additional supplies and then to join him at the Four Roads, the best inn inside the Crossroads. Daerahil registered with the local guard commander as required of any captain. The young commander, superior in military rank to a captain, returned Daerahil's salute stiffly and promptly, then asked if the prince had any special needs he could attend to.

'Nay, lad,' replied Daerahil. 'I have been here before; I just need quarters for myself and my aide-de-camp, Hardacil.'

The captain showed Daerahil to the best room within the barracks kept for visiting captains. Gray stone walls surrounded a tiny chamber, barely ten feet by eight feet, which contained a narrow cot on which lay a thin reed mattress covered by a crude cambric sheet, with a straw-filled pillow. A small chipped washbasin lay on a wooden table crammed against a flimsy pine wardrobe on the wall opposite the bed. A heavy tin pitcher and mug completed the rude furnishings of his temporary home. To Daerahil, it smacked more of a prison cell than an officer's quarters, and he began to see how difficult it was going to be to not only give up his rank and power but all of the privileges and comforts that had gone along with it.

Stowing his gear in the room, Daerahil decided to unpack later; he paused only to change into fresh clothes and use the small washroom at the end of the hall outside his door before heading to the inn. Wearing a cloak with his hood drawn, Daerahil had no desire to attract attention. Entering the Inn, he asked for a private room and the best wine and food to be brought to him promptly. Tasting each dish as it arrived, he found while the fare was certainly not up to his own cooks' standards, it was much better than what was to come when he left for Ianus Malus. Daerahil resolved to load the new pack animals with what preserved food products and wine were available and affordable so that his exile would not be as grim as it promised to be. Hearing a knock on the door, Daerahil said, 'Enter.'

Hardacil came into the room. 'My lord.'

'A sight for sore eyes,' said Daerahil, smiling. 'Sit down and eat, my friend. And tell me how you came to be here.'

'Yes, lord.' Between bites, Hardacil quickly and quietly complied. 'Larissa, who is still free from Mergin's clutches, came to see me before we left the City and presented legitimate travel and reassignment orders for me to take to my guard captain. Where she obtained them, I have no idea, but my new guard captain did not seem in the least surprised that I was going to be allowed to accompany you into exile, as I was still your aide-de-camp. The captain insisted that I take a fine horse and wanted me to wish you his fondest hopes for a speedy return.'

'Well, he might be a toffee-nosed little weasel, but he does have manners,' replied Daerahil. 'It was thoughtful of him to provide you with a fast horse.'

'Yes, Lord, it was. Larissa also sent a large purse of gold and silver. Where she got it she did not say and I did not ask.'

'Excellent, Hardacil. Once you are done eating, go and buy the best supplies for our trip—as much you think we can conceal from the men.'

After the meal was done, Hardacil left to buy supplies, while Daerahil returned to his room. There he changed into somber clothes, with darkened armor, the better to blend into the black night that awaited them, for the moon was young and set early. Besides their torches, there would be little light upon the road.

Once dressed, he hastened to the stables, where Hardacil was already waiting with their horses. Mounting up, Daerahil told the chief groomsman that they would not be gone long. 'And make certain there is someone on duty to care for our horses when we return,' he finished.

The groom inclined his head but said nothing.

Daerahil and Hardacil rode for the East Gate. Daerahil knew this was where his greatest danger would be, both on his departure and his return. Speaking to the guard sergeant, he said, 'Open the gates so that my escort and I may ride forth.'

Stammering in surprise, for it had been months since the gates had been opened after sunset and then only to receive men who had desperately marched west to reach the Crossroads, the sergeant asked, 'Captain, are you sure of your decision?'

'Must I have everyone in this realm question my orders day in and day out, Sergeant?' demanded Daerahil. 'Should I go and extract your captain from his place of comfort so that I can ride forth?'

Opening his mouth to speak, the sergeant saw his lieutenant arrive and gave way to the superior officer. The lieutenant asked, 'Do you intend to ride far this night, Captain?' thereby skillfully avoiding questioning Daerahil's orders while still attending to his duty.

Daerahil beckoned the officer near. 'I have a comely wench waiting just west of the Elven encampment,' he whispered, 'and it would be unseemly for a former Prince of the Realm to be seen gallivanting in public. I will be away until just before dawn. I am sure that we are both men of the world enough to know that where I am heading, there will be no such amusing companions.'

Chuckling at Daerahil's disclosure, the lieutenant smiled knowingly and said, 'Well, my Lord, for I hope that will soon be your title again, I can see that you are a man of superior taste and accomplishments. Be safe on the road.' He then ordered the gates to be opened and, turning to Daerahil again, confided that he would tell his replacement the prince was expected back before dawn and to ask no questions.

Turning their horses eastward, Daerahil and Hardacil cantered along the road and soon reached the Elven encampment, where they were greeted by the Elven guards and escorted across the compound. These Elves, tall and dark-haired, with typically reserved expressions on their faces, had little of the common speech and directed them more by gesture than words to a large tent: the headquarters of the Elves of the North Forest.

Smaller in size and scope than the Crossroads, the Elven encampment contained the headquarters for the representatives of the North Forest Elven government, merchants, and army within its walls. At a distance, there were two small, heavily guarded barracks, one for Dwarves and one for Men, neither of which was used much by either race, as they did not like the standoffish attitude of the Elves. Tonight, however, a raucous din could be heard from the Dwarven barracks. Otherwise, it was quiet.

Leading them to the headquarters of Ferox, the Elves nodded their respects and turned them over to two other Elves guarding the tent. Two bright torches illuminated the Elves, who gestured for them to enter. Daerahil saw a non-descript large tent made from heavy canvas, with a small stove-pipe rising from the far left of the tent.

As they entered, Daerahil saw an Elf sitting behind a beautiful ornate desk piled with papers. Standing, the Elf was quite plain by Elven standards, rather shorter and more slender than many Lesser Elves, without the unearthly beauty normally associated with Elves, Greater or Lesser.

'Felorad is my name, Prince Daerahil, chief counselor to Prince Ferox. Please be welcome and sit.' He indicated two comfortable leather sofas set at an angle toward each other, with a low table between them. Felorad's mousy brown hair and a high-pitched voice would lead the common observer to believe that he was weak until you felt his presence and knew that you were meeting someone who was not to be trifled with.

Clapping his hands, two servants that Daerahil now noticed, standing next to a small iron stove, approached and set down a platter of fruit, cheese, and wine on the table. Though he was full, Daerahil sat and took some of each, nibbling so as not to offend his host. Hardacil reached for the wine and cheese hungrily, as Elven fare was never served to Men unless they had a great errand with the Elves.

'My Lord Ferox is nearby, Lord Prince,' said Felorad. 'We will leave for him as soon as you and your friend finish eating and as soon as it is safe to do so.'

'Safe? How are we in any danger here?'

'Patience, lord, it should only be a few more minutes until we can leave. Word has reached us of the events in the City and your current status. We offer our sympathy and our aid.'

'Your sympathy is well met, but how could you and your Lord aid me, unless you know more about the assassination attempt on my brother than you have admitted to?' asked Daerahil darkly.

'No, Lord, we are as confused as you are about who might wish to kill your brother. But even if we did know, the knowledge would be of no use to you.'

'Why not?' asked Daerahil in surprise.

'Because, Lord,' interjected Hardacil, 'if you discover knowledge about the plot, everyone, including the King, will think that you set it up all along and now wish to betray part of your own treachery to atone for your misdeeds.'

Starting at this suggestion, Daerahil at once saw the merit behind the thought. 'If I prove my innocence, I admit my guilt at a subtle level, while if I act at all suspiciously I am guilty on a more obvious level. Either way, I am guilty in their eyes.'

'So it would seem,' said Felorad. 'Therefore, your only course of action is to do what?'

'Nothing,' replied Daerahil bitterly. 'Absolutely nothing, but ride to my command; endure my exile there, and petition the King for my return once I have served my time.'

'Precisely,' said Felorad. 'As to aid, we will certainly be able to help make your exile more comfortable. A train of pack horses is being assembled now that will arrive at Ianus Malus shortly after you do with their baggage disguised as routine supplies. Inside you will find many things not usually provided to the Men guarding Plaga Erebus, which should make your stay within the forts of the black land less wearisome.'

'Thank you,' replied a startled Daerahil. He could not imagine why the Elves were going so far out of their normal customs to indulge him in this fashion; clearly, they wanted something from him, but what? 'I am curious,' he went on, 'about a warning I received while I was in Nen Brynn.' He described the circumstances of the mysterious visit he had received while in the bath and asked if the message had come from one of Ferox's Elves.

'Not that I am aware of, Lord. I will speak to my Lord Ferox and ask him if he has any knowledge of these events,' said Felorad.

At that moment, another Elf entered the tent and began whispering into Felorad's ear.

Daerahil studied Felorad's face for a moment but could detect no obvious subterfuge. He gently brought his mental powers to bear, but all he was able to sense in the most highly disciplined mind he had ever touched was a steadfast resolve to obey his master's will. There was no trace of deceit. Suddenly feeling a change in the mind in front of him, Daerahil knew that he had been found out and quickly withdrew his mental focus.

Felorad said sternly, 'That was not courteous, Lord Daerahil. I can see that the rumors of your powers are true. But do not try that again with me, and certainly, do not try it with Lord Ferox, or the aid of the Elves shall be withdrawn.'

Daerahil began to apologize when, with a wintry smile, Felorad said, 'No matter. You are young, desperate, and reckless. Let us not speak of it again.'

Daerahil breathed a sigh of relief then politely made small talk while Hardacil watched and ate.

At last, the same Elf who had earlier whispered to Felorad returned. Catching sight of him, Felorad gave a nod and spoke to Daerahil. 'It is this for which I craved your patience. Now you shall see something that will interest you greatly, I think.'

Before Daerahil could reply, three Elves entered the building, dragging a cloaked body with them. Then the cloak was pulled aside. Daerahil gasped at the sight of a Shadow in dark hues of green and black, his body bleeding slightly onto the wooden floor.

'How?' he asked Felorad. 'How could you know that a Shadow was there, much less surprise him in such a fashion?'

'A small group of Elves has been trained by the Hagar tribesman, for they promised loyalty, not exclusivity to your King. Our healers were of particular service in saving the life of their tribal chief's favorite grandchild, and they have agreed to train some of us as well. When you combine their training with our natural skills, you will find that we are more than a match for these so-called Shadows. I hope that we have not upset you by disposing of this man?'

'Not at all. These Shadows have plagued me for years. They are personal minions of that vile serpent Mergin; if you rid the entire kingdom of Eldora of them you would be doing me a tremendous service.'

Felorad smiled with relief and spoke softly but quickly with the other Elves in their language, then said to Daerahil, 'There are two more Shadows waiting outside the encampment for this one to report and to follow you back to the Crossroads. They followed you from there, and we have been watching them the entire time. It is lucky for you that they were ordered to follow you rather than slay you.'

'Slay? What do you mean?'

Drawing the Shadow's dagger from its sheath, Felorad held it up to the light, where it glimmered with an unpleasant sheen. He then thrust the knife tip into the candles on the table in front of them. A bright flame came off the knife, followed by a foul, smoky odor.

'This blade was poisoned with the plant that you call Falls-bane,' said Felorad.

'A Night Blade," said Daerahil, his eyes widening in horror. 'They are issued to the Shadows only when an order for assassination has been given.'

'Yes. Only one antidote to this poison is known to us Elves, and it is difficult to make and keep. Be careful on the rest of your trip, Lord Prince, when we are not there to watch over you.'

'I cannot believe that even Mergin would dare to order my death,' said a shaken Daerahil.

Felorad shrugged. 'Perhaps, then, the blades were issued for your protection. In any case, we will keep the other two Shadows under watch and see that they do not follow you to your meeting with Ferox. When you leave here, we will supply the necessary makeup, perfume, and other subtleties that will confirm your story of a romantic tryst. When you return, the Shadows will see only what they are meant to see.'

'Why not just kill them, like you did their fellow?' asked Daerahil. 'Certainly, they are our enemies.'

'Enemies?' asked a quizzical Felorad. 'They are not Elven enemies, except for this one who breached our boundaries. He would still be alive if he had stayed outside the encampment. We are not at war with any segment of mankind. We simply wish to be allowed to tend our own affairs.'

'Then why are we having this meeting?' asked Daerahil.

'Sometimes our own affairs and the affairs of mortals overlap. In your case, my Lord, the result will be positive for both of our peoples. Come; let us ride east to meet Ferox so we can have you on your home road in time to complete the ruse.'

Striding out of the building, they quickly walked along the dappled darkness of the main road through camp so that the Shadows on the western end would not see them depart. Following closely behind Felorad, Daerahil saw that a troop of twelve Elves was ready, bearing long spears in addition to their bows and daggers.

'Even we are not immune from whatever haunts these woods at night,' said Felorad. 'Since our arrival in Ackerlea many years ago, no less than five Elves have vanished without a trace. It is not easy to surprise an Elf in the forest, my Lord.'

Climbing on to the horses provided for them, the troop moved east at a walk for the first half mile to reduce the noise from their horses. Daerahil felt the night breeze blow softly over his cheek and saw the last moonbeams glimmer through the foliage before the moon set in the west. The stars were brilliant here, and only a faint glow from distant Titania disturbed the night sky. Haunted or not, Ackerlea was indeed beautiful, and Daerahil well understood why the Elves had been drawn here. His father believed that sooner or later they would claim the forest as their own, wresting it from Eldora. But Daerahil was less inclined to credit his father's fears than ever. He would judge Ferox on his actions rather than on rumor.

As they reached a slight rise in the road, Daerahil saw faint lights ahead. The Elves led the two Men through a cleverly disguised gap in what appeared to be a thick, impenetrable wall of trees and brush. Indeed, it seemed to Daerahil that the vegetation parted of its own accord to admit them and then closed behind them in eerie silence.

Here was a large, opulent Elven tent, surrounded by three smaller tents. Faint music could be heard from the smaller tents. Dismounting, Daerahil, and Hardacil strode toward the entrance of the main tent. Pausing for a moment, Felorad spoke briefly to someone inside the tent in the Elven tongue, and then the tent flaps were pulled back so Alfrahil could enter, while Hardacil was asked to remain outside.

Walking into the tent, Daerahil saw opulence everywhere. Silk couches, ornate tables, and beautifully wrought silver lamps that hung from the center beam of the tent. Several cabinets with glass fronts revealed bottles of wine, and, having controlled his thirst earlier in the evening Daerahil could only hope that wine would be served. Thick, beautiful carpets were laid upon the tent floor, and Daerahil, seeing that Felorad removed his boots just inside the entranceway, bent to pull off his own boots. Daerahil then saw Prince Ferox lounging upon a comfortable divan at the far right end of the tent, with a small brazier in front of him. The self-styled Elf Lord of Ackerlea arose to greet him.

Tall and fair, with jet black hair streaming down past his shoulders, Ferox brought all of the usual stereotypes of Lesser Elves to mind. His presence filled the tent. Dark gray eyes under slender dark brows above chiseled features completed the picture of the quintessential Elf Lord. Aside from Felorad and Hardacil, there was no one else in the tent. He could hear soft voices speaking in Elvish from the neighboring tents, but for all intents and purposes, they were alone.

'Well now, Lord Daerahil, please sit,' said Ferox warmly. 'Felorad, if you would not mind, would you pour some wine for our guests?'

Felorad went to a cabinet and, after musing for several moments, chose a bottle and presented it to Ferox.

'Yes,' said Ferox approvingly. 'Such a splendid vintage is called for tonight.'

Uncorking and decanting the wine into a crystal vase, Felorad served Daerahil first, then Ferox, Hardacil, and finally himself.

Raising his glass in a toast, Ferox said, 'Prince Daerahil, you are most welcome. Please enjoy the hospitality of the Elves.'

Daerahil took a strong sip and tasted an extraordinary red wine. The garnet color in his crystal glass was rich and dark, supporting the dark cherries, leather, and hints of wood smoke that emanated from the wine.

'Thank you, Prince Ferox. This wine is truly exceptional.'

'You are more than welcome, Prince Daerahil. It is seven years as Men count them since last we met. How have you fared amongst your mortal kin in that time?'

'Until recently, quite well,' replied Daerahil.

'Indeed,' said Ferox. 'We have heard of the extremely disturbing events in your City, and we are saddened to hear that you are being sent to the gates of the black land in exile and that your return to your home in a position of strength and honor is not an assumption anyone can make.'

Tired of talking about his predicament, Daerahil simply replied, 'Felorad said that you wished to speak with me.'

'I wanted to assure you of the support of the Elves of the North Forest during your dark times and ask if there is anything we can do to help.'

'Felorad has already offered supplies for my comfort, Lord, but otherwise, I will have to suffer in exile until my father relents from his current course of action.'

Smiling, Ferox said, 'We can offer more aid than you might think. In addition to provisions, you will be able to exchange messages securely with those in the City. Information from our sources in the City will also come to you by discreet means. You shall always have an Elven messenger within a half day's ride if you need anything—food, drink, information, or even companionship. We can and will provide all these things to you so secretly that even Lord Mergin himself will not suspect a thing.'

'This is indeed a generous offer, my Lord,' said Daerahil. 'But you will forgive a soldier for speaking bluntly, I trust. What do you want in return?'

'Your goodwill is sufficient for our purposes, but if there comes a time when we need your help, we would ask that you give it willingly and with all of your power,' said Ferox.

'Power,' muttered Daerahil darkly. 'The only power I currently have is to oversee the garrison at Ianus Malus and patrol the evil road from the gate to the tower ruins to the smoldering pits of the fountain and back, waiting for the excavation expedition.'

'That is true now, Lord,' said Ferox, 'but we believe you will be returned to your former rank at the end of your exile and that you may eventually wield more power than you think.'

Suspicions rose in Daerahil's mind at this last remark, but before he could voice them, Ferox stated, 'We had nothing to do with the ghastly attack upon your brother, for we do not wish any Man ill, but if those that tried to succeed in the future, then indeed you will have power, Lord Daerahil.'

Nodding his head, Daerahil stated, 'I love my brother, though that feeling is somewhat diminished since he failed to save me from this predicament. Still, I want nothing to befall him on my or anyone else's account. I will settle his debt with me in my own time.'

'Of course,' stated Ferox, 'but your love for your father is gone, or so we suspect—and rightly so after the terrible way he treated you.'

Burning with remembered shame, Daerahil looked into Ferox's face and saw only sincerity there. After Felorad's warning, he did not dare to use his powers. 'Yes, you are correct. There is no love left between my father and me, but he is King and I must do his bidding. If there is nothing else, Lord, I should be getting back to the Crossroads before any more of Mergin's vile creatures come stalking me.'

'There is one last thing, something of delicacy that I wanted to discuss with you,' said Ferox.

'*Now we have finally come to it*,' thought Daerahil.

At a gesture from Ferox, Felorad removed a small leather purse from his cloak and pulled open the drawstrings. Reaching his fingers within the pouch, Felorad handed a small glass phial to Ferox that glowed with a dark ruby light.

'This is **gurth sogan**,' said Ferox, 'an extremely powerful yet painless poison. It takes effect in less than a minute, and mortals and immortals alike are then free from the bounds of Nostraterra. We have never given this to mortals, as it is a final release for Elves that have grown too weary of the pain of this world.'

'Why show it to me? I am not in need of it,' asked a perplexed Daerahil.

393

'Lord, we have heard of the exile of your female friend and of her current condition,' said Ferox. 'If you like, we can make certain that she receives this phial and knows of its properties. The choice to use it or not will be hers to make.'

Stunned by the depth of information the Elves had in their possession and feeling the black, raging grief well up within him again, it took all of Daerahil's will power to hold himself in check. Thinking for a moment of how much he missed Hala, he hoped she could survive and be with him again. But he knew that it was likely she would not survive her captivity in Shardan, and, if she did, she would not be the same Hala he loved.

'Thank you, Prince Ferox. I would be grateful if she were given a chance to escape her captivity.' Bowing his head in acceptance, Daerahil rose to his feet. Ferox did likewise, and the two exchanged the Elven parting ritual of grasping each other's forearms for a moment while bowing slightly. Sealing this bargain with its unknown price made Daerahil uneasy, but he needed every ally no matter their actual motives. Daerahil then exited the tent, where he found Hardacil waiting. The two men mounted their horses and, conducted by an escort of Elves, began traveling back to the road and the Crossroads.

As they neared the encampment, Felorad handed Daerahil a small bag with the contents of Daerahil's disguise: bits of makeup and perfume so the ruse would succeed.

'You may tarry here, Lord, for another few hours,' said Felorad. 'Sleep if you like, or drink the wine we have brought with us, but you cannot return to the Crossroads until well after midnight.'

'Why stop here rather than at the encampment?' asked Daerahil.

'Because, Lord, the Shadows may have moved or been joined by others. This is as far as we can go without some risk of being seen. When our scouts report that the way back is clear, you will be informed that it is safe to proceed.'

Daerahil dismounted and accepted a glass of wine from one of the Elves.

As he sipped, Hardacil led him several paces away, where the Elves were not likely to overhear them, bent close, and whispered, 'Lord, what do they want for their help?'

'I have no idea, but right now I don't care; I need all the help that there is. I will give Ferox whatever he wants in the future, within reason, of course. We must be wary, that much is plain. It is clear that Ferox wishes to curry favor with me, but I can only guess it relates to the internal politics of the Elves. All we can do, unless and until we get any specific information casting suspicion on Ferox, is to take him at his word. But once our exile is over, we will be able to ask deeper questions and pay for better information. The alternative would be to offend our only ally at this point by refusing his help, in which case we will have no one to aid us in the future.'

* * *

Two miles away a Shadow turned his attention back to the Encampment waiting for Daerahil to return as his primary mission was to watch and report what and where the former Prince went on his way to Ianus Malus. He was quite concerned at the absence of their leader, but his orders were clear: remain with his comrade south of the Elven encampment and wait until his leader returned. When Daerahil left the encampment then they were to rendezvous with their leader and follow Daerahil reporting to the Shadow that remained behind at the Crossroads. His leader was going to infiltrate the Elven encampment keeping Daerahil and his friend under close surveillance. What could have delayed his leader he could not fathom, for there were no warriors besides their instructors from Hagar that could defeat them at their own game. If his leader did not turn up by tomorrow, then presuming he could gain permission from the sub-leader at the Crossroads, he would look for his leader while his comrade continued to look after Daerahil. Perhaps reinforcements could be dispatched from Titania, or from their secret training site above the Pale Crags.

The Shadow recalled their home training camp with bittersweet memories, sweet for the glory to serve Eldora, and the ferocious loyalty that comrades would always show to one another. There was a great strength in knowing that while you would willingly die for your leader and for your comrades, they were equally willing to die for you. All that ultimately mattered was your absolute loyalty and devotion to the Over-commander of the Shadows, his commander, Lord Mergin, and above all, Creon, King of Eldora, leader of the North men. Even the Hagarian instructors, while deserving of loyalty from their students, knew and reinforced this linear pathway of obedience.

The bitterness was because of tremendous sacrifice, ten years of personal hardship, brutal exhausting training under constant duress; pushing many candidates beyond their breaking point to an untimely death. Not one in ten of recruited candidates completed their training to become Shadows. The initial selection process was performed at a restricted, but not secret, camp in the fens of the swamps where the river Aphon spread out for tens of miles south and west of the City. First, all candidates had to prove their pure blood of Northern origin prior to consideration for training. Many young men spent much of their meager fortunes having researchers examine their lineage back into ancient times. While the blood of Kozak, if diluted enough, would not bar them from training, any taint of Southern blood or significant amounts of the blood of the lesser men of Nostraterra was sufficient to keep them as simple men. Regardless, Shadows by their very nature were meant to be few in number. Less than two hundred were active at any given time, not counting the instructors within the program and those Shadows permanently assigned to other Kingdoms or realms.

Their initial teachers were senior Shadows, who put all the recruits who could prove their purity through an intensive year-long initial program of strengthening, conditioning, and fighting techniques. At the end of the year, roughly five in ten were sent back to their former lives, having ultimately failed to become the raw material that was necessary for formal training. Those who remained were taken into the wilderness that still existed in Nostraterra to learn how to survive both off and with the land. Climbing the slopes of the Never Summer Range and the Icy Mountains, traversing the plains of Hagar, navigating the trackless meres of the Miasmatic Swamps, and finally, surviving upon the open sea south and west of the Delta. This training lasted two full years, and the survivors usually amounted to two or three of the original ten. A final evaluation was held by their teachers, weeding out the last few weak candidates, who were not sufficient to warrant the last years of training.

The remaining candidates were then taken to the secret training facility in the Encircling Mountains above the Pale Crags. Prior to departing, they were told they would either emerge as Shadows or shades, and they must make this ultimate commitment before they left to train. Each candidate was interviewed at length by the instructors individually to see if he had the requisite level of commitment prior to leaving for the hidden camp. Once there the candidates met the Hagarian nomads, who were in charge of all senior training. What their actual name might be in their own tongue was unknown, and only Shadows in their last year of training were taught the rudiments of the Hagarian language.

The first year of the seven that awaited them was completely unlike their prior training. There was regular training to keep them at the physical and mental level they had acquired in their first three years, but they were taught nothing new. Instead, they spent the first year as servants to senior students and the instructors, not allowed to question any orders. The Shadow recalled the day his best friend from his early years had objected to remaining on duty cleaning latrines for a third straight day when other students had been on duty for only one. With a sad smile, the short, powerful teacher drew his sword from its scabbard on his left hip, in a blinding hissing arc, severing the student's head from his body. It took less than a minute for the headless body to stop bleeding and twitching, and the instructor gestured for two other students to pick up the remains and deposit them high upon the shoulders of the mountains so that the scavenger birds might pick the bones clean and the very existence of the candidate be forgotten. The two students dispatched to this task were shaken by the sight of so many other bones of so many other students that had been laid to rest there. Unfortunately, one of these students decided to try and sneak away from the training camp that night and the next day the carrion birds were again descending to that high plateau.

As the years went by, the students learned the arts of Hagarian fighting, stealth, and concealment, the ability to perform tasks that the student would have thought impossible only months before he learned them. Overall, there was a constant tension of the fear of failure. Students steadily disappeared as they failed to complete the tasks set before them. You never knew if you had failed until it was too late; one morning there was just one more empty chair at breakfast and you knew that someone that you had trained with, slept next to, eaten many meals with, and gotten drunk with on the rare nights you were allowed to relax, had perished at the hands of the very teachers you were supposed to respect.

Finally, the Shadow reflected, came the day you had waited for ten years, the day you were given the tattoo under your left armpit that identified you like a Shadow and given the mottled clothing that allowed you to blend into many different environments without appearing obvious. You were then given your orders by your instructor to report to a specific troop of Shadows, where you would follow orders without question during your apprenticeship and slowly acquire additional skills that were individually suited to each particular man. The Shadow knew he had been chosen for this night's assignment for his exceptional ability in concealment, an art that few excelled to his level. Returning from his musings, he saw that Daerahil had exited through the south gate of the encampment and was proceeding back to the Crossroads. Following at a discreet distance, the Shadow saw nothing unusual and watched Daerahil enter the Crossroads. Slipping quietly behind Daerahil's party the Shadow climbed a remote part of the walls and seeing Daerahil enter into his quarters dared to go and sleep in a nearby hay loft prior for a few hours before coordinating with his fellow Shadow.

* * *

Early the next day, having safely returned to the Crossroads shortly after midnight, Daerahil led his men out on the final leg of their journey. Nodding wearily in the saddle, he did not reprimand his men for their smirks and whisperings at the cause they believed lay behind his obvious fatigue.

'Better to let rumor convict me of my usual transgressions,' he thought.

The clouds hung sullen and dark, coming from the west. After nuncheon, the rain came in fits and starts, with distant thunder rumbling in the river valley. Gusty winds portended the arrival of even worse weather, and Daerahil called a halt, ordering tents to be erected for protection. The horses were corralled under the trees, their saddles removed as they were allowed to graze the lush underbrush that supplemented their fodder.

As the afternoon drew on, the rain fell harder, pooling in the gaps between the great paving stones of the road. Feeling as dispirited as his men, Daerahil ordered them to pitch camp for the night and prepare the cooking fires. The sergeant relayed his orders, and the soldiers, while grumbling customarily, went about their routine, happy not to march farther that day.

Daerahil was sipping Frostfields ale and looking out grimly from the flap of his tent when a sudden crack of thunder and a blinding flash lit up the dark afternoon. Twenty yards away, a tall ash tree, struck by lightning, was set ablaze. A screaming whinny came from the horses, and six bolted back down the road to the west, while three ran down the road ahead. Cursing, Daerahil ordered the guardsmen who were in charge of the horses to go after them. Twelve men rapidly saddled up at his command, eight of them heading west and the remaining four to the east.

An hour later, as the rain ended, the guardsmen who had headed west returned with the missing horses. After receiving their admonishment from Daerahil, they secured the horses and returned to the warmth of the fires.

Shortly thereafter, Hardacil said, 'Lord, where are the men that you sent east? Unless the horses ran all the way to the black gate, they should have been back by now.'

'Indeed,' said Daerahil. 'Well, there's nothing for it—we had better go and look for them. Assemble ten men as a guard detail. Hopefully, we will be back before nightfall.'

'I suspect the men we seek have just volunteered to take over the latrine work and kitchen detail for the next month,' Hardacil said sardonically.

'No,' said Daerahil. 'A month is too short. I think at least six weeks will be required to teach them not to tarry and force their captain to ride out into this damp.'

Daerahil bent his gaze eastward as he and his guards began to search for the missing soldiers. A golden haze lay upon the road. Soft tendrils of mist gathered and drifted along the ground, as only the faintest breath of breeze was present. It seemed peaceful and tranquil, the woods of Ackerlea lush and hale along the ancient stonework of the road.

Today, Daerahil felt the age-old compulsion to travel upon its unyielding surface more than most days, but there was something new that had not appeared before now. A subtle reverberation of power rang along its periphery, hinting of terrible darkness, a hunger that could not be sated, but only placated. Daerahil tried to put this off as an echo of the dark land of Plaga Erebus imbuing its horror on the present, but a visceral part of his mind refused to dismiss the sensation quite so easily. Instead, dark thoughts intruded from his past, particularly those of his father humiliating him repeatedly as a child fighting against his active will for supremacy, and only after an effort was he able to shake them off with his mental powers and focus on the task at hand.

'Do you sense anything unusual about this stretch of road, Hardacil?' Daerahil asked softly, not wanting to spook the rest of the men.

Hardacil started as if he had been on the verge of sleep. "No, Lord—only I do feel strangely tired as if the mist through which we are riding has drained my energy. And there is something else … I don't know quite how to put it. A vague sense of a dread uneasy, I suppose you could say.'

'You are not usually one for lyrical turns of phrase,' joked Daerahil. 'Whence comes this?'

'I do not know, Lord. The words seemed to form themselves in my mind, almost as if someone were speaking them for me. Indeed,' Hardacil added reflectively, 'it feels as if another nightmare waits to encroach upon the day.'

'Now I know there is something truly out of place here,' said Daerahil with genuine anxiety, 'when you recite poetry for the first time in your life.'

'Yes, Lord,' said Hardacil with a grim smile. 'Let us ride carefully.'

Daerahil and his men cantered eastward. The only sounds were the dripping of moisture from the trees of Ackerlea, the measured ringing of the horses' hooves on the stones of the road, and the occasional whistle of a soldier to his mount. After twenty minutes or so, Daerahil heard the sounds of hoof beats from the road ahead, and the missing horses came into view, along with the four horses of the guardsmen sent to retrieve them. But of the guardsmen themselves, there was no sign.

'Bare your weapons,' said Daerahil. 'It would seem there is trouble ahead.'

'My Lord,' said Hardacil, 'perhaps we should send back for reinforcements.'

'I do not abandon men under my command,' said Daerahil, loudly enough for the whole troop to hear him. 'Nor do I delay when my soldiers are in need of speedy succor. We ride at double time!"

After another fifteen minutes, they reached a point at which the signs of a scuffle were visible in the mud along one side of the road. Daerahil dismounted and searched along the verge until he found a chain-mail shirt that had been torn asunder. It was covered with blood.

A general search ensued. But nothing more was found, and soon enough the encroaching night put an end to the hunt.

'We will find nothing more this day,' said Daerahil, and bid his men back into their saddles. 'We will return to camp and come back in greater force tomorrow. There is no other recourse.'

They had not gone far when Daerahil experienced a sudden and unmistakable feeling of being watched. He whirled around in his saddle, and as he did so seemed to hear a high-pitched whisper on the wind, like words in an unknown tongue. A cold shiver ran down his spine, and he felt a feral hunger pluck at his soul. Yet there was nothing in the deepening gloom and mist.

It took Daerahil a moment to realize just how accurate that perception had been, for with a start he realized that he had indeed seen nothing where something was supposed to be. The soldier riding point was gone, missing from his saddle, with his horse still trotting along with complete lack of concern. Calling to the rest of his men, Daerahil exchanged looks of wonder with Hardacil, for the soldier had literally vanished into the thickening mist and night without a sound. Daerahil reined in his mount and turned to go back, but Hardacil stopped him.

'No, Lord,' he said. 'Whoever it is that is stalking us—for that seems to be what is happening—clearly wants us to stop and go back for our missing men. That way it can take us one by one. There is safety in numbers; let us return swiftly to camp. There is nothing more we can do tonight.'

'Are you saying that you credit the rumors of strange creatures haunting this stretch of the forest?'

'Rumors, my Lord?' asked Hardacil. 'Could rumors have taken one of our guardsmen five yards in front of us without noise and without disturbing the horse he was riding upon? I think not, Lord. We must retire.'

'Do you think me a coward?' demanded Daerahil in a hissing whisper. 'Afraid to face the unknown?'

'No, Lord. No man thinks that. Yet it would be brave but foolish to place yourself and your remaining men at risk from whatever is out there. Wait for the morning, Lord. Tonight we are the hunted. Tomorrow, in daylight, we shall be the hunters.'

Acknowledging the logic in this statement and conceding that they would have little chance of finding wounded or unconscious men by torchlight, Daerahil ordered the men to continue back to camp.

* * *

Back at camp, the tale rapidly spread of the Haunted Road claiming more victims. Demanding that the rumors cease, Daerahil stated clearly, 'The men sent out earlier have gotten lost. The missing point guard may have had a fit and simply fallen off his horse. Tomorrow we will find our missing men, and they will pay for their intransigence. In the meantime, double the amount of guards posted through the night.'

Little was heard during the night and all the men and horses seemed accounted for in the morning, but when a bedroll was uncovered at breakfast, the form of a sleeping soldier was revealed to be nothing more than leaves and bracken left in his place. '*Perhaps he deserted,*' thought Daerahil, '*perhaps not, but the men must think that this is the truth, or I may lose control over the situation.*'

Later that morning, Daerahil and his men rode back to the place where the rider had disappeared the night before. As they drew near, Daerahil noticed a round object swinging back and forth at the end of a rope some five feet above the stones of the road. The rope was fixed to a branch at least forty feet high. The first soldier to reach the object slumped over in his saddle, throwing his breakfast violently over the shoulder of his horse.

Cursing, Daerahil spurred his horse forward and, nudging the soldier's horse aside, saw that the object was a common helmet. He reached out to steady it, then recoiled in shock as the helmet spun, bringing the face plate into view.

The head of the missing soldier stared back at him—or, no, not stared, exactly, for the man's eyes had been gouged from their sockets. Tears of blood streaked the pale face, whose expression was one of utter horror. A crude rune Daerahil did not recognize had been drawn in blood upon the forehead.

Daerahil had Hardacil remove the head for proper burial while the soldiers dismounted to look for the body of their comrade. Two hours later, Daerahil called a halt to the fruitless search. Once the men had reassembled, two more soldiers were found to be missing.

Muttering under his breath, Daerahil ordered the men to proceed to the location where the missing horses had been found. There another search yielded nothing at all; only the whisper of the wind in the branches and watery sunlight spilling down through the leaves. There was nothing to do but return to camp.

Not wanting to spend another night on this section of the road, Daerahil had the men pack up the camp and quick march to a more suitable location just west of the island of Innis Mallow. They made camp that night in a fortified circle. Outside the perimeter, Daerahil heard the same eerie whispering he had heard the night before. This time, Hardacil and some of the other men caught it, too, but none could make out the words—if words they were—and nothing could be seen save a thick mist that rolled in from between the trees, carrying a wintry chill that their fires did little to dispel. Daerahil had to keep himself from shivering. 'It's the cold and damp,' he said to himself, 'nothing more.' But in his heart, he knew that there was reason indeed to fear the Haunted Road.

-The End of Book One-**Assassins**-

Dear reader,

We hope you enjoyed reading *Assassins*. Please take a moment to leave a review, even if it's a short one. Your opinion is important to us.

Discover more books by David N. Pauly at https://www.nextchapter.pub/authors/david-pauly-fantasy-author.

Want to know when one of our books is free or discounted for Kindle? Join the newsletter at http://eepurl.com/bqqB3H.

Best regards,
David N. Pauly and the Next Chapter Team

The story continues in :
Conspiracy by David N. Pauly

To read the first chapter for free, head to:
https://www.nextchapter.pub/books/conspiracy-the-fourth-age-shadow-wars-epic-fantasy

About the Author

Hailing from suburban Chicago, David Pauly attended the same high school where they filmed the 80's classics, Ferris Bueller's Day Off, 16 Candles, and the Breakfast Club. College at UW-Madison was awesome, where David majored in History, minored in beer drinking, and enjoyed his first taste of freedom. Working for a year after graduation for Domino's Pizza convinced, David that law school was preferable to food service so off to Washington and Lee he went.

Another graduation brought yet another re-location, this time to sunny New Mexico. Practicing law in the Land of Enchantment, David spent several years building up his practice, but always felt that something was missing. While David loved the turquoise skies and spicy food, he was looking for something more.

A life change prompted David to take a sabbatical from practicing law, and move to Paris, where he obtained a certificate in cuisine and pastry, from Le Cordon Bleu in 2003. Unable to find work, David left the wonderful magic of Paris behind, returning home to New Mexico, to revive his law practice, and care for his five rescue dogs. Single for the first time in 10 years, David took refuge in re-reading his favourite Fantasy and Sci/Fi books, returning to his childhood refuge, distracting him from a mundane depressing existence.

Voraciously re-reading books like Lord of the Rings, The Chronicles of Narnia, and Dune, The Martian Chronicles, and the Foundation Trilogy, David always wondered what would have happened after these stories ended. So, one snowy night he let his imagination run free and began typing a few sentences of what would eventually become an epic fantasy novel. Ten years later after countless re-writes and edits, begging family and friends to re-read it all, David published his first novel, The Fourth Age Shadow Wars.

Currently busy with his law practice, and precocious 6 year old daughter, David writes the sequel to Shadow Wars, Dark Shaman when he has time. Dreaming of having more time to write and cook, David soon hopes to put away his legal shingle for good, never having to answer the most frequent question asked by his clients "Am I going to Jail again?" with the response, "Yes, yes you are."

Lightning Source UK Ltd.
Milton Keynes UK
UKHW021116021120
372650UK00005B/931